LOVE'S INITIATION

He put her hand on his naked chest. She felt his heart pounding beneath the lightly furred skin. "Here, feel that?" he asked, but now she was feeling the steely muscle moving beneath that heated skin, and almost forgot what he'd asked. "We'll be very good with each other, even though you say it's your first time."

"It *is*!" she cried indignantly, snatching her hand back, the passion of her anger blotting out all the other passion she'd just felt. "You don't believe me?" Her whole body stiffened at his words.

"I wasn't thinking," he muttered. "I'm sorry, I forgot. Good God, Bridget, I told you, I can't think with you so near. Just look at you!"

She did—and felt her face grow hot.

"I want you now, Bridget. What is it that you want of me now?"

She gazed at him. His dressing gown had half opened, and she could finally see the strange and exciting furze of dark hair on his chest and how rapidly that wide chest rose and fell. She waited for maidenly fear to make her tremble. It didn't. There was none. She wanted him as dearly as he wanted her. Maybe not for the same reasons, because she wasn't sure what was ahead. But she wanted him happy, she wanted his love and approval, and she *so* wanted to know what he wanted to do with her.

The Cad

Edith Layton

HarperPaperbacks
A Division of HarperCollinsPublishers

HarperPaperbacks
A Division of HarperCollinsPublishers
10 East 53rd Street, New York, NY 10022-5299

This is a work of fiction. The characters, incidents, and dialogues are products of the author's imagination and are not to be construed as real. Any resemblance to actual events or persons, living or dead, is entirely coincidental.

ISBN 0-06-108706-8

HarperCollins®, 📚®, and HarperPaperbacks™ are trademarks of HarperCollins Publishers, Inc.

Cover illustration © 1998 by Jim Griffin

First printing: September 1998

Printed in the United States of America

Visit HarperPaperbacks on the World Wide Web at
http://www.harpercollins.com

For Mary Van Deusen, who came when
she was most needed

1

She was enjoying herself until she saw the man watching her. Or at least until she realized the others saw him watching her. She could have ignored him; she was good at that. She couldn't ignore them.

So she steeled herself and raised her head high. She turned it to the light, looking fully at him with all the pride and dignity she could muster.

He didn't flinch at what he saw. He didn't look flustered or embarrassed. He didn't quickly glance away. Instead, he raised an eyebrow. The corners of his mouth lifted. He inclined his head, as though he were sketching a bow to her. And kept staring. *That* she wasn't used to.

She felt blood rush to her cheeks, and ducked her head.

She knew the dance went on, even if her heart had

almost stopped. The couples in their sets on the ballroom floor danced under a chandelier of blazing candles.
From where she sat in the shadows on the sidelines with
the dowagers, chaperones, and wallflowers, the dancing
couples looked as though they were onstage. She was
used to being the audience, used to being in the dark—
how *dare* he single her out?

He dared.

"Bridget!" Aunt Harriet whispered sharply. "You must
not ogle the gentlemen!"

"I'm not ogling," she said miserably. "I was *being*
ogled. I just looked back at him."

"Indeed?" Aunt Harriet asked, every word etched in
acid. "But if you hadn't been staring at him, you wouldn't
have known, would you?"

Bridget's shoulders slumped. There was no answer to
that. It was only the truth. Of course she'd been staring
at him. He'd come into the warm room like a breath of
cool night air. She'd noticed him instantly. Most of the
women had.

It wasn't because he'd prowled into the room, ener-
gizing it, causing such a flurry of attention. Or that his
dark head was easier to see because he was taller than
most, or that his face was so tan compared to the fashionable pallor of the other gentlemen. It certainly wasn't
because he was so handsome. He wasn't. Not with that
high-bridged nose, those hard, defined cheekbones,
those long, narrowed, amused eyes. Not handsome.
Just devilishly attractive. Bridget bit her lip. She was the
reason for his amusement now.

But he'd caught her attention and held it. She'd
stared at him, of course she had.

He'd gazed around the room and seen her reaction. And stared back. In that moment she'd been thrilled . . . until she remembered who she was, where she was, and what had caught his attention. Then she'd turned to the dancers and only noted him out of the corner of her eye.

Liar, she thought, and sighed. She'd enjoyed her brief foolish game of glances with him. She imagined that because of the darkness where she sat, he hadn't seen her clearly.

"It's Sinclair," the women around Bridget whispered. The sound went through the group of watching women in excited hisses.

"Sinclair? Here? He must be looking for a wife!" one of them said.

"Sinclair? Looking for a wife?" another laughed. "W*hose* wife, I wonder."

"Nonsense," an elderly lady said sharply. "Even Sinclair knows he cannot come to an affair like this with rakish intentions. I've heard he's on the catch for a new bride, and here he is."

"Indeed?" a lady next to Bridget purred, gazing at him now. "If so, why is he staring . . . ?" She turned an amused eye on Bridget and left the comment unfinished. It nearly finished Bridget. It was more than enough for Aunt Harriet.

"Bridget," she said in icy tones, "I saw your cousin shivering. The night air can be so treacherous. You know how fragile she is. Do get her wrap for her."

Bridget jumped to her feet.

"Wait!" Aunt Harriet said. "Not in the cloakroom. I remember now, she left it in the coach. Go to the hall and tell a footman to get our coachman to fetch it for you. Wait there until he brings the wrap, will you?"

Aunt Harriet was mistress of the question that required no answer, Bridget thought. But what answer could there be? She was being politely sent into exile. She'd wait in the hall until it was time to go home, because they both knew Cousin Cecily hadn't brought a wrap at all. Why should she? It was mid-May, warm in the house, and almost as warm outside.

"Yes, Aunt," Bridget said. Then, with her head down and watching her feet so not to see the expressions on the faces of the women around her, she picked her way through their circle of chairs and quickly stepped around the edges of the ballroom toward the great hall outside.

She didn't mind missing the dance. She would have been shocked if anyone had invited her to take a turn on the floor. She was cousin to a fashionable young lady, but she was not that young and certainly not fashionable. Apart from her most obvious defect, she hadn't a penny to bless herself with. She was not an eligible young woman.

But she was a perfect companion, and had been one for seven years, so long she'd almost forgotten what a poor name that was for what she did to earn her bread. Because there was no companionship in it for her. She was a warm female body present in order to watch over a young lady being presented to society. She didn't mind. In fact, she was thrilled. She'd been a warm female body to fetch and carry for elderly relatives for the past seven years, and now she felt she'd come up in the world. At least she had dancing and not just knitting to watch now.

She'd only been in London a month, but she hadn't been so happy in years. At least not since her father had died, leaving her in the less than tender care of his family. It was amazing that when they'd heard of his death they'd unbent enough to offer his now fatherless daughter houseroom, since they'd been estranged from the day he'd married her mother. They hadn't unbent enough to offer his widow the same, of course.

That didn't matter; Mama would have gone home to Ireland anyway. But Ireland wasn't Bridget's home. And at eighteen years of age, she'd refused to be a burden on her mother. With hope and curiosity, she'd taken her father's family's offer.

She wasn't a burden on them. The first two years she'd been an unpaid nursery maid for Cousin Sylvia in Suffolk. Then she'd been asked to companion crabby Cousin Elizabeth in Derbyshire. Bridget had thought of joining her mother in Ireland after all, but Mama had remarried by then, and was actually increasing! No room there for an older daughter, or so Bridget had told herself—glossing over the notion that she might be jealous or hurt or heartsick at the thought of Mama and her new baby, when she herself would never have one.

Then there were those dreadful years in exile with daft old Cousin Mary in the north. Cousin Mary's loss of wits was the only reason Bridget remained with her, because it was easier to forgive a mad woman for all the nasty things she said. Besides, as Cousin Mary got older she forgot all the really dreadful things she would have liked to say or do.

But then this offer! Companion to sweet, silly Cousin Cecily? In London? *Bliss*. In one short month Bridget had seen the Tower and Regent's Park, gone shopping in dazzling arcades, gone to the theater *and* a concert—and now a ball! Of course, she went as an accompaniment, but it was more life than she'd seen for seven years. Besides, Cousin Cecily smelled of rose water, not camphor.

Bliss. No more criticism, no scolding, no complaining. Of course, there was no friendship, no confidences, and no praise, either. Cecily's brothers were at school, but she had her own set of friends, and if she thought of her older cousin at all, Bridget realized, she thought of her as a necessary accessory, like one of the footmen who always trailed after her. Still, there was no fetching, no carrying . . . except for tonight, of course. But this was in the nature of a lesson, after all.

The hall in the townhouse where the ball was being held was immense, with a ceiling as high as a cathedral's. There were urns with towering floral arrangements in the niches in the wall, and the floor was all black and white tiles in patterns, polished so highly that Bridget's slippers fairly skimmed over them. The company was in the ballroom, so the hall was empty now except for two footmen standing by the door.

"Miss?" one said when he saw Bridget come into the hall.

"Excuse me," she said, "but could you summon the Brixtons' coachman? My cousin has left her wrap in the carriage and needs it now."

"Of course, miss," he said, bowing. He passed the word to the second footman, who called a page. Bridget waited as they relayed the message to him and he went running out the door.

Both footmen looked at Bridget. She shifted from foot to foot. "Um," she said in a low voice, "I'll wait here for it."

"That won't be necessary, miss. We'll be happy to bring it to you."

"My, ah, express orders," Bridget said, "were to wait for it."

She saw the quick look of sympathy the two footmen exchanged. But she was used to that, and so she put up her chin and tried to pretend she was invisible. She was used to doing that, too.

"Perhaps you'd care to have a seat whilst you wait," one of them said, pointing to a chair in a niche at the side of the vast hall. She hadn't seen it; it was a spindly thing set in a recess next to one of the immense marble columns that supported the ceiling.

"The very thing. Thank you," she said, and walked to it, head high. Now all she had to do was to pretend the two silent footmen weren't there. Three strangers alone in a room, spending the evening together, not speaking—or would they have spoken to each other if she hadn't been there? Bridget sighed a little at how absurd the world was. She'd have liked to chat with them, but their job was to be invisible, too.

Well, but there are worse places to spend an evening, she told herself as she settled on the chair. It was a pity, though. She'd worn her best gown, the blue one, with darker blue ribbons at the high waist. She fidgeted with the ribbons now, thinking she might buy new ones—pink, for contrast? But maybe new slippers were a better idea, for she needed them. She raised a foot and contemplated it . . . and saw another foot suddenly appear in front of hers: a large foot in a shiny black shoe. Her eyes widened and her gaze flew up.

"Good evening," Viscount Sinclair said, his mouth tilting in that wicked, curling smile that had sent her into her present exile.

"Good evening, my lord," she said quickly, looking

down at her hands in her lap. She hoped he wasn't going to apologize, and she wished he would.

"Do you dance so badly you insist on doing it in the hall?" he asked quizzically.

She smiled in spite of herself. "I don't dance," she told her hands in her lap.

"Or look at a gentleman when he speaks with you," he chided her. "But I'm not a vain fellow. I came to ask if you'd care to dance."

She raised her eyes to his in shock. A cruel jest or an innocent blunder? His glittering brown-and-gold eyes were amused. "I—I cannot dance," she said. "Thank you anyway. Good evening, my lord."

"You said that already. *Cannot* as in don't know how?" he persisted. "I'd be glad to teach you."

"*Cannot* as in I am a companion, my lord, and companions do not dance at balls!" she said with spirit, because it looked as though the gentleman was having fun with her after all, and she was bitterly disappointed in him for it, and in herself for expecting more.

"I wasn't aware that companions were supposed to pass their nights companioning footmen," he said in his deep voice, a hint of laughter there, too.

"If you must know, companions are not supposed to be ogled by gentlemen, either. That's why I'm here. But I'm new to London, or else I wouldn't be in such difficulties. I won't be again, that I can tell you," she muttered. "But I do know companions aren't supposed to be chatting with gentlemen alone, as we are. Please, my lord, let it be."

"That I cannot do," he said. "Pity there isn't another chair here. I do wish you would look at me when I speak with you."

"I do wish you would go away!" she blurted, and then, because she was miserably aware of the two footmen pretending not to listen, she added in a whisper, "You could cost me my position, if not my reputation! Please—if you've come to apologize, I accept. And if you haven't—well, I suppose you should. In any case, I'm to stay here until my family is prepared to leave, and it wouldn't do for them to find you talking to me."

"Your *family*? Harsh treatment from kin. Are you the black sheep?"

He was prepared to have fun at her expense, then. She sighed. There was nothing she could do but answer him and hope he soon grew tired of his sport. "No, my lord. I'm the impoverished sheep. And likely to become more so if you stay here now."

"No," he said thoughtfully, "just the opposite, my dear. So you're newly come to London. That's why no one seemed to know your name."

"I've been here a month. I wish you hadn't asked about me. I'd like to remain in London, you see."

"Oh, I don't think that's any problem," he said, and when she gazed at him in confusion, he added with a grin, "It can certainly be arranged. . . ."

It was a pity, she thought, that his fascinating looks weren't matched by his disposition, which was miserable. He had such presence. He was tall and straight, his shoulders wide, hips narrow, abdomen flat. Not above thirty and five, she guessed, and a fine specimen of a gentleman.

He wasn't dressed as lavishly as a dandy or with the studied casualness of a Corinthian. But he was outfitted impeccably in a dark tight-fitted jacket over snowy linen and dark breeches. The only color about him was his wine-and-gold vest and his hazel eyes. His dark hair was cropped to discourage curls, but she could see it needed cutting again. Or did he wear it that way because it made a woman yearn to brush it back from that high forehead? After all, Viscount Sinclair was a rake, or at least that was what she'd heard.

She could believe it. He had the sort of dark magnetism a rake was supposed to have. She'd never met one before. The only gentlemen who had tried to toy with her were the kind who attempted to dally with powerless females: the sneaks, the shy, the devious. There was the pinch-and-run type, like Cousin Howard, who was the reason she'd left Cousin Elizabeth. And there was the grab-and-grapple sort, like hearty Squire Evelyn, who was the reason she'd always stayed in her room whenever he visited Cousin Mary. There was also the let's-pretend-my-hand-slipped kind, like Vicar Hanson, of all people!

But Viscount Sinclair was supposed to be a real rake. She wouldn't have guessed a real rake would bother tormenting her. That was usually what bitter men or heartless boys did. Perhaps, she thought suddenly, he hadn't really seen her. Perhaps he'd thought what he'd seen was a shadow or a trick of the leaping candlelight.

"Of course I know it's awkward," he suddenly said with such fellow feeling, such a gentle smile, that she doubted her estimate of him and looked at him with hope. "Embarrassing and foolish, isn't it? My following you into a dim hallway, creeping around like a fellow in a bad farce . . . but you disappeared. Now you say I can't dance with you. And I can hardly call on you, can I? In short, then, my dear Miss Bridget—yes, your cousin knew your name, at least—I have a proposition for you."

Bridget's heart sank.

"Being a companion is not very lucrative, and there's not much pleasure in it, either. And as I've noticed, there's no companionship in it at all—for you."

This was so true she forgot to be wary and just stared up at him.

"But that all depends on whom you companion, you see." He stepped closer and put his hand on the back of her chair as he bent to talk to her. He smelled of cognac and sandalwood, she thought absently. But not too much cognac; he certainly wasn't drunk. And there was the scent of fresh linen and soap, clean and masculine. Her nostrils fluttered as she took in his scent. He noticed and smiled slightly.

"Now, if a young woman such as yourself," he went on, "were to companion an amiable gentleman, she not only would find it much more profitable, she'd have a great deal of pleasure from it, that I can promise you."

She gaped at him.

"Yes," he said softly, nodding and smiling down at her, "nothing wrong with your ears."

"You're offering me . . ." She could not bring herself to utter the words.

"Carte blanche," he said helpfully.

"Carte bl . . . a position as your . . . *mistress*?" she gasped.

He nodded. "*Companion* is a better word, though, and a much better description of the position offered. Think of the advantages: a place of your own, your own servant, jewels, fashionable clothing, pocket money . . ."

"You're mad!" she said.

"No, my dear, merely entranced. And how else am I to get my hands on you? Think of the logistics, the difficulties, otherwise."

She arched her neck, flung back her head, and looked him in the eye. "You can't have seen," she said, "not clearly. It's not a play of light or something I should have removed with my napkin at dinner. It's there, and it's real, and it's part of me."

"Yes," he said gently, gazing at the long, deep dark line on her cheek, near the side of her nose. It curled down to the margin of her upper lip. His eyes studied it. "Yes, I know."

"I see," she said, so beside herself with outrage she forgot he was a nobleman and she nothing at all to him or to the world. "And so you thought my morals as cracked as my face, did you? Or that I was so desperate for the touch of a man that I'd take leave of my senses? The shame's on you, my lord! My face may be ruined, but my reputation is whole, and will stay that way—that I can promise *you*!"

"I see nothing wrong with your face, my dear," he said. "Had I, I wouldn't have offered."

"Now I understand!" she raged, more disappointed than shocked. "Oh, I understand very well. You're one of those men who find scarred females more attractive than whole ones! One of the kind who hate us, or fear us, or have a score to settle with us—a man who's pleased to see one of my sex disfigured so cruelly."

"If you say that seriously, you must need spectacles," he said, frowning. "My dear, has no one ever told you? You're lovely. The scar? It only points that out, as a beauty spot might. It doesn't diminish your beauty; rather, the contrast merely heightens it. Your skin is pure, and your eyes are amazing, gray as night fog. A small straight nose, and such lips . . . shapely, plump, they were made to be kissed. And that's not all. It's astonishing, because although you're slender, your form is nothing short of magnificent. Delicate, yet so ripe— lovely. Surely you must know that, too."

Bridget stared at him, astonished and chagrined. No one had ever said such wonderful things to her, and the someone who was saying them was only a rake. He was making love to her with words, right there in the hall! The worst part was that she felt her body prickling with pleasure in reply to him.

But she knew the truth—who better? And she knew it would free her from his spell.

She rose to her feet, lifted her chin, and faced him squarely. "This 'beauty spot,'" she sneered, "is so lovely. You're right. How fortunate I am. Why, I don't even have to bother drawing it on. It's always there. See how deep and well defined it is, too. Some females wear beauty spots in the form of flowers or hearts. But see mine? How unique. It's in the shape of a snake or a worm, how delightful. Cut line, my lord rake. It's the plague of my life. Haven't I seen people look at it, then away, then back again, as though they can't help themselves? I have, time and again. Haven't I heard people whisper, 'Oh, how pretty she'd be—if not for . . .'? Be sure I have, time and time again.

"A woman's face is her fortune," she went on bitterly, "and I have neither, my lord, nor any luck. I've had other offers such as yours over the years. In fact, I've had no other kind . . . well, only one other. But I know—too well!—that a certain kind of man considers a female's damaged face evidence of damaged goods."

"Do they?" he asked, obviously diverted. "Odd, I've never found it so. Most courtesans don't have any scars."

"*You* would be an expert on such women, I suppose," she spat, and then stopped, aghast at herself for speaking to a gentleman that way, appalled at having such a conversation with any man. She steadied herself. "I must again ask that you leave, or I'll have to leave myself," she said stiffly. "And I've been asked not to do that. You see my problem. So I give you one last chance to be the gentleman I thought you were. Well?"

"I'll leave, of course," he said, backing away. "For now. But think about what I've said, will you? The position I offered is still open. And I remind you that you mentioned your supposed ineligibility for it long before you mentioned your morals. Be that as it may. Think about those spectacles, too, will you? Because it occurs to me you can't have seen me clearly, either. Not that I'm vain. But I'm not an ogre."

"No," she breathed as he bowed. "No," she whispered to herself, watching him turn and leave, strolling down the hall back toward the ball, "not an ogre—just a monster."

She stood straight, but her lower lip was trembling as she fought for control again.

"Miss?" a voice said hesitantly. She looked up to see that a footman had left his post and stepped closer to her. "Good for you!" he said softly.

"And y'can double that from me," the other footman said. "'Ere's to you, my lady!"

"No, I'm not a lady," Bridget said, smiling through her tears.

"Mebbe not, but you're a lady right enough for our money," the footman said.

She inclined her head, just as a great lady might do. But only because she was too touched to speak right away.

"One thing he said that was true is that you're lovely, miss, and that you are!" the first footman said staunchly.

She nodded. How lucky she was, she thought sadly; she'd just received two of the best compliments of her lifetime. One from an unprincipled rake with possibly the most evil intentions she'd ever come across, and the other from a footman who felt sorry for her.

The front door opened. The page returned with her aunt's coachman in tow, looking grieved.

"Miss Cecily din't bring no wrap tonight," the coachman said. "I would've remembered. Only her shawl, and she carried that in with her. I looked, too, everywhere, but weren't nothin' else there."

"I know," Bridget said. "But . . . can we let that be our secret?"

"Oh," he said, and looked hard at her. He sighed. "Aye, lass. We working folk have got to stick together, don't we?"

"Aye," she said, and sighed, too, envying him, because he, at least, was paid in coin for his labor.

When he left she settled herself back on her chair. The footmen marched back into their places. That left her sitting by herself, thinking about the offer she'd gotten, puzzling over how her mind worked. Because wicked as it was, and certain as she was that she could never accept such a terrible offer as the rakish lord had made—still, there was no doubt that in some strange way she felt as good as she felt bad about it.

That was undoubtedly wicked, too. But pleasantly and safely so, because there was about as much future in such thoughts as in any of the other air dreams she regularly indulged in to enliven her life. She smiled to herself as she kept her lonely vigil in the drafty hall.

Being offered carte blanche from such a gentleman? And to imagine accepting it, even for a second? That was even more of a delusion than her usual fantasies, since she had a better chance of having some previously unknown ancient relative pass away and leave her a vast fortune along with a castle somewhere in Spain.

2

The Brixton family departed the ball as night was beginning to leave the sky. Cyrus Brixton, exhausted after a night of small-stakes gambling in the room set aside for the gentlemen at the ball, folded his hands over his paunch and slept as his carriage bore him home again. But his wife and his daughter couldn't stop talking.

"A triumph," Cecily's mother told her daughter again. "You danced every set and behaved as prettily as can be. You'll have your pick and be wed before the year is out, see if you're not!"

"Well, I had my eye on James Worth, you know, but Lord Montgomery is ever so charming, too, isn't he? And the Viscount engaged me in conversation for ever so long and danced with me right afterward," Cecily said smugly. She didn't have to name the viscount in question; her mother smiled just hearing the title.

"He's looking for a wife," her mother said with satisfaction.

"Which is wonderful, isn't it? Because I'm looking for a husband," Cecily giggled.

"Viscount Sinclair?" Bridget gasped.

Both women turned to stare at her.

"And why not?" her aunt asked. "We are not titled, of course, but your own grandfather was a baron. You never met him and may have forgotten, being out of the family so long. And Mr. Brixton's family has been here since the Conqueror."

"N-No, it's not that," Bridget stammered. "Viscount Sinclair is—he's—he's a rake!"

"Any gentleman would act the rake if he found himself being ogled so openly," her aunt said stiffly. "As to that, you're fortunate he didn't do more than mock you with his attentions when he saw you gaping at him like that. As who did not? Truth to tell, Bridget, we're very disappointed in you. Thank heavens Cecily had attended other balls before tonight's, or else I'd worry she'd be considered ill bred, having such a companion.

"I suppose you knew no better, coming from the wilds of nowhere, never having attended a young lady before. But listen, Bridget: You're here to watch our Cecily and lend her countenance, not to call attention to yourself! Poor child, I know you can't have thought—but we never considered you'd behave so, *especially* a person such as yourself, with such a deformity. We thought you'd be perfect for our Cecily, a perfect . . ."

A *perfect foil for her beauty* were the words her aunt left unsaid. But it was true, so Bridget said nothing. Instead she held her breath, afraid the next words spoken would send her back to mad Cousin Mary. *Anything but that*, she thought nervously, and waited.

". . . a perfect companion. And so you yet may be. But you must remember Cecily needs someone modest and unobtrusive—not bashful, mind, but refined and retiring—as her constant companion. We thought that with your handicap, you'd be shyer than you are. I suppose it's not your fault, given the relatives you've lived with. But Cecily does *not* need a lively young person to keep her awake. She *certainly* doesn't need you offering her advice on gentlemen. Indeed, I can't think of anyone less suited for that than you!"

There were insults and there were insults. Bridget drew in a breath, ready to announce her leaving. She didn't know where she'd go, but she had her limits.

"You don't know society or London," her aunt went on. Bridget let out her breath with relief. "I'*ll* advise her about gentlemen, thank you very much. As for the Viscount, he's been a widower for more than a decade, and of course a healthy man must have his outlets. But he's all that's correct when he's in society, and since he's come in search of a wife, he's the unexpected catch of the season.

"Besides, it's precisely your job to see that Cecily is never alone with him—until he declares himself. So you see, ogling him so brazenly was potentially disastrous. Still, we can mend matters. We'll tell him it was because you're new to London and were astonished to see such a fine gentleman."

"No need, Mama," Cecily laughed. "I told him already! Well, he asked about Bridget while we were talking."

Her mother gasped.

"I knew he felt sorry for her, and so I told him we'd taken her in, and he looked at me with *such* approval for it."

"Clever puss," her mother said, and went on to discuss first the Viscount's income and intentions and then the best gown for Cecily to wear when she saw him again.

Listening to them, Bridget hoped they'd get home before she cast up her accounts. She made herself feel a little better by realizing that if they didn't, at least she could say it was the motion of the coach that was making her sick.

But she was still upset as she prepared for bed. They wanted him for Cecily? Fine! Wonderful life poor Cecily would have with him if they did marry; she'd have to comb the women out of his bed before she got into it with him. But she couldn't warn her aunt or Cecily or even tell them what he'd offered her, because they wouldn't believe it. And if they did, they'd believe she'd asked for it. Well, she supposed she had, in a way. She shouldn't have indulged in that fantasy, she shouldn't have thought he couldn't see her scar, she never should have played peekaboo with a rake.

But now they were ordering her to be modest and unobtrusive? Ha! She'd be as silent as a deaf and dumb clam if she ever had to be in the same room as the rakish Viscount again. If he actually had the audacity to court Cecily with her there, Bridget thought, she'd pray to become invisible!

The thought of the Viscount's reaction to an invisible women retching while he was wooing Cecily cheered Bridget—almost enough to make her stop seeing that curling smile, those amused and knowing eyes that watched her through the last of the night into the dawn, following her down into uneasy sleep.

The invitation came three days later.

Cecily had almost given up hope. Other men had come to call. The Viscount hadn't.

"Just so. He is exactly right," Aunt Harriet said with satisfaction as she read the Viscount's note again. "A day later and it would be an afterthought; a day sooner and he'd look overeager."

She'd say "just so" if the villain had Cecily's dress half off in her front parlor, Bridget thought grumpily as she sat sewing and listening. *An inch lower and it would be a scandal, an inch higher and we wouldn't know he cared*, she mocked to herself, imagining what Aunt would say if she did discover her daughter in that monster's lustful embrace.

"Congratulations, my dear future son-in-law!" is the most likely thing, Bridget thought, and found herself depressed. Well, and why not? When Cecily married, Bridget would have to go to another relative, find a new home again. There was no knowing if the next relative who took her in would live in London, or if she did, whether she would even so much as leave the house to take tea with the local vicar. There might never be another ball or party or . . .

"I'll wear the yellow silk—no, the figured satin . . . no, not for an afternoon," Cecily was saying. "My new white gown! Yes! It's sprigged with those cunning violets. Oh, it's the very thing!"

"Perfect! I'll wear violet, too," Aunt Harriet said happily. "We shall look a pair."

Bridget doubted it. Cecily was an artless girl, naive, almost a little foolish in her conversation. She was tiny, shapely, with a halo of fat sausage ringlets around her pretty little face. Her mama was all show and ambition. She was tall and stately and looked as though she could balance a tea tray on her bosom. But they were both blond, Bridget thought fairly, trying to suppress her smiles at the idea of Aunt Harriet promenading with a silver tea set on her breast.

She saw Cecily looking at her quizzically, and bit her lip. She was so used to being on the outside of other people's conversations, having to make her own amusements, that she'd gotten into the habit of doing it more and more often. If she wasn't careful, she thought in sudden alarm, she'd be mad as poor old Cousin Mary before she knew it, walking around constantly smiling at jests no one else could hear.

"What will you wear, Bridget?" Cecily asked again.

"Oh, sorry. Wear to where? I mean," Bridget said as Cecily giggled, "where are we going?"

"We've been invited to a pleasure garden with the Viscount."

Somehow Bridget wasn't surprised that pleasure would be involved in whatever the Viscount wanted to do.

"Bridget will look neat," Aunt Harriet said. "What she wears isn't as important as *how* she wears it," she added, sending her niece a significant glance.

"Oh, a *pleasure* garden! Like Vauxhall Gardens!" Bridget said excitedly, as what they were talking about sank in, "Or Raneleigh! Or the Spring Gardens! I've read about them for so long and longed to see one! They say they have flowered walks and fountains, and great rotundas for music and dancing, and galleries for art, and fireworks displays, too!"

"And dark garden walks for other things," Cecily said with another giggle.

Aunt Harriet exchanged an amused look with her daughter. "Which a young lady should not know about," she chided Cecily gently, "or at least not *speak* about.

"You must have read old books," she told Bridget. "Most of the pleasure gardens are closed, made over into estates or public parks. In my youth there were dozens; now there are only a few, and many of those have been converted to botanical gardens. As for the ones left intact—*everyone* goes to Vauxhall now. You might find yourself falling over your own dressmaker there! The Viscount has more exquisite taste than that, of course. He's taking us to an exclusive garden, he says, with an ornamental lake and swan boats."

"We'll promenade, he'll have a chance to get to know me better," Cecily said happily.

"And we shall walk a step or two behind the couple," Aunt Harriet told Bridget, "far enough back to give him privacy, close enough to remind him we're there."

All Bridget's desire to see the gardens fled. "But if you're going, Aunt, why do you need me?"

"Do you want him to think we're peasants? A girl of good birth needs more than her mama in attendance. Besides, that way I can have a seat if I get weary, and Cecily will still be properly chaperoned."

Wellington's legions would be needed to properly chaperone a girl in the company of the Viscount, Bridget thought. But she nodded. At least she'd see a pleasure garden, even if there was little pleasure in it for her.

There was less pleasure in dressing for the actual day.

Bridget stared glumly at herself in the mirror, or tried to. She couldn't really see past Cecily, who was twirling in front of her looking glass, trying to see herself from every angle. Cecily was radiant in her violet-sprigged gown, with violet ribbons twined through her ringlets. The color enlivened her wide blue eyes, and she looked young and charming. She was whirling so much that Bridget saw only glances of herself. She thought she could have saved herself the bother. She had five day dresses, and the best that could be said of the one she wore was that it was one of them.

The good thing about the current fashion was that it didn't matter if a girl had a fortune or tuppence. She didn't need yards of fine fabrics, hoops, and crinolines, as women had in the past. Now fashion called for all dresses to be basically alike: simple, high-waisted, and round-necked, falling straight from beneath the breasts to the toes. Bridget's was a dark green. Of course, silk would be nicer than muslin, but the color suited her, and the fashion showed off her—

Not that it mattered. She could wear a gown of spun gold and it wouldn't matter, she thought miserably. Viscount Sinclair had come to her secretly, in the dark, and asked her to whore for him. He was taking her cousin out into the light, with an eye toward asking her to be his wife. And for icing on the cake, she had to pretend it hadn't happened and walk behind the two of them, pretending not to mind that either.

Cecily stopped spinning, content that there couldn't be any improvement in her appearance. Her maid, watching her adoringly, had told her that many times, and she could see it for herself. But Bridget was silent. Cecily noticed her at last. She tilted her head to the side and gazed at her cousin's reflection behind her in the looking glass.

"You know," she said thoughtfully, "you look very

well, Cousin Bridget. And it's not just because I'm getting used to your face."

Her maid gasped.

Cecily's laughter was bright. "Oh, Meg," she told her maid, "Cousin Bridget told me to be honest with her from the first, and it isn't as if it's any secret. No use pretending that scar isn't there—it would be like ignoring the nose on your face. But it doesn't look bad, Bridget," she said thoughtfully, watching her cousin. "Indeed, it does not. In fact . . . it gives you a certain air, you know? With your dark hair and those dark eyes, it gives you a certain savage look. Like a gypsy, or a woman with a strange and exciting but violent past. Not exactly brutal, but certainly turbulent. If you were a man, it would be dashing. As it is, it's . . . wild-looking. Many men find that attractive, I believe."

Cecily is young, Cecily's foolish. Cecily never has a private word with me, and she has no reason to be cruel to me, so it isn't that, Bridget thought frantically, and said calmly, "If you say so, Cousin."

"Well, I've heard gentlemen say so," Cecily said, and giggled. "Which is why Mama's so right, you know. If you stare at the Viscount today, he'll definitely get the wrong idea."

"Shall I change to a white frock, then?" Bridget asked in a monotone.

"Oh, no! I was just saying how well you looked in the green, silly," Cecily laughed.

Bridget looked at her cousin with new eyes. Yes, she thought, she did spend much too much time listening to her own interior conversations. She ought to have listened more in the month she'd been here. Cecily and her mama really were a pair. "Thank you, Cousin," she said.

*   *   *

All her worry was for nothing. He didn't even notice her, or if he did, it was in that first and only look he passed over her when he was welcomed in. One brief glance, and then those bored eyes swept past her and back to Cecily, and he smiled, at last. Bridget almost wondered if she'd imagined the whole thing, if it had been some fantasy she'd cooked up to pass the long hours she'd sat in the hall that night, waiting for the family. But no. If it had been a fantasy of hers, he'd have declared his love and admiration for her, not his lust and low estimation of her.

Bridget watched that dark head lower as he bowed over her cousin's hand. She should be pleased, she told herself. She was being granted a rare opportunity to watch a supreme rake at work . . . or play.

He had a carriage waiting for them. He sat opposite Cecily and her mama while Bridget shrank against the carriage, looking out the window and trying to pretend she wasn't there. She must have been successful, for no one paid the least attention to her.

But she soon discovered she could watch the Viscount without his knowing, because she could see his reflection in the window. It wasn't a patch on seeing him real and whole in the sunlight. But it was more than enough for her; she didn't think she could stay so calm and keep her face so serene if she saw more of him than that.

He looked even better by daylight, she thought sadly. Her quick glimpse of him had confirmed it. His hair wasn't just dark, it was thick and black. His face wasn't merely tanned but seemed brushed with tawny bronze, lending color to his changeable topaz eyes. He wore a dark blue jacket, a casual but cleverly tied cravat around his strong neck, a canary vest over his dazzling white shirt, skintight fawn trousers, and gleaming Hessian boots. He was vivid, alive, devastatingly attractive.

The Viscount might prefer to spend most of his time between the sheets, but it was clear he didn't, Bridget thought. Such exercise, spirited though it might be, couldn't account for those shoulders, the muscles in his long, hard thighs . . .

She blinked. She'd actually shocked herself. She shook her head and tried to watch the scenery outside the window, not the vital man reflected there. *Might as well try not to see at all*, she thought wretchedly, for he dominated her view.

Aunt Harriet, meanwhile, dominated the conversation. Cecily just kept giggling—although to be fair, Bridget thought, she sometimes simpered, too.

"The gardens are west of town," the Viscount finally said when Aunt Harriet took a moment to clear her throat, "which is why it's taking so long. But it's worth the trip, I think—ah, we come in sight at last!"

They passed through iron gates and drove down a long tree-lined avenue before they pulled into a circular drive in front of a manor house. There were a few other coaches there.

The Viscount helped the ladies out, Bridget last. He took her hand with casual indifference and released it as soon as she stepped down, turning his attention back to Cecily and her mama.

"Shall we?" he asked, offering them each an arm.

And so Bridget walked alone, behind them.

They strolled the garden's paths. Bridget saw some other well-dressed people walking by. They nodded as they passed. But she was disappointed. It wasn't because the strangers acted as if they didn't notice her, trailing behind the trio as though she were a servant; in fairness, even though she was a relative, she wasn't more than that to either Cecily or her aunt.

She wasn't disappointed because the Viscount ignored her, either, she kept telling herself as she straggled behind them. She had his measure now, and of course she wasn't unhappy about that! But she did feel a little deflated. She'd braced herself for having to endure and ignore his secret glittering glances, knowing smiles, or meaningful silences—and instead she'd not gotten so much as a glance or a grin.

She decided she was disappointed because the place was just a botanical garden. She loved flowers, but she'd spent her life in the countryside, and when she'd heard they were to visit a pleasure garden, her head had been filled with thoughts of entertainment that didn't grow on a vine or a stalk. She'd thought of spectacles: grand rotundas, orchestras playing, long art-filled galleries. Or if gardens, then gardens with cascades of dancing waters and grottoes filled with fascinating statues or living tableaus, as Vauxhall was said to have. This was only a garden.

There was birdsong, but not much other sound except for their voices and the crunch of their steps on the crushed-shell paths. Cecily had a little parasol to protect her from the sun, but Bridget wore a bonnet. It cut off all vision except that straight in front of her, and when she lowered her head to watch her step, she could hardly hear the light conversation in front of her—apart from Cecily's occasional giggles, the drone of her aunt's voice, and an occasional rumbled comment from the Viscount.

It was a mild day; sunlight filtered through the tree-tops, and the play of light and shadow was soothing. Bridget followed the trio, staring at her slippers as she walked. It was better than focusing on his broad back or on how gracefully he moved for a man who was so tall, with such wide shoulders and long legs. . . . She started drifting away in her mind, diverting herself with her own thoughts, as usual.

"You don't care to accompany us?" she suddenly heard the Viscount ask her.

They'd stopped. Bridget halted abruptly. If she'd continued to walk on mindlessly, she would have found herself ankle deep in water, because they stood on the banks of a wide ornamental lake.

"Miss Cooke?" he asked innocently.

He stood in front of her with a look of polite inquiry on his face. She searched for more but saw only that. His eyes were so bright and knowing, though, that her heart picked up its beat as she continued to stare up at him, speechless.

"The Viscount asked if we'd like to get into a swan boat and explore the island in the lake, Bridget," Aunt Harriet said loudly and with a warning tone. "We're wondering why you needed a separate invitation."

"Oh, I don't! I . . . just was wool-gathering," Bridget said nervously.

"Spring fever," the Viscount said lightly. "Unless, of course, she has a fear of the water?" he asked her aunt.

Oh, it's "she" now, is it? Bridget thought, bridling. The rogue, the cad, the wretch! "She is not afraid of the water," she snapped. "I was just being inattentive, and I'm sorry. Yes, of course, Aunt, I'd like it very much."

The swan boat was really only a glorified rowboat,

made to look as though it were a giant swan floating on the lake. A carved representation of a huge swan's body covered its hull, with the head jutting out in front and the high slope of its white wings protecting the passengers in the middle from any watery spray. A man with a pole stood in the front by the swan's head; there was a long seat at the wing level, and one behind, by the jaunty tail.

"You ladies can sit in the center; I think there's room for all of you. You're slim, you should fit," the Viscount told Cecily, giving her his hand. She lifted the hem of her skirt to show him a glimpse of her ankles as she daintily picked her way into the boat. "I'll be in the back. It will be a squeeze, of course . . . unless you'd rather stay ashore, Mrs. Brixton? There's a seat in the shade there, in the gazebo on the hillside. We won't be long."

Aunt Harriet hesitated, looking back at the lacy white gazebo longingly.

"They serve tea and cakes there, and you should be comfortable," the Viscount added.

"I should," Aunt Harriet said crossly. "That is to say, *if* I could be sure Cecily would be attended to." She shot a look at Bridget.

"My dear Mrs. Brixton!" the Viscount said with shock. "You don't think I'*d* let her come to any harm?"

Aunt Harriet gasped. Bridget had never seen her at a loss for words, and she almost felt sorry for her aunt when she saw her face as she scrambled to make horrified apologies.

"Neither would I," Bridget said quickly. "Don't worry, Aunt, I'll be awake on all suits." She took the Viscount's hand, stepped into the boat, and settled herself alongside Cecily.

Cecily twirled her parasol and gazed up into the Viscount's face as the boat was poled out into the lake. Bridget watched the pair, promising herself she'd be alert now. If the man had been able to sneak around and shock Bridget's stockings off that night, and then come out this morning and pretend he'd never done it—and with such ease—who knew what else he was capable of?

But it seemed a man in search of a wife was a lot less inventive and much more boring than one in search of a mistress.

They left the swan boat when they reached the island, and strolled some more. This time the Viscount and Cecily walked together as a couple, with Bridget three paces behind them. The island was another disappointment to Bridget. She'd hoped for something exotic, but it was only more heavily treed and less formally landscaped than the gardens they'd left. The biggest difference was that Cecily didn't have much to giggle about now. Bridget could hear the Viscount's deep voice as he kept telling Cecily about the flowers, bushes, and trees they passed, and there wasn't much humor in that. *He's much wittier when he's looking for sport,* she yearned to tell her cousin.

"Yer lordship!" a voice called excitedly.

They all turned. The man who'd poled the swan boat to the island came running up behind them. "Best be headin' back now," the fellow puffed. "A storm's coming up from the west. Sudden squalls come 'round here this time of year. Ye'll be drenched like drowned rats if ye stay here now."

"Oh, my!" Cecily yelped. She hurried back to the boat slip with the Viscount, huffing as she tried to move fast and still tell him how dreadful it would be to get her new gown wet. It wouldn't be dreadful for him, though, Bridget thought sourly; if the gauzy fabric got drenched, it would cling to her cousin like a second skin.

"Don't worry," the Viscount assured her. "We'll get back before the storm."

Bridget glanced up at the sky as she hurried behind them. What she could see through the treetops looked clear and sunny to her. But it was the season of sudden downpours, and she didn't know the district.

They stopped short. "What's this?" the Viscount demanded when they reached the shore again.

The swan boat was swaying low in the water. Three elderly, terrified-looking people sat huddled in the middle. There was obviously room for only one more, at the tail end.

"Had to pick up some others at the far end of the island," the boatman explained, "an' they was there first. Besides them needing to get back more, if you know what I mean. Only room for one more, or the boat founders. Quick, who is it to be? Which one of ye will be comin' with me now? I'll be back soon as I can for the others."

Cecily looked at the elderly passengers and then quickly back at the Viscount and Bridget. Her lovely blue eyes revealed her uncertainty. She didn't want to get wet—who would? But it was clear she didn't know what to do.

As Bridget weighed her own options, she was sure she looked as panicked as she felt. She didn't mind getting wet, but she'd rather wade back than stay alone with the Viscount. On the other hand, if she took the remaining seat in the boat, her aunt would certainly kill her for abandoning her duties and leaving Cecily alone with him. He might be playing the gentleman today, but he was just playing—they all must know that. The man was a rake.

Which was precisely why Cecily was worried, wondering if she should leave Bridget alone with him. A rake might someday make a reformed husband—for a gently bred girl. Or he might forget that idea if he became protector of an impoverished one.

The Viscount, his face impassive, strode into the water, ignoring what it did to his high polished boots. He held out his hand to Cecily. "Come, my dear," he said. "I promised your mama I'd take care of you, and so I shall. Go now, be safe and dry. I'll be along as soon as I can."

Cecily hesitated.

Bridget bit her lip. After all, he hadn't even looked at her. Why should he? Maybe he had been drunk that night. He was certainly cold and sober now.

"C'mon," the man with the pole insisted, hopping into the boat, "or I'm off without any of ye. If the rain ain't enough to make ye hurry, I got to tell ye, the lightnin' be fierce in storms this time of year. And if one of them monsters is hit and falls," he said, gesturing to the towering trees, "there won't be nothing for me to pick up on my way back."

Cecily squealed. Suspicions were one thing, lightning and thunder another.

"Go now, my dear," the Viscount said kindly, and handed her into the boat.

Bridget stood at the water's edge, watching the swan boat diminish to the size of a toy as it made for the distant shore.

She looked up and around then, wondering where to take shelter. Not under a tree, of course. But the place was all trees except down at the water, where she was—and she knew that near the water was the worst place to be when there was lightning around.

"Come," the Viscount ordered her, holding out his hand.

She took it and followed blindly.

They ran around a turn on the little sandy beach. She got a stitch in her side trying to keep up with the long strides he was taking, but she kept running with him until he finally slowed. Then she looked up to see he'd led her to another gazebo. It was a simple wooden one, almost hidden by flowering hedges. She ran up its steps with the Viscount and saw it was a rustic retreat, with a wooden bench built all around its interior. She sat down and caught her breath, relieved.

The latticework above would be some protection from the rain when it came, because it was covered with bright yellow laburnum. The pink and white hedges would keep wind-driven rain from getting in the sides. It was a lovely place, actually, a fragrant and bright flowery bower.

The Viscount sat beside her.

She stiffened, but he didn't seem to notice her. Instead, he was taking in the view with apparent pleasure. Bridget relaxed. She wouldn't say a word, and maybe somehow they'd get through this with no embarrassment. There was no question about it—he *had* been drunk that night, after all, and was trying to forget the whole thing as much as she was. She sighed, folded her hands in her lap, and waited for the storm.

He turned to her.

"I thought they'd never leave," he said, and smiled.

3

She blinked. For a moment it seemed the only thing she could do. But then Bridget found her wits.

"I beg your pardon?" she asked, because she was sure she'd heard wrong.

"Why should you?" he asked lightly. "You haven't done anything—yet. I have, though, and it took a lot of planning, I can tell you." He leaned back, his arm on the rail behind her, and smiled down at her. "How can a fellow winkle an attractive young woman out of her house and arrange a way to get her alone without actually kidnapping her or setting her household in an uproar? A problem, certainly. But all in all an enchanting one, for a change. I carried it off simply and smoothly. Wellington couldn't have done better. But enough of me applauding myself. Aren't you impressed?"

"Impressed?" Bridget said as her eyes widened. "Impressed?" she cried as she shot to her feet, looking around wildly. "I'm—I'm appalled! How could you?"

"Oh, please sit down," he said calmly. "I won't hurt you. I'm a rake, not a cad." He shrugged as she stood staring at him. "Or don't sit down—it's as you like. But as for *how* I could, it was so simple it's almost embarrassing. Boatmen are underpaid, and there are too many old people who need money in London to mention. Poor old dears. Being paid to take a pleasant walk in a garden and then getting a free boat ride in the bargain is almost a vacation for them, or so they said. I feel such a pleasant glow—it's nice to do charitable work."

"But the storm, the danger . . ."

"There's no storm coming, Bridget. Yes, I can see you're beginning to understand that. You're not slow. It's one of the things I like about you. Oh, and you can stop looking for a place to run and hide. You can, of course; I won't stop you. You've read too many novels if you think I will. But all you'll find here are bushes and trees, and a long, lonely wait for the boatman to come back. He will. There's no reason to run away. I simply want to talk with you."

She continued to stare at him. He didn't look as though he'd pounce. The awful thing, she thought as she slowly sat again, was that he looked as though he'd never have to pounce on a girl. They'd be too busy trying to pounce on him, if they'd eyes in their head.

"Why me?" she asked simply. She said what she thought. Being alone so much had bred that trait in her. It was hard to keep trying to stop it. Now she didn't have to.

"Look in the mirror," he said, his gaze on her face.

"Oh. That again," she said, a little sadly. She lifted a

finger to her upper lip, almost unconsciously touching the indentation as she felt it. "It's from a childhood accident. There's no terrible story to go with it. It says nothing about my character."

He frowned, looking puzzled. "Why should it?"

"Well, Cecily said, just today, that she'd heard some men talking. . . . And I have, often enough," Bridget said, looking anywhere but at him. "There's something about someone like me that excites a certain kind of man. Somehow they think I'm less of a lady, more of a wanton . . . whatever, I hardly understand it myself. But it's not true. I'm no less because of what's on my face; it's just not so." She raised her eyes to him, hoping he'd understood.

He was frowning even more fiercely.

"So little Cecily has more wit than I'd supposed," he said in an angry rumble. "Or at least more bile, which passes for wit these days. Listen, I wasn't talking about that." He gestured to her lip in annoyance. "I'm not attracted to it, nor does it detract from your appearance. I told you that the other night. If anything, it enhances you, nothing more."

"Nothing more?" she asked in outrage. "Are you blind? It's changed my entire life!" She reined in her temper, remembering he was a nobleman, and that she was at his mercy now, besides. But she was still angry that he made light of something so painful to her. "It's fully two inches long! Or would be," she admitted, "if you straightened it out. It's too deep to cover with powder, too. I suppose if I were a man, it might be nothing. Or even attractive, as Cecily said. Huh! If I were a man, I'd grow a mustache and be done with it! I can hardly do that, you know."

He smiled. "Faint heart! You could try."

She conceded a grin.

"But if you were a man, you wouldn't, you know. You'd show it off, claiming it was a saber wound from your student days, or a reminder of the war, and all the ladies would swoon over you. It wasn't either of those things, was it?" he suddenly asked, pretending to be nervous and afraid of her.

It was too bad such a terrible man could seem so likable. She took a deep breath. "Look . . . ," she began slowly.

"I am," he told her amiably. "I can't seem to stop. You don't know how lovely you are, do you? Such fine skin, so clear. Such an insignificant nose, but straight as a die, and adorable, even when pinched with fury, as it is now. Your eyebrows could have been painted on by a master, but I see they weren't; there's no artifice about you. And such eyes, gray, glowing with light. Your passion becomes you, you know. Your lips—I've praised them before, but why not? They're perfectly etched, full, tempting. You have a scar, yes, but it distorts nothing. Your neck is lovely, smooth, and graceful. And that form! Those magnificent br—"

"Stop!" Bridget shouted, clapping her hands over her ears.

He cocked his head to the side. "I was merely going to say something about your bright eyes again," he said innocently, but his own eyes sparkled with mirth. "I haven't got round to your hair yet. If you'd take off your bonnet? . . . I suppose not. Then I really will have to get on to your form."

"*That*," Bridget cried, "you shall not!"

"I meant metaphorically, of course," he said with a little smile.

"I know what you meant," she said vehemently, "and I wish you'd stop. It's not decent."

He lifted an eyebrow.

"I'll bet that if I were Cecily, you wouldn't say such things!"

"Of course not. Cecily's all curls and giggles—it would be like making love to a baby. I have my faults, but that's not one of them. I'm surprised at you, Bridget."

He really seemed offended. She almost apologized, but then she got a grip on herself. He was very dangerous. Sitting there, all indolence, all relaxed strength, bold and masculine, with those laughing eyes, and clever as he could stare, to boot. He had an attractive face, a fascinating form, a deep, dark purr of a voice with a lilt to it she couldn't quite place, though it wound its way into places in herself she dared not name. Oh, very dangerous.

She'd never felt the lure of a man like this before. But she was confident in her virtue, and too terrified of disaster if she should ever stray. She was amazed to discover she was a little sorry about that now, but it gave her some much-needed confidence.

"Well, I'm sorry to have wasted your time," she said primly, "but you can praise me to the skies and it won't matter. I won't be your mistress, or anything like it. You can ask me again and ag—"

"I won't," he said simply, cutting her off. As she stared, he added, "I asked twice. That's enough. More than that is pleading, and I don't do that. Pity, though. It would have been good for both of us, suited both our needs. I've plenty of money, and you've none."

"I have morals, and you've none!" she shot back.

"Yes, but I don't need morals, and you do need

money," he said gently. She fumed silently, finding no way to rebut that. He nodded and added, "You work and are unappreciated. With me, there'd be nothing but play, and you'd be incredibly appreciated. No, don't fuss, I'm just explaining. I was attracted to you by your face and figure. But you're quick and I'd have liked talking to you, too."

"You were attracted to me by my condition!" she declared, sitting up straight. "You wouldn't have asked any *lady* at the ball what you asked me."

"Oh, they were complaining about it, were they?"

Impossible man, she thought darkly. "No, they weren't— or if they were, I didn't hear it. All they said was that you're a rake. That I did hear."

"And that is what's discouraging you?" he asked mildly.

"No!"

"Well, if it is," he went on, as though he hadn't heard her, "it shouldn't. What's in a name, after all? Especially *rake*."

"It's a warning to women. It means a man who— who—" She struggled, trying to find proper words for an improper thing, and, watching his growing amusement, decided to spit it out. "Who has many women!"

"No," he said, "not necessarily. For instance, there were at least a dozen men I could have pointed out to you at the ball who have had more women. But those women were social equals, and the men had what society calls 'discreet affairs' with them. Most of the men were married, and their affairs were with women married to other men. They're considered men of the world, while I'm called a rake. But I don't dally with married women; it's a peculiarity of mine. And I can't dally with any other kind of lady without providing a ring for her finger first.

"So then, who *can* I 'have,' as you so discreetly put it? Street women? Too vulgar. Women provided in certain establishments? Too crass. I'm trying to be delicate about this, you know, but if your face gets much redder it will go up in flame. To be brief, then. I've had mistresses, yes. And in the plural, yes. Mistresses are usually of a lower class, thus I'm a rake."

"I'm not of a lower class," Bridget said furiously. "My father was the third son of a baron, but they cut him off from the family when he married my mother. She wasn't lower-class, either. She was the daughter of a bookseller, that's true, but worse than that in their eyes, she was Irish."

"Hence the temper," he mused.

"That is a vile thing to say. Worse, it's a cliché and—"

"Mind, I'm part Celt myself," he said. "Half my ancestors come from Wales."

"Oh," she said, "I see. Hence the accent."

He laughed. "Touché. Yes, hence the accent. I was brought up near the border. So. Two Celts. We have so much in common."

"We both breathe and eat, that's true, but otherwise we're as far from each other as Ireland and Wales are," she said, enjoying herself now. She hadn't had so much fun in a long time. Each time she got frightened, thinking she'd said too much or gone too far, he'd meet her and make her go further. But it was only talk, she reminded herself, and only for a little while, and she was beginning to feel sorry about that.

She eyed him warily. He smiled back at her serenely and crossed one long, well-muscled leg over the other. She looked away, trying to ignore her reaction to his powerful physical presence. The man only had to move a muscle, and she felt a corresponding movement in the pit of her stomach. When he looked at her steadily, her heart beat unsteadily. And he kept looking at her. But she hated silences, and they had to pass the time until the boat came back. She wondered if he'd laugh if she commented on the weather.

Bridget no longer thought the Viscount would pounce on her, but she was beginning to feel he had some kind of supernatural magnetic force, because she felt him drawing her even nearer. His arm was draped around the rail in back of her. But only that. He was within arm's reach, no closer. She kept thinking, though, how easy it would be for him to just reach out those long arms and take her.

"Who was the one man who had a proper offer for you," he asked suddenly, "and why didn't you take him up on it? Surely it would have been better than playing companion to Cousin Cecily."

She stared at him.

"That night we met, you said you'd had many offers like mine, but only one proper one. You see, I remember everything you said."

"Rakes have to have good memories," she grumbled, "so they don't call their women by the wrong names."

"Exactly!" he said, clearly delighted with her. "I suppose it was a tragic relationship, and that's why you're not telling me?"

"Oh. That. Well, if you must know, it wasn't, not at the time, though it turned out that way. He was a boy I grew up with. When my father's family cast him out, Papa went to live with Mama's father and tried to help run the bookstore. When that failed, he got a position as a tutor in the north. Jeremy was one of his pupils, the local squire's son."

"A bully and a fool, I suppose."

"No!" Bridget flared. "A very decent boy. We were friends. I was surprised when he offered, though. I thought it was because he felt responsible, since it was his mother's dog who'd given me the scar, but he said no, he'd known me for so long he never noticed it anymore."

"A dog?"

"Yes. Sorry to disappoint you," she said, stiffening again, as she always did when she thought of the scar. "A spaniel, old and mean, and gone in the wits. I was petting it one day and it snapped with no warning. Unfortunately my face was in the way. At least, that's what Jeremy's mother kept crying. I only half remember, for I was just seven at the time.

"The worst part was that it wouldn't let go and they tried to drag it away. Hence," she said, bitterly echoing his comment about her temper, "the long and jagged scar. It could have been worse. The squire put me on his horse and raced to the doctor. He decided to reopen it and cut it more neatly, drawing the ends together so it would heal without pulling my features crooked. It didn't so much hurt as horrify me, I remember. Or else I was so horrified I didn't feel the hurt of it. He was supposed to cure me and he came at me with a knife? I squalled the roof down, until he promised he'd make me look pretty again if I'd only be still and let him do it."

She sighed. "I was so disappointed. I'd thought he meant he'd heal it, erase it entirely. When the bandage came off, I was shocked to find it still there."

"I see nothing I can say can heal what you thought all those years ago," he said softly.

"Not *all* those years ago, my lord," she said, stung, "I'm five and twenty, old enough, but not ancient."

"I see that the snapping stayed with you, too," he said.

She glowered at him, but not for long. The sun was in his eyes, finding gold there, lightening them to glowing amber with accents of sparkling green. They turned down slightly at the corners, as did his thin dark brows. That, along with his long, high-bridged nose, gave him almost a haughty expression, aloof and distant. But when he turned his gaze on her, that notion vanished. His eyes kindled, promising something warmer than she'd ever known. She gazed back at him, too fascinated to be aware she was staring.

"You know," he said thoughtfully in that low purr of a voice, "I do believe that if I just kissed you once, it would settle the matter. . . . Oh, sorry. You think I was asking you again, do you? I wasn't, I promise. But did I mention that the offer still stands? If you change your mind, you can always let me know."

"That was asking," she said in a shaken voice, dragging her gaze from his.

"All of this is asking, if you want to be precise," he answered softly, "but all I promised was not to ask you again in so many words. No, not fair. But I am a rake, you know. So. What happened to Jeremy?" he asked in more normal tones.

"He fell in Spain, at Badajoz," she said sadly. "He was army-mad, so his father bought him a commission. He asked me to marry him when he was home on leave. I said no, and how I've regretted it since! Only I think he offered just because he hadn't seen me in years and was a little shocked to find me not married yet—and living with mad Cousin Mary in the bargain."

"Ah! Now there's something I hadn't known about."

Bridget was grateful for the change in subject. She turned to him again, feeling safer because she'd saved up such a hoard of amusing stories from those unhappy years. Because he shared a sense of the ridiculous with her and would appreciate—

Better not to think of what he'd appreciate, my girl, she told herself, and quickly began to tell him about mad Cousin Mary.

He did laugh. And then told her about his mad cousin Martin and his collection of cheeses. She laughed until she saw him cock his head to one side, watching her. Then she stilled, embarrassed. It had been a long time since she'd laughed from the heart.

"I wish you hadn't stopped," he said. "Your laughter sounds like tumbling water, refreshing to hear. There's nothing stifled about it—it reflects your hidden spirit, I think. Still, I wonder if I should be laughing. I may become mad Cousin Ewen someday, after all. Oh," he said, watching her expression, "you didn't know my given name? How remiss of me. We never were properly introduced, were we?"

He arose in one smooth motion, stood before Bridget, and made her an old-fashioned, sweeping bow, one hand to his heart.

"Ewen Kenton Philip Sinclair at your command. Viscount Sinclair, Baron Paige, and lord of all he surveys—except for one lovely, stubborn young woman, that is to say."

She stood and curtsied low. "Miss Bridget Cooke, my lord. Mistress only of her own self, and proud of it."

"Unkind," he said, smiling at her. He took her hand as she rose from her curtsy, and kept holding it. His hand was warm and dry and big enough to swallow up hers, and his thumb slowly stroked the back of her hand as he held it. Her eyes flew to his, shocked. They were alone. If he tried, she certainly wouldn't fight, she thought in a flurry. After all, such a struggle would be undignified. How near he was, how intent his gaze . . .

He slowly released her hand. "How you tempt me," he murmured, still staring at her lips. "But I gave my word."

She sat again, shaken. "I wonder when they'll be back," she said nervously, for something to say.

"Wonder no more," he said, sitting beside her again, this time a little closer. He drew a watch from his pocket. "Not long now, actually. Just long enough for me to tell you something about myself. Because I want you to know me."

"I know what you want," she muttered.

"Do you?" he asked in amusement.

"Well, I'm not deaf. You asked me already. And if you wanted me to know you in any other way but the biblical," she said, greatly daring now that she knew the boat was coming back soon, "you would have gone about it differently. This has been a strange afternoon, my lord, an interlude I won't forget. But of course I know what you want. They say you came to London in search of a wife. You came to me in search of a mistress. There's no mystery there."

"I don't think you know what I was in search of— maybe because I didn't either," he said slowly. "So. You refuse to be my mistress. Noted. What would you say if I said I was interested in you for a wife?" he asked abruptly.

"I'd say you were a liar, and there's the truth!"

"If you were a man, I'd make you fight to defend

those words," he said, eyes glittering, suddenly so serious she was taken aback. Then he sat back, smiling, his tone intimate again. "But you aren't, or we wouldn't be here, would we? And as for me fighting you, there is that scar—you got it from your fencing master at Old Heidelberg, you said? In that case, I think I'd be better off to let the insult pass."

It took a moment, for she had never had a man joke about her scar to her face before. And then she began to laugh with him, and only stopped when he did, abruptly.

"Oh, too bad," he said, cocking his head, listening to a far-off sound. "They're calling."

She heard the distant shouting, too.

"Too soon, but not too late to make plans," he said briskly. "Now then, Miss Cooke, when shall we two meet again?"

She sobered. "I thought you weren't going to ask that again!"

"Elevate your mind, my dear," he said, grinning. "I only meant I'd like to see you again. But how?"

"If a gentleman was interested in me in any respectable fashion, he'd come to call on me at my home," she said. "But how silly of me—you know that."

"Do I? Have you really given some thought to the consequences of my doing just that? I don't think so. You're cousin to sweet Cecily, and yet you're treated like a lackey. You think you'd be pleased if I called on you properly? Think about it again.

"I'm a very careful man, Bridget. I was married once and know too well that marriage is a serious business. It's a lifetime tie no one can put asunder, at least seldom legally. You're charming and lovely and very unique. But I'm not a boy anymore. I can't—and won't—declare myself to any woman after only meeting with her a few times. I can't and won't raise her or her family's expectations by calling on her too often, either. A man must walk a fine line in such matters. A nobleman must walk an even narrower one."

She looked at him in confusion. He sighed. "I have to tell you that if I call on you as you say I should, I might decide to go no further than that. I might decide we do not suit. A man is entitled to decide that, you know; it happens every day. But your situation is not an everyday one. You'd have to live with the consequences. You don't understand? Then just imagine what your aunt and cousin would say. No, it's far better to arrange to meet me in secret and keep it hidden from them until we do come to some decisions, you and I. You could meet me at a tearoom, the park, or even a bookseller's, if you're so inclined. Anywhere but where you suggest, I'd think."

She frowned. "I'd think not, my lord. You want to know what I think? I think you're a rake, but I know you talk in circles. I also know what's right and proper, for I can't afford not to. We will *not* meet again."

He shrugged. "As you wish."

"But thank you for behaving honorably this afternoon," she said. "I was at your mercy. I am grateful that you had some for me."

"*Far* too many novels," he said, "but what can you expect from a bookseller's granddaughter?"

He rose, offering her his hand. She ignored it and stood by herself. He smiled sadly. "Over here!" he called into the distance, and led her from the gazebo.

Bridget almost laughed at the sight of her aunt and Cecily goggling at them from the swan boat as she and the Viscount came out of the trees and walked to the shore.

"All is well?" Aunt Harriet demanded, her eyes darting from the Viscount to Bridget, as though looking for evidence of some wild sexual excess still clinging to them.

Bridget blushed at her thought. Aunt Harriet's lips tightened.

"How else should it be?" the Viscount asked. "But Cecily! Why did you venture across the lake again? I'd hoped you'd stay onshore, where it was calm and safe."

Cecily tittered. "It never rained, my lord."

"So we were parted for nothing!" he said in chagrin, and got into the boat, ignoring Bridget entirely. At his gestured command, the boatman helped her in.

He chatted with Cecily and Aunt Harriet. Bridget sat in the boat watching him, marveling at his duplicity. He was two men, both vile, she decided as he tenderly escorted Cecily from the swan boat without so much as a backward glance at her.

He ignored her on the ride back, too. He didn't even look at her as she stood by the wall in the salon when he said good-bye to Cecily and Aunt Harriet. Bridget couldn't leave until she was dismissed. Hurt gave way to anger, and then she felt sorry for herself. She bitterly regretted even being civil to him, wanting to hurt him as he had hurt her, wishing she could dismiss him from her mind as easily as he had dismissed her.

"Bridget," her aunt said, snapping her out of her thoughts of revenge, "the Viscount wishes to have a private word with you."

She was astonished. She looked up to see him bow over Cecily's hand, then walk out into the hall. He stopped at the front door and waited there, looking bored.

"Go, go," Aunt Harriet hissed, prodding Bridget. "He can't leave his horses waiting."

Bridget wanted to say no. She wanted to go up to him and snap her fingers in his face. She wanted to weep. But her cousin was staring at her, her aunt was frowning, and she hadn't the luxury to do anything she wanted.

Cecily shot Bridget a dark look. "Why does he want a few words with her?" Cecily whispered fiercely to her mother.

"He wants to assure her he won't tell anyone they were alone, unchaperoned, on the island today," her mother said. "I told him it didn't matter. He said he ought to calm her anxieties anyway. He's a gentleman through and through," she told her daughter with a smug smile, "a stunning catch for you. You see? In spite of his reputation, he's everything that's proper."

Bridget walked into the hall. She stopped in front of him but lowered her eyes, refusing to look at him. She'd hear him out and then leave him with a nod, walking away with her head high, whatever he said. She had some dignity left. Her aunt and cousin weren't near enough to hear, so she wouldn't have to answer him, whatever he had to say.

"Bridget," he said, his deep voice low and soft and slow. "Ah, Bridget. I'm sorry, but in spite of my better judgment, I've decided we really must meet again."

Her eyes flew to his. "But—why?" she asked, all thoughts of revenge swept away because of the regret in his voice, all hurt swept away by the look in his eyes.

"Because I burn for you," he said.

He gave her a crooked smile and bowed. And as she stared, he clapped on his high beaver hat and walked out the door.

4

"What *is* the matter with you?" Cecily demanded when Bridget startled, dropping the book she held. "I'm patient as can be, Bridget, but I don't want a companion who acts like she's going to be shot every time someone comes to the door."

Bridget picked up her book. "What *do* you want in a companion, Cousin?" she asked as calmly as she could, to divert Cecily's attention.

It was true she'd been on pins and needles since the Viscount had left with that strange promise to return. But it had been three days now and there'd been no sign of him. He'd been joking, he'd forgotten, or some other woman had come along to put out the fire he'd said was burning. Somehow Bridget found that idea as insulting and alarming as what he'd said. She was confused, wishing she could

51

forget the whole thing. But every time someone came to the door, she remembered.

And every time someone did come, it was only another note or invitation for Cecily that was being delivered, or some young man come to court Cecily. *You're being a fool, my girl—worse, a fool who's been duped and acting even more foolish*, Bridget told herself bitterly. She waited for Cecily's answer but kept an ear half cocked to the front door. There was no further sound. It must have only been someone delivering another note or a card.

"What do I want in a companion?" Cecily asked thoughtfully. "A very good question. I'm glad you finally asked it."

Bridget bit her lip. She hadn't meant to divert Cecily that much.

"I don't need a companion," Cecily said, and nodded with satisfaction when Bridget's head shot up. "I have one because Mama insists, but you and I both know you're not necessary. I'm not being cruel, just honest. I mean, why should I need one? I'm not going to do anything to stain my reputation, you can count on that. I want to marry well. I'll leave stupid flirtations to other girls, thank you. They're a waste of time. You're here as window dressing, we both know it. So what do I need in a companion? Nothing. What do I want? Someone who doesn't annoy me, I suppose. That's all."

"Do I annoy you, Cecily?" Bridget asked, too shocked to be angry or hurt yet.

They were in the salon overlooking the street. Cecily sat by the window, holding an embroidery loop in her little white hands. The sunlight angled in so it struck gold in her curls, and she tilted her head so it didn't cast harsh light on her face—or any at all on her embroidery, for that matter. But she wasn't sewing; she was posing in case a gentleman caller arrived. She looked over at her cousin, drawing the moment out.

"Yes, you do annoy me," Cecily finally said. "I'm glad you asked that, too. I didn't like the way you acted around Ewen, if you want to know the truth."

So it's Ewen now? Bridget thought. The devil was free with his name, wasn't he? Giving it to a lady he was courting as well as the companion he was trying to trifle with.

She hated herself for the twinge of jealousy she'd felt. Of course he'd ask his chosen lady to speak his given name.

"I wasn't aware that I acted any way at all around Viscount Sinclair, Cousin," she told Cecily quietly, "and I'll wager he wasn't, either, because I'm nothing but wall covering to him when you're around. And since I don't see him when you aren't with him, I don't see what the problem is."

"The problem is that he does look at you," Cecily said. "Mama says it's only human—when someone stares at you, you can't help but look back at the person, wondering why."

"I do not stare at him," Bridget said, feeling her face getting warm, because of course she did, and she hated to lie.

"But I think it's also because he's a rake," Cecily went on as though Bridget hadn't spoken. "He can't help but wonder how available you are when you're so obviously fascinated by him. You've no money, no family to speak of, except for us, of course, and you're terribly scarred. That makes marriage impossible for you. But I wonder if he thinks you'd be willing to settle for less. Are you?" Cecily asked, watching her closely.

Bridget put her book aside and stood. She smoothed down her skirt so Cecily couldn't see how her hands were shaking—also giving her something to do so she wouldn't pick up the book and throw it at her. She'd leave, of course. Mad Cousin Mary likely needed a nurse now, and cranky old Cousin Elizabeth was doing all her complaining to the angels, but maybe Cousin Sylvia needed her again or knew some other relative who did.

"I am not going to answer that question," Bridget said in a tight voice. "I find it beyond insulting. But since I am a lady, as you are not, I won't insult you in turn. I think that's why you need a companion, Cousin, and I urge you to find another after I leave—which I'll do, now. You think it's charming to act like a child, and maybe in London it is. I don't know, for as you say, I'm not a fashionable creature. But I know manners and breeding never go out of fashion, and if you're looking for a good marriage, you'd do well to remember that. Of course, I suppose there are dozens of wealthy men who won't care. I wish you luck."

But Bridget suspected the Viscount would care. It wasn't much in the way of retaliation, but it was all she could say, and because it was the last thing she would do in this house, she felt a little better for it.

Cecily was silent for a moment. Bridget suspected that she too knew the Viscount would care. And she knew Cecily considered Sinclair the most elegant man she'd ever met. And maybe the richest.

"Bridget!" she cried, leaping up from her seat. "Oh, where are you going? You thought I meant to insult you? Never! I just wondered—and, well, you know what a goose I can be. We girls talk about the most intimate things, and I felt so close to you, I just forgot my tongue.

But see?" she asked gaily. "That means I think of you as just another of my friends."

That was such an awful lie, in every meaning of the word—being monstrously untrue *and* ridiculous, too— that Bridget couldn't say a thing.

"Don't be so prickly, Cousin," Cecily said. "Forget what I said." But, being Cecily, she couldn't help adding, "Just think: I've become so popular, I can try to find you a fellow of your own—some acquaintance of one of my beaux—if you stay on. And Mama would never forgive me if you left like this. Oh, do forget this silliness, won't you?"

Bridget would rather not. But she was a realist. There was nowhere for her to go, after all. She was passed through the family by word of mouth. When Aunt Harriet had no more use for her, another place would be found for her. That was how things had gone since she'd been taken in by her father's family. In fact, she'd never met them all. She'd have to wait for Cecily's wedding for that. Her father's relatives lived far apart and were cold at heart, at least toward each other. They only assembled when they had to, at funerals and weddings.

Bridget sat, picked up her book, and nodded. She still didn't trust herself to speak.

"Well, that's much better!" Cecily said, arranging herself by the window again.

They both sat silently, pretending to read and stitch. Bridget wished she could just get up and go out for a walk. But she was Cecily's companion, which meant that if Cecily chose to pass a glowing day indoors, so must she. She didn't even have a half day to herself on Sundays, as a servant would, Bridget thought sadly. If Cecily were old and infirm, Bridget might have more time to herself . . . but then, she mused, gazing into the distance, watching dust spinning in the sunbeams, there'd be no excursions, no dances, no concerts, no Ewen.

She sat up straight and looked around guiltily. Cecily's head turned to her, but fortunately this time there were voices in the front hall.

"Of course. Certainly. At three, then," they heard Aunt Harriet say, and the door closed again.

A moment later Aunt Harriet stood poised dramatically in the doorway. She looked pregnant with news. Her bosom swelled and a huge smile appeared on her face as she looked at her daughter.

"He will be here at three," she said with suppressed excitement. "His messenger said something about a drive in the park. Just you—he's got an open carriage and you don't need me or your cousin for propriety. Now, to dress!"

So are wars announced in Shakespeare's plays, Bridget thought sourly as she saw Cecily's eyes widen. *But this is a kind of war, after all.* Aunt Harriet didn't have to say who "he" was. The fact that three o'clock was three hours away didn't matter. Of course Cecily would try on dresses for three hours. What she wore as she rode off to war was of prime importance. The battle for the title of Viscountess Sinclair had begun in earnest.

Ordinarily a few hours' notice wouldn't have been enough for Aunt Harriet. A lady didn't move on the spur of the moment. Had it been anyone else, she would have turned down the invitation with polite regrets and, if she wanted him to call again, a light reminder that notice was needed. But Sinclair was Sinclair, and Bridget thought he could have called from his carriage waiting at curbside and they'd have bundled Cecily out to meet him without blinking. At least now they had hours to prepare.

And Bridget had hours to feel sorry for herself—and scold herself for it. *He never was more than a dream, and a bad one at that. He wouldn't have offered you what he's offering her, and there's an end of it,* she kept telling herself. But getting herself to accept it wasn't so easy.

She'd been alone for seven years now. She hadn't had an admirer in all those years, or if she had, she'd managed to ignore them. What was it about Ewen that enthralled her?

Could it be his face, his form? There must have been more attractive men, though she couldn't think of any. Was it his wit or his laughter, or just the sound of that deep voice purring and the way it wound itself around her heart, forcing it to pick up its beat in his company? She'd never felt that before. It terrified her—even more so when she realized how much she enjoyed that strange terror.

Oh, she'd be glad to go off into the wilds of the countryside with some infirm relative now—in fact, she yearned to go, she told herself. Her brief glimpse of London had been wonderful, but who needed such distress? If she stayed, mightn't there be other such men here?

No, she thought sadly, *never,* and felt even worse, because she must be deranged to feel bad about missing such misery.

She wished she could leave right now. But she'd have to stay for the wedding; it surely was part of her duties. How else could she meet the rest of the family, anyway? After that, she could go away with one of them if they needed her.

So she was very pale and quiet when Cecily was finally ready for her ride with Ewen Sinclair.

Cecily was, of course, magnificent. She was a symphony in white and yellow. Her day dress was white with yellow stripes and a yellow overskirt, and on her yellow curls she wore a pert straw hat with a cunning yellow plume that curled down to caress her cheek on one side. Very dashing, simply adorable. She looked like a smug, happy, plump little canary, Bridget thought enviously, unconsciously fingering the ribbon at the waist of her own plain green dress.

"A pity your father isn't here in case the Viscount wants a word with him," Aunt Harriet sighed as she gazed at her daughter. "But perhaps I'm being a wee bit premature."

And *very imaginative*, Bridget thought, considering that Cyrus Brixton was almost never home in the afternoon. He was seldom home in the evening, either. Whether he spent his days at his club and his nights there, too, or spent all his time with his mistress, no one knew or cared. He was as profoundly bored with his stay in London as his wife and daughter seemed to be with him.

Bridget had heard the servants say he came to life only in the countryside, where he could spend both days and nights drinking or riding. She wasn't sure which, because they always stopped talking when she entered the room. She was one of the family, even if she wasn't treated as such, and she had the servants' pity and distrust because of it.

Cecily sat in the front salon, her mother pacing by the window. Bridget sank into her own world of regret. As the hall clock chimed three bells they heard the door knocker sound.

"Wait, wait," Aunt Harriet cautioned Cecily. "Patience, my dear. Let him come in, let him ask for you, and then wait a moment before you appear."

Like landing a fish, Bridget thought gloomily.

The butler came to the salon in some dismay. "Madam," he told Aunt Harriet, "the Viscount Sinclair is here, and ready to take the young miss up in his carriage."

"I'm ready!" Cecily caroled, leaping to her feet.

"Ah, but no, it's Miss Bridget he's askin' after," the butler said, so perturbed that his perfect accent slipped.

No one said anything for a long moment.

"You've got it wrong," Aunt Harriet said.

"I asked him twice, I did," the butler protested, "and so he said twice, madam."

Aunt Harriet closed her eyes and frowned. "I can't believe it! That can't be right!"

"Oh, knowing what a rake he is, it could be! What did his message say, exactly?" Cecily asked, pacing furiously.

Her mother's brow furrowed in thought. "The messenger said, 'The Viscount wishes to take the young miss for a ride at three.' The villain! He never said which! Well, I won't have it!"

Cecily stopped and cast a murderous glance at Bridget. "But if you say he *can't*, he'll tell everyone, and we'll look like monsters. It will look as though we beat her or starve her or make her sweep ashes or some such," she said wildly, "like in the fairy tales."

"We can say we don't want her compromised, that we are looking after her," her mother said.

Cecily stamped her little foot. "We can say it, but I know what those cats will say—they'll say I was jealous! As if I could be! She's old and disfigured, that's why he's asking. He knows she'll say yes to *whatever* he asks!"

"Don't be ridiculous," her mother argued. "He can buy the most beautiful females in all London. Why should he want her?"

Astonishing, Bridget thought. *They talk as though I'm not here.* Well, that was fair enough; she didn't feel she was anymore. The whole thing was taking on the qualities of a strange dream, the disjointed half-real kind you had if you fell asleep in the afternoon. That notion gave her the courage to speak up.

"He knows I'm your cousin," she said, "a member of your family. It may be he doesn't see anything wrong with asking me to drive with him. There wouldn't be, you know."

They looked at her as though they'd forgotten she could speak.

"Yes. He hasn't been back in London very long . . . ," Aunt Harriet said, her eyes narrowing as she thought about it.

Bridget felt her heart lift. She was going to be able to leave the house, go for a drive with a strange and wonderfully dangerous gentleman. But there'd be no danger. It would only be words and possibilities, and she was good with words and knew her future too well to consider his possibilities. Even if it was only for a few hours, and even though she knew better than anyone that he was a villain, it still would be a marvelous day. The threat of him would only make it more exciting, and more unreal.

"It may be he wants to ask Bridget about you," Aunt Harriet told Cecily. "Perhaps he wants to know your tastes—he may have a gift or a surprise in mind for you and wants her advice. As you say, she's older, certainly not marriageable, and obviously your chaperone. He may feel uncomfortable asking me, but her? Yes, it is a possibility. We have to let her go."

She turned to Bridget. "But hear me well," she told her sternly. "I want no hint of impropriety. It's not logical that he wants anything wicked, but he does have a certain reputation. Who knows what notions the man may have? Behave yourself, you understand?"

Any other time Bridget would have been so insulted she'd have said good-bye to her aunt and cousin and left them then and there, even if she had no idea of where to go. Or *at least I'd leave the room*, she thought more honestly, *and start writing letters to other relatives*. But not today.

Today she felt light and foolish with relief, and strangely flattered and thoroughly excited. She was still young, or almost so, she thought. She'd go, if only so she'd have a few wicked remembrances to cheer her old age. Cecily had been prepared for war; she herself was only looking forward to some fencing. And if he just wanted to ask about Cecily—which she strongly doubted—why, it was still a beautiful day, and she'd be out in it!

"Let me get my bonnet," she said.

He didn't like the bonnet. "You look like you're wearing a coal scuttle on your head."

"It's the fashion," she said.

It wasn't anymore, of course. Cecily's hat was the fashion. But Bridget thought her old bonnet was the best fashion for her, as it covered her face on all sides. He was sitting on her right, driving, and so if he could only see her profile, that was grand. She sat on the driver's seat with him, so high from the ground she was terrified—at first. Then she found the thrill of it.

He drove a high-perch phaeton, delicate and gilded, with the driver's seat fully six feet off the ground. It was the most dashing thing she'd ever seen, pulled by two matched black horses. The fragile carriage swayed and shook, and though it was well sprung, she felt every cobble in the road below. She loved it. She felt the wind on her face and imagined she was motion itself. They must be going at least eight miles an hour, she thought in delight.

There were coaches, carts, wagons, carriages, and other rigs crowding the busy roadway. But she was in the finest one, and he was the most elegant escort, and she knew she'd never forget this. He was a powerful presence as he sat steering the horses with confident ease. He wore a long driving coat with many capes at the shoulder, a high beaver hat, and luxuriously soft kid-skin gloves on his strong hands—she knew how strong they were because she'd held his hand as he helped her up into her seat—and he wore fashionably skintight tan pantaloons and high shining boots. And she was sitting next to him just as though she were a woman of some consequence, just as if she were really desirable, eligible, enviable. *Bliss.*

"We're heading toward the park," he said, or shouted, because of the noise in the street.

She nodded, too thrilled to try to be heard over the sounds of heavy coaches rumbling over the cobbles, the hoofbeats of horses, and the shouted conversations of their riders, all mingling with the raucous clamor of street vendors crying their wares.

But the park loomed ahead, green and leafy—and surprisingly quiet once they rode along tree-lined roads.

"Better," he said, "but it will be better still."

He drove past other fashionable rigs, nodding here and bowing his head there. Bridget sat still and straight, very much aware that the passengers in those other carriages were trying to get a look at her face.

"I see," he said with a smile in his voice. "That ghastly bonnet acts like a turtle's shell, does it?"

"Yes, and it's much better this way," she replied.

She was suddenly aware they were almost alone. She saw few other carriages now. He'd driven to a shaded lane, and she could see water glittering ahead. A *lake and a secluded spot near it—trust him to know where to find a secret rendezvous in the heart of London*, she thought nervously.

It was quiet enough to talk now.

"Have you thought about what I offered?" he asked idly as the horses slowed.

She nodded. "Of course. I wish I could stop thinking about it. You're right, you know," she said, and had the pleasure of seeing him blink and swing his head to her. But she'd decided to be completely honest with him. It would be embarrassing, but lying would be foolish and futile.

"It would be an easy way to earn a living," she admitted, telling him everything she'd told herself all day, "and probably would be a pleasure, too—if I were a different kind of person. But I'm not, so I can't. I just couldn't be any man's mistress. I'm sorry—believe me. But there it is.

"You see, if I did—apart from the fact that I could never live in polite society again, or ever hold down any kind of respectable position again, or ever have my family talk to me again, or be able to look myself in the eye in the mirror each morning—there's the problem of perhaps finding myself less alone after you left me. And you would, of course, in time. I mean," she said, because he looked blank, "I might have something to remember you by." She swallowed hard. "A child."

She looked away from his fascinated stare. "So, you see, it would be impossible for me to consider your offer. Although," she admitted quickly, because he didn't answer and she wanted to be fair about it, "I also have to say that—and it may be wrong to say this—I really do regret it, for many reasons. I do believe you don't find me disfigured, and I do, of course, like to be appreciated, since no one else seems to do that. And my life is not a happy one. Plus you are attractive, as you are far too aware. I know all that, you see. But I know myself, too. I can't, and there it is."

She folded her hands in her lap and looked at them, because she was afraid to see his reaction.

He was too preoccupied with the horses to have a reaction yet. He stayed silent for a moment more, but only because he was angling his horses in under the canopy of a huge, spreading oak tree. When he'd stopped them, he braked the coach. He put down the reins, and then he spoke to her.

"You've been thinking it over, all right," he said. "Well, I have to say I'm sorry—and surprised." The dappled shade couldn't hide his small smile.

"Surprised?"

"Most women don't expect their husbands to leave them. Most like the idea of having children."

She caught her breath. *Cruel*, she thought, because she'd dreamed of children. "Most women don't like the idea of having to raise bastard children," she said bravely, and went on quickly, "I suppose you'll tell me I could go someplace where no one has ever heard of me and say I was a widow, and you'd give me enough money to get by, but I don't want to live a lie. Oh, what am I talking about? The answer is no, and no, and no again, no."

"You *have* been thinking about it," he said with pleasure. He turned to her casually, one hand resting on his knee. But there was nothing casual in his expression. His face held such tenderness that she caught her breath. "Bridget, sweet Bridget," he said in his soft purr, "didn't you hear me? I'm talking about marriage, my dear, and you can't have been thinking about *that*."

"You can't have been talking about marriage!" she said with a squeak. "I've nothing, no money; I'm old; and I have—"

"The scar. I know. God, I know about the damned scar," he said angrily. He put his arms around her and dragged her close. He tipped up her chin with one hand. "Blasted bonnet," he murmured as she stared up at him, amazed. But it didn't get in his way.

She took a long look into those hazel eyes, seeing green and gold and heat and desire and laughter there. She knew very well that she should draw away. But she discovered she couldn't, because she didn't want to. She closed her eyes. He was coming so close. . . . Her pulse was racing so hard she could scarcely breathe. Then she forgot about breathing altogether, because he put his warm, firm mouth on hers, and she couldn't seem to think at all anymore.

His lips were warm, his mouth was hot. He touched her lips with his tongue. She startled and opened her mouth to ask why, and he gave her his tongue as an answer. So strange, so sweet, so shocking . . . but he was intoxicating. He tasted dark and winey, sweet and astonishing. She felt the strength of his body against hers, his hard hands holding her still for his kiss. He didn't need to. Her hands went to his wide shoulders, her mouth opened to him, her body yearned toward him.

"Yes," he said triumphantly when his lips finally left hers, "it's all there, everything I imagined. You *have* been thinking about me, sweet Bridget. Here, something else to think about," he murmured, lowering his mouth to hers again.

She wanted to warn him someone might see, she wanted to tell him she didn't do that kind of thing, she needed to say she was sorry, sorry . . . But she was floating. All she could do was drink in his kiss and try to get closer to the warm and solid reality of him, the worst man she could ever have needed so badly.

5

"**Y**es," Ewen breathed with satisfaction as he lifted his lips from hers again. But now the world was returning to Bridget, and he could see the worry springing into her eyes. He knew how to deal with that. He knew what he most wanted to do, too. They were the same thing. He bent his head to hers again.

"No!" she said quickly, blinking as though waking at last. "You mustn't—" She stopped, because she really ought to have said "we mustn't," and she was shamed to realize it.

"Mustn't I?" he purred, his lips on her cheek, his cheek against hers.

There were so many other denials she could make. But it was herself she had to plead with, not him. *One last kiss, just one, please?* she asked herself. She answered herself by closing her eyes, tilting up her head, waiting for his kiss. He did something even more intimate.

She felt his fingers at her neck, by her breast. Her eyes flew open. It was done in a moment. He undid the string of her bonnet, took it off, and flung it away. She gasped, her hands flying to her hair. He put his hands over hers and cupped her head so he could look fully into her face.

"Lovely," he murmured, gazing at the tumble of soft dark brown hair that rippled around her face. "Rich chocolate, with the sunlight finding cinnamon in it. Thick, lush—a crime to cover it. But if you must, we'll find you something to set it off, not hide it."

But she was near tears now. The sun was full on her face and she couldn't cover her scar from him. He held her head so she couldn't lower or turn it from his gaze. Her heart was surely in her eyes, she knew it had been in her kiss, and she couldn't hide that from him anymore, either. She was exposed, completely. She writhed, feeling like some kind of insect of the dark suddenly revealed, attempting vainly to scuttle from the light of the day, as she tried to look away from the heat of his stare.

"Don't," she whimpered, looking for a place to hide her face. His chest was as good as any. Too good, she discovered when he held her close, crooning to her, stroking her. Too warm and strong, and scented too interestingly of clean linen, sandalwood, and Ewen. His big hand made slow, gentle circles on her back as he made soothing noises low in his throat. Too soothing. Too close. Too many wonderful sensations at once woke her to her situation.

She hadn't been hugged in seven years, much less

held—and never like this. She tried to pull away, trying to pull herself together as well. He let her go at once. She accepted his wordlessly offered handkerchief and wiped her eyes. She hesitated to really use it, but had to, and was embarrassed by the forlorn honk she gave.

"I don't know what came over me," she said.

"The name is Ewen, I thought I told you that," he said with amusement.

She almost smiled, but tried for composure. She sat up straight and ran her hands over her hair, finally grabbing the mass of it, skinning it back, and winding it up in a knot at the nape of her neck. It began to fall apart almost instantly, of course. So did her composure when she saw the light dancing in his eyes as he sat watching her, but she still tried to be dignified.

"I'm sorry," she said, and meant it.

"I'm not," he answered, and clearly meant it, too. "I'm glad that's over with and done."

She hadn't thought she could feel more embarrassed, but she'd been wrong. "Of course, it won't happen again," she mumbled in humiliation. She'd made a terrible mistake. Had she moved to him first? It hardly mattered. If a woman sat with her eyes closed and her lips near, a man might just be being polite.

"Oh, it will happen again, even more will happen," he said, "but not just now. We have to talk. I meant I'm glad we got it out of the way so we could concentrate on other things. It was just as delicious as I thought it would be. Now that we know, you see, we can move on."

"Yes, I think we should go home, too," she said, her eyes cast down.

"Miss Cooke," he said, "I'm trying to make a declaration. Why should you look so astonished? I invited you out, I kissed you soundly, you won't be my mistress, we've talked that through. So now I'm asking you if you'll be my wife."

"You're joking!"

"I have a better sense of humor than that. Listen, my dear. I came to London in search of a wife, you know that. But now it seems I need one much sooner than I thought." He looked down at the reins in his hands, uncomfortable for the first time. "My father's been in poor health. The one thing he wants of me—and I'd do anything for him—is to see me marry again.

"I married young," he said, concentrating on smoothing the separate strands of the reins on his knee as he spoke. "I married to please him. No, to be honest, I was a young fool, and thought one woman much the same as another. And so if the match pleased him, it suited me as well. Well, I wasn't *that* noble. She was lovely. She was young, too, and obedient to her father's wishes. It wasn't uncommon for our class: an arranged marriage for the profit of our families. Still, I was attracted to her and thought it would work. It didn't."

He scowled down at his hands, "As it turned out, we didn't like each other at all. Had she—had we had more years together, we'd have ended up detesting each other. So please don't feel sorry for me or think I remained single so long after because I was looking for another like her. I was not. I am not.

"Truthfully, I never wanted to marry again," he admitted. "But my father . . . My mother was an invalid. I was taught at home so I could be near her. When she died, my father became everything to me. With reason. He's a good man, much better than I am, and I'm fortunate enough to call him friend as well as father. I came to

London to find a fiancée to present to him, because he's sick and says he can't rest easy until he's sure there'll be more of our line. He asks nothing more of me. I can't blame him. My sole heir's my uncle, but he's old and even more foolish than I am."

He looked up, smiling at her again. "My father asks only that I choose a woman with a good head on her shoulders and that I have enough sense not to pick someone altogether ineligible. So, I came to London, went to all the right parties, dances, and teas in my search for a bride. And yes, I've been to all the wrong places, too, in my search for . . . entertainment."

His face grew suddenly grave. "I thought I had the whole Season, but I've just got word from home. His health's deteriorating. I have to marry immediately, then go home and reassure him by introducing my bride to him."

"You mean me?" she asked, astonished.

"I do indeed," he answered, smiling at her surprise.

She shook her head. It didn't make sense. "I'm sorry about your father," she said, "but there are so many more eligible women. Almost any of them would have you. You must know that. Why, Cousin Cecily would snap you up, as would most of her friends."

"I don't care to be snapped up. I much prefer to do the snapping," he said with a grin that made her wonder if she'd said something risqué—but then, he could make anything sound that way. "I know Cecily would have me. But in all seriousness, if you were a man, would you have her? Not only for your life's mate, but even in your bed?"

She gasped. "That—that's such an improper question. I can't even imagine it."

"Of course you can," he scoffed. "A woman can see if a man might desire another female. Take a close look at your pretty little cousin. Is there any real passion in the girl? Yes, but only for her own advancement. That's all right, I suppose; the best courtesans are the same."

Bridget stared. No man had ever spoken to her that way—as though she were an equal. She was as shocked as she was fascinated.

"But she wouldn't even pretend passion in a man's bed, and that's important to a man such as I," Ewen went on. "She couldn't, because there's none in her. Not for matters of the flesh. She only has social ambition. Look hard and you can see her mother staring out of her eyes. Look at her friends, too. They act as though finding a husband is only a game to play against the other girls they know. The object? To win the man the others want most. There's no passion there, and I won't wed where's there's none—this time."

"Surely there are older ladies, widows, any number of worthy women for the position—I mean, for you to marry," Bridget said earnestly. Since he was talking to her as an equal, she found it easier to speak with him as such. The whole idea of marrying him was too fantastic for her to accept. She had to make him see that, she had to see it herself, because she was still afraid it was some strange, cruel joke.

"I'm penniless, Ewen. I'm . . . flawed, even if you don't think so. I have nothing and can expect nothing. Why should you want *me*?"

"I want you in my bed," he said, his eyes clear and bright as they studied her. "I want you in my arms. I realize there's more to marriage than that," he added as her eyes widened. "You do have more. I enjoy your conversation; you're clever. I know you're virtuous—after all, you resisted me."

She gaped at him. *Of all the monstrous, self-important creatures*, she thought, but before she could say it, he went on. "I've asked about you, I've found out all. There wasn't much to know. If you erred long ago, it hardly matters now. Did you, by the by?"

"Never!" she gasped.

He nodded. "I thought not. And so there you are. I find you desirable. Intelligent. Well-born enough to suit my father. Why should you be surprised at my offer?"

She took in a deep breath and let it out. Why should she be surprised? There were so many reasons that if she started telling him, they'd be there until nightfall. So she seized on the one reason that lurked beneath all the others, the one that hurt the most. "You feel sorry for me," she blurted. "You feel that if you must marry, it might as well be a charitable act."

He sat still. His head cocked to the side as he considered what she said. "And I am *such* a charitable fellow," he said slowly, with a curling smile that made a mockery of the statement.

"I mean, you could get to know some other woman."

"To what purpose? I have you. Or at least, I want to. On that score . . ." He leaned closer and spoke seriously, his eyes daring her to doubt him. "Don't mistake me, Bridget. My choice has a lot to do with my desires. I'm called a rake because I enjoy women's bodies and the pleasure a man and woman can share. I *was* a rake, that is to say. Because if we wed, I'd be as faithful to you as you are to me. That I promise. But don't mistake me: I expect an eager partner in my marriage bed."

"B-But . . . I . . . ," she stammered, blushing at even

the thought of the kind of eagerness he expected, "I don't know how, I mean . . ."

"Maybe not the mechanics," he said, watching her intently. "They're simple enough, or else there wouldn't be so many stupid people—or so many happy ones. But you already know the rest, in your heart at least. I'd swear it, and I'm not wrong in these things. It's my field of expertise, so to speak," he added wryly.

"You're all banked fire," he said. "It's what I first sensed in you. I've felt it, too. Lord, have I felt it! You're driving me to distraction, you know—you must know. I saw your reaction to me in your eyes when we met, I felt it in your kiss, I feel it when we so much as touch hands, for God's sake! It took all my control not to try to tumble you that day on the island. I believe you're just right for me in other things as well. I'd try to be right for you. And so?"

He sat back and watched her struggle with the question. Her emotions were clearly readable—that was why her desire was goading him so badly, making him act so rashly. Her thoughts came and went in her eyes—desire, fear, and doubt. And then he could see growing hope lighten her eyes and erase the line of concentration that had marred her smooth forehead, and at that moment he knew he'd won. She raised those clear gray eyes to his.

"I—I'd like to think about it . . . Ewen," she said shyly.

"Fine. You have a day."

"What?" she squawked. "You're mad!"

"No, I told you I have no time. I need to wed you and go home immediately. It's a long journey. Our estate lies on the border, remember?"

"But why can't you marry there? Your father would certainly like it."

"He may not live to see it," he said harshly. "I'll get a special license and we can marry at once, then I'll send word to him by a rider with a swift horse as soon as it's done. I can't have it any other way."

"Oh," she said a little sadly, "so that's why. You really *don't* have time to find another lady."

"I've been in London three months now and know any number of ladies, my dear idiot," he said. When her head snapped up, he added, "That's a form of endearment in Wales, you know." Her eyes narrowed, and he laughed. "Welsh—yes, another thing I'll have to teach you. Well?"

Surely the most unromantic offer any woman ever had, that "Well?" But she wondered if any woman ever had a more exciting one.

"May I let you know?"

"Certainly. By tomorrow. But as for today, let's make the most of it."

She braced herself for his kiss, excited but worried, wondering frantically if she should let him, because maybe it was all a lie to get her in his arms, or maybe he'd think she was—

She felt a jolt, and opened her eyes. The horses were moving again.

"No rain clouds yet, and the sun is still bright. Let's take advantage of it. There's a Punch and Judy show near the Serpentine," he said, shaking the reins. They went rolling out of the shade and out into the sunshine. She sat back, now worrying about why something so respectable should make her feel so disappointed.

He paid a lad to watch the carriage and hold the horses while they got down to see the Punch and Judy show. He bought her an ice, and they watched the puppets, as entranced as the children around them were. They strolled the park paths afterward, sharing the walk with children rolling hoops and chasing balls, old ladies and gentlemen out for their daily constitutionals, and nurses pushing babies in prams or invalids in rolling chairs. They smiled at the children and nodded to the old folks, just as if they were a staid old couple themselves.

He placed her hand on his arm and she walked by his side. Her head came to his shoulder and he had to tilt his own head in order to speak with her, and she loved the unusual feeling of protection and security that gave her. When she looked up at him she had a hard time looking away again. It was fortunate for her composure that he kept pointing out things for her to see, because that way she didn't see that he seldom took his eyes off her.

They saw the milkmaids and their cows, the sheep in the meadow, and all sorts of dogs on their romps. He bought her a bunch of violets from a ragged little girl standing by a gate, and then another when the little girl was so overjoyed by that. They talked about nothing and laughed over everything. There weren't many young adults in the park because it was an ordinary weekday and high afternoon, when common young men and women were working, and ladies and gentlemen were shopping, having tea, or visiting friends or clubs.

Bridget had a marvelous time even though there wasn't a fashionable person in sight. *Especially* since there wasn't a fashionable person in sight, because she knew she must look bedraggled in her old dress, with no bonnet, and her hair mussed by the breeze and his hands.

When no one was near, he stopped, drew her behind a tree, pulled her even closer, and kissed her witless. She'd been kissed a few times in her life, mostly against her will. Nothing had ever felt like this. He took her in his arms, bent his head, and curved his body against hers, pouring himself into his kiss, concentrating on her utterly. She felt the heat of his mouth, the expertly teasing touch of his tongue. It was even more astonishing, disturbing, and wonderful than when they'd kissed in the carriage, because now she could feel the urgency of him pressed against her entire body.

Extraordinary, frightening, delicious. He made her forget to worry about being seen, and chuckled at her confusion when she emerged from his embrace. She was flustered, but also pleased to note that his chuckle was strained.

But then she remembered something. Her eyes searched his. "Ewen. One thing. Your first offer, that I become your mistress, was that only in the nature of a test, then?"

He seemed surprised by her question and tilted his head as he considered it. "Testing you? Or testing myself? What is courtship but a testing process? Whatever it was, I have no more time for games." He cupped her face in his two hands and kissed her lightly. He gazed down into her face and said, "Tomorrow."

Then it was time to head home.

"Tomorrow," he said again as he stood with her on her aunt's front step. He paused. He reached into his vest pocket, withdrew a small silver case, and took a card from it. "It occurs to me that you don't know where I live. A small thing, but maybe large in your mind. Here is my card. If you need me, send word to me."

She took the card without looking at it, frowning. "You wouldn't have given Cecily your card," she said, her face and voice troubled.

"I wouldn't have asked Cecily to marry me, either. Nor do I doubt her mama has my direction—as well as my assets, properties, and funds, all neatly and completely listed by now."

She grinned in spite of herself. "Tomorrow," she said, nodding. She watched him drive out of sight. She still didn't believe what had happened. She still didn't want to doubt it. She buried her nose in the violets he'd bought her, breathing in their sweet, elusive fragrance. They were warm and fragrant and velvety against her nose. She gave a long shuddery sigh at the feelings of yearning they aroused in her. But she'd felt so much today. . . . *Enough of feelings, my girl*, she told herself, *now you've a lot of thinking to do.* She went into the house, bemused and bewildered, wishing she had someone she trusted to talk to now.

Instead, she had Aunt Harriet and Cousin Cecily. They were waiting in the salon. It was as if they hadn't moved since she'd left. But the sun had been pouring in then. Now, Bridget realized, there were only the lengthening gray shadows of twilight.

"*Where*," her aunt asked with awful haughtiness, making the word sound as if it had three syllables, "have you been?"

"With the Viscount, but you know that," Bridget said, taken aback.

"Why is your hair like that?" Cecily demanded, but she was looking at Bridget's lips.

"I was riding in his rig, and the wind took my bonnet away," Bridget said, trying for an innocent explanation and ruining it by blushing.

"It's been hours," Aunt Harriet said in outrage. "No decent woman would stay out until dark!"

Bridget was about to mention it was only twilight but had no chance.

"And no man with decent intentions would keep you out so long!" Cecily snarled.

"Well, as to that—his intentions couldn't be more decent," Bridget flared. "He's asked me to marry him!"

Cecily and her mother fell still. It was so quiet Bridget could hear her own pulse pounding. They just stared at her. But not for long.

"Mama," Cecily screeched, "it's not fair! Look what she's done!"

"Be quiet," Aunt Harriet commanded her now wildly weeping daughter, "or I'll send you to your room! I'm only letting you stay so you can learn from this. If you can't control yourself, leave!"

Cecily fell sulkily still, glowering at Bridget. Aunt Harriet closed the door to the salon and then turned her attention to her niece. "I was afraid of this," she said, as though to herself.

"He asked me to marry him," Bridget said, holding her head high. "I can't help that, nor will I apologize for it."

Her aunt dismissed what she said with a withering look. "Don't be a fool. He's silver-tongued, but you're not stupid. He couldn't have asked you to marry him. It's too soon, for one thing. For another, look at yourself. You're no longer young, you haven't a penny to bless yourself with, and you have a disfiguring scar on your face. He is one of the wealthiest men in England, titled, disastrously attractive, and an acknowledged rake."

"He wants my answer tomorrow," Bridget said bravely, but in a small corner of her mind she was already beginning to doubt what he'd said. More precisely, since she doubted herself much more than him, she was wondering if she'd heard him right.

"If his proposal was honest, don't you think he'd have come to your uncle first, or, failing that, to me?" Aunt Harriet frowned and her voice grew a little softer as she gazed at her niece. "Life hasn't been fair to you. But life isn't kind. We marry where we may and hope for the best bargain our family can make for us. Some do very well," she said, and added bitterly, "and some have to do the best with what they're given. But we marry through our families, Bridget. You have none to watch over you, except for us."

"My mama," Bridget said, and grew quiet when she saw the look on her aunt's face. They both knew that if her mother could have offered her better, Bridget wouldn't have been a drudge all these years.

Aunt Harriet nodded, as though the thing had been discussed. "We can't do more than offer you a roof over your head, since you've nothing to offer in marriage except yourself. And that is little, and imperfect to boot. I'm not being cruel, merely honest. Which he was not."

"He said he came to London for a bride and must marry instantly."

"Instantly?"

"He said his father was gravely ill and—"

"And a load of other utter nonsense, I don't doubt! Which you believed because you wanted to. Come, Bridget, think!"

"I have, I am," Bridget cried. "I do believe him. Why should he lie to me?"

"So you will lie *with* him," her aunt said bluntly. "You came perilously close, I think. But you're unaccustomed to any flattery—certainly to the wiles of such a man. I could cast you from this house for almost ruining Cecily's reputation, because what people would say if they knew her companion had spent such an afternoon, I shudder to think! But I understand your inexperience with such attentions, so I'll do my duty by you. Just give me your word you'll never see him again."

"I can't do that!" Bridget protested. "I promised to give him an answer." She didn't know what that answer would be, because now she even doubted his question. But she knew she had to see him again.

"I forbid you to see him, Bridget."

"He's coming tomorrow."

"If he does, he will see me, not you. You'll stay in your room."

"Aunt," Bridget said, trembling with outrage and the effort of containing it, "I'm five and twenty! I can't be sent to my room like a child."

"If you can't, you can't stay here with us any longer. In fact," her aunt said, "I think that's the solution. I'll write to my sister-in-law in Devon immediately. She has an elderly mother and lives in the countryside. I suppose the gaiety, the excitement of London and Cecily's life, turned your head. You made a fool of yourself by forgetting you are not like her. Clearly you can't be a companion to a young person. In time you may be suitable for such pleasant duties. A long stay in the countryside will calm you. Perhaps in years to come you'll suit some young lady very well."

"Yes. Perhaps you can come companion *my* daughter when it's her turn to be presented to society," Cecily said sweetly.

"Don't you dare gloat!" Aunt Harriet ordered Cecily. "So there it is," she went on as both her daughter and her niece looked at her, amazed. "Go to bed now. I'll take care of the Viscount, you'll be off to the country-side, and all of this will be but a memory before long."

"No," Bridget said quietly. Her aunt and cousin stared. But she knew what she had to say. "I know you mean the best for me, Aunt." *And she does*, Bridget thought in won-der. Her aunt had been kinder to her in the last moments than she'd been since she'd met her. "But you didn't hear him and you don't know him. I haven't made up my mind yet, but I must see him tomorrow."

"He has nothing to offer you but dishonor!"

"He has offered me marriage," Bridget said, clinging to that one thought desperately.

"That will turn out to be false, or falsely postponed, or impossible in one way or another," her aunt said. "Let it be. Forget it now while it only hurts, before it destroys you. What is there for a woman with no family and no honor? Nothing. Enjoyment for a brief while, perhaps. But when he tires of you he'll pass you on to a friend, and then there'll be nothing but other such men, and then, if you haven't been clever enough to save money, the streets."

Bridget laughed, relieved. Her aunt was the one who had read too many novels! She was talking like a street-corner savior, ranting about morality. It gave Bridget some perspective. "Oh, Aunt, no! Rogue he may be, but never so desperate as that! He's a gentleman, after all. I'll talk to him, he'll reassure you—you'll see."

"I will not, nor will you," Aunt Harriet said stonily. "You know nothing of gentlemen. You can't run wild, Bridget. This is my house, and it will be as I say. If you refuse me in this, you may as well leave my house *and* my protection."

"You really mean that?" Bridget asked, astonished.

"I do. Think about it, Bridget, think long and well. Rules are disobeyed at one's peril. I care for your welfare. He cares for . . ." She paused, openly inspecting Bridget—her rumpled dress, tumbled hair, swollen lips. Bridget flushed under her slow appraisal. "He," Aunt Harriet went on, "cares only for his pleasure. Give me your word now and this will be forgotten. Refuse me in this and I'm through with you—I and the rest of the family, I assure you. And so? I'm waiting for your answer."

Cecily was staring at her avidly. Bridget tried to think, but she was wild with hurt and anger. This went beyond pride and longing. This had to do with trust and love, fear and folly. It was her whole future she was considering now. Aunt was right about one thing: It was hard to believe what he'd said was real. It was even hard for her to believe her time with him had been real. It had been too wonderful. Her head and her heart hurt. She was not brave.

"Well?" her aunt demanded.

6

Ewen sat back and stretched out his long legs, resting for the first time that day. He was content for the time being. There was nothing more to do now. He was at his favorite club, deep in his favorite chair; the evening was soft and gray outside the great bow window overlooking St. James Street. He could barely see the lamplighter making his rounds, making the new gas lights wink on one by one. Ewen closed his eyes. He had brighter things on his mind.

He'd ordered his dinner and had nothing to do now but wait for it—and everything else he wanted. He had nothing to do, and could do nothing, either, he thought with the first spurt of annoyance he'd felt all day. He was a man who was sometimes a spy; he'd grown used to laying traps, setting snares. The planning and the execution of the plan, however dangerous, were always exhilarating. The waiting was the worst part. He'd done it before and it never got easier.

Would she or wouldn't she? Could he have made it any easier for her? For him? Should he have been more ardent or less so? But how could he have been less so? She made it impossible. He thought of Bridget, that almost perfect face, made more fascinating by its blemish, and those magnificent eyes she had. They showed the striving spirit that animated that lovely face—and form. Oh, that exquisite little body. He remembered it and her passion very well, too well for his complete comfort now. He couldn't forget that slender, curving shape pressed against him, those firm breasts dimpling against his chest, the tentative way she'd taken his kiss, how eagerly she'd accepted and then learned from his mouth. The very scent of her—

"She must be something extraordinary," an amused voice commented.

Ewen's eyes snapped open. The wing chair opposite him was now occupied by a tall, gaunt gentleman with a harsh face and flaming red hair clipped in a fashionable Brutus crop. Ewen said nothing. Instead he cocked an eyebrow at the new arrival.

"The look on your face," the redhead explained. "The word *voluptuous* doesn't do it justice. Even with your eyes closed it would've got you slapped—or arrested—if there was a female nearby."

"I'm hungry and waiting for my dinner," Ewen said simply.

"Ha! I know that look. I'll bet the main course you were thinking of is much tastier and a lot more tender. Spicier, too. Who is she? Not the buxom little dancer you've been seeing; I hear you just gave her a healthy severance check, but no one knows why. Wait—you were on the prowl at that ball the other night. But it couldn't be the blonde you danced with; you were smiling, but your eyes were glazing over. Whose wouldn't? The Brixton chit's adorable, but I've met smarter geese. And less avaricious lawyers."

"Yes," Ewen said, "too true. But as for the woman in my thoughts, it doesn't matter who she is. She's only a daydream to fantasize about, for now. I wouldn't tell you who she is, anyway. I don't know why, but otherwise sensible females get the urge to warm themselves at your red hair, Rafe, and what I do not need is competition from you."

Rafe snorted. "As if you worried about that! Damme if I know why, but women bet on the black—like your hair and your soul—instead of the red when we're together."

"Liar. How goes it with you?" Ewen asked lazily.

"As it goes with you," his friend said, shifting in his seat restlessly, "We helped get the cursed little emperor out of France, into exile, and on his new throne at Elba, but I swear if I'd known how dull it would make my life, I'd have given him a rifle, a fast horse, and wished him Godspeed."

"Yes, which is why you almost lost your life getting him on that new throne. How's the arm?"

"Still attached," Rafe said with a scowl, "though sometimes I wish it weren't. So. What's there to do tonight, then? You may be content to just sit and dream, but I'm not."

"I'm not content to just dream, either. What have you got in mind?"

"New things, untried things, for us bored old rogues

to do. There's a new farce at the Haymarket, there's a new opera, too, and Freddy Winthrop swears that Madame Gold's got herself a parcel of new stunners in her house. And aside from White's and Brook's and the usual gambling spots, I hear there's a new hell where Hazard may actually be played honestly."

"Life's a farce for me these days, Rafe. I have no ear for screeching. I don't patronize houses of pleasure, even if they have the Venus de Milo and her twin sister in residence; I thought you knew that. Because however charming the merchandise may be, I don't like to be next in line—at least, not so obviously. But as for high-stakes gambling . . . well," Ewen said, a slow, sensuous smile curving his lips, "I'm doing that right now. It's what I was thinking about. That, and other new things to do, too, should I win."

"You always win," his friend complained. "Everyone thinks you're so lucky at love, you should lose at cards, but you don't."

"Lucky in what passes for love with us," Ewen said softly, "but as for *love*—how should I know?"

"Oh, philosophy, is it? Then I'm off to find more congenial company."

"My lord?" a footman said, bowing to Ewen. "Your dinner is ready to be served."

"Care to join me?" Ewen asked his friend. "The philosophy usually disappears along with the roast beef."

"Why not? It's time to eat. Maybe I can talk you into doing something else after."

"We're not joined at the hip, like a pair of babies in a bottle at a country fair," Ewen said mildly.

"If you're going to cut up sharp, be damned to you!" Rafe snapped, jumping to his feet.

"Softly, softly," Ewen said, rising and putting a hand on his friend's shoulder. "Why do you redheaded fellows take that myth about your terrible temper so seriously? Or is it that it's true?"

"No calmer fellow on earth than me," Rafe said grouchily. "It's you who's the firebrand."

"I apologize. Forget it, whatever it was, will you? We've worked together too many years for our friendship to fall apart now. Peacetime is hard on both of us. Join me. I need someone to talk to who knows what secrecy, stealth, and danger are all about."

"Ah. She's married," Rafe said.

"No," Ewen said, and laughed. "And I'm not ready to talk about her, remember? So forget that, too. I'd rather talk about the old days, since the new ones are so damnably dull."

"Aren't they? Yes, I'll share a bird and a bottle or three with you, Ewen, damme if I won't! We'll share some laughter, too, talking about the bad old days."

Their dinner was served with many courses and many wines. They talked about the old days in the past decade, when they both had traveled the Continent making public reputations as pleasure lovers and careless rakes. And private ones for boldness and valor, as they also made themselves busy evading foreign agents, freeing English ones, and ferreting out secrets to send home. But as the evening wore on, they laughed less and less, remembering those men who hadn't been able to come back to England, as they had.

"Enough! We're going to be bawling in a minute if we don't stop," Rafe finally said in exasperation. "They don't need our tears any more than they can use them now. They knew what they were getting into, as we did.

Which is more than we do now. Damme, Ewen, a fellow knew what he had to do then! He had a purpose for getting up in the morning, and no guilt about whom he went to bed with at night. It was all so clear then—them or us, and squeeze as much pleasure as you can in between. Now, what? Raise turnips on our estates? Sit in the House of Lords and squabble with each other all day? What if we don't want to farm *or* bicker? What are we supposed to do now?"

"Have lives, I expect," Ewen said, "a thing we didn't care about before because we knew we could lose them at any time. It's what most men do, you know. Make a choice and get on with it. Raise a family or raise Cain. Seek pleasure or permanence. Or go to some other country and get involved in their war, if peace is too boring for you."

"Ha!" his friend said mirthlessly. "No more war, thank you. At least I know that's one thing I had enough of. And you? What are you going to do now?"

"What do you think?" Ewen asked, raising one dark brow.

"That's easily answered, as I've seen you doing it: pursue pleasure, of course, as usual. Don't know why I even asked," he said moodily. "Don't know if it's right for me, though. Don't know what is. Ewen, you're a fine fellow and a good companion, but the truth is your company's driving me to drink tonight. And I've got no room for another glass. So if you'll excuse me, I'm off to someplace you don't want to go. You've got some rig running, and I don't.

"Unlike you, I don't expect much, so I'm happy with what I get," Rafe said as he got to his feet. "I can sleep through anything onstage, so if it's a bad farce, who cares? I don't mind gambling, because I expect to lose. As for females, I don't mind being one in a line of men, if I don't actually see them standing there. I have *some* discretion and a *bit* of taste, you know. But still, whom am I deceiving? Whether she's a lady or a whore, I know I'm never the first and won't be the last."

"Thank you, that's cheered me considerably," Ewen said.

Rafe chuckled. "Oh, you're cheery enough underneath," he said wisely. "I worked with you long enough to know that. You can't hide from me. Your face might be bland as butter, but you're all anticipation—you're practically licking your lips. You've got eyes like crystals, Ewen. You can make them flat and hard, but I can see them glittering. It's the only thing that gives you away, and you're lucky the Frogs never twigged to it. You've got some prize in mind that makes everything else seem dull by comparison. But me? I'll take whatever I can use to get through this night. I bid you a good evening, Ewen. And good luck."

But will luck be enough? Ewen wondered as he strolled home from his club, alone. He hadn't had much time. She had to act on what she knew now. It was just as well. As things stood, he wouldn't have been able to let her know more, even if they'd had three months instead of three meetings for her to judge him by. Three months? Impossible to even imagine. For one thing, he wouldn't have been able to keep his hands off her for another three minutes. For another, her aunt and cousin wouldn't have let him woo her that long anyway. It needed to be done as it had been done, quickly and in secrecy.

He was obsessed with her now, a strange thing for

him. He wasn't sure just what it was about her, and that was new for him, too. He was usually very certain of why he wanted a woman. This went beyond that delightful body, though. Did he pity her, as she had said? Certainly the surge of pure lust he felt every time he thought of her wasn't pity; the way he felt in her company didn't resemble pity; the way his body reacted when she was in his arms wasn't remotely like pity—unless it was pity for himself, because the thought of being without her bothered him very much.

The scar? It was nothing but a lure to him. Her lack of a dowry? Why should that concern him? Her obvious loneliness? Ah, *that* he pitied. But these days he pitied it in himself just as much.

No. No use wondering about it. He might regret what he'd done in some ways, but he was used to that. He could not regret his choice. She needed him. She was lovely. She liked him, in spite of herself. She had a sense of humor and a quick tongue—and a delicious one, he thought, a smile springing to his lips.

It was easier to think about pleasures than puzzles tonight. She had *such* lovely breasts, he mused as he strolled the fashionable streets toward his townhouse. How he'd like to see them. Her skin was so white and smooth, they could be no less. He'd felt them taut and tilted against his chest, felt them rise to him and wondered how they'd feel in his palms, but he'd dared not go so far. She was skittish with him, with good reason. But that would pass, he knew it from her body's response.

He became aware of a hard arousal, his own body responding to his thoughts. He frowned, surprised and annoyed. He was too old for such nonsense. A man learned to control such things as soon as he was out of the nursery, or at least a gentleman certainly did—especially in today's fashions, he thought wryly. Skintight pantaloons and form-fitting trousers ensured that a man had to learn to master outward manifestations of his desires. Which forced them inward, where they burned. Yes, he thought, he'd told her the truth in that; he did burn for her.

He'd given her a day. He wondered how he would get through the night.

He took out a book, but the words made no sense. He tried to write a letter, but he couldn't concentrate on it. He glanced at the clock on the mantel again, but it was moving slowly tonight, as though it didn't believe in tomorrow.

Well, but it was time for bed, Ewen thought. Not that he knew what time that was anymore. London had no time for sleep. No matter what hour it was now, he could have been at a ball, a gambling hell, a party of friends, or any number of amusements until dawn. He could have shared his bed with any number of women, too. But he wanted only one now. He wouldn't know her decision until daylight, and he refused to spend the night with less than what he wanted. Not now that he knew who that was.

But it was stupid to sit waiting for tomorrow, reviewing his tactics, wondering about his chances. Ewen prepared for bed at last. He went upstairs, took off his clothes, washed, put a dressing gown on over his nakedness, and sent his valet to bed. He lay down on his own bed. But someone seemed to have put pins in it; it was too hot, too hard, too lumpy. He couldn't get comfortable on his side or his back. He got up and went downstairs again.

He went to his library, rekindled the fire in the hearth, and stared into it. He was annoyed with himself as well as on fire for her now. Three and thirty years old, and he had no patience—nor any belief that she'd come to him. Why should that be? Women had always liked him. But that was *women*, not ladies. He didn't know very much about ladies. And even though she'd no money or family to protect her, she was definitely a lady. He knew it too well.

He'd married a lady, but he couldn't say he knew her when he did or wanted to know her much better afterward. His mother had been a lady, not that he'd known her very long, either, poor lady—and poor lost boy. Ewen smiled bleakly. With all the pain they'd dealt him, on purpose and by accident, he should avoid ladies like the plague if he had any sense. But he'd done that for most of his adult life, since his marriage, and what good had that done him?

This went beyond a question of birth and breeding. Bridget Cooke was singular. She appealed to the man as well as the gentleman in him. She badly needed rescuing. He didn't know if what he wanted to do could be considered rescuing her, precisely. Surely heroes were more virtuous, with nobler intent. But he believed he could better her situation, certainly. And his own, of course. If only she said yes.

He'd go to her aunt's house at noon and discover his fate, he decided. But then Ewen thought better of it. The less he had to do with her well-connected relatives, the better. There was little chance of running into the father, for he was never home. But he didn't want to meet up with that socially ambitious aunt or her fashionable daughter again.

So he'd have the house watched. It'd be easy enough to find a footman or a maid to do that, and he could wait until she was alone before he called. But was she ever alone? A companion wasn't engaged to pass her time by herself, after all. Probably he'd have to send a note by private means—which entailed giving the butler a very handsome bribe for his silence—asking her to meet him, if only for a moment, outside, and alone. Yes, that would do it.

But he'd only ask her once more, and never again. He wouldn't demean himself, even if he had the time or inclination.

Oh, but he had the inclination. Ewen's hazel eyes glinted, reflecting the firelight as he stared into it as though hoping to see the future there. All he saw was flames. *Now there's a just and true vision*, he thought cynically. *Because flames are all I feel now.*

The clock had chimed three bells, his eyes were just beginning to grow heavy, and the decanter at his side was empty when Ewen heard the sound at the front door. His head shot up and he listened closely. The house was still, the servants asleep; indeed, he wouldn't have heard it had he not been so bedeviled and jumpy and aware of every little thing tonight.

He heard another scratch, and then the tiniest thump, and then another. Then, after an agonizing pause in which he wondered if he'd heard right, there was another. Timorous, embarrassed, but determined—someone was hesitantly but definitely tapping at his front door.

He rose to his feet and went swiftly through the sleeping house to the door, but he knew what he'd find before he got there. And that alarmed him.

He swung the door wide. She stood there, a traveling bag in one clenched hand, a crumpled handkerchief in the other. Her eyes were wide with fright as she stood on his doorstep in the darkest hour of the night, wavering.

"Bridget," he said, and waited, because he didn't trust himself to say more. She looked so lost, he was suddenly afraid for more than her state of mind. Her aunt's townhouse was blocks away from his door. She'd come to him alone in the night. London wasn't safe for a woman alone in the day, much less at this hour.

He searched her face for bruises, her clothes for disarray. But she seemed sound. All he saw was the bruised look around her eyes. She'd been weeping. It was only her spirit that was in chaos.

"I—I came to say yes. Yes, I will, Ewen," she said hurriedly, her voice soft even in the quiet night. "That is, if you still want me, and if I heard you right. I know I should have waited for morning to tell you, I *wanted* to wait until morning, but I didn't know where to wait anymore. It's not easy to be alone in London at night."

"You're not alone anymore," he said, taking her hand and her bag, leading her in and closing the door firmly behind her.

7

Now that she'd left her aunt's house, Bridget wasn't being screamed at, abused, or belittled. Nor was she alone, wandering through London, wondering where to go, running down dark streets to get away from strange men who thought she was for sale—or darting into the shadows at every noise, hiding from them.

She was in an elegant but cozy room, with a glass of something bracing in her hand and a comforting fire in front of her. The man she'd been thinking about all day and night was standing by her side, watching over her. She felt much worse now.

"I wanted to think it over, come to a reasonable decision," she said into her glass, because she was so nervous about meeting his glittering eyes, "but they didn't give me a chance. Aunt said if I didn't promise not to see you, I must leave immediately. So I did. It was a matter of honor, you see."

"Ah, so you didn't precisely want to come to me," he said in that disturbing, rumbling voice.

"No. Well, yes, I did. But not like this," she said uneasily. Which was the truth. After all her indecision and worry, she was at last here—alone with a man in his house in the middle of the night, and he a rake she'd been warned about, a man she was so attracted to that she could hardly think when he was near. Which he definitely was now. Plus he had nothing on under that brightly colored dressing gown, or at least she thought not. She'd got a glimpse of a muscular, lightly furred, and very naked masculine leg, and didn't have the courage to look further. Did gentlemen wear clothes to bed? She gripped her glass tighter. She didn't have the time—or safe vantage point—to even think about that now.

What she wanted to know was what he expected her to do now. Or rather, what it was *he* would do.

According to everything she'd ever learned, she was utterly ruined now, completely at his mercy, socially and physically. The rash thing she'd done must be inspiring the wildest notions in him. It certainly did in her. She couldn't say no to anything he asked, not after this. The worst part was that she didn't know if she wanted to.

"You see," she said, explaining it to him and herself, "I had to leave or never have their respect again, or my own for that matter. I was so angry I saw everything outlined in red, I really did. There was a buzzing in my ears, too, the whole time I was packing. It was like some kind of seizure. I threw everything important I owned into this bag and rushed out of the house. I felt wonderful when the door closed behind me . . . for about a minute, because then I realized I had no place to go. It was terrifying," she said, finally looking up into his eyes.

There was such warmth and understanding in them, she swallowed and looked away. *The man's sympathy is as thrilling as his lechery*, she thought in dismay. She wasn't sure how to handle either one.

"It must have been dreadful," he agreed calmly. "You and your aunt must have been fighting a very long time." He glanced at his mantel clock. "Until at least two in the morning, I'd say."

She squirmed. "Um, no. I left at about dinnertime."

He said nothing. His silence said it all for him.

She picked her head up. "Well, it would have looked awful for me to come rushing here right after you asked, wouldn't it? As if I couldn't wait. As though I didn't have another place to go to in the whole of London. Like I was some urchin, some street girl, without a home, connections, or a place of her own."

But it was hard to explain the rest while she was crying. Her chin had started quivering at the word *home*, and then came the deluge, even as she fought for control. That was almost impossible to get now, because when her voice had started quavering and tears pricked her eyes, he'd come and perched on the side of her chair and taken her into his arms. She wept into his chest.

His chest was hard, yet resilient and warm, and soft hair prickled against her smooth cheek as it rested there. She was mortified, terrified, and much too interested in the strange new textures she felt and the feelings they caused in her. She pulled her head away and looked up at him, her eyes wide and expectant, fascinated and frightened in equal measures.

"You look terrible when you cry," he said with a crooked smile. "You haven't got the hang of it at all. You're supposed to let tears fall like rain, not fight them back like that. It makes your face red and your nose—"

"Thank you very much," she said, snatching a handkerchief from her reticule.

He smiled. He liked her better this way: striving, valiant. An equal, not a victim. He intended to keep it that way—no illusions between them from here on.

"Where did you go, then, when you left your aunt?" he asked.

"I wandered. But that was a terrible thing to do. London is not the same at night—you've no idea. Well, I didn't. There are men who dress like gentlemen and act like animals. One group of them saw me and cried 'Halloo!' and chased me, but I hid behind some shrubs. When I stayed in the light, I was noticed too much. The dark places were even worse. There were women in the shadows who thought I was going to compete with them," she said indignantly, remembering what they thought she was competing for.

"Finally I found a church and sat in there," she added more quietly. "It wasn't my faith, but that didn't matter; I wasn't there to pray, but to think. No one bothered me," she said, and hesitated. She decided not to tell him that nobody had troubled her but herself. Her conscience hadn't let her alone. That had been what finally sent her away from her sanctuary.

"The quiet was a good thing," she said staunchly. "I asked myself what I wanted to do, what I could do, and what I should do. And pride be hanged once my mind was made up, because it was madness to stay out all night. So then I came here."

"Madness indeed. I'm glad you came to me, Bridget. I'm only sorry you waited so long. But I knew how your aunt would react; if you'll remember, I did tell you so. Yes, you may wrinkle your nose at me; I hate people who say that, too. Was she very cruel?"

"Very," Bridget said sadly. "I doubt we'll ever speak again."

"You don't want her at our wedding, then?"

"I don't ever want to see her again," Bridget said with a sniff, remembering how many euphemisms for a fallen woman her aunt had called her when she realized she was leaving, before she finally settled on *whore*. Cecily's glee had been painful to see.

"Oh, I doubt that you'll never see her again. The reverse, I'd say. She'll come to see the advantages of having a viscountess in the family soon enough," he said lightly, though it was hard for him to contain his exultation—she was here, she was his, he had won!

Bridget fidgeted. She'd been so busy considering the details of sharing his bed and his life, she realized, she'd never really thought over all the particulars of being a viscountess. Her eyes were troubled as she sought his. "Are you still sure?" she asked.

He knew what she was asking. "Those are slender shoulders, Bridget," he said, putting his forefinger at the base of her neck and skimming across her collarbone, as if to illustrate, "but I'm sure they can bear the weight of my title. I promise you, it doesn't hurt. And in time you may come to enjoy it very much."

How did the man manage to make everything he said sound so thrilling and illicit? Or was it just her? She felt as though the insides of her bones were itching, and she shivered. He sat back, but he still sat next to her. They didn't touch, but she was very aware of him. He was such a large man, and she could feel the heat radiating from him. And now he was toying with a strand of her hair: curling it around his finger, letting his fingers graze her neck now and then. Just that. It was enough.

"So then," he said, "I'll get a special license and have the wedding as soon as possible. Is there anyone else you'd like to invite?"

"My mother!" she said, suddenly delighted. *Wouldn't that be something? To see Mama again and have her see me marrying a viscount!*

"Yes, that would be nice," he said, "but as I recall, she's in County Clare, isn't she? I don't think she could get here in time. I'm sorry, but the whole point is that time is of the essence."

"Oh," Bridget said, "yes, that's so, I see. But wait," she said, her eyes narrowing, "I never told you that! I just said she was in Ireland. How did you know?"

"I told you I'd looked into your situation, remember?" he said mildly. "I'd be a fool not to have, wouldn't I?"

"I didn't look into *your* situation," she said, now a little anxious.

"Yes, you did." He laughed. "I'll wager you stored up every scrap of gossip you could get about me."

"Well, it wasn't much," she admitted. "The servants didn't consider me one of them, exactly, and so they didn't share stories with me. The ladies certainly wouldn't lower themselves to gossip with a mere companion. And I didn't know any of the other companions well enough; I've only been in London a month, you know. Of course you know," she finished gloomily.

"So you had to eavesdrop. Oh, too bad."

She laughed with him. *Wretched man*, she thought, *to insult me so prettily*. But when she stopped laughing she saw that he was very still now, and staring at her.

She didn't utter a word of protest when he bent to her, lowered his head, and feathered a kiss across her lips. It was brief and sweet for both of them. He left her dazed, her mouth unconsciously searching for more as he drew away. He tilted his head, considering her.

"It's late," he said very softly, touching her cheek lightly, "past time for bed. Where would you care to sleep?"

Well, that's done it, he thought with amused disappointment as her face flamed and her eyes flew open wide, *she's definitely willing, but not able—yet*.

What will he think of me? she thought, and bit her lip, because she knew just what she thought of herself. "I thought I might take a room in a hotel?" she said carefully, because she had begun to realize she had nothing to fear from him, but everything to fear from herself when she was near him.

She didn't know if she had enough money in the world for a room in a proper London hotel for a night, but she didn't know if she had the nerves for a night in an improper situation. She was wildly attracted to him, and he was a nobleman, and she was going to marry him, but all in all, she didn't know him, and her aunt's doubts and accusations were still ringing in her ears.

"A woman alone engaging a room at this hour?" he asked. "My dear, I don't think a respectable hotel would admit you. And if I got the room for you . . ." He left the thought unspoken.

"But if I stay here, my reputation . . ."

He looked at her. She hung her head. *Of course. I left Aunt's protection to go to a gentleman, unaccompanied. That it was in the middle of the night hardly matters. I have no reputation anymore.*

"Bridget," he said gently, "when we marry, my name will restore yours. But as for what's left of tonight . . . are you afraid of staying here? Afraid of me?"

"That depends on what you want to do," she blurted, and thought she'd die, right there in his comfortable chair, because now the thing was out and they had to talk about it and she might have to make that decision right away—as if they both didn't know what it was already, she thought sadly.

But he didn't want her sad. He wanted her joyous and giving and ready for him, entirely. He could wait. The thing was as good as done. A man with taste lingered over his pleasures, he didn't gulp them.

"I want you to be happy," he said with perfect truth, "and so to bed. Alone. Don't worry, you'll have your own room and bed. Until we're married."

It was a promise and a caution, and they both knew it. She nodded. He stood, took her bag, and led her up the stairs.

He showed her to a room and said good night.

"My servants are all asleep. Is there anything you need? I can wake them, or I can try to help you myself."

"No, this is fine, this is lovely," she said, wondering if he was going to kiss her again.

But he only nodded and left, closing the door behind him.

What she could see of the room in the rosy glow of lamplight was charming. There was a canopied bed with a satin coverlet, heaped with pillows. The fireplace was ringed by a fine filigree firescreen. The chairs and settee were in the latest Egyptian style, light, with delicate legs and inlaid designs. The stretched silk on the walls was green and yellow, in the pattern of a Chinese garden, all over bridges and trees. It was a luxurious and tasteful room.

Bridget was uneasy for a moment, wondering if this was where he usually took his women. But then she saw a military-looking silver-backed brush on the vanity and realized it was probably his best guest room.

She yawned. It was very late. The ewer and basin on the table were empty. As much as she wanted to wash the soot off her hands and face after her hours of wandering the streets, she wouldn't disturb him by asking for water. *Let sleeping rakes lie*, she thought with a smile, which faded as she realized that particular rake was going to be her husband in no time at all. She brooded as she took off her gown, wondering about the wisdom of her decision again. Her head had just emerged from the nightdress she'd slipped on when she heard tapping on her door.

She opened the door hesitantly, peering out. It was Ewen. She clutched the neck of her gown, although there was no reason to. Her grandmother might have worn such a nightdress without embarrassment. In fact, she thought, it might have belonged to her grandmother at that. She'd had it for longer than she could remember, at any rate.

"Fetching," he said with a grin, looking at the long, enveloping plain white woolen gown. She actually felt herself blushing for not being more seductive. "I just wanted to tell you where the conveniences were. They're down at the end of the hall. There are towels and such there, too. If you've any needs or questions, let me know. My room is there."

Just opposite hers, she saw, nodding mutely.

"It's *very* late. You look like a little owl." He laughed. "Good night, sleepyhead."

The glow from that sweetly innocent endearment lasted until Bridget got to the facility he'd mentioned. She was astonished. Aunt had a lovely townhouse, but no indoor plumbing on the second floor, and certainly nothing as lavish as this. Here there were fine porcelain basins and bowls and a bathtub big enough for two.

When Bridget was through blushing over the thought of which two that might be, she decided a bath would have to wait for another time when she wasn't so tired. Certainly a time when she was more comfortable about staying in this house. Right now she was hesitant to take off all her clothes and leave them off for that long. She looked at the big tub longingly as she hastily used a washcloth and a basin instead. As soon as she was done, she tiptoed back down the hall to her room.

She crept into bed, realizing how exhausted she was when her head touched the plump pillow. She worried one minute more. But the sheets were sweet-smelling and the bed so very soft that her worries faded into the dawning light, and she slept at last. She was still alone, although she felt less so than she'd been for years.

She woke to a kiss.

She was between sleep and awareness, and the kiss was so light and sweet it seemed part of some amazing but fading dream. She stretched and half rose, seeking, trying to follow it into the light.

She opened her eyes and saw Ewen bending over her. She shot up in bed, pulling up the coverlet, blinking in the full light of day.

Ewen was fully and magnificently dressed. He wore a dark green jacket over dazzling white linen, his vest was embroidered green and gold, and his cravat was tied casually but elegantly. He had on tight-fitting tan breeches and high boots with gold tassels, and he wore one gold fob. "I let you sleep for hours," he said, smiling, "but I have to leave now and didn't want you waking and finding me gone. I could have sent in a servant to wake you, but I decided to spare them the risk—I didn't know how you'd react. Some people are very cranky in the morning. You could have been quite savage."

But now she was fully awake. "Brave of you, indeed," she said.

"Yes, well, I thought so," he answered, and sat on the bed beside her.

She stiffened for a moment, until she saw him raise one eyebrow at her reaction. She realized how foolishly she was acting. He was fully dressed, and it was broad daylight, after all. He read all that in her face and smiled to himself. He was amused and pleased by how naive she was.

"A liberty, to be sure," he said in answer to her unspoken concern, "but not an outrageous one, considering we'll be man and wife as soon as I can rattle enough cages here in London. That's what I'm off to do now. We need more than a vicar. I need a special license, and quickly. So I must call in a few favors from a politician or two, be charming to some friends at the House of Lords, and then pay a visit to a magistrate I know, to push the thing through. Otherwise it could take weeks. We don't have them. But after I set matters in motion I'll come back. I also have to do something about the things you need."

"I don't need anything, Ewen. I took everything I have with me. Well, I left a pair of shoes and a bonnet because they didn't fit in my bag, but they were old anyway, and I have the rest."

"Ah, we finally see the end of the coal scuttle. That's good," he said, gazing at her hair. It had come free of its night braid and tumbled around her face.

"No, that's not the one I meant," she said, brushing back a lock of hair, ready to defend her taste. But it was hard to argue with him, hard to even speak with him now.

He was so dashing he took her breath as well as all her resistance away. His dark hair was brushed back, still damp from his morning toilette, and she could smell some crisp, delicious scent left from his shaving soap. His eyes were dazzling with green and gold light, and his mouth, she saw now, was really perfectly shaped, and wonderfully tender for such a strong man.

"You need new clothing, my dear," he said.

Her musing about his mouth stopped abruptly. She was not a beggar to his king. Well, she supposed she was, but it was embarrassing to have it so obvious. "I have clothes!" she retorted.

"Yes, I know, you do," he said, "and very lovely you look in them, too, or you wouldn't have attracted me. They were perfectly correct for Cecily's companion, but not for mine. It's a question of job requirements."

It was unarguable. He lifted her chin with his finger. "Don't be so unhappy. I want you to look beautiful. I have money, a great deal of it. We'll sit down one day and go over it together so you know the extent of it should anything ever happen to me. But for now let me spend some on you; it would please me to see you looking as elegant as you can. And I know you can look magnificent. No, not another word about the scar—I can see it forming on your lips. I have something better for them to do than argue."

He did. His mouth was warm, then hot. He tasted of coffee and toothpowder, and something tartly sweet that was like dark nectar to her. He pulled her close, though he didn't need to, because she found herself clinging to him, trying to get closer to the wonderful taste and touch of him. She'd learned to open her mouth to his, and he murmured something congratulatory when she did. She wasn't doing it for him, though; it was all for herself now.

When one large hand slowly caressed her shoulder, she shivered. When it caressed her breast, she shook. It felt so strange, good and bad all at once, because it had to be wrong. He felt the change in her lips even before she could speak.

He wanted to strip off his jacket and press her back into the bed, to swamp her fears with the same sensations that were riding him, stunning her with the delicious knowledge of where they were going. He thought he could. She was so warm and muzzy with sleep; pliant, dreamy, delicious. Her mouth was so welcoming. Her smooth, curved breast just fit in his hand. The tip of it pebbled into his palm, and he felt the reaction stirring throughout his body. But her mouth grew taut just as her breast did, and he felt her slight withdrawal. It was enough to remind him of the hour, the day—and the days that would lie ahead.

"Quite right," he said, dropping his hands and drawing back. "I must be going. But hold that thought, will you? Not the doubt and fear—the pleasure. It *is* a pleasure, Bridget, and there's nothing wrong with it."

She bit her lip. "Perhaps if we were married . . ."

"I see. If I were your lawful husband, I could do anything and it would be good and acceptable to you?" he asked, watching her closely.

"Well," she said slowly, beginning to think of any number of unmentionable things she could hardly imagine that he might do and she might not like, "that's what I was taught."

"Then you were taught rubbish," he said curtly. He stood, straightening his jacket. "Married or not, you have to like whatever I do or else it's not right. If you like it, then it is. Understand? I don't enjoy pretense, I don't like victims."

She'd never pretended anything to him. But she was a victim of what life had done to her, and they both knew it, so she didn't know what to say.

His voice became gentle, he touched her cheek lightly, and his eyes grew tender. "Don't worry about it. It'll sort itself out once we're married, you'll see. Oh— since you don't have a maid yet, you'll have to go downstairs for breakfast. I've asked for it to be left out for you in the morning room. Enjoy; I'll be back as soon as I can." He dropped a kiss on her forehead and left.

She washed and dressed in her best frock; anything else would be unacceptable in this lovely room and house. Thinking of the house, she hesitated. Hungry as she was, she was nervous about going downstairs. *But you'll be mistress here one day, my girl*, she told herself, held up her head, and went down the stairs.

The butler was a large man of middle years with distinguished-looking gray hair and a sober face. He smiled politely enough and directed her to the morning room. She wanted to exchange a few words, but remembering how her aunt behaved with servants, Bridget merely nodded and thanked him. *Not so difficult*, she told herself happily, and went in to get her breakfast.

The room was well named. Morning sunlight streamed in through the windows, spotlighting a table big enough to seat a dozen. Bridget's eyes flew to the sideboard laden with dishes and servers, silver tureens and urns. The rising scents of fresh bread, pastries, eggs, bacon, porridge, and coffee made her mouth water. But she stood stock still. A tall, harsh-faced, well-dressed man with red hair was selecting his breakfast from the assorted dishes. His head swung around when she stepped into the room.

He paused, his fork arrested in midair over a server heaped with golden shirred eggs. "Well, well," he said with a slow smile, looking her up and down.

Without even thinking about it she turned her face so that her scar was shadowed and lowered her eyes, as she was accustomed to doing in the company of strange gentlemen. "No wonder Ewen was so distracted last night. Look what he had to come home to!" he said. "My name's Rafe, little darling, what's yours?"

"My name is Bridget Cooke, and I am Ewen's fiancée," she said stiffly.

"Oh, lord, here's a romp!" he said with a wolfish smile. "Ewen's promised bride, is it? Getting a head start on the honeymoon, are you?"

"I stayed here last night, but nothing untoward happened," she protested, trying to hold her head high again. "Ewen was a perfect gentleman."

"Oh, to be sure, to be sure," he said, before he started laughing so hard he dropped his fork in the eggs.

8

The red-haired man who'd introduced himself as Rafe sobered instantly. Maybe he saw her face clearly at last.

He sketched a bow as best he could while still holding a plate full of food. "Apologies," he said seriously. "It was just that I didn't expect to find Ewen had such lovely company." He put his plate down. "May I help you to some of this delicious food, Miss . . . Cooke?"

"Thank you, but I prefer to serve myself," she said, though she'd lost her appetite. She went to the sideboard. She refused to leave the room, though every instinct shouted that she should. She had to face reality, though the redheaded man's interested gaze was so disconcerting, her hands shook as she picked up a plate.

"So," he said casually, putting some biscuits on his heaping plate, "you're from the countryside? Have to be.

No London lady would be up this early. Your family coming down to breakfast a little later, then?"

"My family," she said evenly, "is not here."

"Ah!" he said.

She filled her plate quickly and went to the table. He seated her, and then himself—opposite her. Well, but it would be unfriendly for him to sit far away, she decided, and much too friendly if he sat beside her. Still, she didn't like the cold blue eyes assessing her over the table. She lowered her gaze and studied her plate, surprised to see she'd put kippers on it. She hated kippers.

"Your chaperone?" he asked negligently.

"I—I don't need one," she said. "Ewen's gone out to get a special license. We're going to be married as soon as he can get one." She stopped. It sounded incredible to her own ears. It had been a wildly strange concept in the middle of the night, and the glare of morning sunlight made it even stranger.

"A hasty fellow indeed," Rafe remarked.

"Well, it's because his father's so terribly ill, you know," she said, wondering how much she had to say to him.

"No, I didn't," he said with a slight frown.

They ate in silence for a few moments. She thought it was toast she was nibbling.

"I haven't seen you before," he commented, his eyes studying her.

"I've only been in London a month."

He frowned more fiercely. "When will Ewen be back?" he finally asked.

"He said as soon as he can."

"Then I'll wait for him in the library, if you don't mind. I won't get in your way. I often pop in—it's a privilege of old friends—but breakfast's usually not so lavish, or I'd come oftener. Excuse my confusion earlier," he said in a softer voice, "but I saw Ewen last night and he didn't say a word of this to me."

"It was a sudden decision," she said.

"Indeed."

She thought about how she looked in her plain blue gown, with her hair braided up at the back of her head. His boots probably cost more than the sum total of everything she had on. He obviously didn't know what to make of her, a scared, scarred, ill-dressed, tongue-tied female claiming to be the Viscount's promised bride. She wouldn't blame him for anything he thought— including the possibility Ewen had run mad. Maybe he had. Or she had.

"Please don't let me change your plans," she added conscientiously. "If it's what you're accustomed to doing, please wait for him."

He nodded, and then, still frowning, concentrated on his breakfast.

When she was done pretending to eat, she excused herself and went into the salon Ewen had taken her to last night. It was the closest she could get to the front door without waiting out on the step for him to return. His friend Rafe disappeared into the library across the hall.

The butler appeared to ask if there was anything she needed. But all she needed was Ewen. A footman asked the same thing a while later, and by then she needed to speak with Ewen even more. She thought of all the things she had to say to him . . . and that maybe one of them had to be good-bye.

Someone came to the door just as she was starting

to worry about pacing a path into Ewen's fine Turkish rug. She heard voices, but not his, and sighed.

The butler came to the salon. "The Viscount has sent these persons to see you," he said, showing three people into the room.

Bridget knew none of them was gentry, because the butler had called them "persons," but they were so well dressed and confident, they awed her by their presence and style. There was a spectacular-looking blond woman, a smart-looking dark-haired woman of middle years, and a willowy, exquisitely dressed man.

"Permit me," the man said, bowing low. "I am Jocelyn, and here are Mesdames Finch and Blau. You are Miss Cooke? Very well, we begin. The Viscount asked Madame Blau to measure you for your new wardrobe, Madame Finch to be sure you have all the accessories, and I shall see to your hair—and whatever else needs my touch."

"*Your* touch, Jocelyn," Rafe said from the hall, where he stood looking into the room. "Here's a flight! Your touch is beyond most men's—financially speaking, of course. I'm amazed. The great Jocelyn coming to a patron! I give you good day, Finch. See you're thriving in your new profession. Too bad; I rather miss you in the old one. And Blau! You've made me fork over half a year's income for my particulars too often to mention, but you never offered to come to my digs."

"You never offered so much," the little woman snapped back.

"I daresay," Rafe agreed. "Ewen must care very deeply indeed. I congratulate you, Miss Cooke, indeed I do."

She didn't like his tone of voice and didn't know what to expect from the trio, who were gazing at her as if already measuring her not only for her wardrobe, but for a clue as to her appeal.

"Thank you," Bridget told them at last, "but I don't need a new wardrobe, accessories, or a new hairstyle."

"Oh, my dear!" Jocelyn said, and Bridget found herself being laughed at for the second time that day. Only this time there were four people laughing at her—five, she decided sadly, if she counted the butler's smirk.

"Apricot silk? Delicious," Jocelyn said, nodding at the design Blau showed him. "The pearl hue? No, no, and no. She has no color in her face; pearl would make her vanish utterly."

"With purple satin ribbons at the neck and a purple sash? I think not!" Finch argued.

"Purple!" Jocelyn cried, closing his eyes in pain. "Only if her gentleman dies, my dear. So funereal, so utterly deadly!"

"Well," Finch sneered, "if you don't do something about that hair, Joss, she might as well be dead."

Bridget scowled. Not that they noticed. Though she stood in the middle of the room, she might as well not have been there. The three were deciding what she would wear and carry and walk with. They'd been at it for an hour. They'd all gone to her room, where Blau had pinned her into a lovely dark gold gown. But then they'd proceeded to discuss all sorts of clothing for her. They didn't ignore her entirely; sometimes, when they were debating something, they'd turn to her and point out the part of her body they were dealing with.

They never asked her opinion. She had none. She'd only observed other young women's fashions and never considered buying grand clothing for herself. But her hair was her own, and there was a limit. "My hair might not be to your taste," she said in a voice creaky from disuse, "but I like it."

"Of course you do," Jocelyn said, "and why not? It's a lovely, rich sable, and with a natural wave. I wish I had such."

"Exactly," Finch said quickly. "I was merely talking about Joss doing his work."

"Which would be a shaping, a style, a look. Do sit down—oh, my dear, what wretches we are! You must be exhausted," Jocelyn said, pulling out a chair and seating Bridget at her dressing table. He deftly pulled the pins from her hair and threaded his hands through it, shaking it out so that it tumbled all around her face. "It would be a crime to savage such hair," he crooned, producing a pair of scissors from a velvet envelope he took from his pocket. "A snipping, merely. A touch here, a taste there . . . watch, you'll see."

Bridget did. She was delighted by what he so deftly did. In what seemed like seconds he'd shaped her hair. He'd cut it into a slightly wedged shape so it was neat even when unbound. It fell into waves that lay in artful disarray against her shoulders. It looked elegant when he drew the mass of it up and pinned it high on her head, letting only a few strands flutter down around her face.

Bridget smiled at her reflection—until she saw Jocelyn exchange a frowning glance with Finch over the top of her head. "Can you do something about . . . ?" he asked Finch.

She nodded. "Yes. I've been thinking about it. Lucky I brought my case. I've just the thing," she said, and went to rummage in a black case she had laid on the bed.

"I wouldn't," Blau said, looking up from a pattern. "Some men like flaws. It's what attracts them."

"Not he," Finch scoffed. "And I'd know, wouldn't I? The girls I worked with would have said something if he'd a queer kick in his gallop. Likes them straight, he does."

Bridget gasped, and her eyes flew wide open.

"The girls at the *theater*, my girl. Whatever did you think I was talking about?" Finch said haughtily when she saw Bridget's reaction. "I was an actress before I chose my present profession. Now, turn around," she commanded. "I'm no prima donna, like Joss. I don't want you watching—it ruins my concentration. And pray do not flinch. I'm not going to harm you, merely . . ."

"*Enhance* you," Jocelyn supplied. "Our dear Finch uses cosmetics to *illuminate* young women. It's provincial to protest. Ladies of fashion do what they must to be beautiful. It is expected."

"It's necessary," Finch told Bridget, "especially for you—as you, poor dear, must know."

Bridget lowered her head—and Finch immediately put a finger under her chin to push it up again. "I must work," the woman told her. Seeing Bridget's expression, she added in a softer voice than any she'd yet used, "Aw, don't worry, luv. Just you wait until you see what I—and some of my potions—can do for you, dearie."

"Powder won't do it," Jocelyn commented as Finch produced a huge, fluffy powder puff.

"What am I, a flat?" Finch snapped. "Don't get your pantaloons into a twist. This'll just be to gild the lily."

It felt odd to have a stranger nose to nose with her, frowning as she stared into her face, Bridget thought. Stranger still when she started slathering Bridget's face with what felt like thick salve. Finch piled it on. It felt cold, and then warm, as though it were heating up as it lay against her skin. Bridget's face felt strange, tight, and hot.

"Don't!" Finch cried. "If you twist your face, it'll all crack. Let it dry and keep still. Up, up, keep your head up," she muttered as she rubbed something on Bridget's eyelids.

All Bridget could do was worry, and not about how she'd look when Finch was done. She could always wash her face when they'd gone, after all. But now she had time to think about how they all acted toward her. They treated her like an object. She supposed a seamstress, hairdresser, and expert on cosmetics might consider the person they were working on as such. It was the way they talked to her that was so worrisome. They were more than familiar, less than friendly. They didn't speak to her as they would have to Cecily or Aunt Harriet, that was certain.

"Done!" Finch said, interrupting Bridget's worrying.

"Well, well, well," Jocelyn said, circling Bridget like a shark around a capsized boat. "You have done it, old girl. Congratulations."

Blau looked up from her patterns and studied Bridget. "Yes," she said, "but I still don't know if he'll like it. Men have odd fancies. She was unique before."

"She's dazzling now!" Finch crowed.

Bridget spun around and finally stared at herself in the mirror. She couldn't speak. Her hand crept up to touch her face, her scar, to be sure she was looking at herself.

"Don't!" Finch shrilled.

Bridget dropped her hand and just stared instead.

Her eyes might look brighter because of the interesting shadows Finch had put there. Her cheeks and lips might be redder, too. But she didn't see that. She only saw that she was beautiful. She was the girl of her dreams. She was the woman she'd have been if that dog hadn't sunk its teeth into her flesh. Her skin was smooth and white and whole. There was no scar. None.

"Maquillage," Finch said with a satisfied smirk. "I wonder no one ever told you about it before. It's nearly your exact color, too. I'll give you a pot and send you more when you need it. No trick to it at all. Pile it on, especially over the scar, and then smooth it out. Put it on first thing in the morning, and only take it off after he's asleep. Don't leave it on all the time, it will kill your skin in time. But what won't? Have a care, though. No tears, and no screaming, unless you learn to do it through your teeth. And you must never, never smile—except with your eyes. It will make you look mysterious. He'll love it."

But Bridget hardly listened. She was staring at herself. Her face was whole at last. All of this—his advances, his proposal, leaving her aunt, staying here with him—had seemed unreal. But this! This was the most amazing thing of all. Bridget closed her eyes. It might only be the best and last part of the dream. She was afraid to open her eyes and find herself not transformed into this lovely perfect creature after all. She dared a glance again.

The unblemished woman with her eyes looked back at her again. Then she knew what bliss was. If she hadn't been so terrified of ruining Finch's work, she'd have cried.

The trio of fashionable helpers finally left her room.

She heard them congratulating themselves all the way down the stairs and out of the house. Now Bridget was ready to go downstairs, too. She took another long look at the elegant, smooth-faced stranger in her mirror. It was very hard for her to follow Finch's instructions and not grin.

She sailed down the long staircase. No one would ever stare at her again and feel sorry for her. Nor could he. Wouldn't he be surprised and proud? Now she could face him with a whole face and be his equal in that, at least.

She heard the deep rumble of his voice the moment she stepped off the staircase and into the hall. It came from the open door to the library, where he was obviously talking to his friend. *Won't that blasted Rafe be boggled, too, though?* she thought in delight. *But Ewen . . . he'll be so pleased.* Bridget ran her hands down the skirt of her new gown. The dress was only basted together, but she hadn't let Blau take it with her. Not today. She couldn't bear to part with it. Her new face didn't match her old clothing, but this dark gold dress did. It was magnificent. Oh, but he'd be surprised.

"I'm surprised," she heard Rafe say harshly. "It's not like you to play games with innocents, Ewen."

"You know she's an innocent?" Ewen said.

"Doesn't take a genius to see it. She's green as grass. Nothing wrong with that; a man's tastes change over the years, I suppose. Anyone might develop a taste for lamb."

"Mind your tongue," Ewen said gently, but with warning.

"Yes, that's just it. The air of sanctity. It isn't like you, Ewen."

"You might not know me after all."

"I might not want to if— Oh," Rafe said.

Bridget stood in the doorway. She held up her head and extended a hand to Ewen, posing for him. He stood staring at her, his eyes opened wide, his expression unreadable.

"I didn't need all the clothing, indeed I did not," she told him, "and so I said, and so I won't have as many things as you wanted. It doesn't matter. *This* does. I never knew this could be. Oh, thank you, Ewen. This is beyond anything, *anything* I ever imagined."

"Apologies, old friend," Rafe said with a twisted smile. "My mistake entirely."

"Good afternoon, Rafe. We'll speak about this again later," Ewen said, not looking at his friend.

Rafe bowed and left, whistling a jaunty tune.

Bridget wanted to smile in triumph. It was good that her face was too tight to allow it. It *won't do to look too conceited*, she thought, waiting for him to praise her, to find words to show how astonished and pleased he was. But Ewen didn't speak for a long moment.

"Go upstairs," he finally said in a toneless voice. "Take that damned mess off your face."

She blinked. "What? What are you talking about? Can't you see? Isn't it wonderful?"

"I see you look like a whore now, that's what I see," he said furiously. "What possessed you? Or is it only your true nature coming out? Did you think that once you were in my house, under my protection, you could finally fly your true colors? We're not married yet, my dear, and the way things are looking now, we may never be. Just as well, just as well," he muttered. "I only investigated your background here in London. I should have been more careful. God knows I ought to have known better."

"What?" she said, her smooth, tight face cracking into a mask of grief as tears began to spill from her eyes. "What are you *saying*? It looks lovely, they all said so. Look." She raised her face, scarcely able to see him through the tears. "You can't have seen. *There's no scar, Ewen*. Look, none at all. It's vanished. I'm not a . . . what are you *saying*?"

He put a hand over his eyes, and his shoulders slumped. "Oh, God," he said, "of course not. What was I thinking? Bridget, don't cry," he said, just as Finch had. But Finch had been right to say it, because when Bridget put her hand to her cheeks to try to wipe away the tears, she felt the smooth surface had become wet and slimy, and when she looked at her hand, she saw a gluey white smear, along with bits of cracked plaster clinging to her fingers.

That made her cry harder, in shame and despair because the lovely image had been shattered.

"But *you* sent them," she said in confusion.

"To dress you, not to change your face." Ewen said, and against her tearful protests, he gathered her in his arms. "Hush," he whispered. "I'm a fool, I didn't realize. Bridget, lovely Bridget, it's a stage trick. Finch, I suppose. Or that madman Jocelyn. It's not for you. Never for you."

"It looked good to me in my mirror," Bridget wept. "It looked wonderful." He could feel her draw in a sudden, sharp breath. She gazed up at him, her voice shaking but determined. "Madame Blau said . . . she said some men like flaws. She said some men have odd fancies. Is it that, Ewen? If it is, please tell me now."

"No," he said in a harsh voice. "My 'odd fancy' is to see you healthy. Actresses only wear that sort of cosmetic for a few hours at a time, and even so they're at risk. Offstage, that concoction's for raddled women or courtesans who are growing old. It poisons your skin. It's only for those who have much worse to disguise than you do." His eyes were dark and serious. He heaved a deep sigh and held her by the shoulders so he could look into her eyes.

But then he felt how delicate those shoulders were beneath his hands, and how shuddering sobs still shook them as she tried to gain control. His thumbs made small circles on her smooth skin as he spoke, as he tried to caress her and speak a difficult truth at the same time.

"Listen, my dear," he said softly, angling his head, trying to catch her eye so she could see his concern. "There are diseases women—and men—can get, diseases of the lower body that come from sexual relations with a diseased partner. These conditions also pit and destroy the skin. Such cosmetics are used then because the reality is so much worse. But you—I told you, I find the scar no flaw in your appearance."

She raised her head. Her face was smeared, the cosmetic cracked into pieces, showing her own pale peach complexion beneath. He looked into grave gray eyes bright with tears and caught his breath. It was as though he saw a beautiful living woman emerging from the marble she had been sculpted from. The sculpture, he thought, could have been titled "Misery." He lowered his lips to hers and kissed her gently, then drew back.

Her eyes widened. "Ewen! Your jacket! It looks as though someone spread plaster all over it!"

He glanced down. His dark blue jacket was ruined. "Someone did."

She bit her lip, and then slowly, unexpectedly—and enchantingly, he thought—a grin formed on her lips, making the last of her mask splinter into a network of cracks. "Serves you right," she said with more spirit, "saying I looked like a . . . talking about investigating me further." Her smile faded. She glanced down at the cosmetic caked on her hand, not at him, and took a steadying breath.

"What you said," she remarked pensively. "I think it's as well we're not married, too. Yes. I see this was a bad, bad idea, after all. I can't go back to Aunt Harriet. But I do have a mother." She looked up at him again. "I only ask—this is so embarrassing, but . . . could you please just lend me a few shillings? I have most of the fare, you see, and I promise I'll pay you back."

"Bridget, forgive me," he said ruefully. "I had a devil of a morning. Trying to get the law to move fast is like trying to get the House of Lords to waltz. It will take a day, maybe more, to get a special license, which is so much faster than anyone else can get one, but too slow for me, even *with* all my connections. And then to come home to find Rafe smirking and you looking like . . . but again, forgive me. Whatever my problems, I'd no right to leap to conclusions, and such stupid ones at that. I'm sorry.

"And if you don't marry me," he added, "I'll sue you for breach of promise, and how will you ever get to Ireland if you have to pay me all your money? Come, let's forget this. Wash your face—or heap on another pound of that ghastly stuff, if you really want—and I'll take you to dinner. We'll enjoy London tonight. That new gown's too lovely to waste."

"But it's only basted together," she said. "It could come apart at a touch."

"Is that a promise?" he asked with a curling smile.

They left his townhouse as evening fell. They rode in his town carriage, a coachman at the reins, a footman at the back. Bridget sat in the luxurious coach, a little nervous, but gleeful, too. If they should run into Cecily, it would be awkward, but Bridget decided she'd greet her and forgive her and Aunt Harriet both. She was feeling very charitable tonight.

She wore no cosmetics. She was through with that fantasy. But she felt as though she were living in one anyway. She wore the gold dress, because Ewen had had the seamstress send over her assistant to stitch it up right. The gold dress, *and* a lovely new paisley shawl, soft as the spring night, fragrant as a bouquet, in shades of rose and gold. She wore new slippers and carried a lovely fan, courtesy of Finch. Her hair was done up at the top of her head, the way Jocelyn had showed her. And she held that head high, because Ewen sat next to her, severe as a priest in black and white, but attractive as the very devil.

"Are we going to a house party?" she asked. "A concert, a ball? Or the theater? The opera? Please tell me! I know you like surprises, but the suspense is dreadful. I'd like to prepare myself, mentally, that is, because I don't know how I could look better—even with a pound of Finch's concoction," she added with a giggle. She could laugh about it now. Tonight she could laugh about anything.

"No, no party or ball." His deep voice was regretful. "Not the theater or a concert, either. We can't go out in public yet, Bridget. Remember, we're not yet married.

We have no chaperone. You've left your family's protection. There's a restaurant I know that is discreet, though."

The restaurant was in a townhouse, the entrance on the side. It was done up with gold statues in the anteroom, and heavy crimson curtains were everywhere. Not that Bridget got to see much of it. The host bowed them into their own private curtained alcove a moment after they set foot in the place. They sat at a small table. Bridget thought it was almost as if they were eating in a very elegant closet. She couldn't see any other diners, but there were flowers everywhere. Hidden musicians played soft music from a crimson-draped balcony.

The food was French, and there were many courses, but Bridget toyed with whatever Ewen put on her plate. Her food and her laughter seemed to stick in her throat. Ewen tried to joke with her, but after a while he too fell silent, his dark face shuttered and thoughtful.

"Are you still angry with me?" he finally asked. He tapped his spoon on the table as he waited for her answer.

She raised sad eyes to his. "No. I told you I understood. It's just that I feel like an outcast—not good enough for society, not bad enough for the streets."

His spoon stopped tapping. "All right," he said suddenly, "we'll go to Vauxhall, it's still early. We'll stroll the grounds, see the displays. It's dark enough to discourage gossip, but they keep it lit well enough to see everything. We've had good times in gardens, Bridget, haven't we?"

She smiled, and was still smiling when he called for the waiter and paid the bill. They went to the door but had to stand aside as several new diners entered on gusts of laughter fragrant with liquor and heavy perfume. The men were dressed like Ewen, but the women weren't ladies; their gowns were too gauzy, their laughter too loud. They didn't wear maquillage, but their lips and cheeks were berry red and their eyelashes were coated with black. One of the men stared at Ewen.

"Sinclair!" he shouted. "Watch your women, chaps!"

"He doesn't need my filly," another giggled. "He's got his own, and she's an original. Damme, Sinclair, if you don't find the most unusual every time!"

"Pretty as a picture, even if the glass is cracked," the first man agreed. "Too bad you saw her first, Ewen. I fancy a bit of strangeness now and then myself."

"Good evening, gentlemen," Ewen said firmly. Since it seemed she couldn't move, he put his hand at Bridget's back and hurried her out the door.

She said nothing until they reached his coach. "I want to go home now," she said in a small voice before she stepped in.

He paused and then nodded. "Home," he told the coachman tersely. "I wanted to go for their throats, you know," he remarked in the silence as the coach bore them back to his townhouse, "but it would've made matters worse. The less talk about us before we marry, the better afterward. It seems my bachelor friends aren't suitable anymore. I wouldn't have realized it if not for you. So now I also see there's no place in London for us to go tonight. But when we return from my father's house, I promise, the King himself will see you."

"The King is mad, they say," she said dully. "They say he sees spirits, too."

He smiled in spite of himself. "Then the Prince will see you, and he, I promise, will be mad *for* you."

Several minutes later, as he closed the front door of

his townhouse behind them, Ewen asked, "Would you care for some coffee? Some tea? Port?"

"I'd like to go to bed," she said softly.

"So would I," he said. When her eyes widened, he shrugged. "I know, not yet. I'll go out tomorrow and tear Parliament down if I can't get that damned license. Not just because I want you in my bed," he added, touching her upturned cheek, "but because I want you everywhere in my life. Good night, Bridget. I'm sorry my outing turned so flat. I've apologized to you twice today," he added in wonder. "You bring all sorts of new experiences, don't you? Unsatisfied desire and guilt, all in a day."

"You bring them to me, too," she said seriously. "Shame and regret, all in a night."

"Is that all?" He wagged a finger at her. "Then shame again, Bridget, because I've caught you in a lie. You forgot unsatisfied desire, didn't you?"

"No," she said sadly, "but, my lord, that's not new to me."

He watched her go up the stairs. He yearned to go with her. They would share the night under the same roof, but not the same bed, and that was dazzlingly different for him. And one of the reasons why he was so obsessed with her, he thought. He'd wanted other women, too many to count. But this was different—or so he told himself, even as he remembered he told himself that every time.

But this time, he thought urgently, he wanted more than just a woman's body; he wanted her mind and heart, too. It wouldn't be simple. It never was. But this was unique and dangerous, even for him. Even so, and perhaps even because it was so, he felt alive again for the first time since he'd left the Continent.

He stood tensely, watching how slowly she moved up the stairs, every step showing her sadness, hesitation, and fear. He held himself in tight check, denying his body's natural impulses, his mind's demands. He knew he could stride up the stairs after her. He could call to her, stop her, turn her around in so many ways. Then he could teach her how they could cure each other's disappointments and doubts. In her present solemn, needy mood, he could press the matter and persuade her. He knew it. He had arts, and she had few defenses. But he didn't want her that way. It was his way or no way. And tomorrow was only hours away.

9

Bridget hesitated on the church steps. It was a small distance to the church, but a huge and irrevocable step she was taking. She stopped in order to think about it for one last time.

Surely, she thought, no one had ever married in such haste. She'd had the leisure to worry about it, too. Yesterday, the morning after that embarrassing dinner out, she'd awakened to find a message from Ewen lying on her pillow.

Bridget, my dear:

I've gone to move heaven and earth to get a special license for our marriage. I'd like to say I won't return until I've

*got it, but I'm a realist. I'll see you at dinner—with luck,
sooner. I cannot wait.*

Yr. Ewen

After luncheon she got another message.

*Triumph! I have gotten the license. But now I have to
remain from home, dashing around London to make all the
arrangements for our wedding. I'll return as soon as I may.*

Yr. Ewen

After a late dinner that she fretted and picked over,
hoping to see him come in the door every second, the
butler delivered another note to her.

*Finally! All is in readiness. I'm told it's bad luck to see you
before our wedding. I also have friends who want to dine
with me on the last night of my bachelor state. Don't worry,
I'll be very good, if only because I want to be very good for
you tomorrow night.*
    Until tomorrow . . .

Yr. Ewen

It was endearing and challenging, all at once. How
like him, she thought. And how like this new Bridget,
she realized in alarm, to be excited about it.

He sent a gown, all creamy antique lace, for her to wear
the next morning. She sat up far into the night admiring
it. She was awakened in the morning by the maid he had

sent to help her dress for the day. There was a bouquet of roses and gardenias for her to carry, and some to pin in her hair. When she was dressed, his coachman took her to an old church in an out-of-the-way district.

When the coach stopped, Bridget gazed out the window at the church, and for the first time since Ewen had set their wedding in motion, she paused. It occurred to her that not only did she not know the neighborhood, she didn't know one person inside the church but her groom! She hadn't even been a *guest* at such a wedding before. She stepped from the coach and hesitated again.

"Miss Cooke?" She looked up to see Ewen's red-haired friend, Rafe, bounding down the steps to her. He was dressed in formal morning clothes, his face solemn. He bowed.

"Lord Raphael Dalton, at your service," he said, offering her his arm. "I hope you'll permit me to be your escort today. The thing of it is, Ewen wanted someone to give you away. I daresay I can do the job well as anyone, though I'd never give such a stunner as you away, had I a choice. Blast—that's not the thing to say to a bride, is it? Pardon. Never done such a thing before, you see, and I'm all thumbs with it."

"Well, I've never done a thing like this before, either, so that's all right," Bridget said, managing a nervous smile for him.

His lips tightened, but he nodded abruptly. She put her hand on his arm and walked up the stairs with him, trying not to think how awful she felt because she didn't know any gentleman who could take the place of her father. Her only male friend was the one she was about to marry, and she really wasn't even sure she could consider him a *friend*.

For a moment she considered flinging down her bouquet, running back down the steps, and going someplace far away. But of course she didn't. There was nowhere to run, and in truth, the only person she wanted to discuss it with was waiting for her inside the church.

The oaken double doors to the old building swung open. A little girl with shining hair the color of sunshine stood there waiting for them. She was dressed in a lovely pink frock and held a basket heaped high with violets. She bobbed a curtsy and gave Bridget a gloriously gap-toothed grin.

"Dashed little charmer, isn't she?" Rafe commented.

"Who is she?" Bridget whispered, half afraid to find out. She could have sworn she'd heard Ewen had no children with his late wife, but then, she didn't know that much about Ewen. Her heart sank. She hated herself for being so trusting, so weak-willed, so dazzled and intimidated by him that she hadn't asked more questions.

"Ewen said you'd know her," Rafe said, frowning again. "Trust him to be ripe for a jest. Well, the little chit's been all smiles the whole morning because he bought her that dress and all her violets, too."

Bridget blinked. It was amazing what a bath and clean new clothes could do. She stared at the girl—who tipped her an enormous wink. "The flower girl, from Regent's Park," she breathed with dawning recognition.

"Aye. Ewen said who better to be a flower girl than a real flower girl? The fellow loves a joke. He said you'd enjoy it, too."

She did, and she felt a sudden glow that took the chill from her hands and her heart. She went into the church and down the aisle, the little flower girl fairly skipping in front of her.

There were less than a dozen people in the old church, sitting together. All the empty pews made it seem as though there were even fewer. She saw Ewen's butler standing a bit apart, watching her approach the altar. She got a quick glimpse of a regal-looking couple around Ewen's age, a dashing soldier in a bright red coat, two sober-faced gentlemen, a neatly dressed little man, the vicar, a plain-faced, hostile-looking woman who had to be his wife—and Ewen. And then Bridget had eyes for no one else.

He wore a dove gray morning jacket, slate-colored trousers, and a silver waistcoat. There was a single creamy rose at his lapel, and a single luminous gray pearl shone from the pin in his elaborate cravat. He radiated confidence and contentment. His eyes approved her. He took her hand and led her to the altar.

Bright daylight shone in through the high rose windows. Even though the rays were tinted mauve and lilac by the pattern of the stained glass, Bridget bowed her head the minute she felt them strike her face. It was a reflex, what she always did in public. But now she was glad of it. She didn't know these people who had come to witness her marriage, and she didn't want to see their expressions as it went forth.

It went forth so fast, it was over before she had a chance to be badly frightened. Surely she must have heard wrong, or time itself had telescoped, because one moment she heard the vicar begin the marriage service, and it seemed only a scant second later that he asked if she agreed. She must have squeaked her consent, because she heard Ewen murmur his, and then she heard the vicar tell him he could kiss his bride. Ewen turned to her and lifted up her chin with his fingers. She gazed at him in confusion and surprise. She was his bride? She didn't know if she was ready for that.

It seemed to her he spent more time looking down into her eyes than the whole marriage service had taken. His face was grave, and she didn't know what he was searching for in her expression; she was too busy trying to read all his secrets in his stormy hazel eyes. Someone coughed, and Ewen seemed to recall himself. He bent his head and brushed a featherlight kiss across her lips, then turned to take his friend's congratulations, leaving her standing alone, even more surprised and confused. But he didn't let go of her hand.

He didn't get many congratulations, Bridget thought unhappily. The vicar shook his hand. The vicar's wife shook her head, scrutinizing Bridget with narrowed eyes. The butler congratulated Ewen and bowed to Bridget.

"You're a lucky girl," the regal-looking lady told Bridget. "He's a gentleman. He'll treat you well."

Ewen heard her. He put his arm around Bridget's waist, "No, my lady," he said, "I'm the lucky one."

"Indeed," the lady's husband said as he bowed to Bridget. "Permit me to introduce myself. I'm Charles, Baron Burnam, at your service. This is my lovely lady, Millicent. It's awkward meeting the bride on her wedding day, and I'm sorry for it, but Ewen explained the reason for his haste. I wondered about why he wanted such a hurry-scurry affair. But now that I see you, I know he was lying."

Bridget blinked. Ewen's face became tight. His friend Rafe's head went up. "My God, Burnam!" Rafe protested.

"Of course he lied," Burnam went on, unfazed. "One can't blame him for it, either. He said you weren't new to London, and that can't be true, because if you'd been here over a week, you'd have found a far better fellow. He had to secure you at once. Ah, don't fret, my dear, I've known him since the dawn of time. Old friends have a responsibility to taunt each other, don't you know?"

Odd friends, not old ones, Bridget thought in annoyance. *Poor Ewen. One of his friends drops in for meals whenever he fancies, the other insults him and thinks it's amusing.* She was surprised at how angry she was—for Ewen's sake, not her own. She was used to disrespect, after all.

The two sober gentlemen bowed over her hand and wished her much happiness.

"Don't blame you," one of them told Ewen.

"Lucky man. Now I suppose we won't be seeing much of you for a while," the other said abruptly.

The soldier wished her happiness, slapped Ewen on the back, and then stood laughing with Rafe.

The neat little man turned out to be Ewen's valet. He was even more formal than the butler had been with her.

"We have to sign the register before we can leave," Ewen told Bridget.

He led her to the vicar's office at the side of the old church. She took the freshly dipped pen she was handed. But when she bent to sign the papers he put before her, there was a dull clanking sound, and a thick gold ring fell from her finger. She hadn't remembered his having put it there. Ewen picked it up before she could, and frowned.

"I thought so. And now that I see it on your finger, I see it's too common, too. It's the best I could do on short notice. You deserve a rarer, better one, and shall have it: my mother's. It's in my father's vault. There are jewels that go with this position, you know. They go from viscountess to viscountess. They're beautiful, but they can't be yours in the sense I want them to be. Fairy gold, my mother called them, since they aren't owned in the truest sense and must disappear with each succession. You wear them for state occasions and then pass them on to your son's wife. Sad stuff, that. What if you don't like her? What if you come to love them? I hadn't thought of it before now." He scowled. "Never mind. I'll buy you more to do with as you please."

His voice grew deeper as he looked down at her. "Something to go with those misty eyes of yours. Sapphires, I think, and opals, to cool the fire of the diamonds. Dulcet and subtle, like the lady they'll adorn. Yes. But I think you'll like her ring."

"I'll be honored to wear it," Bridget said.

"No, it is I who will be honored," he said, dipping the pen again. "Here, sign once more, and we are done."

Bridget hardly noticed what she signed, but Ewen snatched up the parchment as soon as she wrote her name.

"I'll take this," he said. "The marriage lines are yours to keep—after we show them to my father," he told her, slipping the paper and the ring into his pocket. "I worked too hard and paid much too much to risk letting this document out of my sight now."

He led her from the alcove. "And now," he announced to the little group by the altar, "I invite you all to adjourn to my house for some light refreshment."

"Heavy refreshment or nothing," the soldier laughed.

"Regrets, must get back to the office, old man," one

of the two sober gentlemen said. The other nodded agreement.

"We should love to," Baron Burnam's wife said, her tone of voice making what she said an obvious lie, "but we've a previous engagement. This invitation was so sudden, I don't know how we managed to come at all."

"Pleased that you could," Ewen said with equal insincerity.

There were five guests at Bridget's wedding reception: Ewen's friend Rafe, the young soldier, the flower girl, the butler, and the valet. There was a table laden with delicacies, and the wine flowed freely. But since the butler and valet only stayed to share the first toast, and the flower girl was more interested in eating her fill, there were only two guests to keep toasting the pleased groom and nervous bride.

After a merry hour, the soldier remembered another appointment. Rafe, realizing he'd be the only adult left with the happy couple, wished them well and left with the soldier. Then there was only one guest left. She was still eating, but more listlessly, picking at one dish, tasting another. But she stayed standing at the table, looking hungrily at all the food and drink.

It was suddenly silent in the room. Ewen stood at Bridget's side, and from the corner of her eye she could see he was staring at her. *Well, but I'm married now,* she thought on a shaky breath. *Still, it's broad daylight, it would be indecent.* But what did she know about what he thought was decent, after all? What did she know about him? Her breathing grew shallow, her heart raced.

Ewen watched Bridget's breasts rise and fall rapidly. He knew if he took her wrist he'd feel her pulse skittering.

Lovely, he thought with irony, *exactly as it should be with a shy new bride*. He sighed. It could only be one of two things, and he knew it wasn't desire. She was clearly panicked.

"We have a whole day before we leave for my father's estate," he said. He saw her shoulders leap. "We could, of course, leave now. But it's better for the horses and the passengers to start in the early morning—keeps them both fresh. I don't want you exhausted our first night together.

"Damnation, Bridget!" he said as she turned paler. "A piece of paper hasn't changed me into some sort of beast. I'm not going to leap at you now that I have the right to, so would you kindly take a deep breath and listen to me? You're making me nervous. Sorry, I just made you more nervous, didn't I?"

He took her hand, found it icy, and put his other hand over it and held it gently. He lowered his voice. "As I said, we've a day to fill somehow. I wish I had a houseful of guests to amuse you. But I've been out of London a long while. As you saw the other night," he said ruefully, "most of the friends I've made since I returned aren't suitable to be in the room with you. My older friends were unavailable at such short notice. So it's just us, my dear, and our little flower seller. What would you like to do? Aside from that, of course," he added with a grin.

Her eyes widened, and he knew he'd spoken her thoughts aloud. He laughed. "You really have to learn to hide your emotions—no, don't. Forget what I said. I could have wed a fashionable lady with a mind as smooth and blank as her expression. I didn't want that. I wanted you." He looked at her hungrily and took her hand to his lips.

She was flattered and dismayed, eager but uncertain. He saw all that. He cleared his throat. "So," he said, dropping her hand, "What would you like to do today? It's a beautiful day, our wedding day, and we've the whole of London at our command."

Before she could answer, the butler appeared again. looking put upon. "My lord," he said, "there is a person *demanding* admission."

"You've got that right, you fool!" a high tenor voice cried. "Ah, there you be, Betsy!" A young man appeared behind the butler and thrust his way into the room. He was reed thin, dressed in threadbare clothing a size too big. His mop of saffron hair was slicked back close to his head; he had hollow cheeks, strangely yellow eyes, and was pale as a wraith. He looked like a small yellow-topped scarecrow, Bridget thought. He sank to one knee and gathered the flower girl close. "Where've you been? What were you doing? I been worried sick, I were, you wretched girl. Oh, Betsy, I were half out of my mind!"

"She was with us," Ewen said in such weary tones he even made Bridget feel small. "And *who*, may I ask, are you?"

"Her brother," the haggard youth said, staring at Ewen. "She didn't come back from her work on time. I knowed she were working a wedding this morning; I took her there, didn't I? But she weren't back in her usual place in the park by noon."

"We invited her to the wedding feast," Ewen said casually. "She never said she was expected anywhere else."

"There was such a lot of good food!" Betsy told her brother excitedly. "I et and et, and when I couldn't no more, I was figgering how I could take some home to you!"

"Don't need no food. I do fine for us, don't I just?" her brother muttered. "But you ought to have sent to me, Betsy, you ought. I were half crazed thinking on what happened to you."

"But why? The gent's a real viscount, Gilly," the girl protested. "He's got hisself a beautiful lady, and just look at this here house!"

"Indeed, what she says is true, miss," Ewen said casually. "I may have a terrible reputation, but for all my sins, no one ever said I fancied children. We wanted to do nothing more than give your sister a hearty luncheon for her efforts."

The young man turned crimson and rose to his feet, his fists clenched. "Miss, is it? Who you think you're talking to?"

"You, my dear," Ewen said gently. "No sense trying to deceive me."

Bridget gaped. When she looked harder, she began to see the youth had smooth cheeks and refined features. His slender form was delicate rather than rawboned, and now he was blushing ruby red. Once Bridget began to see the female in her visitor she didn't know how she'd ever mistaken her for a boy.

"How did you know?" Bridget asked Ewen.

"I *am* a rake, you know," he said, and then with a gentle smile, he added, "Or I was."

The girl shrugged. "It's a fair cop. You rumbled me, all right. Most gents don't. Good thing for me, that. It's a hard life in the Rookery, y'know. Any age, a girl don't fare as well as a lad does, that's certain sure. You are a one, though," she told Ewen with grudging admiration.

"Is that so?" he said. "Now, take the food that's been packed up for Betsy, and don't worry—it's not charity.

My lady and I are leaving London tomorrow, and there's no sense letting so much good food go to waste. Then you may take Betsy with you; she did a good job." He paused, thinking. He grinned at Bridget. "Shall we go to the park, too? It's a fine day and as fine a way as any to pass it. What do you think?"

"Yes! Oh, yes. You *are* a one," Bridget said with relief and admiration. "Just let me get my bonnet. My new one—Jocelyn said it's all the rage."

"I don't doubt it. And even if it weren't, I wouldn't dare defy Jocelyn!" Ewen said, smiling.

Betsy's sister made her change her clothes, too, instructing her to carefully fold the new dress and put her rags back on. "I can look after her, but no sense making it harder," Gilly explained. "Having her to go to work in such fine togs is just asking for it! There's them that'll want it off her to sell. Others would take her with it, thinking she's a nob's kid they can hold for ransom. Rags gets her more coins. Lace will only buy her trouble."

Bridget and Ewen said farewell to the odd pair at the gates of the park, Betsy the richer by a new frock, a basket of food, and an extra coin Ewen gave her for a job well done.

Her sister frowned as he handed the gold coin to the girl, her eyes filled with suspicion again.

"It's the custom for the groom to bestow coins on his wedding day, my dear," Ewen said. "I have no other motive."

"Didn't think you did," Gilly grumbled as the coin disappeared in her pocket, "but a girl can't never be too sure. Thank you kindly, my lord, and good luck to you both, I'm sure."

Betsy and her sister bobbed their curtsies and then vanished into the green depths of the park, leaving Bridget and Ewen alone, their wedding day before them. There was an awkward moment as Bridget looked up into Ewen's eyes, saw the leafy green of the park reflected in their sparkling depths, and couldn't seem to drag her gaze away again.

There was another when Ewen smiled down at her, saw the faint color rise in her cheeks, and lowered his head to hers without thinking, only realizing that they weren't alone when he heard the sudden laughter of a child.

And then there was the time when their thighs happened to touch as they sat on a bench to hear a impromptu concert by a trio of roving street musicians. They grew still as stones, intensely aware of the shape and warmth of each other's bodies. It was only natural. Ewen wore thin, close-fitting clothing, and Bridget's fashionable new frock was all gauze and style and very little fabric. And, of course, they burned for each other now. The more they ignored it, the more intense it became:

Their hands touched as he handed her an ice he bought from a passing vendor. She looked down at their hands. He didn't wear gloves. She noticed his hands were lean and tanned. He felt the smooth skin of her palm, and felt her hand shake a little as she took the ice from him. Their eyes met: hers wide and alert, expectant, as wary as they were excited; his half concealed by his eyelids, hiding his knowledge of the growing excitement consuming them both.

It was nothing like their last visit to the park. This time they hardly spoke. They didn't kiss. They didn't smile at passing children or stop to pat any prancing dogs. They strolled. They looked at the sights. But they only saw each other. All they could do was think of each other, so close, so near. *So nearly really married*, Bridget thought. *So nearly mine*, Ewen thought.

They headed back to his townhouse as the day faded to pastel shadows.

Well, at least it will be dark soon, Bridget thought nervously. She knew what would happen. She was twenty-five years old, after all. And mad Cousin Mary had led an interesting life that she insisted on sharing with everyone in her advancing years—which was one of the reasons the family had finally sent Bridget away. They'd been mortified by the things Cousin Mary said. Bridget was more realistic. She had an open mind about what was to come. Mad Cousin Mary had quite enjoyed herself, although Bridget thought that what she described sounded . . . fascinating.

It may be fine or it may be dreadful, but either way I won't complain, Bridget thought as she walked, head down, to her wedding night, *because he's kind and so attractive, and he's my husband, after all*.

Sheep have cavorted more gaily on their way to the slaughter house, Ewen thought, smiling to himself, *as if I'd bring anything but pleasure to my tender lamb*.

"We can't go out tonight because we have to leave so early tomorrow," he told Bridget as they entered the house again, "so I've asked Cook to prepare another wedding feast for us. He's such a perfectionist, it won't be ready for hours. That's as well, as it was a huge wedding breakfast, wasn't it? I've a message to write to my father and travel plans to make in the meanwhile. But I don't like leaving you alone on our wedding day. Tell you what—why don't you go up and rest? Better yet, have a nice luxurious soak in the tub until dinner's served. Then you can dress in something magnificent and we'll pretend we're at a banquet."

"That sounds wonderful," she said with relief.

"I'm sorry you don't have your own maid yet, but I thought that as we were leaving London so soon, there'd be no point in hiring one now. There'll be plenty of servants to attend you when we get to the manor; my father keeps a full staff. If you need any help in the meanwhile, I'd be glad to assist. . . ."

"Oh, no, I can do for myself, I always have," she assured him nervously, and hurried up the stairs to her room.

My room? she thought as she took off her new dress and slipped on a new dressing gown. Would he expect to come in here tonight? Or would she be expected to go to his room? For that matter, would they share one room, or have separate bedchambers, as fashionable couples often did? *Later, later, later,* she thought as she went down the hall to the bath. She had time, and he'd know what to do. *The good thing about rakes is that they've done this all before, it's nothing new to them.* But that thought made her feel a little blue, too.

The bath *was* luxurious. She found a bottle of salts and tipped some into the tub. They made the water smell like sweet pine and flowers. It foamed and fizzed deliciously around her body when she sat down in the water. She'd pinned up her hair to keep it from getting wet, and the scented water came up to her collarbones. *Ahhh, a body could drown in pleasure in this house,* she thought languorously as she floated there—and then, as she thought about what passed through her mind, she sat up again and started to wash a little too vigorously.

But the washcloth slowed as her thoughts did. She'd have to be sure and wash everywhere, because one never had a notion as to what a man might do. Mad Cousin Mary had known a dragoon with the strangest preferences . . . or perhaps, Bridget thought as she relaxed in the water, her mind slowing and her senses heightening, perhaps not so strange, after all. She couldn't see some of the parts mad Cousin Mary had cackled about. But when she looked down, what she did see made sense of some stories she'd heard. Her breasts were actually very pretty, weren't they? With their pink tips and pleasing shape, so buoyant in the water before her, no wonder a man might like to . . . and as for the other parts . . .

Your mind ought to be scrubbed up, too, my girl, a scandalized Bridget told herself, because the water was cooling, her body was heating, and the time was passing. She concentrated on washing. When she was sure she was done, she stepped out of the high tub and reached for a towel—

And found herself being gently wrapped in one instead.

It was good that he took her outstretched hand, else she would have stumbled. She whirled around, her eyes wide. He was also wearing a dressing gown. His hair was damp, and though his voice was calm and deep, his face was hard and tight.

"I was washing up, too," Ewen said as he folded the towel close around her, "and it occurred to me you might need some help. That leaves you speechless, does it? I don't blame you. I certainly never heard a worse lie. I didn't want to go through the uneasy dinner, the awkward conversation after, and then all the uncomfortable, insincere maneuverings to get you upstairs, naked, and in my arms. I simply cut the process short. Ah, but you are exquisite!"

He had whisked the towel away. She stood, head down, not daring to open her eyes to see her own nakedness, or the naked desire she heard in his voice now.

"Bridget," he said, taking her in his arms, which was better for her in one way, because he obviously couldn't see her, but worse in others, because she could feel every inch of his long, hard body against her. And there was considerably more than she'd felt before. Now there was no doubt what was under his dressing gown: nothing but that strong, lean body, which had changed. She felt the unfamiliar hard contour of his sex pressed against her belly, and it made her breath catch.

"If you can honestly say you don't want me . . . ," he whispered, angling his head so his lips were by her ear.

"You'd wait until another time?" she asked breathlessly.

"Certainly not," he said on a huff of a laugh. His hand caressed the silken skin on her back, her sides, down to the curve of her rear. "Lord, you're good to touch," he murmured, and added in her ear, "Aren't you curious? How can you listen to me, talk to me, understand a word I'm saying, when you're so busy wondering how we'll be together? I can't think for wanting you. How can we get to know each other better if we don't know each other now?"

Well, that was definitely a good point, Bridget thought dazedly, feeling his hand tracing circles on her body, feeling her arousal in the strangest places, feeling his arousal clearly as he cupped her bottom and pulled her against himself. *Definitely a good point, oh my!*

He tilted his head back and looked down at her. "Bridget, if you hate this . . ."

"Oh, but I don't," she said. "I'm just a little . . ."

"I know," he said with a wolfish smile. "We can do something about that. We will."

"You don't know what I was going to say," she protested, and then squeaked in surprise as he lifted her in his arms as easily as if she were a child. No one had carried her since she'd been one. She felt very vulnerable as he bore her out of the room and down the hallway. It was wonderful.

"You were going to say you're afraid or nervous, but you didn't have to; your heartbeat said it for you," he breathed. "Mine's beating just as fast, and I know what's to come." He put her hand on his naked chest. She felt his heart pounding beneath the lightly furred skin. "Here, feel that?" he asked, but now she was feeling the steely muscle moving beneath that heated skin, and almost forgot what he'd asked.

"Just so," he said. "We'll be very good with each other, even though you say it's your first time."

"It *is*!" she cried indignantly, snatching her hand back, the passion of her anger blotting out all the other passion she'd just felt. "You don't believe me?" It was as well that he'd already put her down on his bed. Her whole body stiffened at his words.

He paused, one knee on the feather mattress. "I wasn't thinking," he muttered. "I'm sorry, I forgot. Good God, Bridget, I told you, I can't think with you so near. Just look at you!"

She did—and felt her face grow hot. But not so warm as the look in his eyes as he stared at her. "Must we begin all over again?" he groaned. "Must I tell you all the nonsense, pretend to be doing something else, pretend to be thinking something else? I want you now, Bridget. What is it that you want of me now?"

She gazed at him. His dressing gown had half opened, and she could finally see the strange and exciting furze of dark hair on his chest and how rapidly that wide chest rose and fell. She looked farther down, blinked at what she saw, and felt the blood rushing to her cheeks. She didn't know if it was from alarm or excitement. She'd never seen anything like it, and didn't know where to look: back at the astonishing evidence of his desire, or away. She quickly looked up to see the muscles working in his clenched jaw, and his avid eyes.

She waited for maidenly fear to make her tremble. It didn't. There was none. She wanted him as dearly as he wanted her. Maybe not for the same reasons, because she wasn't sure what was ahead. But she wanted him happy, she wanted his love and approval, and she *so* wanted to know what he wanted to do with her.

So she told him exactly that.

His head went up and his nostrils flared. Her hand went to her mouth. She couldn't believe she'd actually said that. He took that hand and brought it to his own lips. "Done, and gladly," he said on a chuckle. "You shall have all of that, and more." He shrugged off his robe, moved over the bed, gathered her close, and kissed her. He opened his mouth, deepening the kiss, straining against her as he stroked and calmed and wildly excited her.

It was more thrilling than she'd imagined. His pleasure—and hers. In the twilight she could see his face clearly. She saw his lashes outlined against his high cheekbones as his lips left her mouth to go to her breast. She could see his wide shoulders moving over her, his face concentrated, hard-edged with passion. His mouth on her breasts, first one and then the other, brought her to a kind of sweet fever, the pangs of sharp-edged pleasure so delicious she wished he'd never stop. His hands were deft, his mouth gentle yet demanding, his skin hot and darkly fragrant. He was so sure, so accomplished, so knowing.

He stopped kissing her and held himself still. He rose above her, balancing himself on his elbows, their bodies barely touching. Then he abruptly closed his eyes and hung his head, taking in a deep shuddering breath and letting it out slowly. And then he did nothing else for a long moment.

"Is everything all right?" she finally asked, her voice stunned with pleasure—and the sudden cessation of it.

"Bridget," he said breathlessly, going to one elbow beside her, his body tense, his voice strained, "do you think . . . that is to say . . . I wonder . . . do you think you might care to participate, my dear?"

10

He could have bitten his tongue, she looked so stricken.

He'd had to say it, but he wasn't sure it had been the right thing to say to a virgin. He didn't know much about them; he'd been more interested in changing her state than researching it. He regretted that now.

He put his damp forehead on the pillow next to hers and drew a shuddering breath. It hadn't been easy to stop. He was almost dying of frustration. But it would have been unthinkable for him to go on, because this was very important to him and he wasn't a man to ignore such an important thing as pleasure.

He cracked open an eye and looked at her. "Maybe I said it wrong, Bridget. Do you really like what I'm doing?" he asked cautiously.

"Oh. But yes, of course," she said, shifting nervously beneath his outstretched body, making him wish he could just be quiet and get on with it, as his body was yearning to do.

But he knew what he wanted. More than that, he knew what he needed and what was required if there was to be any future in this for them. "Well, then," he said carefully, "the thing of it is, it's something for two people to do, not just for one to do to the other.

"Bridget," he said, raising his head and gazing down into her confused eyes, "you kiss deliciously. You allow me everything. But you haven't touched me. Is there a reason?" He held himself up above her on his arms now, and, muscular as they were, they trembled as he waited for her answer.

"Oh," she said, and thought about it. "But I put my arms around you."

"I know, and thank you," he said with hard-won gravity. "But that isn't what I meant."

She raised a serious face to his. They were almost nose to nose, and it was a ridiculous time to hold a conversation, but he had to know.

"Oh," she said in a little voice. "Why I don't do to you what you do to me—is that it? Am I supposed to?"

"Not exactly," he said, damning himself for starting a debate when his sex was clamoring for satiation and his body was thrumming with the discomfort of interrupting a promised treat. "I simply meant, why didn't you touch me at all?"

Her brows went down as she frowned in thought. "Well, you see . . . I didn't dare, I suppose. I didn't know you wanted me to, and well, Ewen, you seem so—so elegant, so separate, so aloof. So dignified. Yes, that's it.

The mighty Viscount Sinclair. How can I say it? I didn't wish to presume, I guess."

"Oh, please presume," he said eagerly.

She put a tentative hand on his chest and felt him suck in his breath. She almost pulled her hand away. Instead, curious, her eyes downcast, she ventured to stroke a tentative finger over the hair growing there.

"Yes," he breathed. "Oh, yes," he whispered when she ran her hand cautiously down his chest to his flat stomach. She marveled at the hard muscles there and didn't know—at first—what it was she then felt below his navel, that warm, smooth, striving length springing up toward her hand.

She snatched her hand away, shocked at herself. There was only so much she could do. This intimacy was thrilling, but leagues beyond what she'd imagined. She didn't know how she'd gotten even this far, lying naked in a man's arms and delighting in it. He'd swept her away. Now she paused and worried. If she thought about what was happening, she might not be able to go on. She'd been taught her husband could do anything— but as for what she could do, she really had very little idea. Her upbringing stood between herself and his passion. She'd been taught to be a good and moral girl.

He saw her difficulty. Lord knew, he thought, if she opened her eyes she could see his.

"Bridget," he coaxed, his lips on hers, "why should your loving me distress you when my loving you does not?"

That made sense to her. And it was what he wanted, wasn't it? He was her husband, after all. Well, then. She could allow herself to be free. Society would expect it, after all. And she so wanted to do it. She dared to discover him then, becoming increasingly bold in fits and starts. Touching, retreating in surprise—and then touching again as his breathing grew ragged.

Her shy, inexpert lovemaking was a delicious novelty to him. It took all his resolve to withhold himself, but that soon became a torturous pleasure for him, too.

She caressed his back, even ran her hands over his tight, hard rear. *Imagine that!* she thought in awe. *He's always so cool and amused, but not when I touch him.* It was a revelation to her, and a joy.

She heard him groan in his throat when she finally dared to touch him *there.* At his whispered urging, she dared hold him in her hand, her confidence growing even as he did. *What an astonishing part of a man that is!* she thought fleetingly. *So large and yet always so hidden. But not now.* She wondered if even the bedsheet could hide it now. So smooth and strong, and yet so sensitive to her lightest, hesitant touch. As was he.

He wasn't reserved now. His body was hot, his skin lightly sheened with perspiration. His focus, his concentration, all his intellect and passion were centered on her. She'd never felt so important.

He was on fire, and there was a limit even to his endurance. He moved over her again, nudging her legs further apart. She grew still. He remembered.

"Don't worry," he managed to say, "I won't hurt you. No, there's a lie. I'm told it may, the first time. I may hurt you then, but I'll never harm you, that I promise." Then he could no longer speak. He moved to her—and stopped, aghast.

What was he thinking of? She'd bewitched him, making him forget years of experience. She was obviously not ready. She was happy experimenting with him, but not ablaze with passion. He'd have her no other way. He took another breath, winning control.

"My turn," he whispered, putting his lips to her neck, his hands on her breasts.

"I thought it was a thing for two people to do," she said nervously.

"So it is, so it is," he said as he bent to her, shaky laughter in his voice. "You don't have to stop, you know."

But she did, eventually, because he began to stroke her again, touch her again, kiss her again, in new places, his breathing growing tumultuous as she closed her eyes and turned her head so she wouldn't see herself enjoying such shocking, intimate, delicious things.

Now he truly burned, now he couldn't wait or stop again, not even if she asked. But she didn't; she moved for him, and everything he knew told him she was ready for him. Her body warm, silken, and damp; she lay in a daze of pleasure.

When he came to her at last, she was beyond ready for him. There was a sudden burning moment for her, and it wasn't desire. But the pain was quickly over and soon forgotten in her delight at their closeness and his obvious enjoyment. It was more than that now. Her easy, laughing lover was suddenly intent, serious, driven. But always gentle, except when he no longer had the choice. When his body strained, the muscles in his back and shoulders bunched, and he drove into her, she accepted him gladly. She moved with him, even if she wasn't as moved as he was. But that was only because she was too astonished by what he was doing. She held on to him as he came to her, and held him as he convulsed in his final ecstasy.

After he finally subsided, he turned on his side with her still in his arms, and lay down with her again.

She touched his damp hair. "*Husband*," she whispered proudly.

He swam up from the haze of repletion he'd been drowsing in. Women had told him many things in the throes of their lovemaking, and afterward. He'd heard profanity in plenty, demands at times, too, and often words of pleasure or praise. But never that. It made him feel strange—rueful and yet triumphant. He sought the right, honest, best thing to say to her now.

"Bridget," he said, and kissed away any reply she might make.

He didn't sleep right away, though he soon heard her soft, regular breathing and knew she'd drifted off. Though usually he preferred to turn on his side and sleep alone, he still held her; she'd asked him to. "I like that *so* much," she'd confessed sleepily, rubbing her cheek against his chest. "It's so good to be held, you know."

That had surprised him. But she'd surprised him in many ways: her modesty, the way she'd been able to blush even afterward, when he brought her a basin and helped clear all traces of their lovemaking and the unavoidable stain of her previous innocence. That had been new for him also. Some men found a quick release best, but he knew women too well. It was her first time, though, and so against all his knowledge of women he'd hurried to spare her discomfort. It still had been exquisite. Though she'd been shy and hesitant with him at first, it turned out nothing he did distressed her. He could hardly wait to do more and teach her how to get more from what he did.

Surprises and pleasures and laughter in the bargain: She was exactly what he'd been looking for, he thought contentedly as he relaxed and began to join her in sleep. He'd been very lucky. He could only hope for her sake that she was, too.

As her eyes fluttered open, Ewen grinned down at her and bent to nip her exposed shoulder. Then he dropped a light kiss on her lips.

"Good morning," he said, his eyes gentle and smiling. "I'd have preferred another way of rousing you, but we're traveling today, remember? No, no, don't jump up like that; you've an hour to get ready. I took the liberty of having my valet pack for you. All you need do is rise and shine . . . and stop looking at me like that or we'll never get there."

As he straightened she saw that he stood at the side of the bed, washed and dressed and scented with shaving soap, immaculate as always. It was almost as if she'd dreamed the impassioned naked man in her arms. Almost—until she saw what was kindling again in his eyes.

"I'll be ready in no time," she promised. Clutching the bedsheet to her breast, she swung her feet over the high bed and stepped down. She winced.

"Another reason not to rouse you that way," he said ruefully. "I'm sorry about that. The soreness will disappear, and you'll become accustomed."

"So I've heard," she said, averting her eyes, her face growing warm. "It's like riding a horse, they say. The muscles soon adapt."

He laughed. "What a compliment! I hope you don't think it's like traveling on old Dobbin. I'll have to do something about that if you do. But not for a while. For now, please just get ready." He went to the door.

But she was still frowning. "Ewen?" she said in a little voice as she stood and studied her toes. "Last night, was it—was I—what you wanted?"

He turned back, strode across the room, and took her in his arms. "*More* than what I wanted. More than I deserve. You were a joy, a delight, and I'm a fool for not telling you so. I don't usually make that mistake. You see? There's proof. You were so dazzling, you made a rake forget his wiles. But what I ought to do," he muttered angrily, almost to himself, "is to stop telling you what I used to do! What a clunch I am. Forgive me. It was wonderful, Bridget, don't doubt it. Now, although I'd love to stay and reassure you, there are things I must do. Breakfast awaits, so please hurry."

"I will!" she promised, and danced her way to her bath.

Her mood was even rosier when she came back to see what she was to wear. Ewen's valet had good taste. Madame Blau had delivered some of her new wardrobe, and he'd packed it all, except for a lovely new dark rose carriage dress. Bridget slipped it on, did her hair up, snatched up a matching shawl, and hurried down the stairs.

There was no one in the morning room this time, so she ate her breakfast in solitary splendor. She was half done when the butler appeared.

"Miss—pardon, my lady," he corrected himself, although he wore the faintest frown and said the words as though they were in some alien language. "There are persons to see you. I hesitate to send them away since they did gain admittance yesterday. Shall I show them in?"

"Of course," she said, because she was curious.

"Or would you prefer to see them in the study?"

She wasn't even sure where the study was. But she was supposedly mistress here now, and it was time to start acting like it. "Send them in, please," she said as loftily as she could, with less confidence at the end because she realized she didn't know the butler's name.

Betsy, the little flower seller, and her older sister, Gilly, were ushered in. "Ma'am," Betsy said, curtsying to her, but eyeing the breakfast laid out on the sideboard. She again wore her new dress. Her older sister still wore boys' clothing.

"Mornin', my lady," the older girl said. "We come because there's a thing I'd ask of you. All I wish is you hear me out."

"Well, you may ask," Bridget said, "but I'm not sure I can grant anything. Would you like to wait until the Viscount . . . my *husband*," she said, tasting the new word with pleasure, "comes back?"

"Nah," Gilly said. "No reason to, 'specially since we waited till he left to come in. Truth is, I don't much like to deal with gents, and it's a thing I think only a lady would understand."

Every instinct told Bridget to ask the girls to have some breakfast. They were both painfully thin, and Betsy's eyes were huge as she stared at the sideboard. But Bridget was a viscountess now. *And you're still a person first*, she reminded herself. *Shame on you, a lady half a day, and already too like your Cousin Cecily.* Bridget's conscience pricked her so sharply, she sat up as though she'd sat on a tack. "Fine," she said. "Would you care for some breakfast?"

Betsy ran toward the sideboard, but her sister put a

hand on her shoulder and held her back. "The lady was just being a lady, luv. You ain't supposed to sit and eat with her. If you're good, I'll get you some to carry away. Now sit in the corner there, and be quiet! I ain't going to sit with you neither, my lady. Wouldn't be fitting, but thanks for asking," she told Bridget. When Betsy had gone across the room to a chair by the window, she went on.

"Listen. I mean, please hear me out, my lady," Gilly said. She held her hat in her roughened hands and raised her head high. *She really has beautiful eyes—tiger gold*, Bridget mused. *She'd be lovely if her face weren't dirty, if she weren't half starved, if she weren't dressed in men's clothes, and if she didn't look as tough as boots.*

"I work at the flower market mornings, and at the cock pits afternoons. Someone's got to take care of them, they fight like devils, but they're only poultry, after all. A step from a fricassee, for all their fine feathers and silver spurs," Gilly added with a little smile, showing small, even teeth.

"Nights, I work at what I can—all decent jobs of work! You'll never see Gilly Giles selling nothing but the sweat of her brow in honest labor, you can ask anyone. Still, there's them that knows I'm a female, and it's true I'm asked otherwise, now and then. But they never ask me more than once! Not that some don't try to take what I won't sell. Them that tries have always got something to remember me by, and I promise it ain't pleasure, neither," she said with satisfaction. She looked so fierce, Bridget moved back a little in her chair.

"Thing is," Gilly went on in aggrieved tones, "I got to take care of Betsy, too, and it's getting harder, 'cause she's getting to an age what attracts certain gents."

"No!" Bridget breathed. Betsy could surely not yet be seven!

"Oh, aye," Gilly said roughly, "I were the same age when one got me. But I ain't going to talk of that, besides saying I don't want the same to happen to our Betsy. I'd *kill* to keep it from happening, I promise you that. But see, our ma's gone, and it's only Betsy and me and I can't be everywheres at once. So I got to thinking, you being such a nice lady and all, and leaving London this very day . . . I'll miss her like anything," she said savagely, "but I know what's good for her.

"Lady, could you take her on? She'd work at anything, she's bright as a new penny and good as gold. But whatever she does, she'd be safer in the country than London now. There's them that got their eyes on her, that's what's eating at me. So?"

Men wanted that little girl? *That way*? Bridget was horrified. She couldn't have been asked at a better time. She was newly initiated into the mysteries of what men did with women. Although she'd loved every moment in Ewen's arms, the thought of *that* being done to a child chilled her to the heart. To do the thing without love at any age would be terrible, she understood that now. But a child and a man?

"Of course," she said immediately—and then bit her lip. "But I'll have to ask my husband. It is his house, after all."

"Ask me what?" Ewen said, sauntering into the room.

Bridget saw Gilly's withdrawal, saw her jut her chin out and put her feet apart as though readying herself for a blow. Quickly and softly Bridget told him what she'd been asked and why.

He listened close, looking Gilly up and down. "I see,"

he said thoughtfully. "And what makes you decide you can trust me?"

Bridget gasped.

But Ewen and the fierce slum girl stared at each other measuringly. "Aw, you don't fancy little ones, that's plain as pie," Gilly finally said. "Nor would you want her even when she were growed. You got your lady there. And even if you tired of her, you ain't the kind what takes your servants to bed. I know. I asked around. Ain't nothing happens in London Town a person can't find out if they asks in the right places. You're wicked with the ladies, and so say all. But you never touched one what didn't want you, and never a kid. I trust you with her, right enough. In your way you are a gent," she admitted grudgingly.

Ewen laughed. "Pragmatic *and* polite. Lucky for you I like flattery. But pass the word round town that now I only care to touch one lady, and she's mine. As for your request? Done. We'll take her this very day. My lady doesn't have her own maidservant yet. Betsy's too young for that position, of course. But she might be useful if she's willing to help where she can on our journey. When we get to the manor, I'm sure we can find room for another girl there." He paused and looked speculatively at Gilly. "How about two? There's a thought. Would you like to try your hand at employment in the countryside, too?"

"M*e*?" Gilly asked, startled. "Nah. Fish out of water is what I'd be. London's my home and I can take care of myself just fine. But thank you for taking Betsy. She deserves more."

As the morning sun rose high, two coaches pulled away from Viscount Sinclair's townhouse, one with the Viscount and his lady, the other filled with luggage, servants, and an awed and fascinated Betsy. Two outriders leading another pair of horses followed.

"Don't worry about Betsy. The other servants will see to her," Ewen told Bridget as he sat back in the carriage. "Don't worry about anything, in fact. The outriders are there for our protection. There's little crime on the roads anymore, but one can never be too careful. I carry precious cargo now, you know."

She gave him a glowing smile.

"Why, my evening clothes alone are worth a fortune—ow!" He laughed. "Didn't anyone ever tell you? Viscountesses do not pinch."

"What do they do?" she asked, honestly curious.

"This," he said, and she almost giggled—but his kiss made her forget it was a jest. He stopped after too short a time, she thought. But he said it was too soon for her to make love again. "And furthermore," he said on a shaky laugh, "I refuse to enliven dinner in the servants' hall by pulling down the shades on the coach windows just now. I won't have them saying Sinclair hasn't changed. I have, you know, Bridget—you do know that?"

"You said you'd be faithful to me as I am to you," she said seriously, "and I believed you."

He was still. "Sometimes," he finally said, "I believe you believe me too easily, but what I said is true."

"You think I was gullible? You think I was a fool to marry you so quickly," she asked, appalled, "or so desperate I didn't care?"

"Bridget, no . . ."

She sat up straight, her eyes blazing like molten steel, but her hands clenched in her lap before her. "Well, I tell you, my lord," she said, "it was no easy decision. I thought and thought about the consequences; I weighed everything carefully and made the decision based on how I felt about you. Not on what I *had* to do. I trusted my judgment and my instincts. Your lovemaking is very fine, but it did *not* influence me! As for your riches and your title, why, I give not a snap for them," she cried, snapping her fingers beneath his nose. "I—"

"Stop, stop!" Ewen laughed, catching up her hand in his. "Why is it I'm attracted to firebrands as friends and as lovers? And me such a peaceable man? I know, I know, I know, Bridget," he said, bringing her hand to his lips. "I'm glad you married me. I hardly deserve you. I know you're right to be guided by your instincts. But how can I understand them? They're pure and good. I'm so far from pure in so many ways, and so newly arrived at the state of goodness, that I can't help worrying about you."

"Oh," she said, and couldn't say more, because no one had worried about her in so long. Besides, it was a touchy subject for her. She herself was still wondering about how quickly she'd been wedded and bedded and carried away.

He put his arm around her, urging her to sit closer to him. She did and put her head on his shoulder. They sat that way, in silence, as the coach bore them through the last great gate of London and headed out on the road north.

"I'd forgotten," Ewen said musingly after a while. He was gazing out the window at the flowering hedgerows, the rolling green meadows, the fields blazing yellow with mustard flowers. "I haven't seen England in summer for such a long time. London's not England. As to that, I never thought to ask—how do you feel about living in the countryside? We may have to stay awhile. Even if we don't, I've always loved it there. I wasn't born on a baize table, you know, nor raised on the pavements of St. James Street. And it occurs to me that now I've found you, I don't need to live in London. I'll have to visit there, of course, from time to time. I suppose we could go in for part of the Season, too, if you wanted. Do you?"

"I hadn't thought about it. I grew up in the countryside," Bridget said. "I spent years there with mad Cousin Mary and the others. I had no choice. I loved London for the novelty of it, but who wouldn't? But do you know," she mused, considering it, "I believe my heart is in the countryside, too."

"Is it?" he asked. "I wish it were entirely in my care instead."

He smiled at her, the look in her eyes made him bend to her, and it was a long moment before he spoke again. When he stopped kissing her and sat up straight, he straightened his jacket and used his walking stick to rap on the roof. "I think I'll ride for a while," he said briskly as the carriage slowed. "I have excellent intentions, but even better temptations now. Resisting temptations is *not* one of my virtues. I'll see you when we stop for luncheon, although you can look out the window and see me anytime."

Around noon they stopped at an inn by the side of the road. There were a few local people drinking ale, and a pair of fashionable-looking men who eyed Bridget when she came in. Then, seeing who she was with, they hailed Ewen loudly. Ewen sat Bridget at a table and went over to chat with them. He soon returned, to see her sitting stiff and still, her head turned aside so that her scarred side faced the wall. He frowned.

"I didn't introduce you because they aren't the sort of men I want you to meet," he said immediately. "My misspent years are coming back to haunt me. Why can't I run into any worthy gentlemen? Probably because I don't know many," he sighed. "That will change. Don't worry about it—look, they're leaving. And so am I, just for a moment. I have to consult with the coachman and outriders about such things as miles and maps."

Bridget relaxed when the gentlemen left, although she saw them slapping Ewen on the back and laughing with him by the door. One looked back and winked at her. She worried for a moment, wondering if her scar was the real reason Ewen hadn't introduced her. But the men were soon gone, and she was able to dismiss the notion as ridiculous and unworthy. She was his wife now. She had to change, too. His past might be filled with excesses, but hers had shadows, too. *And nothing can grow in the dark except mushrooms and mold*, she told herself. She had to get rid of so many old hurts and fears.

It wasn't a grand inn, so there was only the common room for everyone to eat in. Bridget was happy to see Betsy giggling at the table she shared with Ewen's footman and valet. The girl had wept when her sister left, but the servants had cozened her into smiling for them. Now she'd obviously twisted both men around her finger. Bridget grinned to see how much food they'd ordered for her. She wondered about the wisdom of their letting her eat so much. It would be a long ride north, and the inside of the coach could end up looking like the inside of the girl's stomach if they weren't careful.

"All's going well," Ewen announced, sitting down next to her again. "A light luncheon, and we're off again. We should be there by sunset."

"How fast are your horses?" Bridget inquired. "I thought it would take two days, at the least, to get to Shropshire."

"So it would," Ewen said, eyeing the sliced cold meats the innkeeper put on the table, "if we were going there."

"I thought we were going to see your father," Bridget said in confusion. "You said he lived in Shropshire. I thought we were in a rush to get there. That's why we married so quickly, why we—"

"Hush," Ewen said, putting his hand over hers. "So we are, and so we were, and so we shall. But as it happens, I've a little hideaway just off the north road, not too many hours from here. It's a lovely place, my favorite for recreation. Close enough to London to reach with ease, far enough away to relax in. We'll lose some time going there, that's true. But we'll make it up. It's better than driving on into the night now, and a much better place to stay than some strange inn on the high road. We don't have to race all the way; I don't want to rattle your teeth out, my dear.

"I get messages about my father's health daily. His condition's stable and has been for the past week. Not good, but neither is it dire. We can take the extra time, and it will pay, if only by preserving your health. You don't know what some of those inns are like—probably not so bad as on the Continent," he mused as he served her a slice of beef. "I survived acts of war, but I swear I don't know how I survived staying in some of those places! I still have the scar from a particularly indignant bedbug I encountered one night in Calais. And that was over six months ago! I'll show it to you later, if you're very, very good," he added with a burlesqued leer.

"You were in Calais six months ago? But—but we

were at war then," Bridget said, her forehead furrowing as she tried to remember exactly when the long war had ended.

"Indeed we were," he agreed. "So was I. Not as a soldier, though. Rather, as a . . . let's say I was in the business of officially gathering information for the War Office. But I was trying to get it unofficially and unnoticed."

"A *spy*?" she gasped.

"Not a nice term. Still, much nicer than the other names I was called—after those who talked to me found out what I'd been up to."

"I didn't know," Bridget breathed.

"What did you think I was doing all those years on the Continent? Oh, of course. You believed all those stories about the conscienceless pleasure seeker rattling around boudoirs and gaming hells all across the face of Europe? Well, good. That's what you were supposed to do. Not that I didn't seek pleasure, too. No sense telling lies anymore now that I'm out of the business of doing it." He smiled wryly.

But Bridget didn't laugh. She was horrified—at herself. How little she knew of him after all! She looked at his face, all hard angles and hidden mirth. Devilishly attractive, yes, and so disciplined that getting beyond that subtle mask had been a triumph for her. But how many secrets lay behind that fascinating face? She knew how well he could kiss, of course, how easily he could charm her, how he could stun her with his attentions so utterly that she forgot everything else.

She'd thought he was the sensualist with one thing on his mind. But now that she considered it, she realized she knew his manners in bed better than she knew his life out of it. He knew her simple life entirely; he'd even investigated to find out. She hadn't looked beyond his appearance or his kisses.

What had they really talked about? Light chatter about light things. They shared laughter and sympathy and lovemaking. She knew he liked music and rare beef, a good book as well as a good horse, spaniels and a glass of fine red wine. But she didn't know his father's given name, or his first wife's name, or anything about his family, for that matter. And she knew next to nothing about his past—not to mention his plans for their future.

She sat stunned by the realization. He had seduced her, saved her, taken her from everything she knew. But they were, in effect, intimate strangers, because there was far too much she didn't know about this man—her husband, her lover.

"I didn't know!" she said again, shaking her head.

"You didn't ask," he said gently.

She bit her lip. That made it worse, because it was true. There was probably much more she didn't even know enough about to think of asking more about. *Didn't think about your life with him much beyond his bedroom door, did you?* she asked herself with sudden guilt and regret.

She sat up straight again and looked at him. He gazed back at her with amusement sparkling in his knowing eyes. She took a deep breath. Clearly there was more she had to find out, even if she was beginning to be a little nervous about the answers, because she realized that whatever those answers were, in so many ways it was already too late to do anything.

11

"You lied," Bridget said flatly.

Ewen raised an eyebrow.

"It's hidden away, but it's not little," she insisted nervously as she stared at the house the coach had arrived at. She stood on the circular pebbled drive, frowning at his "little hideaway." When they'd turned off the road she'd thought they were driving into a forest, because the trees were so tall and old. She'd expected to see a charming cottage.

But the road became a private drive that led to a long meadow with grazing cattle. Then she saw the house—a huge brick and timbered structure with a wide entrance. It was at least two stories tall, and sprawling. It was not only bigger than ten cottages cobbled together, but even grander than his townhouse in London.

"It's only a hideaway now," Ewen said. "It used to be an inn, a coaching stop, actually, in the fourteenth century. But the main road went elsewhere as the centuries went on. An ancestor snapped it up and closed in the courtyard, making it part of the house. He used it as a hunting lodge in the days when there was something larger than rabbits to hunt this close to London. It's not very big once you get inside."

"Only fifteen bedrooms," she muttered.

"Twelve," he said. "Shall we go in?"

"Ewen," she said a little desperately, "if you consider this small, your father's home must be a castle!"

"It is," he said gently. "What of it?"

"How shall I fit in there?" she mourned.

"Much more easily, I assure you," he said. "It has twenty bedrooms, you see."

"That's not funny," she said.

"It would be if you weren't being so foolish," he said, taking her arm and leading her to his house. "You're usually quick to get the joke. But you must be weary, we've been traveling all day. A good night's rest will do you good." He bent to whisper in her ear. "Too bad I'm not going to let you have one."

A dozen retorts sprang to her lips, only to die there as a footman flung the front door wide open. It was easy to see that the front of the house had once been a courtyard, and a huge one. They'd closed it in on all sides and made a domed ceiling of glass to cover it. It was bright as day inside. Potted palms flourished in planters by each of the two curved staircases, one at either side of the vast space. The stairs met at the top in a long balcony that overlooked the room. In back, to the

right, she could see another room with an immense fireplace. To the left a corridor led to other parts of the
house.

Ewen waited for Bridget to step inside, but she was
so awed, she hesitated. He laughed, lifted her in his
arms, and carried her in. After the first startled moment,
she flung her arms round his neck and planted a quick
kiss on his cheek. "Ewen! How lovely, you remembered."

"Remembered?" he asked, stopping still and looking
at her.

"To carry the bride over the threshold. I confess, I'd
forgotten it myself. But I'm so glad you didn't. It's good
luck, they say."

She'd seldom seen him embarrassed, but the skin
over his high cheekbones grew ruddy in the bright light.
She saw regret and something else, something sad and
lost, shining in his eyes. But in a moment he was his
usual self again.

"Truth to tell, I forgot, too," he said as he set her feet
on the floor, keeping his hands locked at the small of
her back so he could pull her close against himself. "It
was a happy mischance. I'm glad it pleased you." As she
gazed at him in confusion he said, "Easy as it would be,
and pleasant as it might make it for me if you thought I
remembered, I don't like to lie. Not if I don't have to."

"Because you had to so much in the past?" she
asked, determined to learn about his emotions as well
as his history.

"Because I don't like to," he said bluntly, closing the
subject by dipping his head to kiss her.

He introduced her to the butler, the housekeeper, and
the cook as the other servants, the footmen and maids,

stood at attention. Like many rich noblemen, he saw them infrequently but paid their salaries regularly so he'd have staff in attendance whenever the whim moved him to visit this house. He paid them little attention now, too. He didn't take his eyes from Bridget. He even insisted on showing her to her bedchamber himself.

It was magnificent, just as bright and beautiful and exquisitely furnished as the other parts of his amazing "hideaway" that she'd managed to see on their hurried way up the stairs. But this room was furnished with modern furniture in the Egyptian style, made popular by Wellington's successes there. There were delicate gilt chairs, lounges with crocodile legs, and graceful inlaid wood tables and bureaus. The bed and wardrobe were from an earlier generation, made of dark, gleaming woods and enormous, but the room was big enough to contain them all with enough room between to make it seem uncluttered.

"Why bother with the outside? A body could hunt rabbits in *here*," Bridget muttered to herself as she moved from the fireplace to the windows overlooking the meadow.

"But a body could find a better body to capture than a rabbit's in here," Ewen said so close to her ear that she jumped.

"I didn't know you were still here," she said, flustered and pleased.

"Where else should I be? This is my bedchamber— and yours, if you so desire. Of course, some fashionable ladies prefer their own chambers, so if you wish—"

"No!" she said quickly. "I'd like to stay with you."

"Done, then," he said, looking pleased. "Now, as for tonight, you'll want a bath. So do I, and not only because of the dust of the road. I've a treat in store. You've no idea of the bathing facilities we have here. They're nothing short of Roman—because they *are* Roman. They're all mosaic tile from an ancient site my ancestor excavated on these very grounds. There was a warm springs here, and it still flows. Nothing like Bath, of course—not so hot, or foul-smelling either, fortunately. The tub is more like a pool, with room for six at least, though I'll be happy to make do with two."

She saw he was serious. Her heartbeat accelerated. *Bathe* with him? What she did with him in the night, in their bed, in the darkness, was one thing. But bathing together? There would have to be light, there would have to be intent, their eyes would be open, and there would be so much to see, even inwardly. She couldn't absolve herself by pretending to be merely dutiful.

She ducked her head and looked away. "I don't think so, Ewen," she said in a stifled voice. "There's much I can do, much I *have* done that I never thought I'd do, but some things seem . . . too much for me to do right now."

"Oh, well, it was a lovely idea," he said, and shrugged. "But if wishes were horses, this old Dobbin would ride." He grinned at how her eyes widened at that reference. "Not to worry, I'll be a gentleman and let you use it first. I'll make do with a basin or the icy little brook behind the house. Your face! No, I'm joking. Don't fret, enjoy your Roman orgy all by yourself, selfish creature. The thought of what you're missing will comfort me. I'll see you at dinner."

Bridget wasn't sure just exactly what six people would do at an orgy, though her imagination was delighted to deal with the problem. But when she got to the room with the bathing pool, she realized that whatever it was, there was certainly room to do it there. *They could play cricket here*, she thought as she tiptoed into the big tiled room.

It was like a Roman temple. There was a long, shallow rectangular pool in the center, and she could see the designs of the tiles on the bottom. Satyrs and maidens, fowl and flowers—*it's an underwater art gallery!* she thought in wonder. She left her dressing gown on a stone bench and, feeling odd about being naked in such a vast place, quickly and gingerly stepped down the wide marble steps into the water. It was delightfully warm, and only came to her thighs, she realized with relief. Letting go of the railing, she sank into bliss.

She passed the first minutes relaxing, trying to make her body forget the miles of road it had been jolted over. Even the most comfortable coach felt like a farmer's rig after a day's traveling. Then she was able to take closer note of her surroundings. She looked up— and shrieked. She wrapped her arms around herself and doubled over.

She dared another glance up, and felt like a fool. It wasn't open to the sky at all. It was only another glass dome. It took a few minutes to convince herself that the only way someone could look in would be if they were strolling on the roof, and she didn't think that was customary. And *what birds can see, they can't talk about*, she told herself, sitting up and relaxing again.

Then she looked down and saw the designs on the floor of the pool from that close. Still, soon she was edging around the pool, walking on her knees, peering down into the water. *The vicar was right:* How quickly one gets used to evil, she thought piously, and then got back to studying the figures again. It was all very classical, she thought when she'd made her way across and back again. All from Roman myths. It wasn't as if one could see *exactly* what they were doing, although she definitely tried. But there was little doubt.

Still, a child might think the bull was merely frolicking with the pretty maiden, and that the satyrs were simply carrying the maidens off to a picnic. *Cut line, Bridget,* she told herself. *The mosaics may not get Ewen arrested, but they're not illustrations from children's tales.*

Thinking of children made her wonder if she and Ewen would have any. Suddenly she blinked, wondering if they'd already started one. As she lazed in the warm water she remembered how they'd gone about that. That memory, along with the mosaics swimming in her mind, made her almost wish she hadn't insisted Ewen resort to that cold brook. Soon she was actually trying to envision orgies, although she could only think of one person she'd ever let join her.

Ewen stood outside the door to the bathing room. He paused, a little rueful, a little embarrassed. Must all their encounters begin with a bath? Cleanliness was next to godliness, but he didn't feel at all spiritual. Last night he'd surprised her in the bath and pressed the matter to spare her the anxiety of waiting for their lovemaking.

Give over, Saint Ewen, he thought wryly. He'd done it because he couldn't wait a moment longer. He'd been on fire. But tonight he wanted to slowly bring her to a simmering flame. Whether it began with a bath or not didn't matter. He'd see that it ended in a blaze that would consume them both. He grinned at the thought.

He wore only a dressing gown and that grin, and he carried a silver tray. It was heaped with plates of finger foods, fruits, and sugared treats, delicacies a man and a woman could feed each other, the sort of treats that were easy and pleasant to nibble at leisure while lolling in a pool. He knew. He'd done it often enough.

The last time, with that big-breasted blonde . . . or was it the dark-haired one who refused to get her hair wet? That *was definitely not a good night,* he thought, raising a hand to ease open the door. He stopped, his hand on the door, before he did.

It was *Bridget* inside. Naive, wise, newly experienced Bridget. Not the buxom blond baggage or the dark-haired one, or any of the others he'd known. She was different in so many ways; that was what he valued about her. If he repeated the pranks he'd pulled in lustful fun, wasn't he somehow making her like the rest? She wasn't. Nor did he feel the same about her, or want to.

He let his hand drop. She deserved better from him. He didn't want to meld her in his mind with all the others he'd coupled so briefly with.

Ewen turned and went to his room. He put the tray down and called his valet so he could dress for dinner.

"It ought to be called a dining hall," Bridget said nervously when she entered the cavernous dining room.

There were no servants to be seen. Ewen held out a chair for her, waiting until she sat before he seated himself. He looked elegant. He was dressed almost as formally as he'd been in London, in a dark jacket with his neckcloth crisp and white. The only concession to the countryside was the high boots he wore.

She was glad she'd dressed in style, too. She'd worn one of her new gowns, silken, puff-sleeved, and pale lime green, simple and expensive as a new banknote. It made her feel elegant, but seeing his utter composure, she became ill at ease. She didn't know how to deal with this formality of his, at least not now that they'd known intimacy. He seemed to be two men. She supposed all gentlemen were like that, and wondered if she'd ever be lady enough to accept that her husband would be intimate in bed but coolly formal outside of it.

At least she sat beside him, she thought with relief. If he were at the head of the table and she at the foot, they'd have to shout about the food or the weather or other dinnertime chat. The room was huge but somehow cozy. There was room for the table and sideboard as well as comfortable-looking chairs and settees. The walls were polished oak, and the windows looked over lawns where late afternoon shadows dappled the scythed grass. It was a cool night, and so a merry fire chuckled in the enormous hearth.

"It must have been a lovely inn," Bridget said.

"You'll find it a comfortable house. So tell me, did you enjoy your bath?"

"I did," she said, and looked down at her glass. She glanced up to be sure there were no servants near. "I did," she repeated, her eyes merry and bright, "but . . ."

"But?"

"But . . . it was lonely," she said.

He thought he'd misheard, until he saw the grin tugging at her lips. He put down his glass and threw back his head, his laughter ringing out, to be met by hers.

It was a good thing that Brook House had no history of ghosts, because when the footmen came in to serve the first courses there was no one left in the room, and nothing to be seen or heard but echoing laughter floating down from the top of the stairs.

"'E's at it again," one footman told the other. "Best

get all back to the kitchen and 'ave Cook make up a tray, as usual when 'is lordship entertains a lass."

"Thought this one were different," the other said, listening to the fading sounds of merriment.

"Different? She's female, ain't she?"

"Thought he said this time were different," the first footman insisted.

"Aye," the other mocked, "when a tiger changes 'is stripes, 'e'll be different, that one. 'E's somethin', ain't 'e?" he added proudly.

Her gown was just a breath of gauze, as easily lifted off as it had been to put on. But she hadn't known an elegant man could remove his clothing, boots, neckcloth, breeches, waistcoat, and smallclothes so quickly. It seemed only a moment after they'd reached their room that they got to the bed, and a second after, she felt the blessed thrill of the warmth and shock of his naked body next to hers.

This time she was as eager as he.

He groaned. "Bridget, wait, let me, let me. Ah, Bridget, what are you doing to me?"

Her arms around him, her hands moving over him, she was so relieved to find *her* Ewen again. Her laughing, intimate, aroused Ewen. She was flushed with desire, heated by the long moments in her bath and the longer moments remembering him.

He did his best to fan the flames, and then, when he could no longer fight her curiosity or his rampant desire, he brought them together, and sighed with the absolute pleasure of it. He tempered himself, fought himself so he could move slowly, battled his unruly desire so he could linger, even though the very thought of tarrying brought an ache to tinge his delight. Then at the last, when he heard her breath catch, he gave in.

But only so far. Because at the end, at the last thrust he could control, he pulled away from her before his pleasure could erupt.

She'd been spiraling upward to some new height she'd never known. But when he suddenly left her the spiral stopped and she came crashing down to reality. She watched in confusion as he flung himself away. He pressed his forehead to their pillow, his broad back convulsing. But he kept one arm around her and gasped in her ear as he came to completion beside her, without her.

"Ewen?" she asked in a little voice when he lay still at last. "Ewen? What happened?"

"What happened," he said breathlessly, raising up on his elbow so he could look down at her, "is that I spared you a child."

"Oh," she said, frowning. Her eyes grew wide and frightened. "You don't want me to have your baby? But why? I'm your wife, Ewen."

He took a deep breath. He toyed with a lock of her hair. His fingers caressed her cheek. "Bridget, you're new to this game of ours. Surely you don't want to be encumbered by a babe, at least not just yet?"

Her eyes were enormous, gray as the twilight. "I'm not that young, Ewen. Is it—is it that you don't want me to bear . . . Ewen, an outer scar doesn't mean the baby will be marked. That's an old wives' tale. I know, I asked a doctor."

"Damn and blast!" he said, sitting up and pulling her up with him, his hands hard on her shoulders. "I know that! I wasn't thinking that. I was trying to spare you. Most women don't want—"

"I'm not most women, Ewen," she said quietly.

"I know you're not," he said, and laughed. "Good God, how I do know that. Very well. I take it you want me, and all of me, whatever the consequences?"

"Would you want less of me?" she asked as answer.

"I want as much of you as I can get," he growled, pulling her down beside him again, his anger turning to passion, her fears becoming tinder.

They lay tangled together, quiet at last. The moon was high and threw stark white shadows across their naked bodies, highlighting a curve of breast here, an outflung leg there. She lay on his chest, her hand playing over it. He lay back on the pillow, one arm behind his head, one hand still stroking her back.

"So that's what you always feel when you make love?" she asked languidly.

"Not always. Never like this, no."

"Thank you," she said, "but I mean what I felt. That moment of absolute . . . well, you know." She blushed in the dark, thinking about how he'd wrung such sighs and whimpers of pleasure from her, until she'd heard herself and even then couldn't stop herself. And certainly not after he'd heard and urged her to utter more. "Is it always like that for a man?"

"It never felt like this for me," he said again, "and so I couldn't say. I suspect that was only the beginning for you. You'll see."

"The *beginning*?" she said in wonder.

"Well, gratifying as it was to see you learn so fast, I believe you could still remember your name and where you were. I'll have to do better than that," he chuckled.

"Oh, my," she said, and lay still, listening to the

steady beat of his heart. There was little else to hear in the still country night. It reminded her of something. "Do you know why my mother named me Bridget?" she asked softly.

"No," he said, yawning drowsily.

"Well, I had no sisters or brothers, and I was lonely. So, sometimes when I didn't want to go to sleep on summer nights like this, she'd tell me to lie very still in my bed in the dark. She said that if I did, and listened very close, I'd hear all the creatures talking to me, saying my name. Listen—they're still doing it. There's a frog. Hear what he's saying? B*ridg-et.* B*ridg-et.* And the crickets, too. Hear them? I'm glad you told them I was here, Ewen."

They each smiled then.

"When I was companion to one cousin or another," she went on, "all those lonely years, sometimes at night I'd listen and I'd feel better, knowing all the animals were calling me."

He smiled. "All the animals, eh? Including me? B*ridg-et,*" he growled as he bent his head, tipping hers up to receive his kiss. "You won't be lonely anymore, my dear."

She settled herself to sleep again, her hand on his heart.

"You didn't ask me," he said, his voice low and rumbling.

"Mmm? What?"

"Why my mother named me as she did."

"Ummm," she said, trying to think of something clever. But she was sleepy and too content to summon more than an echo. "Why Ewen?"

"Exactly. '*You win.*' Music to my ears. She said I'd always hear people saying that to me, whatever I challenged them to do." She thought a minute and then giggled. He added more seriously, "But it's true. Bridget, if you think to test me, remember, I always do win."

"Well, fine," she mumbled, and fell asleep, still smiling.

But he didn't. He'd had wide experience and thought he'd little conscience, and he'd never finished lovemaking and lain awake brooding before. She was unique; he'd hadn't been wrong about that. She was a joy and a delight; he hadn't been wrong about that, either. He felt better than he had since he could remember. And yet he had a certain history, and an uncertain, unplanned future. Now he'd linked her future to his.

He *would* make her happy, he promised himself. Easy enough for now. It seemed that all he had to do was make himself happy in order to do that. But later? He wasn't accustomed to thinking of that. He stretched, yawned, and drew her close, just to hear her sleepy murmur. And just to take her murmurous kiss. And just to move her closer still and let her help him forget himself and all his troubling questions tonight.

Bridget smiled as she came awake. Early light filtered through the windows. It was a fine morning. Finer, because for the first time in her life she'd woken to find a man in bed beside her. Not just a man—her husband. Not just her husband—her Ewen.

She spent a few minutes watching him sleep. His hair was growing and beginning to curl around his ears, which were flat to his head and very shapely, she thought with pride. His eyelashes were really quite long, she noted. A faint dark beard outlined that hard jaw. Now that he was utterly still, she could see that half his attractiveness came from the spirit that animated his face, because while it wasn't unappealing, it wasn't classically handsome in any sense. Just enough to make her lose her senses, she thought, sighing with happiness.

She passed a few more glad moments merely watching him and then began to wonder if she ought to wake him—nothing too presumptuous, just a feather touch, really, just to see if he wanted to— *Madwoman!* she chided herself. *You have a day of hard traveling ahead, and a night of lovemaking behind you. Up with you, and off you go.*

She started to slip out from under the covers. A long arm snaked around her waist and held her back.

"Done watching over me?" Ewen asked, a smile in his voice. "Or did you take a good long look and decide to leave such a bad-looking fellow?"

She fell back into bed, laughing. She knelt over him, holding herself up on her hands and looking down at him, her hair falling to form a curtain around his face. "Wretched man! Do you never sleep?"

"I don't dare. I might snore, and you might leave me," he said comfortably.

"I might leave my senses, you mean. But I have to get up now. We have such a long trip before us. Another thing I never thought to ask," she said in chagrin. "Is it two days or three to get to your father's house?"

But now he was staring into her eyes. "Gray in the dark, silver at dawn—you have the most astonishing eyes," he murmured.

"Well, I'm glad of it, but I don't see them much," she said, dismissing his compliment to get at the facts. "How far must we travel today, Ewen?"

"How far? To the convenience and back, to the dining table and back—that is, if you really feel you have to get out of this bed at all," he said, brushing a kiss along her brow.

"Don't joke. I'd like to know."

"I've never been more serious," he said, and she did see serious intent in his eyes. But it had nothing to do with leaving the bed and traveling on.

"Ewen! Really, we have to get going."

"Precisely my thoughts," he said with a smile, and tugged at the bedcovers she held to her breast.

"I meant to your father's," she protested. "You said we have to leave early."

"So I said," he murmured as he put his lips to her shoulder, "but I was wrong."

"What?" Bridget put her hands on his chest to hold him off, her eyes troubled. "Ewen, we wed in haste, we rode like mad things to get here, and now you say we don't have to hurry anymore? I don't understand."

He took her two hands in one of his and held them to his heart, his eyes narrowing when he saw how the bedcovers had fallen away from her breasts, showing them coral-tipped and tilted. *She wears them like ornaments on that slender frame*, he thought.

"I wake early," he explained, forcing himself to gaze back up into her eyes. "A most un-rakish trait, I agree; please don't let it get out or my reputation is ruined. I went downstairs at dawn, while you were sleeping, to see if there was a new message from my father. I told you I get reports daily. Since we're closer to him here than we were in London, I thought a message might come earlier. It did. He's better, Bridget. I don't know whether it was the news of my marriage or God's own will that did it, but he's better."

She gazed at him, looking adorably confused. He smiled and his voice was soft as he went on. "You see, he's not a sickly man, in the normal way of things. But he contracted an ague this past winter. It grew to a fever, and then worse. Much worse. He had a crisis. But it's passed! His fever finally left with the dawn yesterday. That's why I dared stop here. Now his doctor says it's all he can do to keep him in bed.

"He wrote to me today. He finally had strength to write to me himself," he said with a wide grin, "to say he'd prefer not to meet you in bed. It's a wonder the fellow is my father, isn't it? I suppose he meant he didn't want you to meet him while he was in bed." He smiled at his joke; he was all smiles this morning.

"And," he went on, touching a finger to the tip of her nose, "he says he wants us to have a proper honeymoon. He told me to take a few weeks to celebrate my marriage to you, and leave him that time to recuperate. Vanity. We're a pair of vain males. *Recuperate*, my foot. He wants you to be impressed with him when you do meet. So there it is. There's no finer place for a month of honeyed moons than this. And so we travel nowhere today, Bridget . . . unless I can talk you into a taking a little journey with me now."

"A journey? Where?"

"I was thinking of someplace where we'd both be happy," he said as he lowered his lips to hers. "To the stars, I think, for a start."

But he lied, because he soon took her to the heart of the sun. She followed where he led. She let him gather her in his arms, she let him lead her back down the paths they'd explored in the night and then take new turns in the growing daylight. If it wasn't for a strange moment of niggling doubt about what he'd said, it would have been entirely exquisite for her. But that didn't matter. Because that made it only blindingly exquisite for her.

12

Bridget came to understand why the period after a wedding was called a treacle-moon or honeymoon. Each day was slow and incredibly sweet, drifting into a delicious night, as days and nights seemed to run together into a pool of delight.

But she had a practical soul—she'd had to have one to survive so long without love. So even in the midst of love, she tried sometimes to remind herself that nothing can live in honey, that a taste of it was always sufficient, that too much would cloy and jade the palate.

That didn't happen.

She came to know Ewen better than she believed a woman could come to know a man. She memorized his body, became fascinated by it, was repeatedly surprised by its power and by how gently he could use it. After only a week she knew what made him sigh or shiver, what simple touch could suddenly fire his passions.

She was astonished by her own passions. She hadn't known she'd had them. There was a whole dimension to life she'd never imagined, and now she couldn't recall how she'd lived without the pleasures he could make her feel. Sometimes just a certain look from him could set her yearning. Even more remarkable to her, sometimes just a look *at* him would do it.

A few days more and she knew his favorite foods and scents and songs. She asked questions and was answered—sometimes with a jest, sometimes with a kiss, sometimes with an embrace that made her forget her questions.

Some facts she did discover. His father's name was Simon Cuthbert Sinclair, his mother's had been Mary Elizabeth. He'd had a brother and two sisters, but none had survived infancy. He enjoyed swimming, he liked to ride and fence, he didn't care if he never hunted again, but he loved to fish. He confessed he liked to watch a good pair of pugilists sparring, he read the newspapers every day, and tried to read a book each week. Of course, as he told her with a sudden kiss as he bore her back on his bed, that was before she'd come into his life and banished books and papers from his world forevermore.

Some things he told her readily.

"Yes, I suppose I might've been in danger sometimes, those years I was on the Continent, acting for England," he said one day in answer to her question as they sat in the gardens together. "But what of it? I had friends who were in constant danger. They were fighting Napoleon on bloody battlefields. I was trying to do it in salons and at balls. They faced sabers and shells. I was gossiping in bedchambers and gaming hells while they were being blown apart in real hells. There was never any question of me stopping because of *danger*."

"But they might have found you out. You might have died," she protested.

He shrugged. "We were at war. I couldn't join the army because I was my father's only son and heir. But neither could I have lived with myself if I'd sat the war out. Some things are more important to a man than life."

"Honor," she said, nodding.

"And love," he said, then turned and took her in his arms, stopping her questions for another hour.

Some things were hard for her to ask, but she summoned the courage—when she couldn't watch his face or he hers.

"Ewen?" she said one night as they lay deep in their bed.

"Mmm?" he murmured, half asleep after their love-making.

"That time when you left me before you could . . . when you pulled away from me when we . . . loved?" She spoke in a rush, her voice higher than she liked, because it was still embarrassing to talk about some things, even though she could do most of them now. But she needed to know. "Why did you do it? I know you said it was to spare me a baby. But you said you married me so you could have a baby for your father's sake." The time ticked by and he didn't answer. But she knew he wasn't sleeping.

"Oh, *that* time," he said. "I suppose that was the time I came closest to lying to you. But I was only lying to myself. Dear Bridget, darling Bridget, it pains me to tell you, but I think the truth was half that I felt you were so new to such pleasures it wouldn't be fair to you. But honestly, the other half was habit."

She was very still. He stroked her back with one warm hand as he spoke, his voice low and cajoling. "You know I wasn't a monk before we met, my dear. I never wanted children that side of the blanket, and I was accustomed. . . . So I wasn't thinking, I suppose. You have a way of turning my wits to water, you know. Let's see if you can still do that."

She learned he could turn the blood in her veins to fire.

Some things he spoke of briefly, and only if she persisted. She often asked about his past, and he freely told her about his childhood, his days at school, his travels to exotic places abroad. But only when she gathered her courage and asked directly did he speak of what she most wanted to know.

"My wife?" he finally told her one mild morning as they strolled by the brook. He paused and then chose his words carefully, being economical with them. "Yes, she was beautiful. And young. As was I. We weren't together very long."

They were under trees, in leafy shade. She could feel the play of light and shadow across her face and was glad of it, because she felt the dappled light somehow disguised her scar. She almost forgot it sometimes. But never when she was outside, and never in the daylight.

"It must have been tragic for you," she said hesitantly, because she'd never dared ask details of his first marriage before, and his demeanor was so guarded.

"So suddenly tentative, my brave Bridget? Do you think that I pine for her? Or compare you to her? Unthink it, then. I don't. I never have. I couldn't."

"But you never told me about her. Nothing. I mean, was she fair? Or dark? Smaller than I am, or—"

"It doesn't matter," he said, picking up a stone and tossing it into the water. "It never mattered. Our fathers wanted the marriage, they arranged it, we agreed. We were both good children," he added with a twisted smile.

"But when she was . . . gone, that's when you started gathering information abroad, wasn't it? Were you trying to forget her?"

"It was what everyone was supposed to think." He stared at the rushing water. "Because a heartsick youth trying to drown his sorrows in mindless pleasures can gain entry to many places."

"But was it true?"

"One thing was: There didn't seem any point to coming back to England right away. The time slid by, months became years. The war lingered, and so did I, my original reasons forgotten. Don't waste your pity. I took a bad situation and made something good from it. Bridget, this is dreary stuff! Speaking of waste—what a waste of a fine day," he said suddenly. "Tell you what: I'll teach you to fish. The water reminds me of it. I'm sure there are some rods back at the house. Or are you afraid of worms?"

"I am not fond of them," she said cautiously, "but if you promise not to dangle them in my face, like Cousin Sylvia's sons did, I think I can deal with them."

"My word on it!" he said fervently, grinning like a boy himself. "Let's get to it before the weather changes." He took her hand and they ran back to the house, laughing.

They were laughing even more an hour later. "Yes," she giggled into his ear as they lay replete on their bed in the sun-drenched bedchamber, "a wonderful rod you showed me, my lord."

"And look what I caught with it," he said, picking up a handful of her hair and letting it drift down to cover them both. "Much better than a fish—she's got warm blood, a sleek body that twists and turns in my arms. Lord, Bridget, no sooner do I catch you than I am caught again. Is there any end to this desire?"

It seemed there wasn't. But they became more accustomed to it, as one becomes accustomed to any luxury.

But Bridget began to be uneasy. Her edginess lay beneath the surface, half noticed, slowly growing as the days slipped by. One morning she became aware of why she felt it. She was writing to her mama again. While she was thinking of the next thing to say, she idly noted the date on the top of the page she was writing. Two weeks had passed. *Two weeks*, she thought in shock. And still they tarried at his hideaway, making love and laughing as if there were no future.

But the summer was ripening; she saw it in the cumbrous roses, the onslaught of butterflies, the growing ripeness in the air as she strolled the peach orchards. The future was coming, and she still didn't know how to take her place in Ewen's life and had no way of learning it. She hadn't met his father or any of his relatives. Except for the red-haired man in London and the few people who'd been at the wedding, she didn't know any of his friends. She hadn't met anyone since then but the servants at this house. Ewen had taken her from London and preserved her in this glowing golden amber jewel of a honeymoon. She worried about the future, even though she felt ungrateful for doing so.

"What a face!" Ewen said as he came into the room from his bath, rubbing his hair with a towel. "Why such gloom?"

She looked up, embarrassed. "I was only thinking."

"Yes," he said as he sat beside her and put an arm around her, "obviously. Because whatever you think is on your face. What tragedy is this?"

"It's only—Ewen, we've been married two weeks!"

"A tragedy," he agreed, "and with any luck, before we know it, it will be three weeks. If you're depressed now, I'd hate to think of how you'll be then."

"But Ewen, no one knows me! That is to say, your family and friends heard we were wed, but I'm just a rumor to them. I might as well be on the moon."

"Oh, I see. You wanted to honeymoon in company?"

"That not what I meant! You know how lovely it's been. I never want this to end. I only mean—we'll meet your father soon, and then eventually everyone, I imagine. But we've been here two weeks, and you must know the people here, and yet I . . ."

"You feel I'm hiding you?" he asked, suddenly as serious as she was. He looked at her grave gray eyes and nodded. "Well, then, that's easily remedied. We'll go to town this very afternoon. Put on your best bonnet and mind your manners, and I'll introduce you to the world of Little Newton."

It was foolish to be so excited about a trip to the tiny town nearby, but Bridget *was* excited. She didn't turn her nose up at such a treat. When she'd been a companion, her only recreation had been trips to nearby villages. And this was Ewen's home, after all. So she put on one of her new gowns, a pretty pink one with a red-striped overskirt. She wore a new bonnet, too, not as a jest, but because it was the most fashionable thing, with a turned-up brim.

Country lanes would have played havoc with the spindly wheels of a high-perch phaeton like the one Ewen drove in London. Here in the country he drove a light carriage instead.

The entire village of Little Newton was a two-street affair. There was a village green, but the only traffic Bridget saw there was a line of ducks going back into the pond. There was a church on the highest slope; below that was a smith's, a grocer, and a few other shops whose signs were too weathered to read. There was even a modest inn, with a little outdoor garden.

"It's not a historic place," Ewen said as he reined in his horses. "The site's old, but not the church. The original burned down several times, and they kept rebuilding. You'd think they might have started wondering if the deity really wanted a church just there. But Little Newton doesn't question itself much.

"We could walk the streets and chance the bustling crowd," he went on with a smile, "but let's take refreshment at the inn and let the town discover us instead, shall we?"

The Stars and Garter was dim and beery-smelling on the inside. A few old men sitting at a table near the tap looked up at them. They touched their caps when they saw Ewen and then went back to talking together in low voices. Ewen led Bridget to a table by a window. The landlord hurried to serve them.

"M'lord," he said, bowing to Ewen. "Ma'am," he said to Bridget, looking hard at her, and then quickly away. "Meat and cheese is our usual fare. Will it do for you? Well, then, Sukie'll be bringing it soon as can be. Ale for you, my lord?"

Ewen nodded.

"And would the lady want lemonade? I make it fresh."

"That would be fine," Bridget said. But when he left she frowned.

"You don't care for lemonade?" Ewen asked, leaning back in his chair, studying her face.

"It's not that. I just thought since this was your hometown, you'd be greeted more warmly here."

He laughed. "Hardly. I only come here now and again for a day, at most a week or two together, and not that often in a year's time. When I do, I usually stay at Brook House by myself or with whatever friends I've brought. Most of them aren't such demons for spending all their days in town, as you are," he teased. "So the villagers don't know me well. And if they think they do, they think of me as a wicked libertine. That is, when they think of me at all."

"Oh," Bridget said, disappointed, because there was little sense meeting people who thought badly of her husband.

The serving girl certainly didn't, though. She came to their table smiling widely, and only at Ewen. She brought their luncheon, and seemed to be carrying her own considerable bosom on the tray with it. She was fair-haired and dimpled, a pretty little thing, even if there was far too much bosom, Bridget thought—nervously, because who knew if a man ever thought there was too much bosom?

Bridget glanced at Ewen. He was admiring his cold beef and not the other sumptuous flesh being presented for his inspection. The girl set down all their dishes and finally flounced away, looking resentful.

"You could have given her a smile," Bridget said. "I wouldn't have minded that. I know you noticed her."

"Oh. Give her a smile? Instead of seething with frustrated lust, I suppose?" he asked too lightly. "My dear, I noticed, but I wasn't interested. And a smile is considered an invitation to that sort of woman. Bridget," he said seriously, laying his knife and fork down, "you either trust me or you do not. Which is it?"

"I'm sorry," she said miserably. "I do trust you. But I also suppose I'm afraid to. Does that make any sense?"

"Too much," he muttered.

A different woman, this one plain and serious, served them the rest of their meal. This time Ewen scowled. He glared at the woman as she left their table.

"What's the matter?" Bridget asked. "Is there something wrong with the food?"

"With the service," he growled. "I think I'll have to have a word with the innkeeper."

The service? Bridget saw nothing wrong; the woman wasn't very friendly, but she was neat and quick. The only thing Bridget could think of that might have upset Ewen made her so nervous she had to joke about it. "Oh, so you miss the blonde already?"

"This one has no manners," Ewen said grimly.

Bridget frowned, too—until she realized what he meant. She'd been aware of it in an absent sort of way because she was so used to it. "Oh! You mean because she keeps staring at me—or rather, at my scar? At least she looked at me," she laughed. "Your blond beauty didn't even see me, I think."

He didn't smile. She put her hand on his. "Don't make a fuss," she whispered. "I'm sure she doesn't mean anything by it. It takes some people that way. They can't look away. I don't mind."

"You should," he snarled.

"Why? It's not intentional. Nor is it any worse than people who look at it and then look away, as if they've just seen a carriage accident and can't bear to see more. The landlord did just that, you know. I've become accustomed. In fact," she said sadly, "it's your reaction I can't understand."

"Mine?"

"You said you don't mind it."

"I said it enhances you. Get my words right, if you please. Ah, Bridget, how shall I deal with you in this?" His hand closed over hers, his voice so low she had to lean forward to hear him. "I have a confession," he said. "Sometimes I yearn to kiss that scar, did you know that? Yes, look shocked. I've wanted to put my lips on it—trace it with my tongue, even—to acknowledge it, for you and for me. I've been tempted to do that so many times but was afraid of what you'd think. It's not because I'm perverse—or *that* perverse." He grinned. "Or because I feel sorry for you, or because I'm trying to heal the hurt, or any of that muck. But because if it weren't for that scar, we'd never have met. Have you ever thought of that?"

"No!" she said, tilting her head to the side as she considered it. "That's the nicest compliment you've ever paid me, I think."

"Then I'll have to do better in the future," he said, and went back to his beef.

They finished their meal and sat looking through the small window. Not many people were walking by. "I suppose if you want to meet the immediate world, we'll have to stroll," Ewen finally said.

They walked up to the church and then down to the carriage again. By that time Ewen's face was thunderous. They'd met few people, and those they did hadn't been friendly. The vicar was polite but distant. The smith greeted them but carefully avoided looking at Bridget when he was introduced, and an elderly man touched his cap to Ewen and frankly stared at her.

"Half of them are dolts, the other half think I'm the very devil. My reputation has preceded you," Ewen muttered angrily as he helped her back into the carriage. "I'm sorry."

"Why?" she said as merrily as she could. "Your reputation kept all the nice young women away from you, didn't it? Your reputation—my scar. How lucky we both are." It didn't sound as funny as she'd thought it would.

Ewen drove back quickly, saying it was going to rain. They talked about the weather on the way home, but all Bridget could do was worry about whether she'd embarrassed him after all.

She was edgy and uncomfortable for the rest of the afternoon. He wrote a note to his father. She wrote a letter to her mother and then tore it up, realizing how it would look to send two letters in a day on her honeymoon. She put down her pen and sighed, realizing the honeymoon was probably over.

Ewen didn't think so. She was still sitting at her desk, brooding, when she felt his lips touch the back of her neck.

"Let's make it a spectacularly good night, to offset the day," he whispered against her throat. "I think we need a delicious dinner lit by many candles, and then perhaps we can think of a way to pass the rest of the evening brilliantly as well. I'll go change now, in my dressing room. We'll meet in the dining room at seven."

"As though we weren't married at all? Why so formal?"

"Because I think I have to woo you back to me again,"

he said, and kissed her so thoroughly she knew he was joking. Surely he could tell she was his completely. She clung to him so long that he whispered, "Perhaps we should . . . no." He stepped back from her. "It was a good idea. It will make it all the better later. A game, yes. But a honeymoon is a fine time for games. You'll see."

When he left, her mood stayed uneasy. *Ungrateful chit!* she told herself as she went to bathe and dress. *Rolling in clover and complaining. What is the matter with you?*

She found out what the matter was when she went to the convenience. Then she worried more.

He said he was courting, and he came to dinner like a man who was. He had dressed in black, so that the white of his linen was dazzling. His dark curling hair was brushed back, and his eyes were bright against the deepening golden tan the country sun had brushed his face with. He looked leonine, proud, incredibly elegant. He took her hand and kissed it when she came into the room. She wanted to cry. One of his dark brows went up in inquiry.

"Ewen," she said, and paused, because the footmen were serving dinner.

When the footmen left, he served her himself, putting ham, beef, and fowl on her plate. Every time he offered her something, she nodded. He finally stopped.

"More and we'll need another plate, though I swear you don't look hungry. Though you do look lovely. What's amiss, my dear?"

"Oh, Ewen," she said with a broken sigh, "I hardly know how to tell you. . . ."

"What is it?" he asked, alarm springing to his eyes.

"Well, it's foolish, but I just don't . . . Ewen," she said in a whispered rush, "you wanted tonight to be so special and romantic. But—well—it's my time of the month."

He frowned for a split second, then threw back his head and laughed long and loud until he saw her face. He stopped, biting back a smile.

"It's not funny," she said crossly. "I don't know what I'm supposed to do—with you, I mean—when that happens. Oh, heavens! I don't even know how to *talk* about it with you."

"The way you'd talk about anything else. My dear, we've been intimate in all else, you know."

"I know," she said fiercely, embarrassed pleasure coloring her cheeks as she remembered the all else. "But we can't now. Or can we? Is there anything I can do for you? Or should we go ahead and . . . ?"

"Bridget," he said with sympathy, though laughter still lurked in his eyes, "we should only do what's pleasurable for both of us to do. I imagine you feel like you've been punched in the stomach?"

She nodded quickly.

"Aching?"

She nodded again.

"Then it's not precisely an ideal time to make love, is it? Even though there are certainly other things we could do, if we wished. We just haven't come to that yet, and now is not the time to begin. Do you think I'm such a hedonist I can't go a night without love?"

"Well, it might be three—or even four—nights more," she said, wanting to be completely honest with him.

"So long? My God! How shall I survive?" Then the laughter left his eyes. "Thank you so much for your high estimate of me," he said grimly. Before she could protest, he murmured, "Still, how can I blame you? I courted you with passion, for passion's sake, and I've treated you to little else since, haven't I? But listen. There are other things to share beside our bodies. We're together, we have the rest of our lives for the rest of our pleasures. Be easy."

She was, for the rest of the evening. He made sure of it. They strolled after dinner. He played the piano for her, she sang a few old songs for him. They went to bed. She lay there stiffly, wondering how he really felt—until she felt his strong arm hook around her waist. He pulled her close, tucking her rear into the warmth of his abdomen, putting his big hand on her aching stomach. But good as it felt, she couldn't relax.

"Go to sleep and stop worrying," he whispered. "I'm tired. And it's too far into town, so I won't nip off while you're sleeping. Besides, how do I know that the lovely blonde from the inn isn't in the same condition as you are tonight?"

She thumped him with her pillow as he lay laughing like a madman. Then she curled back against him and slept, satisfied that for the moment, at least, he wanted her for more than passion.

But in the morning he told her he was leaving.

He sat at the breakfast table, and the early sunlight showed nothing but dismay in his eyes. It was nothing to what he saw in her face when he told her he'd gotten a message and had to go at once.

"No, it's not my father, thank God," he reassured her quickly. "It's from London—from the office I worked with when I was on the Continent. I can't tell you all. But I can tell you they're having a problem. There are stirrings—rumors from Elba. The man they have in my place now doesn't know whom to trust. But I do. They need me there."

"In *France*?" Bridget gasped.

"No, no, my purposes are too well known now. Not only would I not be safe, my presence would endanger anyone we had there. They need me to speak to the man they're sending out in my stead, and they want me to answer some questions that have been sent back from abroad. I won't be long. A day to get there, a day there, and a day to get back. Three days, four at the most. But I must go now."

"I'll go see to the packing of my things," Bridget said, jumping up from her seat.

He took her hand to stop her. "No. There's no reason for you to go. You can't, in fact. I can't travel by carriage. Too slow. I'm riding, taking nothing but my saddlebags. My valet's coming with me, but only so he can pick up the rest of your wardrobe while he's in London. You'll be more comfortable here, I'll be back before you miss me."

"Impossible," she whispered.

She was in control as she said good-bye to him, though it was clear to him she found it difficult. They stood in the drive. His valet sat on his horse, waiting for his master. Ewen's horse was saddled, waiting, too.

"Don't fret so," he said, his eyes steady and sober, holding her gaze as he held her two hands in his. "It's only for a few days."

"I know. It's only that I don't want you to go. Foolish, I know. But now that you're going, I realize there are so many more things I wanted to ask you." She had to stop to swallow the tears that threatened. But it was only for a few days, and he thought her state of mind was influenced by the state of her body now. Even so, he too had the idea that this was an important, dangerous parting, but he didn't know why, so he brushed off the feeling.

"I wanted to ask you some things, too," he said, "and there was something I meant to tell you as well." He paused, considering each word before he spoke it. It made his voice more hesitant, slower and more deliberate. "It's a thing I never thought I'd want to tell you. But then, I didn't know how it would be with me and you."

What he said was so true he couldn't go on speaking. He paused, shocked at himself. Something significant was happening. He'd said good-bye to dozens of women in his time. He hadn't known it would hurt so much to leave her now. He wouldn't have believed it so much as a week ago.

But there was nothing more he could say—at least not here and not now. Or rather, there was too much he wanted to say, and he had to think about it before he did. He wasn't a man to act on impulse, except in matters of the flesh. He wasn't used to listening to his heart and didn't trust it.

He lowered his head and kissed her gently instead. Muttering something under his breath, he took her in his arms and kissed her hard. Then, utterly beguiled, he kissed her tenderly. Her mouth was warm, quivering with desire and sorrow. It was very difficult to let her go. But he couldn't let her see that.

When they parted he could see her eyes glistening with tears. Her scar stood out in bold relief on her ashen face. It hurt him to see it, and he had to stop himself from brushing his lips against it.

"How theatrical we are become, my dear," he said lightly as he dropped her hands. Laughing, he swung up on his horse. "I hope my welcome home will be as ardent as my leave-taking is. Fare thee well, my lovely Bridget. Keep thinking of me—I won't forget you."

That too was new to him, surprising and true. He raised a hand, turned his horse, and rode away. He yearned to look back, but didn't dare.

13

"**O**h, but you're crushing it!" Betsy cried.

"An iron will set it right when I unpack," Bridget told her little helper through gritted teeth. She dared to pick up the trunk's lid and look at all the clothes she'd squashed inside. She sighed. Betsy sat on Bridget's high bed watching her, making a steady commentary on the mess she was making of her packing.

"I meant the hat," Betsy said, looking sad as she saw what had become of a once perky bonnet.

"I know," Bridget snapped, "but I'm sure I can have it blocked when I get to London."

Betsy sat still, her blue eyes wide. Bridget's voice had held impatience and threat. And what she said was nonsense; they both knew it.

"I'm sorry," Bridget said quickly. "You're right, of course. But I never liked that bonnet anyway."

Betsy's eyes got wider. She knew it was Bridget's favorite. And Bridget never lied.

Bridget was having trouble getting her clothes neatly stowed. She'd always done it for herself. But it had been easy before, because before she'd met Ewen she'd never had much to pack. His valet had made swift, neat work of packing her new wardrobe when they'd left town, but he hadn't come back from London. Neither had Ewen. That was why Bridget was packing.

The promised three days had come, another three had gone, and Bridget was packing to leave because she didn't know what else to do. At least packing was doing *something*. The only other thing she'd done since he'd left was to wait. She was tired of it.

She'd missed him with painful intensity for two days, and then looked for him to return all day on the third. She went to sleep that night with her eyes half open, ears straining to hear the slightest sound of his arrival. She'd heard nothing but crickets and frogs, and no matter how often they called her name, she could only think of him.

The fourth and fifth and sixth days had been unbearable, so now she was going, too. Or *at least*, she confessed to herself, *getting ready to go*. She flung a shawl from her wardrobe onto the bed.

"Shawls are easy," Betsy said happily, catching it and laying it down on the bed so she could fold it.

"Indeed they are, shawls and sheets. Roman ladies had nothing but sheets to pack, or at least their gowns looked like sheets and they wore them wrapped around themselves."

The child needed tutoring, Bridget thought, so why

not make a task into a learning game? She enjoyed Betsy's company. The girl had stared at her scar the day they'd met, and never again. Children were that way. A person could have a tulip growing out of their nose, Bridget thought, and a child would stare once and then get over it. She never had trouble with children.

Betsy was an eager helper, too, and Bridget could use a little company. Betsy had become the darling of the household, but Bridget wasn't. The servants at Ewen's hideaway were polite to her, but only that, and she refused to grovel in order to win a smile from them. Besides, she didn't think it would work.

If they didn't exactly dislike her, they seemed determined to ignore her. The butler might have been built with the house, he was that wooden and that old. He treated Bridget with polite distance. Of course, then, so did his staff. Even the gardeners were wary and taciturn with her. Betsy was the only person she'd had to chat with since Ewen had left.

She certainly wouldn't dare going into Little Newton again. If the village folk had been rude and standoffish when Ewen was there, she hated to think how they'd receive her alone.

He'd sent a message on the fourth day.

Dearest Bridget,

Do you miss me as much as I miss thee? Hardly possible. But things have not gone as swiftly as I'd hoped. Delay and more delay. I'll be back as soon as I may. Yes, I know it's a trivial verse, but I like to think of you smiling.

Yr. Ewen

A charming note, but it did not inspire confidence. She'd wanted something warmer. What she really wanted was his warm body next to hers, his arms around her, blotting out the real world. A world that probably wondered why an elegant nobleman would marry a scarred spinster without a penny to her unknown name, and in such haste—and then hasten to hide her away. That was what she was wondering now.

So if he didn't come by the end of the week, she resolved she'd go to him. Or go to his father's house and meet him there. This place had been her honeymoon heaven. Now it was limbo.

She'd given him her hand, her heart, and her body, all he had said he wanted, as well as her soul. But she wondered about the coincidence of his leaving the moment her body became temporarily unavailable to him. And now that he was in London, and staying there, she couldn't help thinking of all the other available women who were also there. She *should* be able to help it, she knew that. It was wrong to suspect him simply because she'd never really believed anyone could want her for more than a day. But what was wrong and what was real were two different things.

"My lady?" a maid said at her door. "There's a message for you."

Bridget dropped the clothing she was holding and took the boldly scrawled message with trembling hands.

Dearest Bridget,

Pray do not part my hair with a hatchet when I return, but the truth is that happy moment won't be as soon as I wish. I

can't say when it will be. I push and push, and it's like
pushing a wall. Fate and events conspire against me. Please
be more patient than I am.

Yr. Ewen

Very nice, Bridget thought. She tried to read it again,
but her eyes had filled with tears. *Four* lines? She
needed at least a novel from him now. She needed tor-
rents of words to reassure her. Words . . .

"Is the messenger still here?" she asked the maid.

"Aye. He's that tired, rode since dawn, he says."

"Then go tell him to rest a moment longer. I've an
answer for him to take back to his lordship."

Why hadn't she thought of that before? Bridget went
to her desk with a smile on her face, drew out a sheet of
paper, and dipped her pen into ink. She held it above
the paper, trying to decide what to write.

Please, please, please come home. I love and miss you. You've
become everything to me. I'm so lonely, and when you're gone for
so long I imagine the worst things. That was exactly what she
wanted to say.

But she didn't want his pity, or to anger him with her
foolish doubts. She had to find a way to tell him everything in her heart, without whining. She had to guard a
little corner of her heart, to save that much of herself
from his keeping, in case her wildest fears were true.
She had to have a little pride. She had to be as witty and
succinct as he was, too; men liked that sort of thing. She
had to be clever.

"Are you gonna write and ask him when he's coming
home?" Betsy asked, interrupting her thoughts.

"No, because he said he doesn't know that yet."
Bridget frowned at the empty sheet of paper.

"Are you gonna ask him when we're going to his father's house?"

"No, he doesn't know that either," Bridget said absently, trying to concentrate.

"Are you gonna ask him to come home 'cause you miss him?"

Bridget looked up at the golden-haired child. She chewed on the end of her pen, thinking furiously. Then she dipped it in ink again and set it to the paper.

Dearest Ewen,

Oh, how I miss you.

                                                            Yr. Bridget

"Would you like to go for a stroll?" Bridget asked Betsy three days later.

Cook looked up from her pastry dough when Bridget said that. A maid stared, and the pot boy gaped. Bridget pretended not to notice that all the happy chatter and clatter in the kitchen had ceased when she walked in. It might have been because it was the first time that she had—or because she had at all. She wasn't even sure if a lady ought to enter her kitchen. But the upstairs maid had said that was where Betsy was, and Bridget was sure that if she didn't have someone to talk to soon, she'd begin talking to the pictures on the walls. Since they were mostly landscapes, she decided talking to a seven-year-old was much better than chatting up some painted shrubbery.

Nine days now. Eight nights since he'd left her. She sent a message to him every day now. He sent one a day to her. But they needn't have bothered, she thought.

They kept saying the same things to each other, in one way or another: I *regret* I'm *delayed*, he wrote. I *wish you were here*, she wrote back.

Her trunks were packed and ready, and that somehow comforted her, even though it was hard to live out of a trunk.

"A walk? Wouldn't I just!" Betsy cried excitedly. She loved the freedom of the countryside, discovering something new and wonderful every day. But then she paused, her little face sobering. "I wanted to finish making pie crust with you, too," she told Cook solemnly, "but it's *such* a nice day, ain't it?"

Cook beamed at her. "Gracious to yer bones, y'are, little 'un," she told Betsy. "Go along, I'll do fine by meself now."

Bridget gave Cook a conspiratorial smile. Her face froze when Cook didn't so much as lift the corners of her mouth. So she nodded in what she hoped was a gracious lady's manner, took Betsy's hand, and left the kitchen with her.

"I thought we'd stroll down to the brook and see if there are any new frogs," Bridget said.

"Oh, yes!" Betsy said excitedly, because she wasn't allowed to go there by herself.

They soon were sitting on the banks of the brook, slippers off, letting their toes be tickled by the bubbling water.

"Cook's teaching me to bake pies," Betsy told Bridget as she paddled her bare feet in the water, "I like that. Mrs. Morton's teaching me how to polish up silver. That ain't so much fun. Mr. Moody lets me help with the horses and that's prime, but he says I can't be a groom no matter how good I gets at it. That ain't fair, is it?"

"I suppose not," Bridget said, lifting her own leg and watching the frothy water sparkle over her ankle, "but that's how it goes. But you don't have to be a cook or a house-keeper. You can learn your letters and be more than that."

Betsy looked up at her, her blue eyes wise. "What's better'n that? They gets a good house to live in and all they eats whenever they want. I can't be a lady, like you. And I don't want to be no whore, no way, even if they does live high. And Gilly, she says they only live good for a while, anyways. Then they becomes dirty bags in the gutters, like them I ain't supposed to speak to."

Bridget blinked. Sometimes she forgot. Betsy knew more about the darker side of life than she did. But she knew a brighter side Betsy did not.

"If you got an education, you could become a schoolmistress or a governess, or a companion," Bridget said briskly. "With a nice family, of course."

"Dunno if I could," Betsy said, "nor if I'd want to neither."

"Well, you could be a maid or a seamstress or a milliner or . . . Well, you could marry some nice man." Bridget's voice trailed off as she tried to think of decent occupations available to an orphan girl with no breeding.

"Like you done," Betsy said with satisfaction. "Aye, that'd be prime! The Viscount's a nice gent, ain't he? Everybody likes him. Mrs. Morton she says he ain't got an ounce of mean in him, and if it weren't for his tom-catting, he'd be a perfect master."

"How nice," Bridget said uneasily.

"She says as how she's tired of him treating the place like a house of convenience, though," Betsy reported chattily as she splashed her feet. "She says she puts up with it 'cause otherwise he's fair, but she got to take special care when his women leaves, and that's hard.

She says after he brings his sport to the house and leaves she gotta put so much lye in the sheets they're going to fall to bits, they are. But Cook, she told her to hush since he pays so good and treats them so good, and besides he don't come here much. Then they seen me, and they hushed and acted like they was talking about something else." Betsy giggled.

"Oh," Bridget said. There was so much she wanted to ask Betsy. But it was wrong to ask the child to parrot things she shouldn't have heard in the first place. And besides, she wasn't sure she could bear hearing it.

When their feet got cold they put their slippers back on and went for a walk, picking wildflowers, watching bees competing with the butterflies in the flowery meadow, and taking care to stay out of the bees' way. Betsy chatted about innocent things. Bridget half listened, only absently correcting particularly awful grammar now and then. She was still subdued and thoughtful as they turned back toward the house.

Then she saw the elegant traveling carriage standing in the drive. It was a glossy black coach with trunks on top, outriders on fine horses standing beside it.

She dropped her armload of wild blooms and began to run. It was a long way down from the high meadow to the circular drive in front of the house, but it had been a long time since she'd seen Ewen. Her bonnet flew back and bounced on its strings at the nape of her neck as she ran. She held a hand to her chest as her slippers flew over the grass, because she was jiggling so much she thought she might bounce out of her low-necked gown. She held up her skirt with her other hand so she wouldn't trip and go sprawling. But she kept running. It was Ewen, come home, and she wanted to run right into his arms.

She didn't. She screeched to a halt so fast she almost overbalanced and fell anyway. She stood panting, one hand still on her heart as she looked at the people who'd gotten out of the coach. Not one of them was Ewen. And they were all gaping at her.

There were three gentlemen and three ladies. Three *women*, Bridget realized, as her gaze steadied. No one would mistake them for ladies. They were beautifully dressed, but too beautifully for daytime. There was too much to see altogether, face and form. Their gowns were too sheer, their hair was too bright, their blushes were painted on, and unless they'd all just had berry tarts, they were all wearing bright lip rouge, too. No, whatever they were, they were certainly not ladies.

The gentlemen were just that, though. Bridget would swear to it. Gentlemen born, if not gentlemen bred. They held their heads high and had *bedamned to you—who are you* looks on their clean-shaven faces, and their clothes were as correct as their companions' were not. Bridget had seen their sort in London, the sons of rich noblemen with nothing to work for but their own pleasure, and they didn't like to work too hard for that.

The tallest gentleman was the first to speak—and not to Bridget, but about her, so she was sure she was right about them.

"What a lovely greeting that almost was," he drawled. "She's poetry in motion, is she not?" He finally spoke to Bridget. "But I confess, I'm wounded. Why did you stop at the last minute?"

"I—I thought you were Ewen, I mean, Viscount Sinclair," Bridget murmured, embarrassed.

"Would that I were," the tall man sighed. "Ewen's taste is excellent, as ever," he told the group behind him. "No

wonder we haven't heard squeak nor whisper from him
in so long. Lucky fellow. She's unique." He raised one
long thin finger to Bridget's chin to tilt it up to see her
better. She slapped his hand away. His eyes narrowed.

"I beg your pardon," she said icily, getting control of
herself again. "We have not met. I am Ewen's wife,
Viscountess Sinclair, and you, sir?"

"And I, dear lady," he said, bowing, as his companions began to fall about in their mirth, "am enchanted.
Utterly enchanted. What theater did Ewen pluck you
from, the lucky dog? For I swear you're the best little
actress I've ever seen—forgive me, dear Charlotte," he
said over his shoulder to one of the women, "but what
an impersonation. My own dear aunt might have been
fooled. And she the terror of the court itself."

The women were hooting with laughter; the men, far
more cool, were treating her to contemptuous smiles or
leers. Bridget grew red, then white with fury.

"Yes, you may sneer yourself silly, and a flock of silly
geese you are, then," she told them angrily, "and how
delighted Ewen shall be, to be sure. When he returns from
London, I'll be sure to tell him. It would be braver of you
to tell me your proper name," she told the tall gentleman,
"but of course, only a gentleman would do that."

He paused. He was a lean man, perhaps Ewen's age,
with straight black hair and a hard, almost homely face,
saved by a pair of strangely beautiful azure eyes. Those
eyes searched her face keenly. "I am Drummond, my
dear," he finally said, his phrasing an eerie echo of Ewen
at his loftiest. "Ewen is not here?"

"He is, as I said, in London," Bridget said with dignity. "He didn't tell me he expected company. Indeed, it
would be strange if he did. He was called to London

suddenly or else he wouldn't have left himself. It's our honeymoon, you see."

The other two men began to guffaw, and the ladies snickered. They were silenced by a wave of the thin gentleman's hand. His eyes continued to study Bridget's face, and it was all she could do to keep her head up as he gazed at her scar in the cruel afternoon light.

"We were wed a fortnight ago, in London," she said, hating the little tremor that cracked her voice.

"Aye, I was there," Betsy spoke up. Bridget had forgotten her. But she crowded close to Bridget's side and took her hand as she gazed at the tall man, who was looking at her with bemusement. "I was flower girl, I was. You know what that is? I din't. I used to sell flowers in the park, but his lordship, he give me a golden boy—a whole guinea, he did—to carry flowers at their wedding. It was grand, there was lobster and chickens and beef and fish, and oysters, and jellies, too, served after, and all the cake I could eat!"

There was a moment's silence. "I see," the man who'd called himself Drummond said. "It must have been lovely indeed. I'm sorry to have missed it. How many guests were there, do you think?"

"There was that man with red hair," Betsy said at once, "and the soldier, two other blokes, and a couple fine as they could stare. Henry the butler was there, and Vickers, he's a valet. That means he takes care of the Viscount's clothes, y'know," she confided. "And me, o'course. Did I forget anybody?" she asked Bridget.

"No," Bridget said softly, wondering why this elegant fellow hadn't been there, or if he'd been invited.

"I see. An intimate party. And you, my dear," he asked Bridget. "May I ask where my cousin met you?"

Bridget swallowed hard. *His cousin*? Then he'd know all—if not now, then soon. It was easier, as always, to tell the whole truth. "At a ball in London, sir."

"I've not seen you there," he mused.

"I am cousin to Miss Cecily Brixton and was her companion," Bridget said, and to make matters sound a bit better added, "It was an intimate wedding—my cousin and aunt were unavailable, my other cousins live too far away, and my mother lives in Ireland."

"Ah, of course," he said, and stood lost in thought for a moment. He came to some decision. He turned his oddly penetrating gaze on her again. "Forgive me, then, my dear, for intruding. I didn't know the way of it. That Ewen! You'd think he'd remember to tell the family."

"We married in haste, because of his father, you see," Bridget said, trying to be conciliatory, because his attitude had suddenly and clearly changed. He looked at her with sympathy now, his azure eyes mild and kind, and he waited for her to continue.

"Because his father was so ill, Ewen wanted to marry to put his mind at ease," she explained. "But then we got word his father was getting better, so Ewen decided to stay here for a while—until he was called away." She hesitated to say why; surely the work he did for the government was secret. "He said he'd be back as soon as he could manage," she added nervously. That was shaky ground for her, and she hoped he wouldn't ask when. He didn't.

He was obviously thinking deeply, his long face troubled. Then he bowed to Bridget again. "Well, then, that changes our plans! Back you go, my friends," he said to the gentlemen and women standing behind him.

"What?" one of the gentlemen bellowed. "Truck all

the way from London on a promise of a week in the country, only to turn around because a pretty bit of tail tells us pretty lies? I should say not."

"Then would you rather say when you'd care to meet me," Drummond asked him mildly, "and whether it will be with pistols or swords? Ah, I thought not. Then kindly close your mouth and pick up your feet. We're going now. And no groans, if you please. We passed a charming inn coming up here, and it will still be there when we go back.

"I regret the intrusion, my dear," he told Bridget. "Please tell Ewen I'm sorry to have missed him, and be sure to tell him I wouldn't have bothered him for all the world had I known what he was about."

He waited until the others, with much grumbling, made their way back into the black coach. Bridget hardly noticed, she was too busy wondering and worrying about whether she ought to have invited him to stay. He was Ewen's cousin, after all, but it was still their honeymoon. And she didn't even know if he was really Ewen's cousin. Ewen hadn't mentioned him, or any close relatives, except for his mad cousin, Martin. The man had called himself Drummond, as though she should know his title—but he could have none and be nobody.

She was called from her thoughts by the tall man's deep voice.

"And please do remember me," he told Bridget, as he paused, a foot on the step of the coach, his sky blue eyes searching her face. "Someday it might be well to remember my name. I shall not forget you. Forgive me, my dear." He hesitated; asking for forgiveness was clearly not a thing he was used to doing. "And please also remember that we all do what we must, even if we sometimes wish to do as we will. One has obligations, my dear, and sometimes it's difficult to know where they lie. For example, now I've angered some of my friends, haven't I? Remember, please, when you think of me, that it was for your sake."

He gave her a thin smile, sketched a bow, and stepped into the carriage.

"He weren't so bad for such a gentry cove as he were," Betsy said as they watched the carriage roll away down the drive.

"No, he wasn't so bad," Bridget agreed, almost wishing he had been, because he left her even more deeply troubled than he'd looked at the last. Which was a very great deal.

His head hurt, but his throat ached more, he'd done so much talking today. *Damn them!* Ewen thought wearily. He rubbed the back of his neck with one hand and stared down at the papers on the desk in front of him. Being a spy wasn't a game. A man had to be fearless, not feckless. The idiot they'd sent in his stead was bold enough, but a fool to his toes. Ewen was tempted to leave the lot of them to their own nonsense, until he remembered it was his country and one of his best friends that the fools could endanger.

For two pins he'd go again himself, and damn the dangers. Then he remembered Bridget and realized there weren't enough arguments in the world or money in the treasury to send him abroad now. He couldn't stop thinking of her, even in the midst of these aggravating days. It wasn't even as though he wanted to, though he knew he had to keep his mind on his work.

But a vagrant scent of warm flowers or even a trace of teasingly familiar perfume could make his heart race; then her face would be before him, and he would yearn for her again.

Just yesterday he had glanced out a coach window and seen the back of a woman's head, the sun finding burnished chestnut in her glowing brown hair. He was about to stop the coach, throw open the door, and run to her, both shocked and delighted that she'd disobeyed and come to find him. But then the woman turned and his heart sank, because it was not her face he saw.

He only saw that in his every dream before he finally slept during these long restless nights since he'd left her. Sleep was always a long time coming, because it seemed to him that his very skin longed for her touch as much as he longed to touch her.

It amazed him. He was too old to be so smitten. He'd known her too long to still be so enraptured by her. But she defied all his rules and was the exception to his every experience. The more he had her, the more he wanted her—now more than ever.

She haunted his nights, and his every spare thought flew to her during the day. And they were the sort of thoughts that did a man no good when he was so far away.

But he was obliged to stay in London that night, and who knew how many more after that? So he had another note to write. He snatched up a clean sheet of paper and paused. There was so much he had to tell her, he needed a book. So much, and such startling stuff it didn't let him sleep sometimes, no matter how tired he was. There were all the things he needed to hear her say, too.

And the one thing he never thought he would tell her—but now knew that he must.

He ran a hand through his hair and groaned. The piece of paper on the desk before him was infuriatingly blank. *Impossible.* There was too much and too little to put in a letter. Too difficult, too chancy, too dangerous. It would be hard enough to bring himself to speak the words he had to. He was no coward. But neither was he a fool. He had to see her; her face would be his guide to how and what to say. So until that day . . .

My dearest Bridget, he wrote. . . .

14

*D*earest Ewen . . .

Bridget's pen paused. Suddenly it seemed presumptuous for her to address the aloof, distinguished Viscount Sinclair as "dearest." It seemed almost too intimate, although she'd known him more intimately than she'd known any other human being.

But she grew less confident with every passing day. He'd been gone two weeks. Of course she remembered his face, his body, the thrill of his loving; she wouldn't forget it if she lived forever. Their jests, their conversations; the touch of his warm lips; the feel of his hair, clean and silken, curling over her fingers as she ran her hands through it; his purring laughter low in his throat—of course she remembered that.

But now, too, she remembered the disparity of their

stations. And the incredible sophistication—and worse—the incredible reputation of the man. Their brief time together was like a fading dream. And dreamlike, it wasn't the feelings she remembered that she questioned, it was the reality of her situation she was doubting. Still, he was her husband and he loved her.

Her head shot up. *Loved?* He'd never said it. She thought and thought but couldn't remember ever hearing that from him.

Yes, that's good. God, you drive me mad. So soft, so sweet. Oh, yes, Bridget, yes, that way. That was the sort of thing he said when they made love. He called her "my dear," and she hoped she was. But he never said more. He said she was lovely, he said she was sweet, but that he loved her? Never.

She swallowed hard and dipped her pen again. He'd married her, hadn't he? There had to be some kind of love there—or was it pity? It didn't matter. Whatever his reasons, what she wrote was no lie. As his wife, she had the right to write it. Besides, it was true. He was her dearest love.

Dearest Ewen,

Your cousin Drummond came to call yesterday. He didn't stay above ten minutes, but said to send his regards to you. He was surprised you weren't here. To tell the truth, I am, too. I know your business is urgent. You say you miss me. But it's over a fortnight since you've gone. I don't want to complain; your servants do the best they can for me. Still and all, I must tell you I'm not happy here. It goes beyond missing you, although nothing is worse than that.

*It was awkward meeting your cousin, not knowing what to
tell him. I only came here because of you, and without you I've
nothing to do and no reason to be here at all. I think it's time for
me to move on. If you still feel there's no need for me to come to
you, then may I take Betsy and go to your father's house?*

*My bags are packed. Only send instructions to your coach-
man and I can leave at once. Or I can take a public coach; I discovered the coaching station is not far from here. I can come to
London. If you send me your father's direction, I can get there.
But I wish to go. Please keep well. I anxiously await your reply.*

                                                            Yr. Bridget

She read what she'd written, and groaned. This was
the third try and she still hadn't gotten it right! She
couldn't just fall in on his father, alone and out of the
blue. It would be awkward, embarrassing. There ought
to be a line asking him to write to his father announcing
her arrival. She took out another sheet of paper.

It would be a day before she'd get his answer—two, if he
was out late tonight. She hated thinking about that. There
were too many dangers in London at night for him and for
her peace of mind. It wasn't footpads or pickpockets she
was afraid of him running into—it was all the lovely ladies
he might encounter at all the balls and parties he might
attend. Them—and the other kinds of women he might
meet at the theater or in the teeming night streets. London
was stocked with tempting females. And he was a man
who was famous for being tempted. He'd said it himself.

The only thing she could do here at night was listen
to the frogs and crickets. Even that magic was gone
without him. They could call her by name until the snow
fell, but it was his voice she wanted to hear.

Dearest Ewen, she started to write again.

*   *   *

The ballroom was aglow. The guests were, too—with perspiration, exertion, and lack of fresh air. It was a mild summer night, but they were sweltering. They were ruddy and sweating to a man—and woman. The hundreds of candles burning in every huge chandelier hanging over the great room made the thick air shimmer in a bright haze. The guests beneath were packed into the ballroom so tightly there was hardly room to bend an elbow—although they did, dancing and drinking and fanning themselves, complaining about the heat and the crowd. But few wanted it any other way.

"A crush, an utter crush," one matron told another with satisfaction, and they smiled at each other. It might be hot enough to make the plumes in their steaming hair droop, so hot the dancers on the floor could be smelled as well as seen as they traipsed by, cavorting in their intricate sets. The air might be damp enough to waste the hours the ladies had spent in curl papers the night before, too, but not a young or old one minded. They were seeing and being seen, and however they looked, it would have been worse not to be seen here at all.

This was a grand ball. The townhouse was one of the best addresses in London, the company was top of the trees. And even if it was hard to breathe, the air was rarefied by the number of wealthy and noble persons present. This was where a woman could find a husband for herself or her daughter, or an adventure she wouldn't want her husband or daughter to know about. Of course, there was prime gossip to be mined here, too, and good gossip was almost better than gold coin in their circles.

The gentlemen suffered more than the ladies did;

their clothing was tighter and they wore more of it, and none of it was gossamer or gauze. They were literally bound and wound into their clothing. Shirts were fastened high at the necks with starched neckcloths wound around them, waistcoats were thickly embroidered, and tight jackets were worn over them. Their breeches were of heavy silk or satin, knit too fine to let air in. The men paid for such elegance in every way tonight. Their neckcloths wilted until they looked like linen fresh from the wringer, not their valets' talented hands. Their own hands were covered by gloves as they danced, and they were glad of it, because their palms were so sweaty their partners would have literally slipped away from them otherwise.

It was a good thing the gentlemen wore dark clothing. That way the damp patches growing under their arms and on their backs couldn't be seen. But everything else could be, which was the whole point. Tonight's ball was where to be if one wanted to be in fashion, or find a fashionable wife, or arrange for a fashionable dalliance or affair.

"Ewen," the lady standing on the sidelines of the dance purred to the gentleman next to her, "why not dance with me?"

"Might as well ask why not swim with you, my dear," Ewen answered, his eyes roving over the crowd.

She made a face. "Of course it's warm, but dancing might move the air," she said, fluttering her fan harder. She gave him a sideways look and added, "Someone might think you don't want to be seen with me."

"We're hardly invisible, Claire," he said absently, his gaze still raking over the room.

A muscle tightened in his jaw. He gave no other sign

that he saw the newest Incomparable of the season, the blond beauty Cecily Brixton, and her imposing mother. He'd greeted them earlier, coolly and politely, and then braced himself, waiting for them to ask about Bridget. They'd curtsied and said nothing more than "Good evening, my lord." From the avid look in their eyes when they saw he was alone, he guessed they might have wanted to say more. But he doubted any of it would be about Bridget's welfare, so he bowed and walked away. Now they were staring.

They were standing together, looking like guests at an amateur charade, one portraying shock and the other scorn. They were openly gaping at him—and at the lady with him. Lady Claire Kensington was well known to the *ton*, as was her husband. She was also well known for not allowing the fact of her marriage to interfere with her pleasures. And her husband was not at the ball tonight.

"But to stand here on the fringes of the dancing like a pair of chaperones or wallflowers," the lady beside him said impatiently. "Come, Ewen, it will not do!" She tapped his arm with her fan.

"On a night like this you'd be better off using that thing for the purpose it was meant for instead of beating me with it," he commented, finally looking down at her.

The lady caught her breath when she found herself suddenly the focus of his erratic attention. The play of the dancing candlelight accentuated the hard planes of his handsome face. Tall, impeccable, he, alone of all the men in the sweltering room, wasn't sweating. He was cool, composed, faintly amused, and slightly distant, as always. She wanted him badly because of it. She wanted to see him impassioned, she wanted to see him grown hot, excited, that hard face harder, taut, and concentrated on her.

She licked her lips and saw his eyes following the motion. She raised her head, knowing her lips were now glistening in the shimmering light. Her gown was low enough for him to see that her breasts were still high and shapely, too. She wore her sable hair high, letting one long dark ringlet fall to her alabaster neck for contrast. Her sapphires matched her eyes, but nothing could complement her fair skin better than her inky hair—she knew because so many lovers had told her so. She was of English stock and nobly born, and intolerant of anyone from a lower class, but she reveled when her infatuated lovers called her "gypsy." Her husband called her his little witch. She wanted Ewen Sinclair to call her name out in ecstasy.

She'd wanted that for a very long time. She'd known him long ago. But the same spring she'd made her first appearance on the social scene, Viscount Sinclair had married his lovely Elise instead of her. Then he'd gone to the Continent. Now he was back, alone, and this was finally her chance.

He was known as a rake, but it wasn't just his reputation that attracted her. Damn the man for being so elegant, aloof, and fascinating. His smiles were infrequent but dazzling because of his even, white teeth. When she won one from him, she felt she'd won much more. Like his smiles, she felt his love would be rare but thrilling.

She enjoyed a challenge almost as much as she loved eventually despising the men she took to her bed for making such fools of themselves once she'd got them there. No man looked refined or remotely worthy of her when he was in the throes of his passion. But maybe such a cool fellow as Ewen Sinclair . . .

She'd been standing beside him for ten minutes now and he hardly seemed aware of her, though she could swear anyone could hear the pulse pounding in her body as she thought of him and her plans for him. He wouldn't dance with her. He appeared content to just stand, listening to her idle comments. He didn't leave, though. Nor did he take it further. It was up to her, then. Damn him, she'd make him pay for this . . . after.

"It's ridiculously hot in here," she said, snapping her fan shut. "I'd like to stroll in the garden."

He inclined his head politely. "Perhaps I'll see you later, then."

"My dear sir!" She forced a laugh, refusing to get angry. Her anger and ridicule of him could come later, as always. "I meant perhaps you'd like to accompany me, of course."

He lifted one eyebrow. "You mean accompany you for a stroll in the garden now, and then in the conversation of all the scandalmongers later? My dear lady, I like your company. The question is whether I like it enough to face the gossips—and your husband on the dueling field tomorrow."

She laughed. "My husband does not, *would* not care if you strolled with me, I assure you! Or did anything else we might care to do," she added in a softer voice. "We have an understanding."

"Really? I'm surprised. I've met him, you see. A hasty man, I'd thought. A possessive man, I'd wager."

"Then you'd lose your bet," she said.

"Indeed," he said. He didn't seem remotely interested. Her eyes hardened and she took a step away from him, but his voice stopped her. "The garden will be as crowded as the ballroom," he added.

"I expect you're right," she said, plying her fan frantically as she thought fast. "Anyplace here would be, wouldn't it? Now, my house fronts on the square, near the park. If it grows warm, we have only to open the windows in the evening to get the most refreshing breezes. It should be delightfully cool there by now."

"How fortunate for you and your husband, the good baron," Ewen said.

"Well, it would be if he were home. But he's not."

"Ah? I wondered where he was. I thought he was in the gaming room."

"He's not even in London, in fact," she said, smiling up into his suddenly interested eyes. "He left two days ago. We don't expect him back for weeks."

"Now, I love the theater, but I've always hated farces," Ewen commented conversationally, though his eyes traveled from her lips to her breasts and back up to her avid eyes. "Lovers hiding in closets or climbing out windows when outraged husbands unexpectedly appear on the scene is not my idea of high humor."

"He can hardly do that," she snapped, and then added more gently, because he seemed actually willing to discuss it now, "He's gone abroad."

"Indeed? How bold of him. These are dangerous times. Political tides may still be shifting. Odd. He didn't strike me as an adventuresome fellow."

"He has a cousin in Italy. He's on his way there."

"Italy?" Ewen laughed lightly. "Easy to say, but I sincerely doubt he'd actually go there. Are you sure? Napoleon is cooped up on a little island now, but that island is off the coast of Italy. Your dear baron seems the sort to hesitate to set foot in the same country, much less on the same continent."

"But of course he's in Italy. Someplace on the coast—Livorno? Yes, that's it. Then he said he was going to Piombino to meet up with his nephew on his grand tour or some such. He didn't want to go, to be sure. But the boy broke his leg, and his great-uncle asked him specifically to see what the situation was. He'd hardly make all that up, would he? So, is that sufficiently far away for you?"

When he didn't answer immediately she wondered if she'd overdone it and insulted him, and so she added in a heated whisper, "I don't know why you hesitate. I doubt you have anything to fear from him in any way. Although," she said coyly, "only time and experience will tell me that, of course."

"Fear him? No. Say rather I fear the consequences, because I dislike scenes. Intensely. So, Italy, is it?" Ewen mused. "Still, two days," he said doubtfully. "He might not have crossed the Channel yet. What if he decides to come home? The stuff of a fine farce, exactly as I said."

"I tell you, he's gone! That is to say," she said through clenched teeth, reining in her annoyance, "I received a note from him yesterday telling me he'd made the crossing safely. I don't expect to see him for at least a month—perhaps two."

"Indeed?" He looked down at her. Small, beautifully curved, white-skinned and dark-haired, with those sapphire eyes. Her gown was so sheer he could see the dark puckered tips of her conical breasts. Small, sharply etched breasts, a small sharp chin, sloe-eyed and cunning, she'd be wild in his arms, he knew; he'd heard it often enough from many men. She was foxlike in face and habits. Her lovers said she was insatiable. And very versatile.

He smiled at her. "How sad for you. You'll miss him sorely. But you'll be comforted by your delightfully cool house, no doubt."

"No more games," she said in a harsh whisper.

That did get his attention. He laughed. "But no more gossip either, my dear. It would look bad if I left with you now. But if I went out now and you left later . . ."

"A fine idea. Good evening, my lord," she said with a triumphant smile. She turned on her heel and walked away from him. She was too much of a lady to wiggle, but her hips swayed as nicely as any barmaid's as she left him, because she knew he was watching.

But so was someone else.

"And so?" the elderly, balding gentleman asked Ewen a few moments later as they were both collecting their hats and canes from a footman.

Ewen didn't answer right away. That didn't bother the old gentleman. He left the overheated house with Ewen and strolled down a few streets with him in silence until they turned a dim corner and walked to where the old gentleman's carriage was waiting for him. There they stopped. After looking around casually but carefully, they spoke at last, in low voices.

"Yes. The baron's abroad," Ewen finally said, as though they'd been talking all along. "On his way to Italy. Probably to meet with Herr Berger *and* Monsieur Ricard, as we thought, and then to Elba, as Rafe heard. He's not expected back for at least a month."

"Good, good," the old man said thoughtfully, nodding. He looked up at Ewen. "Now, that was simple enough, wasn't it? For you, at least. It was so easy for you to get information that would have taken us days and many costly bribes to ferret out. And we'd have risked the baron's knowing we were making inquiries. I suspected he was just fool enough to tell her. But why not? She's usually more circumspect—she has her wits about her except when her glands are involved. She told you immediately, as I thought she might. Your reputation was the making of us. This was simplicity itself. Why did you fight me so?"

"I'd better things to do."

"Hard to believe. Look at the other reward you get for your labors," the older man chortled. "A night in the arms of one of the fairest charmers in all of London town!"

"I don't care for crowds," Ewen said coolly.

"But she's beautiful, lad!"

"Beauty is easy. In this case, in every way."

"Ah. A young man's answer."

Ewen's smile showed briefly, "No. It's only that I prefer a challenge. The reputation you speak of is for being a rake, not an opportunist. There *is* a difference."

"Why so touchy? I remember a time when you thought *rake* a fine description of yourself. It served us well—and you, too—in other ways, as I recall."

"You've forgotten what I told you? I suppose you must have, though your memory is usually more accurate than mine."

The older man looked down at his walking stick. Ewen's voice matched his twisted smile, and there was a hint of hurt in it. That shocked him. He hadn't thought elegant Viscount Sinclair could be hurt by what any man said—especially about him and any woman. But the Ewen Sinclair he used to know so long ago could be hurt. And had been.

"Forgive me, Ewen," the older man said softly. "I've known you since you were a boy, and your father since he was one, too. You did tell me. I did remember. I suppose I thought you were jesting."

"Why shouldn't you?" Ewen shrugged. "Given my past and what you obviously believe to be my future." He cut off the older man's feeble protests. "And you were not that far wrong, after all. Because if a rake is a man who passes over what's easy and instead exerts every effort to win someone different, unique, with depths that are his alone to discover, then I must still be one, I suppose."

"No. That's not a rake, that's a connoisseur. And a wise man. My apologies. So! The fair Lady Claire sleeps alone tonight?" the older man added, seeking a lighter note. He shook his head. "Gad! That's like throwing back a thirty-pound salmon after you've landed it. Were I only ten years younger . . . hmmm. Considering the lady, best make that fifteen. Still, though you have the years for it, you do have the right of it, too."

"Then I may go?"

"Go? Certainly. It's late, and you've told me what I wanted to hear. Good night to you, then."

"I meant go home," Ewen said patiently.

"Home? Have you forgotten everything?" the old man asked gleefully. "Aha! Lady Claire must be more potent than you admit!"

"I live to amuse you, sir."

"Forgive me, lad," the older man said without a trace of regret. "At my age I prefer to believe the worst; it enlivens things wonderfully. Seriously, though—no. If you mean to leave London, I'm afraid you can't yet. Don't look at me like that. We need you to advise us. The mission isn't done, Rafe isn't safely on his way home yet. You know that. Be patient. It won't be much longer. This was only a diversion I thought of as a reward, a panacea for your restlessness."

"The only cure for restlessness is travel."

"Soon, lad, soon."

Ewen's messenger usually came at noon, as regularly as luncheon was served in well-organized Brook House. But now it was past three. Bridget had had a forkful of lunch and a mile of pacing, and the messenger still hadn't arrived.

"Maybe his horse broke his leg," Betsy said helpfully. "I seen that once and they shot him."

"Hard on the messenger," Bridget muttered as she patrolled the salon. Every so often she glanced into the big, bright courtyard room. But nothing moved there, not even the palm fronds.

"No, they din't shoot him." Betsy giggled. "They shot the horse, he was screaming so much. It were awful to see," she said with horrified relish. "Such a lot of blood! The horse's head was streaming blood, and his legs, they—"

"I understand," Bridget said hastily. "I was only joking."

"Maybe he fell offa the horse, then," Betsy offered. "I seen that once, too."

Betsy had seen too many things, Bridget thought grimly. But she merely said, "Doubtless he's just delayed."

"So we ain't gonna leave today?"

"I don't know," Bridget said, glancing at the mantel clock again. "It's getting late. If he doesn't come in an hour, we won't be able to go until tomorrow morning. It stays light long this time of the year, but there's no sense setting out if we can only get in four or five hours of traveling. If we'd put our cases in the carriage, we'd be able to leave right away. But we haven't, so loading them in and saying our good-byes will take up even more time."

She hadn't wanted to actually put her things in the coach and take formal leave of Brook House until she'd heard from Ewen. Now she regretted that. But now she was also so wound up she was ready to walk to London— or Wales. So when the butler came to the salon she spun around and looked at his hands. She expected to see him bearing Ewen's latest message on his silver tray.

He carried no tray. He wore no expression. "My lady," he said stonily, "there's someone to see Miss Betsy."

"Send them in," Bridget said.

He hesitated, obviously struggling for the right words. "The person to see Miss Betsy," he finally said stiffly, "is not the sort of person the Viscount would ordinarily permit in his salon."

"If it's a dangerous person," Bridget said, alarmed, "then Betsy can't see him anyway."

"Not dangerous. Perhaps the better word would be *unfit*," the butler said stiffly.

"She can't see that sort of person either. What can you be thinking of?" Bridget demanded, so upset that for the first time since she'd laid eyes on the butler she didn't watch her words with him.

He looked at her with respect for the first time, too. "That is correct," he said, "ordinarily. But it is, I believe, imperative that Miss Betsy see this person."

"No more riddling," a tired voice said from behind the butler. "I'm here. She can see that with her own eyes, can't she? Want to toss me out, Miss Bridget?"

The bright light of the courtyard room was behind the visitor, so it took a second for Bridget to recognize her. It took Betsy no time at all.

"Gilly!" she cried, flying across the room to fling herself into her sister's arms. "Gilly! Gilly! It's you!"

"None other. Here now!" Gilly said, holding her sister away after giving her one hard hug. "Don't want to get the dirt of the road on that fine dress, do you? The road and more, besides. I hopped a coach or two and rode in a farmer's cart, so I stink like a horse and look like a haystack."

She did, Bridget thought. Gilly's ill-fitting men's clothes were covered with dust, her boots with dirt—at least Bridget hoped it was only dirt. Her face was so grimy it was hard to see who she was, much less what sex she was, even if anyone could see it clearly under her battered floppy hat. She looked less like a man than she had in London, but nothing like a woman, either.

"Look at you, though!" Gilly said, holding Betsy away and staring at her. "Fine as fivepence. They treated you good?"

"See for yourself! I got four other dresses good as this, and a fine gown to do nothing but sleep in besides. There ain't a rat in sight nowhere. Nor nobody sleeping in the hall or under the stairs in this whole house, neither. Ain't nobody living rough outside round here—there ain't even got gutters here, Gilly! I eats regular as that clock there chimes, and they lets me play and I'm learning to cook, and there's kittens and horses in the barn, and oh, Gilly, there's a brook I can put my feet in and—"

"And hush! I can see you're doing fine. Hold your tongue now, do. For I've come to say a hard thing and you have to listen close. No time nor sense in putting sugar on it, so I'll say it flat out. It's time for you to come home, Betsy."

Betsy fell silent, her eyes wide. But not as wide as Bridget's. Even the butler stared.

The quiet in the room didn't stop Gilly. "I want you to thank Miss Bridget kindly, and take what they lets you, and then come back home with me," she told her sister sternly.

"Oh, Gilly!" Betsy said, her lower lip quivering.

"I don't understand—I think we need to talk about this," Bridget said.

"I don't think we do," Gilly said harshly.

"You may go," Bridget told the butler, who reluctantly backed away. "What's happened?" she asked Gilly as soon as he'd left. She was confused, shocked, and worried. The more she came to know Betsy, the more she realized she and Ewen had saved the child from a disaster, not just the slums. To send her back now—especially now that she'd seen a brighter new life—would be more than cruel, it could be deadly.

"You go get your things," Gilly told Betsy, "whilst me and Miss Bridget talk. What can she take with her?" she asked Bridget.

"Nothing, for you haven't told me a reason for taking her away, and it's 'my lady' and not 'Miss Bridget'!" Bridget said angrily, because the look on Betsy's face was so painful to see.

"Nah. No, it ain't, and there's the reason, missy," Gilly said harshly. As Bridget gaped at her Gilly prodded Betsy. "Now hop it," she said, "and don't you dare cry, mind? Me and Miss Bridget will have us a talk whilst you're gone. It's past time, and more, for that."

Bridget stood still as stone. Betsy backed away and

then, sobbing, ran to her room. Gilly stood, her dreadful hat in her hand, looking at Bridget. But before she could speak, the butler returned. This time he carried his silver tray.

"My lady," he said, offering Bridget a note. He'd obviously heard everything Gilly had said; Bridget had only a moment to glance at him, but she saw the contempt in his eyes. She snatched up the note and unfurled it, her hands shaking badly, her nostrils flaring. It was from Ewen; she knew his bold writing. Just holding it made her feel steadier. Reading it did not.

My dearest Bridget,

I can't come back just now. Words can't express how angry and sorry I am about that. But you cannot leave now, either. Wait for me. I'll come as soon as I may. I have every reason to suspect that will be soon, but never soon enough for me. I can't wait to see you. Among all the other things I yearn to do—and I can only hope you wish to do them, too—I have things to tell you, things too difficult to put into written words. I must see you. I will see you. But I ask you to trust me, and to wait. Wait there for me.

Yr. Ewen

15

Bridget read the note twice but learned no more from the second read through it. When she looked up she saw Gilly waiting for her to finish, so she slipped the note into her pocket and closed the door, motioning Gilly to sit. She seated herself opposite her visitor before she spoke again.

"Tell me," she asked, "why did you say such strange things about me? Why would you want to take Betsy away? This place is good for her, surely you can see that for yourself."

"Aye, so 'tis—*now*," Gilly said, turning her hat round and round in her hands. Those small hands were red and callused, the fingernails stained and blunt. They were hands that worked, and worked hard. Gilly hunkered down over the wretched hat, but then looked up, her peculiar golden eyes full of sorrow and fury. "*Now*

240

she's fine, I see that. Any fool could. But what about in a year or two?"

Bridget smiled in relief. "Oh. I see. Don't worry, I'm only waiting here; my husband will be returning from London anytime now. That's why I'm still here by myself and why Betsy's not settled yet. But when we get to his father's estate we're going to foster her to a worthy family there. I'll make sure of it. Don't fret; she'll be educated, she'll learn."

"Huh! That's what I'm afraid of." Gilly scowled, then she sighed heavily and ducked her head, staring at the hat in her hands.

"Listen, Miss Bridget," she said in a gruff little voice, "you don't have to do no fancy dancing with me no more. I ain't green—can't be in London, can you? Plain talk between us, then. If you don't mind being a gent's convenient, why then, more power to you, says I. It's a good life for some. But not for the likes of me and Betsy. Maybe some can do it, but me? I don't even like to have to touch a gent's hand."

Bridget couldn't speak. What Gilly thought of her was so awful she felt a pang in her chest, as though she'd been hit with a fist.

"But Betsy ain't so bad as me. She ain't got cause, thank God," Gilly went on relentlessly. "But she ain't petticoat goods neither. She's too kind and too loving for the game. See, it's hard to keep your heart whole if you're a gent's mistress, 'specially if you learn to care for him—like poor Annie Haynes, her that attached that handsome young baron? Oh, she was the envy of all the tarts on the street. But she kilt herself when he lent her to his friend, she did. And more's the pity, 'cause she was a good girl with a warm heart till she give it away to the wrong man."

"Gilly!" Bridget gasped, as horrified by what Gilly was implying as she was by what she was saying. But the girl went on relentlessly.

"So you got to have a cold heart *and* a hard head to walk that road," Gilly insisted. "Even if you get a good ride for your money with a fair protector, even if you keep your wits about you, it ain't your wits they're paying for, is it? As for keeping them and your profit, why, you got to be shrewd as you can hold together. It ain't easy hanging on to your money once your looks go. Some can—not many, though. Just look at where I live in London. Them that don't keep their gold wind up as low as they lived high. They end up walking the streets. Streets? Hah! *Gutters*, more like."

"Gilly," Bridget said firmly, "that *is* terrible. I understand your fears. But you can't have understood. I'm *married*. Betsy was at our wedding. I'm not the Viscount's 'convenient.' I'm his wife now."

Gilly sighed. "And if you really believe that, then I'm that sorry for you. For it ain't true. You ain't no viscountess, nor his wife neither. Listen," she said wearily, "why'd you think I come tearing up here to get Betsy? I don't want her living with a demi-rep and that's that. The whores who don't work in houses, them that call themselves 'demi-reps'"—she snorted in derision—"like giving a thing a Frog name makes it better. The ones with protectors and fancy places of their own to live in, I mean. They live soft, and they like to take on little girls, like pets, I s'pose, for company, 'cause their days are so lonely until the nights, when they work. She coulda lived pretty as you please with her own room and a soft bed, 'stead of sharing a blanket in a corner with me. But I wouldn't let Betsy go to them, no matter how good they live, nor will I let her stay with you neither.

"A girl learns from her elders, and there's truth. I work like a dog, and that ain't the best thing for Betsy to learn. Granted. But it's a sight better than working on her back until no one will buy her anymore. A woman can always find decent work if she's willing to work hard. But the other kind of life, soft as it is, don't prepare her for nothing but nothing, in the end."

Bridget was appalled at Gilly's knowledge of the world—a different world from any she'd ever seen. But how could the girl know that? She opened her lips to set her straight, but Gilly fixed her with a golden stare. "I don't know what Betsy was doing with them flowers that day," she said ruefully, "nor why you had a feast after it, 'cause near as I can tell—and I can find out anything— you ain't married to no one at all."

Bridget's gray eyes flew open wide.

Gilly went on with difficulty, because Bridget's reaction was upsetting her. "You look sick, Miss Bridget. But things have to be said. See, there weren't no notice in the *Times*. Now, if a gent gets married, it would be there. Everyone knows that. I can't read, o'course, but I know them that does, and it weren't never there, they said. I asked and I asked. And I know where to ask. Nor did anyone who knows the Viscount know he was wed neither. He was, o'course, all them years ago. But not since.

"And if he did marry again, it would be to someone high as he, or someone whose looks . . ." The dark scar on Bridget's face stood out in bold relief across her sudden pallor, and Gilly paused. She gazed at the hat she twisted in her hands. Her voice became lower and sadder.

"Miss Bridget, you may be greener than grass, but you got to know some gents will do anything to get a female they fancy into their bed. You *got* to know that. And Sinclair, well, all know he's a rake. And this place— it's where he takes his women. Well-known fact, even in London. I kept track of Betsy, I got my ways. When I heard you was here, that's when I started worrying. Now I see he's gone, and I ain't wondering anymore."

"It can't be," Bridget said, shaking her head. "It's not!" she said with more vigor. She remembered Ewen and raised her head.

"I *am* married, Gilly. My husband was called to London. That's why I'm still here and not at his father's house yet. I just received a message from him—why, that message I got just now was his. He sends me a message every day. . . ." Her voice trailed off. Being a good correspondent was no proof of anything.

And so what? Bridget told herself, her chin coming up higher. *I know him.* "He asked me to wait. He'll be here soon," she said staunchly, holding out the note with a trembling hand before she remembered Gilly couldn't read—before she remembered she didn't have to prove herself to anyone. She pocketed the note, took a steadying breath, and spoke with all the authority she didn't feel.

"He'll explain everything when he gets here. Why, I hate to even ask him about this. I'm sure he'll be hurt by my doubting him." She laughed, but the sound came out shrill. "Let Betsy stay until then. Just until he comes home. Then you'll see. It would be a crime to take her away now."

I'm not pleading, Bridget told herself. *And it's not just for Betsy's sake; the girl's only a slum child I'm doing something char-*

itable for. It's the principle of the thing. But suddenly she was terrified at the thought of being alone here, although she didn't want to dwell on that.

"In fact," she added quickly, "why don't you stay, too? At least until my husband comes back. I'm sure we can find a room for you, although that mightn't be necessary at all." She laughed, hoping it sounded like she was laughing gaily. "Why, he could be back any hour now!"

"Might as well," Gilly said resignedly, "but if I have to stay the night, I'll share with Betsy, thanks."

Bridget relaxed.

"Could be I can do you a good turn, too. Who knows?" Gilly asked sadly, rising to her feet and looking around the elegant room. "Maybe you'll want to come back with us when he gets here—if he ever does, that is."

Gilly had traveled hard, and she went to bed early that night, after eating a huge dinner. The kitchen staff may have winced to see such a grubby creature at their table, but Gilly insisted on eating in there instead of with her hostess.

"I can scrub my mitts," she told Bridget, "but I'm too tired for a proper wash and too dirty for such a fine place the way I am. And I only got the clothes on my back. I'll wash them out and let them dry overnight. Tomorrow I'll give myself a proper soak in a tub full of suds and dress from the skin out in clean clothes. Then I'll be fit for dining with a duchess—if you got one around. But now? All I need is something to stick to my ribs, a place to kip, and I'll be right as rain in the morning."

Betsy ate with her beloved sister, so Bridget dined alone. She walked alone after dinner, too, pacing the salon until it was time to go pace in her room—their room, as she kept reminding herself. Not that she had to. His presence was stronger in their bedroom than anywhere in the house. The implications of that notion didn't comfort her much now.

But when she lay down in their bed at last in the broad moonlight, she imagined his dark head on the pillow next to hers. She reached out a hand and stroked the cool sheet, remembering the warm, muscled body that had lain next to her own, remembering the way her slightest touch could make him wake and take her in his arms, remembering how she'd shared warmth and ecstasy with him. His hair had been silken as the coverlet she stroked now. His hands on her breasts had been harder and yet gentler on her skin than her own, the scent of him had been warm and musky. At the thought her body seemed to swell, tingle, yearn—a dry patch that had once known such sweet rain.

She remembered the quick pace of his breath on her neck, his voice in her ear, urgent, wanting, willing. . . .

She flipped over on her belly and groaned, pulling a pillow over her head. She missed him body and soul. And she was very, very frightened.

Gilly cleaned up amazingly well. Her hair looked like corn silk, not dirty straw, in the morning light. Her complexion was fair under all that removed dirt. And she was much younger than Bridget had thought—until she looked into those strange yellow eyes and saw how old they were. But at least now she looked like a presentable, if strange, young lad.

They actually made a pretty picture as they strolled through a meadow pied with purple clover and busy with butterflies. Bridget was shapely and graceful in a cream-colored gown, her bonnet swinging from her fingers, her hair glowing with rich mink tones in the summer sunlight. Gilly looked like a slender flaxen-haired lad striding along by her side, and bright little Betsy skipped before them.

"And so then it was give Betsy over to the beadle and go on by myself, or keep her. Well, that weren't no decision at all, I can tell you," Gilly was saying as she told Bridget her story.

"You had no relatives?" Bridget asked.

"I had them—just lost them somewheres along the way," Gilly said with a grin. "Like I said, my dad worked like a mule, lading on the docks. He just dropped down one day, stone dead. Folks said it was his heart. He was a good man, that I do remember. Ma took in washing and such to keep us going, but then when she got the fever she was so worn out she just laid down and died. They was both from the country come to the city to make their fortunes. All they made was Betsy and me."

"And they didn't keep in touch with home?"

"More like they didn't want to, I think. The land was all taken and there wasn't room for no more mouths to feed there."

Bridget nodded. She understood. Her parents had come from a higher class, but it was much the same for them. Decently bred daughters from the middle class found themselves in the same no-man's-land as the poor did these days.

Everything was changing. War was changing the face of the world, and industry was changing the face of England. People couldn't work at home anymore; common land was becoming private as property was fenced off. Even the rich knew life wasn't going to be the same as it had been for their fathers. An extra mouth to feed and an extra body to dress were often hardships or threats to the well-being of those who had just enough for themselves, or thought they did.

"But you can't go on working like a man, much less dressing like one," Bridget argued.

"Oh, can't I?" Gilly said, bristling. "Listen, Miss Bridget, I got no use for men. But if I can act like one, that's fine with me. I don't want to make my bread serving them, and if a girl got no one else to depend on, how else is she to earn her keep? If not serving them in bed, like some do"—she had the grace to look down as she said that—"then she'll be serving them in taverns and such, bringing them vittles and drink. They don't make much, anyway. I don't want to work in some rich man's house scrubbing up his messes neither—besides, I don't know no one who'd recommend me for such. The rich don't hire no one they don't know, and who can blame them? I can't read nor write. Don't got a family in a proper business, like selling milk or coal, or sharpening scissors or selling fish," she said enviously.

"Selling fish?" Bridget said, startled. "You think that's a fine occupation?"

"I'd do it in a flash if I could," Gilly said fervently. "Good money and brisk business. But where am I to get fish from, I ask you? Standing with a pole on London Bridge? Huh. Them that does sells fish, even in the streets, has connections," she said bitterly, "family and friends with boats, and such. Fresh fish ain't easy to come by elsewise."

Bridget had never considered fishmongers as particularly lucky people, but she now could see why Gilly did. She'd never thought about it. Her parents might not have been wealthy, but they'd been from a different world than Gilly. Her father had been a learned man, her mother an educated woman. She had never actually met a girl like Gilly before—although she supposed she'd been surrounded by men and women like Gilly all her life. She'd never felt particularly privileged before, either. Now she realized she was.

At least she could work at something decent for a living, she thought . . . and paused in her thoughts when she did. When her aunt had told her to leave her house, she hadn't had anywhere to go or any way to earn a living. Selling fish would have been preferable to walking the streets. She'd gone to Ewen because he'd been her only refuge. She'd gone along with his proposal because she'd been thrilled by it—and maybe, she admitted now, because she'd been afraid not to. She listened to Gilly with new respect.

"So I dresses like I does, and I does a man's work for a man's pay. Hard work. But it don't kill me. Starving would. That way I can keep Betsy and me safe and fed. Betsy does her bit, too, don't think she don't. She's young, prettier than she can stare, and she's got taking ways—that's how come she sells flowers in the park. I take her to the flower market at dawn and she gets a tray of them. The girls that sells good get more to sell the next day, and choicer blooms, too. The flower vendors get to know which girls do good and them that don't sell don't get no more, 'cause there ain't nothing worth less than flowers you get in the morning by that night. Could be, with luck and hard work, she'll have herself a regular corner to sell flowers on when she grows up. That's prime work for a girl."

"What about marriage, children, a proper home?" Bridget asked.

"Nothing wrong with that, but where's a girl like Betsy going find a gent?"

"I was talking about you," Bridget said gently.

"*Me?*" Gilly said, looking just as shocked as the boy she was pretending to be might have been by that notion.

"Gilly, you can't pretend to be a boy forever. How old are you now?"

"Be sixteen in a month, but no one got to know that," Gilly said angrily.

"But they will," Bridget said, looking at Gilly's smooth face. She saw the way the light breeze blew her baggy shirt against her slim body. It showed evidence that her days masquerading as a youth were nearly over. "You've already got the face of a woman, Gilly, and your body is changing, too. Will they hire you to do the jobs you do now when you look like a woman?"

"Oh, *that!*" Gilly said, her fair skin growing red, "I binds 'em at home, keep 'em wrapped tight, and who's the wiser? And I keep my mug dirty, so no one notices it much. Listen, Miss Bridget, I ain't a fool. Them that knows me knows what I am. They know I carry a knife, too, and that I know how to get revenge. I just dress like this so them that don't know me don't get any ideas.

"I know you mean good, but don't tell me fairy stories about a good man and a good marriage, for it ain't for me. I told you. A man grabbed me once when I was about Betsy's age. I don't want *no* man to ever touch me again."

"Did he . . . ?" Bridget asked, and then stopped. It wasn't fair. It wasn't her business. And suddenly she didn't want to know.

"Yeah," Gilly said bitterly, "he did, all right. A big tub

of a man, who liked little girls and liked it even better when they screeched. I knew he was a bad one, we all did. I even stayed away from his shadow. But I was young, like I said, and couldn't watch every second. He got me in an alley. I got away, but not in time. He done me, hard and hurtful and laughing as he did. But he paid for it."

"They arrested him?"

"For grabbing a slum brat like me and having her? What of it? Who'd listen? Who'd care? They'd just think I was dumb for not asking for money. As to that—there's some that would've tried to hire me if they'd known, and I ain't talking about the folks from my part of town. Who do you think buys the kids there?" she scoffed. "Men from my neighborhood ain't got that kind of money.

"I had no family. My ma was sick as a horse after having Betsy. What could she have done even if I told her, eh? I just had my friends in the street, and they was mostly my age. But I got him, all right. I ain't never nosed on anyone." She saw Bridget's confusion and explained, "Never laid information with the Runners, I mean, though I knew enough even then to put half London on the gallows. But I watched, and then I told them about a purse he grabbed."

"They arrested him?"

"They hung him high," Gilly said with grim satisfaction. Her eyes grew a distant look, and Bridget knew she wasn't seeing the country scene anymore. "I was there to make sure. I jumped up and shouted and waved at him as he walked from the cart to the gallows so he could see me. I cheered when they put the noose on his neck, and I shouted 'Coward!' and 'Chicken guts!' when he asked for a hood for his head. I watched every second. I cheered when he was kicking and spinning like a top, and I kept cheering till he was dead as a mackerel.

"There was some wild boys at the hanging that day, gents like your Sinclair, young and dressed fine. One sees me shouting and laughing and he says, 'Damme! But there's a girl with spirit,' and he laughs and tosses me a coin, yelling, 'For your enthusiasm!' A whole golden boy, just for being happy to see a man hanged," Gilly said, shaking her head. "Easiest money I ever made."

Bridget saw some dreadful conflict in Gilly's eyes. "And you spent the coin?" she asked carefully, wondering if Gilly had kept it as a trophy of that terrible day.

"Did I just! I had me a fine dinner that night to cap a fine day!"

Bridget said nothing. It was the pointed silence that made Gilly speak again. Her thin shoulders slumped. "Yeah, don't say it. I'm 'shamed of myself. Cast up the lot of the best dinner I ever et, right afterward. Guess it was too much all at once."

"I'd guess it was the way you earned the coin," Bridget said softly. "You're not as hard as you'd like to be, Gilly. You've a good heart, and in spite of all your efforts, you're only a young girl, after all."

"I ain't been young for a long time, Miss Bridget," Gilly said.

It was true. Bridget couldn't imagine Gilly's pain or her life; she knew that now. But she tried to think of something to say to take the terrible look from the girl's eyes. "They hang people for snatching purses?"

"God love you, but they hang them for a handkerchief," Gilly said in wonder, looking at Bridget as though she'd stepped down from the moon. "See, that's what

I'm trying to tell you," she said urgently. "You know a lot, Miss Bridget, but nothing about life. Or men. You're the one that got a good heart. But you're living in a dream. You ain't married, and you're just making it worse for yourself by staying here."

Bridget looked at Gilly and was suddenly amazed she'd been upset by what she'd said about Ewen. She saw the pathetic imposture for what it was: a young girl dressed as a younger boy. Gilly was brave, but small, defiant—pathetic, really. She was uneducated, even with all her hard-won street sense. Her sad experience colored her thinking. With all she knew, there was so much she did not—could not—know.

"Gilly," Bridget said firmly, "my husband didn't lie to me. I know that. You will too someday. But you don't trust men enough to even try to see it. Do you believe all women are as immoral or foolish as the ones who sell themselves are? No, of course not. Not even all the women who sell themselves are that. Then you must see that not all men are brutal. You remember your father. Was he a good man?"

"None better!" Gilly said quickly. "As I recollect," she added conscientiously.

"Then you have to realize there are others like him. Perhaps not many where you live. No, even there I'm sure there have to be some who are decent men, men of nobility even if not nobly born, men who treat women with loving respect and gentleness *because* of their own strength, not in spite of it." She paused, wondering how she could possibly explain gentlemanly behavior, loving behavior, much less all the wonderful, secret things men and women said and did with each other, in love and for love.

"There's so much you don't know about a grown man's gallantry," she went on, "his code of honor that won't permit him to hurt anyone weaker, or any woman, especially one he loves. When such a man loves you, and you love him, then there's no question of doubt, or fear of him."

"Aye!" Gilly said savagely, "that's it. When a *good* man loves you, maybe. Aye, I can maybe see that. But your Viscount, he's another piece of work, he is."

"Gilly, I told you—"

"I know, but you don't know what you're talking about," Gilly said in exasperation. "Listen, I ain't talking through my hat. He's up to no good. I seen your aunt and your cousin, and they know it, too. Yeah," she said as Bridget drew in a sharp breath, "the one that looks like a doll in a shop window, and that long Meg of a mother of hers. I went to the kitchen at their house to talk with them that works there to find out about where Betsy and you were, and they told me the whole of your story. But one of them ratted, and so then in comes your aunt *and* your cousin, all noses and whiskers twitching. When they heard what I asked, they give me an earful, too. I know they wouldn't have wiped their feet on me most days, but they didn't care what I was, they were that happy to tell the world about you and the Viscount."

"They're jealous. They wanted him for Cousin Cecily. They—"

"They seen him at a big fancy ball the night before, Miss Bridget. With another woman."

Bridget stopped walking. Gilly looked at her shoes and went on sadly, "Aye. With some fine-looking lady, a *real* lady and married, too, but one what's famous for being free with her favors. I ain't saying I blame you for leaving them two, but there's truth for you, though I'm that sorry to tell you. Listen, it ain't your fault. Who could blame you? You're a good girl, I heard that, too. And he couldn't get you no other way, could he? So I'm betting he spun a pretty tale, and you wanted to believe him. Maybe most women would of, for he's handsome and sweet-talking, but he's a rake and no doubt of it.

"Some men like that," Gilly said with a world-weary air, "they take a girl to Scotland and hire a blacksmith to tell them they're wed. But they ain't really in Scotland, and when the honeymoon's over she never sees him again. Some don't even want to bother traveling that far. They get their friends together and one poses as a vicar and says the words, but there ain't no law behind it, God nor man's. Then they all have a laugh after. All but the bride, who wasn't nothing but a pigeon ripe for the plucking. I heared lots of stories like that.

"I was at the church that day, Miss Bridget," Gilly said with dull finality. Bridget's heartbeat accelerated, making her feel dizzy and light-headed. "You think I'd let my Betsy go somewhere new I didn't know about? It looked like a wedding. Maybe it fooled me for a time, too. But even then I was suspicious, 'cause no one was there. No one but a few of his friends, and them leaving shortly after."

Gilly shrugged. "You and me, we got a lot in common, though you wouldn't think it to look at us. You're full-growed, you got looks and an education and more manners than a duchess. But a man done you wrong, and you don't have family nor money neither. At least I had some friends and more than a pretty face to see me through."

Bridget's hand went involuntarily to her scar.

"Yeah, 'pretty,' I said, and that's what I meant," Gilly emphasized. "More than that, too. Them eyes and that hair and that figure—you look fine, the scar ain't nothing. No—it *is* something. It gives you a look, you know? It makes folks look at you harder, and what they see is so pretty it makes them stare. You're beautiful but different. I guess that's why he wanted you so bad. But he didn't marry you, and there's God's truth."

"He did!" Bridget said automatically. For if he did not, then she knew nothing of life, or men, or love, or trust. "He did," she said again, remembering his voice, his face, his presence—so strongly it was as if he stood beside her now, tall and straight, with all his strength and certitude and power of personality upholding her. She could almost hear his deep voice and feel the warmth of his big hand enveloping hers. She stood in his shadow even though he was miles from her now. But he was in her heart. And for good reason. She wouldn't even consider the notion that he'd lied to her, betrayed her, taken her the only way he could and then left her when he'd grown bored with her. It couldn't be. She might know little about men, but she knew him.

How well, though? She hated the sudden thought, but she wasn't stupid. She had to think of the possibilities. How many other men had she really known, after all? Her father, a few neighbors, her relatives, men in whose homes she'd worked, men who had either patronized or ignored her or tried to dishonor her. She'd never had a real suitor before Ewen came along. So how was she to know that wasn't what a rake would do—could do? He'd said he was a rake, he'd admitted it the night they'd met and never denied it since.

But he'd also said he wasn't a cad. He'd made that distinction himself the first time they'd met.

Because only a cad would take a woman's love and say he cherished it, seem to return it threefold, while all along playing a game for his own pleasure. A cad would grow bored with the game once it had been won. Then he'd lightly discard his hard-won prize because there was another woman beckoning to him—a newer one, and so a richer prize to him.

No. Bridget drew in a sustaining breath. He might have been a rake, but Ewen was not a cad. Some men might do such things, but not he. Never Ewen. No matter what they said about him, no matter what they claimed they'd seen him do. She knew better. His eyes hadn't lied, and his lips hadn't lied, either, not in their kisses and not in what he'd said.

But before he'd left he had said there was something he'd wanted to tell her: *"a thing I never thought I'd want to tell you, but then, I didn't know how it would be with me and you."*

And he'd just written that he'd something to tell her: *"I have things to tell you, things too difficult to put into written words."*

His own words—the very things she counted on to keep her courage now—came back to haunt her.

He'd also written, *"I ask you to trust me, and to wait."*

And she did trust him.

"He did marry me," she told Gilly, her head held high, though her hands were clenched together. "There can be no love without trust, and I tell you, I am not a fool. I'd *never* have given my love to a man I couldn't trust."

And so maybe it just might be, she thought in desperation, *that what he wants to tell me is that he's done the wrong thing and he regrets it bitterly, but he means to make it right now.*

16

It had been another terrible day, so bad even the fine whiskey Ewen was drinking couldn't take the bitter taste from his mouth. He was stuck here, and he couldn't like it, or change the situation by himself. He sat in a deep chair and tried to relax. He thought he had, until he realized his foot was tapping on the floor. When he stopped that, he discovered his hand was clenched so tightly around his glass his knuckles were white. It was no use. He felt like a coiled spring. He could almost feel the insides of his bones itching. He longed to leap out of his chair, get on a horse, and go pounding out of London as fast as he could. But he couldn't.

They told him leaving now would jeopardize everything. He took another swallow of the liquid fire. He wondered if staying was jeopardizing everything, too—

everything that was important to him, at least. How long would she be content to be alone? How long before her doubts about him—doubts he'd seen in her eyes and could now read in her letters—seeped through her thoughts like slow poison?

She was growing impatient, asking him to let her go in every letter, and he got a letter from her every day. As if he'd let her go. When would she stop asking and actually leave?

"Another," he told the footman, indicating the empty decanter on the table by his side. He was in his favorite club, and a long summer twilight was softening the view of London, but he wasn't looking anywhere but within himself. That, he decided, was part of the problem.

He was alone too much these days. He had a small family; most of them lived in the countryside. He'd hardly any real friends in town and had no patience with any other sort now. Years abroad had limited his friendships to those few men who had traveled the Continent as he'd done. His recent profession hadn't encouraged more than acquaintances, but even with his wide circle of acquaintances, he didn't know many people in London. When he'd returned, his weeks here hadn't gained him many new friends. He hadn't been looking for any. The truth was he'd been looking for sport when he came home, not companionship. He'd found both. But she wasn't here now.

He was blue-deviled and needed someone to divert him. Rafe, damn his rascally red head, had been sent to France. That was the reason Ewen was still in London: because Rafe was a good man, an old friend, and a fine soldier, but no spy. The fool who was working with him might cost him that fiery red head if Ewen didn't guide his every move.

Ewen looked around the room. It was late afternoon, and the club's salon was almost full. The members hadn't gone to dinner yet. Some old men were arguing politics by the fireside. Some young blades were standing by the big bow window, looking out and making what they hoped were quotable sarcastic comments, and in the corner . . . *Drum*?

Ewen smiled. His cousin, the Earl of Drummond, was sitting with a few other men not fifteen feet away. And he hadn't seen him? Ewen got up and walked over.

"Having trouble with your eyes, Drum?" he asked when he came up to his cousin. "You must have passed right by my nose, old man. How are you? I haven't seen you in months!"

The elegant gentleman slowly turned his head away from the men he'd been speaking with. His azure eyes were as cold as the north wind's soul when he looked up. "So you have not," he said coolly, and turned his back.

Ewen froze. The cut direct? From *Drum*? Apart from being cousins, they'd been close as boys, friends at school, and friends whenever they met since. And now this?

His thoughts raced. A gentleman dealt with a cut direct one of two ways. He could skulk away, his tail between his legs. Or he could make an argument of it so he could challenge the other man to a duel. Drum was a worthy opponent. At school he'd been the pride of fencing class. He was a demon with pistols, too. It was said he could put out a candle at twenty feet, even after four bottles. They'd been well matched in those days. But then they'd competed for the fun of it. Since those days Ewen had been trained to kill too well, in too many ways. He was now so lethal he refused to duel with a civilian . . . especially not Drum! But he couldn't ignore the insult. It wasn't just a matter of pride.

"Drum," he said in a dead cold voice that made the other men fall suddenly still, "I *will* know why. I choose not to accept your insult until I know why you've given it. You can tell me now or on the dueling ground. Entirely your choice. I doubt the family will be thrilled if you choose to make a killing point of it, though. There are few enough of us, and they won't happy with one less. Nonetheless, I'll oblige you if you wish. Or talk first, if you prefer."

Drum's gaze raked contemptuously over his cousin. "Talk? Very well," he said. "Here and now?"

"Here and now," Ewen said, "but not with an audience." He gestured to a far corner.

The Earl of Drummond rose and followed his cousin to where two high-backed sedan-style leather chairs sat facing each other across a small table. Excited whispers hissed in their wake. The two gentlemen were of a height, broad-shouldered and slim-hipped, with a certain grace and elegance. They were witty and immaculate, both famous for being men of the world.

The Viscount Sinclair was a few years older, his strong face had the irregular features that women found wildly attractive, and his crop of thick dark hair curled as wildly as a poet's, too. The Earl of Drummond was leaner, even his best friends could only claim his face was expressive, his dark hair was straight, and his eyes were azure instead of glinting citrine. Their family resemblance was more in their wit and style than in their faces. Both men were always worthy of notice and conjecture.

Ewen sat, crossed one long leg over the other, and stared at his cousin. Drum settled himself, paying close attention to his boots and nothing else.

"I don't want to shed blood, apart from the fact that your mother would shed mine if I harmed you," Ewen said in conversational tones. His cousin didn't smile at his words. Ewen's expression grew tight. "All right, no jokes. Out with it. Why? We've got too much history behind us for such nonsense."

"Indeed," Drum said coldly, "too much history. But no future. I thought I knew you. Now I think those years apart made you a different man."

"I suppose they have. I hope they have. But not one who deserves your contempt."

"I wonder," Drum said, fixing his cousin with a chill gaze. "After Elise died you had my sympathy. She was lovely. I always envied you, did you know that? But of course she fancied you. So when I heard stories of your wild life abroad after she'd gone, I sympathized. When I visited you there and saw the dissipated life you led, I thought you'd get over it. Now I know you didn't."

"Hold!" Ewen said, frowning, putting up one lean hand. "I don't understand. We haven't seen each other much since then. You were with the Iron Duke in Spain until you were invalided out by that cannonball. I was out of the country all that time, too. I'm back now, to stay. But you know that. We met when I returned, just months past. We took up where we'd left off. Or so I thought. What could I have done to offend you in the short time since? I'm honestly surprised."

"Are you? Perhaps that's the only thing honest about this. I'm recently returned to town, too, if only from the countryside. Oh," Drum said, too sweetly, "you didn't know? I'm surprised. Didn't your *wife* send word to you? I visited her just the other day."

Ewen blinked. Only that. His face remained reserved, though his hazel eyes grew bright with some emotion his cousin couldn't name.

Drum leaned forward, his words harsh whispers. "I knew you once, Ewen. The man I knew wouldn't stoop to such games. You're only two years older, but I always looked up to you, tried to pattern myself after you. Remember? We played together in the old days, as both boys and men. I learned from you, I admired you. You had standards, even then. And when I met you on the Continent, after you lost Elise, you had them still. We were men then, no longer hunting for bird's nests together, but on the prowl for more tender ladybirds. It was you who showed me to seek only those who knew our aims. We went to houses of pleasure, or assemblies where everyone was up to snuff. You never took advantage of innocents, even then. There's a line between rake and cad, Ewen. You taught me that."

"And you believe I've crossed it?" Ewen asked calmly, though his hand knotted to a fist on his knee.

"I went to Brook House," Drum said. "I thought you were there; it's where gossip had placed you, at least. You never minded my joining you for sport in the old days, and I'd brought my own diversion. When I got out of the carriage, she came running to meet me, thinking I was you. When she saw I was a stranger, she was deeply embarrassed. As was I—after I spoke with her. I had Storm, Turner, and Bryant and their ladybirds with me."

"And you *dare* criticize me?" Ewen said angrily, his voice rising.

"The females with us were paid for their time. They

were experienced tarts, hardened cases, women in the business of pleasure. She is not. It didn't take five minutes in her company to see that. She's lovely, even with that scar. She speaks like an educated woman, and there's a sweetness about her. . . ." Drum shook his head. "But that doesn't matter. If she were a common trollop, I'd still be upset. The woman thinks she's your *wife*, Ewen!" he said in a fierce whisper. "There was a little girl with her, from the slums, obviously, with an accent from the Rookeries you could cut with a knife. She said she'd been the flower girl at your wedding. Your lovely friend agreed, and again claimed to be your bride with all the pride and decorum a wife of yours should have. Your *wife*? Your *wedding*? She told me about it, too. Gads! There are wretches who get decent women into their beds that way when they can have them no other way. I've always been contemptuous of them. I'd thought you would be, too.

"And last night, at the ball. That was the final straw. I saw you with that Kensington woman, the foolish baron's famously unfaithful wife. Who did not? She's not the sort of female a newlywed ought to be seen with. Or should want to be with."

"Do you happen to know who the lady went home with?" Ewen asked acidly. "But no. That didn't matter, I suppose. A man may not be seen with another female if he's married? You've gotten some strange notions since we've last met, Holy Father."

"*If* he's married. *If* is the relevant word here, Ewen. Ah, what's the point of trading insults?" Drum asked, the pain clear to see in his eyes. "You could always best me in that. But I'm not playing now. No games, Ewen. I met her. She deserves better than such a cheap charade.

When Barrymore or Dearborne or one of that sort of man tricked a girl into thinking she was wed in order to bed them, we sneered, even then. But this, now, from you! *You*, Ewen!" he said, raising his voice in pained fury. "It's even more disgusting because of who you were—or who I thought you were!"

Ewen's face was deathly still except for a muscle that bunched tight at the hinge of his jaw. "I see," he said through clenched teeth. "You think I'd never marry her because she's scarred?"

"The scar be damned! I told you! It makes her even more lovely, though I don't know why. But she's poor and unconnected; she's nobody, Ewen, from nowhere."

"And you think I'd care about that?"

"What do you think I am, a fool?" Drum shouted.

"Of course I do," Ewen snapped.

"Then damn you!" Drum bellowed, shooting up from his chair.

"It is you who'll be damned, my boy," Ewen shouted, slowly rising to his feet, his eyes narrowing on his cousin.

The other men in the room had been still for a long time, though the two hadn't noticed. Now they no longer pretended not to be eavesdropping. They frankly stared. Shouting? Threats? Standing glaring at each other as though they were about to come to blows, here? Such behavior was unheard of in this club, impossible to even imagine coming from these two polished gentlemen. But there they were, almost nose to nose, snarling at each other.

The sudden utter stillness in the room occurred to both men at the same time. They looked away from each other and around the room. They stared at those watching.

A heartbeat later halting conversation broke out. The other men turned their faces away. Gossip was delicious, and many of the men in the room lived for it, but none was willing to die for it. No one in his right mind wanted to challenge either man. At any other time Ewen and his cousin would have laughed. Not now.

As the sudden babble rose, Drum sat again, and so did Ewen. But both men were on the edge of their seats. Drum spoke first, and low. "So, you claim you did marry her?"

"I *claim* nothing," Ewen said dangerously.

"How strange. You didn't ask me to the wedding."

"Did I not? You were out of town."

"There was no written invitation. There was no notice in the *Times*, no letters to the family, no word to anyone."

Ewen closed his eyes. He muttered a curse. He ducked his head and ran a hand over the back of his neck, but when he looked at his cousin again, his expression was pained, frustrated. "We have to talk. There are strange circumstances involved. Drum—" he said, and paused, collecting his thoughts. His eyes, usually so guarded, were now alive with emotion. "Sometimes a man, even the most sensible of men— which I am not, as you know too well—is driven so hard by his desires he forgets the most elementary things. If you haven't experienced that kind of desire, I envy you—and pity you, too, I suppose. But believe me, sometimes you can become so obsessed, not just for a woman's body, but for the very essence of her.

"Well, no sense trying to explain it here and now," Ewen said with a grimace. "Too much to tell, too little privacy. Suffice it to say you're right about some things. I've been a fool, and I've botched things badly. You can't know how badly! I'll tell you, if you'll let me. Give me ten minutes to write some notes and send them out. Then we'll talk. There's so much I haven't told you, couldn't tell you before . . . but I'll explain all at dinner. Please. For old times' sake?"

Ewen was not famous for asking, for saying "please." His cousin studied his face. Then he nodded. "For old times' sake," he agreed warily, "and the hope of new ones."

Ewen gave him a tight-lipped smile. The stilted conversation around them grew more normal; laughter was heard. A footman who had been hovering nearby decided it was finally safe enough for him to interrupt the two dangerous gentlemen.

"My lord?" he said nervously, offering Ewen a note on a silver tray. "There's a message for you."

Ewen picked up the square of paper. He read it and then crumpled it in his fist. His eyes were bleak, and then afire. He sprang to his feet. "Damn! I have to go," he told Drum. "Damn and blast, damn them all!"

Drum looked at him curiously. "Surely it can wait a moment?"

"I wish it could, but I must leave. Now."

"Your father?" Drum asked anxiously. "I'm so sorry. . . ."

"No, no, he flourishes. It's . . . something else, entirely."

Drum frowned, then his eyes opened wide. He rose and put a hand on Ewen's sleeve. "I won't ask your reasons. But I don't lack funds, and I won't ask for interest or a quick return. If you need something to see you through, you don't have to throw yourself to the loan sharks. Whatever you've done doesn't matter. As you said before, I'm family."

Ewen's stern expression vanished. He threw back his

head and laughed wholeheartedly. "That's rich," he said when he'd done, his voice softer, "and I don't mean money. You're ready to slay me for an imagined slight to a woman you never really met, but you're also ready to empty your pockets for me? Well done! Even I'm not so befuddled." He sobered. "But there's no need. We aren't boys anymore; I haven't spent my allowance. I'm well to grass. It isn't money troubles. But thank you."

"Then why do you have to rush away? Who has such power over you? I saw your face when you read that note. You're in trouble, Ewen."

Ewen's face grew graver. "No. A friend of mine is. Don't ask, because I can't tell you yet. Just trust me." He winced. "I'm asking that of a lot of people these days," he murmured, his eyes bleak again. "Damn and blast it all! I'll see you when I can. Hold a good thought for—and of me—until then, will you?"

"I'll try," Drum said, but he said it to the air because his cousin was already striding from the room.

Dearest Bridget,

How tired you must be of my excuses, how impatient and out of sorts with me. Even I am weary of my excuses. But hold on, please. Only a little while longer. I'll come to you soon. Soon, I promise. There is much I must tell you, too much to put on paper, even if I dared. But I need to see your face when I speak to you next. I need to hold you in my arms when we speak again. I badly need to hold you in my arms in my bed, if truth be told. But we must speak, too. We will. Only a little longer. You are not the only sufferer. I burn for you.

Yr. Ewen

*   *   *

Well, Bridget thought as she carefully folded the note, *that's something*. It might only be desire talking, but it was something. But what exactly did he mean by "only a little longer"? *Forget about that, my girl*, she told herself. *What did he mean by saying*, "*I need to see your face when I speak to you*'?" That was worrisome. She sighed. So many questions, and only one answer: Ewen.

"So, from your face, I guess he ain't coming today neither?" Gilly asked.

"No, but soon."

"Oh, aye, and soon it'll be winter, and where's Father Christmas? Huh," Gilly said, glancing out the window at the verdant lawns that made her statement seem even more foolish. "Listen, Miss Bridget, I can't stay here all summer. Longer I'm away, less work I'll find when I get back. Folks get to thinking you're dead if you don't show up after a week's passed. And how long do you think they'll hold Betsy's corner for her? It's been given away to someone else already, you know. I'll have to talk sixteen to the dozen until they gives it back to Betsy, as it is."

"Oh, Gilly, you could be a storyteller on that same street corner and make your fortune—you've only been here a week, and you know it!"

Gilly shrugged. "Feels like more."

"Because you're idle. Come along, we'll go for another walk," Bridget said, snatching up her shawl.

"Oh, good!" Betsy cried, skipping after Bridget as she left the salon and went to the door.

"Be an inch shorter when I does get back, we does so much walking," Gilly grumbled. But she followed the pair out the door, into the enclosed courtyard, and then out into the sunlight.

They walked toward the little village nearby but never actually got there. They never did. Bridget always found a reason to turn back before they came in sight of it. She did again now.

"It looks like it's clouding up to rain," she said, screwing up her eyes and staring at a cloudless sky.

"It always rains. So what?" Gilly asked as she trudged along.

"And it's nearing teatime," Bridget added.

That did it. Gilly never passed up a chance for a meal. They turned back. Bridget was relieved to have thought up yet anther excuse not to go into town. It was bad enough that Gilly saw how the household staff was treating her these days. Going to the village would be worse, because Bridget knew that they didn't like her there. She was only learning that about the Brook House staff now.

The longer Ewen stayed away, the worse his household staff behaved toward her. They did it in a way that made it hard for her to complain to Ewen, because there was nothing precisely to complain about. But they made her life more uncomfortable every day and night. It was done cleverly, but she suspected servants were masters of the art of subtly showing their distaste for someone they had to serve. Each day she was subjected to a dozen little things that showed what they thought of her, so little they were never enough to write to Ewen about, things that could be seen as her imagination—if you weren't there to see them. An inflection in a voice here, a sneer on a face there, a slow look or a fast retort, and things never done the way she asked: a fire lit an hour after she asked, a cup removed long before she was done drinking from it, luncheon served late, dinner cold, and always with foods they'd have to have been blind not to notice that she'd left on your plate the night before. Sometimes she suspected they were the same foods, too. All these little things added up to a miserable whole.

Betsy was still treated charmingly, and they'd even grudgingly accepted Gilly, for Betsy's sake. Not for hers, Bridget knew. That was clear.

Brook House had been a terrible place for him to take her for her honeymoon, she thought. But then she admitted it really wasn't. Hell itself wouldn't have been bad if he'd been there with her. But he wasn't, and this was where he'd always taken his light ladies, and so why should they believe her to be any better? Especially since the only title on her name was his. And now Gilly had introduced doubt that he'd even given her his title. Bridget refused to explain herself to servants. She knew they wouldn't have listened, anyway.

This was her honeymoon, and she'd never been more wretched in her life. She no longer wrote to her mother. She hoped her mama thought it was because she was too busy spending every hour in her doting new husband's arms. Messages or not, Bridget wasn't even sure she was in his thoughts. He was constantly in hers— both the remembered joy of him and the new fears about his intentions.

She could hardly sleep at night, though she walked every hour of the day, either taking country rambles or pacing the time away. It showed in her mirror. She grieved to see that her finest feature, her gray eyes, weren't so fine when they were so red. Her complexion looked more haggard than fair. More and more the scar dominated her pallid face. Less and less she looked like the beloved bride of a nobleman, she thought as she and Gilly and Betsy straggled home from their shortened walk again.

So she literally stopped breathing when she looked up from her dusty slippers as they came to the top of the slope that overlooked Brook House. She only stood staring.

"Lookit that fine carriage!" Betsy cried. "Is it him, do you think, is it, Miss Bridget?"

"Him or the King hisself," Gilly said, eyeing the fine carriage, with all the cases on top of it, stopped in the drive.

"Four horses!" Betsy said, dancing in place. "Matched blacks, too. Coo! It's gotta be him!"

More likely some more of his rakish friends, Bridget thought warily. Whoever it was, she wasn't going to run into embarrassment again.

"Well, I don't think it's my husband," she told them as she began moving toward the house. She refused to run, but that didn't mean she couldn't hurry. "He left on horseback, and I think he'll come home the same way. Maybe it's guests." *None of whom I know*, she thought miserably, *and many of them I'm afraid to know*.

Still, it was company. And maybe news. So Bridget picked up her pace. She made her way down the slope as quickly and as daintily as she could, in case anyone was watching from the coach.

They weren't. She saw some figures alighting, and they went right up the stairs to the front door. A party of three. Two women and a young boy. Might it be Ewen's relatives? He had no sister, she knew, but perhaps another cousin? Now Bridget hurried faster.

The door swung open. The footman stared. The butler, Mr. Hines, appeared a moment later, and even from a distance Bridget could see his astonishment. He gasped like a fish and swayed, and she feared he might actually fall. But then his sour old face broke into a huge smile. She almost didn't recognize him.

She hurried on, Betsy skipping beside her, Gilly lengthening her boyish stride. Even so, the group at the front door was about to move inside when she at last came close. They were going inside? But she hadn't invited them in!

Then it must be relatives. Bridget reached the front stair before she slowed, smoothing her tousled hair, hoping she didn't look too windblown and frowzy.

The butler saw her first and frowned. That made the trio in the doorway turn back to look at her. The woman closest to her was obviously a servant, because she stood in back of the other two and was dressed in the sort of shapeless, subdued brown dress that Bridget remembered all too well. The boy, a handsome youngster with a sulky mouth, stared openly and rudely at Bridget, Gilly, and Betsy. But the women with him stopped Bridget in her tracks. She felt like curtsying. This was obviously a lady, anyone could see that.

She was some years older than Bridget, but not many. The stranger was tall for a woman, and slender, and blond and fair as the meadowsweet blooming in the fields around them, but with all the refinement of an exquisite rose. She wore a perfectly cut black carriage dress that showed her shapely form. A dashing little pink and black bonnet tilted rakishly over smooth golden tresses, accenting a classically elegant face. Thin brows arced over blue eyes as she beheld the trio before her.

"My lady," the butler said, "this is the young woman I was speaking of, and her . . . friends."

But he was speaking to the visitor and not Bridget— the mistress of this house, and so then, however much he disliked her, *his* mistress. His *lady*. Bridget sucked in a breath. She may have been belittled by the staff in small ways, and so unable to fight back before. But this was outright rudeness and insubordination. Her chin went up. Her gray eyes grew dark with wrath. She knew her place, even if he did not.

"Oh, dear!" the strange woman said in dismay before Bridget could say a word. "This will be more difficult than I thought. Well, needs must when the devil drives. There can be no help for it, I suppose." She pulled off her lacy gloves as she turned her perfect profile to Bridget and addressed the butler again. "Dear Mr. Hines," she said, "would you please introduce me?"

"Of course, my lady," he said with glee. "Viscountess, may I introduce Miss Bridget, from London, and her friends, Miss Betsy and Miss Gilly. Girls," he said with a look at Bridget, "this is Elise Sinclair, Viscountess Sinclair."

"Ewen's mother?" Bridget said in confusion. "But— but I thought she was dead."

"Alas," the strange woman said, "so she is. I am not she. For one thing, I'm not old enough. Still, I suppose you might think a second wife—but the Earl never got over her death. Although how could you know that, poor thing? I'm sorry, truly I am. But I am Ewen's wife, my dear."

"His . . . ," Bridget said, staring.

"Yes. That's right. Elise, Ewen's wife. Ah!" the lady said, her voice beginning to crackle and fade in Bridget's ears, "do see to her, Hines, would you? I fear the poor thing's going to swoon."

"No, I'm not," Bridget said as the faces before her wavered and drew together. Finally, and mercifully, they were eclipsed by all the darkness that was rushing toward them.

17

She hadn't been dreaming. Bridget knew that the minute she opened her eyes. It wasn't just because she woke choking on the lingering smell of burnt feathers or the stench of the salts that they'd used to revive her still scalding her nose. She knew because she hadn't wanted to wake up.

She'd fainted, for the first time in her life. And as she woke she immediately remembered, too clearly, why. The woman downstairs *had* said she was Ewen's wife, back from the dead. Only she looked very alive and well, and worst of all, exactly the way Bridget had always thought his first wife looked. She woke in a second, sitting straight up in the next one.

"They said as to how you wasn't to get up right off," Betsy said in a small, worried voice. She was sitting on Bridget's bed with her, looking anxious.

"Huh! Them! They wisht she wouldn't wake at all," Gilly said, frowning fiercely as she studied Bridget. "They said as to how we should let you be until they calls for you."

"They did, did they?" Bridget asked. She swung her feet over the edge of the bed. "Well, I'm not a servant, to be ordered about. This is my husband's house. No one else has the right to tell me what to do."

Gilly's face was somber, and Betsy's lower lip was quivering.

"Aw, Miss Bridget, the game's up," Gilly said sorrowfully. "Leave your losses, and let's be gone from here."

If she doubted now, she was lost. That alone, Bridget knew for certain now.

"He told me his wife was dead," she said, as much to herself as to them. "Why should I believe otherwise? Because some fine lady says so? Who is she? Any number of women could claim anything at all. She looks like a lady . . . maybe more than I do, I grant that," she added, her voice wavering. She pulled herself together and straightened her back. "But his wife is dead. He told me so, but you don't have to believe him. Everyone knows that. You said so yourself, Gilly."

"Aye," Gilly said slowly, "so I did. Y'know, there's something to that. I'll be blowed if I wasn't took for a flat! She looked so fine, I thought, Well, Gilly old girl, that's that. Poor Miss Bridget's been hoaxed all right and tight—bammed, led right round the garden path, she was. But come to think on, there's something smells funny here."

Gilly began to pace, her voice picking up excitement, her strange eyes glowing yellow. "All say she's dead. Yet here she be, no ghost at all. Now, where I come from, there's them that would pretend to be a dead man's son, or brother or father, or even his wife or mistress— don't matter which, they might try to be any—just to get the boots he left. There's more at stake here. Much more. Aye, there could be some rig running.

"Now," she said, holding up a finger to stop Bridget from interrupting, "I ain't saying your Viscount ain't a rogue, mind. Nor that it mightn't be him at the bottom of all this, even so. Remember that. But I'm just thinking that this fine lady may be a bigger rogue than him, or any you've met yet. See, like I said, I know London, and who to ask what there. One thing I know as sure as my own name: One person tells you a thing, bet your life it could be a lie—or not. Two or three people tells you the same thing, maybe it ain't a lie. But *everyone*? Ah. Then either you got the biggest lie ever told, or the truth of it."

"One thing I know," Bridget said, getting down off the bed, "is that if Ewen told me something, it's true. Don't look at me like that, Gilly, I know what you're thinking. But that's what I believe, or I'll believe nothing else. I'd bet *my* life on it."

But hadn't she already? Because what was her life but her reputation? And what could she do if he had lied to her? She'd burned all her bridges when she came with him; she'd known it then. If he'd duped her, she had no reputation left, and so no life to speak of: no possible way of finding decent employment without references, not even the goodwill of her father's wretched family. She could only go to Ireland and seek out her mother and be a burden to her.

But luckily, she thought determinedly as she went to her wardrobe, that was not the case. Ewen hadn't lied to her.

"You going to go talk to her now?" Gilly asked as Bridget cracked open her trunk and stared into it.

"Of course," Bridget said absently. It had to be soon, because the more she thought about it, the more frightened she'd be. And she was already afraid.

"Then Betsy and me, we'll go belowstairs and do some talking there, too," Gilly said. "That's where everyone knows everything, the servants do. And I'll try to get a word with that lad who came with her. He's a nasty piece of work, that one. Got little beady eyes, that's always a sign. But he'd never guess what the game is with me, and since he don't speak to servants, he might not know. He just might have a word with another lad, though—that'd be me. Or he might be willing to chat with a cunning little doll like our Betsy. No one can refuse her. We'll sort this out for you, not to worry."

Bridget gazed at Gilly, so fierce in her defense. She had more than a friend in Gilly, she had an ally. Impulsively she reached out and gave her a hug. She didn't know who was more startled. But just hugging the girl—who turned out to be unexpectedly fragile beneath her baggy clothing—made Bridget feel stronger, better, less alone. She couldn't have done that before her brief time with Ewen. He'd given her that—the ability to touch, to know how good it was to hold another human being.

Bridget let Gilly go, grinning at how surprised she still was. "Now," Bridget said briskly, "you to your tasks, and me to mine. You're right, we'll get to the bottom of this."

Gilly gave a tentative smile in return. A real smile, if a shy one. The first such Bridget had ever seen from her. Then she blinked, straightened her thin shoulders, and

took Betsy by the hand. "Aye, you to yours and us to
ours, but be sure and call if you needs us. I can fight like
a cornered rat, and Betsy here can screech the rooftops
down if she got to. I taught her how to use her knees,
nails, and elbows, too."

Bridget grinned at the thought of the two tussling with
the elegant lady who claimed to be Ewen's wife. But the
moment they left her room her smile faded. She picked up
a gown, scrutinizing it. What she wore was important now.
Her dress had to be modest, expensive, and elegant.
She'd have to arrange her hair simply and neatly, too. She
had no jewels to wear, but she'd paste on a small, secre-
tive smile and never let it slip. She'd raise her head high
and forget her scar, pretending there was nothing but a
dash of powder on her face. She'd dress in her finest, so
that she could be the finest lady to ever grace this house.
Finer even than that paragon downstairs. Who was not
Viscountess Sinclair. She'd bet her life on that.

Now she only needed to forget that she already had
done just that.

Bridget finally choose a gray high-necked dress. It wasn't
servant gray, not remotely like the gowns she'd had to
wear when she'd been little better than a servant. It was
expensive gray, the color of heirloom silver. It was softly
draped, the color shifting from that of a storm cloud to
the quicksilver shade of fish flashing though clear water.
The overskirt was slate silk with a tiny floral design. It
had been cut by a master's hand and flowed over her
body like a lover's caress, making her fine gray eyes shine
as though they were touched by moonlight. She didn't
know that. She only knew it made her look like a dignified lady.

She went downstairs and found a footman.

"Please tell our visitor that I will see her in the library," she said.

She'd thought it over carefully. If she sat behind a desk, the woman she'd summoned standing before her, then she'd clearly be seen as mistress of the situation, and the house. It would be a small advantage, but Bridget needed every advantage now. She knew she herself was Ewen's wife; she knew the woman was some kind of impostor. And she was very afraid the woman might be Ewen's wife, too.

She didn't know how all these things could be at the same time, but so it was. She didn't have time to sort it out. One thing was clear: She had to act before the interloper did.

The footman hesitated, clearly uncomfortable. He was a young man and a quiet one. Bridget had addressed only a few words to him in all the time she'd been here.

"The lady is in the salon," he finally said, his eyes blinking rapidly, "and she asked me to tell you she wants to see you there . . . miss," he added unhappily.

Bridget's head snapped up as though she'd been slapped. *Miss*, was it? Not even *mistress*, so there was no chance at her misunderstanding her demotion? He'd taken sides, had he?

Now Bridget wavered. She could go to the library and wait there anyway. But she had a sinking feeling she'd be waiting there a long time. The thing had to be out and in the open, discussed and resolved long before evening. *Before another hour passes*, she thought, taking a deep breath. There was only one course to take, and she could carry it off if she took it with the style and elegance Ewen himself would. This was *her* home now.

Bridget turned and marched to the salon. The door stood open. She paused in the doorway, looking in.

The lady was having tea there. It looked as though she'd been having tea there in just such a way every day for years. She was posed on a settee, her son lolling at her side. His hair was brown and lank, not curly as Ewen's unruly crop, and he didn't resemble him much in any other way. *But what of that?* Bridget thought with sinking heart. She didn't look like her own father. And the boy *was* dark ... but his face was made darker by a perpetual scowl. The lady didn't share it; in fact, a small smile seemed about to appear on her lips at any moment. Otherwise her face was as smooth and fair as her blond hair; she was altogether calm and lovely.

She was pouring fragrant tea into little china cups from a fragile teapot Bridget had never seen. It was painted all over roses. The lady looked like some sort of rare rose herself. She wore a gauzy gown, a cloud of pink, with trailing skirts and puffed sleeves, the sort women of fashion wore in their homes on slow summer afternoons.

But it was *not* her home, Bridget thought, and, gathering her courage, she marched into the room.

"Ah, Miss Bridget," the lady said, barely looking up, "I've been waiting for you. Would you like a cup of tea?"

"No, thank you," Bridget said abruptly. "I would rather talk with you, I think. *Alone* would be best," she said with a pointed look at the young boy. A pointed look and one of censure, a governessy sort of silent reprimand, remembered from the days when she'd worked as one—because the boy hadn't gotten up at her entrance. He was at least ten years old, on the brink of leaving boyhood behind him. Even if he were younger, he ought to know better. A boy ought to rise from his chair for any female but a girl younger than he—or a servant.

Bridget's chin went up to keep it from quavering. She was in the right, she told herself fiercely; it was absurd the way this strange woman had taken over her home.

"Louis, my love," the woman told the boy gently, "I'm afraid she's right. This is not for your ears. Do find something to do, will you? Perhaps upstairs? I'll call you later."

With an ugly look at Bridget, the boy rose and slouched past her and out of the salon.

"Now, please sit down, my dear," the lady said. "Some refreshments, perhaps?" she asked, nodding toward a plate of tiny cress sandwiches, little jam tarts, seed cakes, and scones and cream. *Such a grand tea!* Bridget thought. *The servants never prepared that for me in this house.*

"No, thank you," Bridget said, standing before her hostess—*the strange woman*, she corrected herself quickly. "There's little point to it," she said, running a hand over her silken skirt for reassurance. "This isn't a social occasion. I heard what you said, and I've thought about it at some length." She took a deep breath and spoke the words she'd carefully rehearsed.

"There is a mistake, and it is not mine," she told the lady, who sat listening politely, no discernible expression on her lovely face. "You can't be Viscountess Sinclair, nor can you be Ewen Sinclair's wife. His wife is dead. We married last month in London. In a church. With witnesses. Now, either you're claiming my husband is a bigamist, or you're entirely mistaken. Or . . . there is some baser motive here. I prefer not to believe that. And so I think it would be best if you admitted your mistake and left this house immediately. I expect Ewen back any hour now. I know he'll be very angry at this imposture. I, however, am willing to let you leave with no repercussions—*if* you leave at once."

She was pleased with herself, she hadn't forgotten a word. She couldn't know that her breast rose and fell as rapidly as her fast-beating heart did, or that her eyes were open wide, clearly terrified. In her gray gown that matched her clear gray eyes, she looked as much fragile as she did elegant and demure, and altogether vulnerable.

"Oh, dear," the lady said. She put the teapot down carefully and wiped her long white fingers with a little cloth. She fixed Bridget with a long sad, look. "My dear," she said, and sighed again. "This is *so* difficult, you cannot know. I know you believe yourself to be in the right, and why should you not? That's the tragedy of it. I could *strangle* Ewen, and would—if I hadn't resolved to forgive and forget. And after all, the poor fellow didn't know I'd finally agreed to his terms.

"My dear," she said again, in an eerie echo of Ewen's favorite expression, "I *am* his wife, you know. We were married eleven years ago, almost to the day. It was at his father's estate. I would have preferred London, but it was Ewen's family tradition, and Ewen is so traditional in some ways. In others, alas, he is not, or we wouldn't find ourselves in this position, would we?

"I've been here before, too," she added, "shortly after we were wed, on our way back to London. We left here and went directly to London, and then to the Continent for our honeymoon. That's why dear Mr. Hines recognized me, you see." Only the faintest moué disturbed her serene expression and showed she was slightly uncomfortable as she added, "He tells me that since then Ewen has taken to bringing his . . . light ladies here—no," she said, holding up one slender white hand, "please understand. I am not calling you such. I believe you believe what you told me. But you've been cruelly misled, my dear, and none can be sorrier for it than I. I'd hoped he'd changed. He promised he'd change. Why do you think I left him all those years ago? Still," she said, cocking her head to one side, "to give the poor devil his due, he didn't know that I'd finally decided to take him up on his promises, did he?"

Bridget put out a wavering hand and found a chair. She sat and tried to collect her thoughts. The only thing she could think to do was attack. "And I'm supposed to take your word—and a butler's—for proof, am I?" she asked to buy time to think. Butlers *can be bribed*, she thought desperately.

"Of course not," the other woman said gently. "Why should you? I've proof. I'm a sentimental creature, you see. When I decided to move back to England, as Ewen beseeched me to, I brought my mementos of him back with me, too. Oh, yes," she assured Bridget, "he did beg me to return, or else I wouldn't be here now. He came to me so many times to plead his case I grew weary of it. But I ask you—would you be willing to forgive a man who betrayed you on your very honeymoon? Mmm, I see that's perhaps not a fair question to ask of you, poor dear. But I, you see, had expected better of him.

"I've come back now only because of his solemn promise to change his ways—and for our son's sake. Yes, my sweet Louis. It's true he boards at school most of the year. But when he returns in the summertime, as now, he needs a man's companionship. More than that, he needs to know his father, and his place in his father's life. It's no good his living abroad with me now. Not to be crass, but whatever their relationship is to be, there *is* the matter of coming to know the estate and properties he will inherit. I've come back for his sake. And for Ewen's, of course. He vows he never stopped loving me."

She paused, looking pained. "I can scarcely blame him for . . . this," she said, glancing at Bridget, "when I, after all, had vowed never to come back to him. A man needs some company, some recreation, and I do realize that. I expected it, in fact."

"I am not recreation," Bridget said, fighting back her tears. "He said he lov—he married me, and I, too, have witnesses to prove it!"

"Indeed?" the lady said, eyeing Bridget coolly. She looked at her closely for a long moment. "And where are they?"

"Well, of course, wedding guests aren't on one's honeymoon," Bridget said.

"And neither is one's bridegroom, it appears," the lady said. "And your family? Where are they?"

"My mother is all the family I have. She's in Ireland."

"I see," the lady said, as if she saw much more. "And if you are wed, then why, pray, do you not wear a wedding band?" she finally asked politely.

"The one Ewen gave me was too big. He said he was going to give me his mother's, but it's in his father's vault," Bridget said, regretting it instantly. *She* ought to be the one doing the questioning, she told herself fiercely.

"No, it's not there," the other woman said, waving one white hand so that the sunlight glinted off the gold ring she wore. "It's here on my finger, as it has been since the day I wed him. No matter how I choose to live out my days, I'm still a married woman. I'd scarcely go without proof of that. I only wonder that you do."

"I'll have the ring," Bridget said desperately. "He said so. And I have the wedding lines to prove it, too . . . or at least," she added, biting her lip, belatedly remembering, "I will when he comes home. He's put them in safe-keeping!" she said triumphantly.

"Indeed? Isn't that usually the case? Mine are in safe-keeping as well. The difference is that I can produce them at will, which is more than you can say. Oh, this is sad stuff, is it not?"

Bridget looked away, trying to rally her thoughts. So she didn't see the lady studying her with a slight frown that marred the calm perfection of her expression. It was gone before she spoke again.

"I've kept my wedding lines only because I—sad to say—never completely trusted him with them," the lady sighed. "Or with anything, for that matter. Well, after finding him entwined with a chambermaid scarcely four weeks after we were wed . . ."

Bridget turned to her, shocked. The lady nodded sadly. "Yes, completely entangled. It was no brief, light peck on the lips or playful pinch on the bottom he was treating her to, my dear. I found him in the most inde-cent position imaginable. Well, I'm sure *you* can imagine it. I became quite ill with despair and disgust, sick to my stomach, really, not even knowing that half of it was natural, due to my condition. Our dear Louis was already on the way. But I didn't know of my condition then. What an innocent child I was.

"He loved that innocence," the lady went on reflec-tively, "the fact that he had to teach me everything for his pleasure. And please him I did. Mightily. We scarcely spent a moment out of his bed. Oh. I've shocked you?" she asked in amused tones. "How odd. I wouldn't have thought I could, not if you've spent your time these last weeks similarly with him, as Hines said you have.

"No matter," she said with another wave of her hand, as Bridget felt the blood rush to her face. "It was much the same with you, I suppose. Ewen strayed because his pleasure didn't last. But then, it never does. We've talked about it often since, every time he came to visit Louis and plead with me. Which he's done regularly ever since that ghastly morning. So you see, I know he always gets bored after a month. It is his pattern, unfortunately. He can't help himself, he says. Nor can the poor girls who tumble into love with him. He's very attractive, well nigh irresistible, to a certain sort of woman. The kind with no family to warn her and protect her, alas.

"So I can sympathize with you, my dear, truly I can. But that doesn't mean I'm willing to let you stay on here. And why should you, after all? How embarrassing, how shameful for you. I'm willing to advance you funds so you can leave now and retain some dignity, spare yourself the cruelty of having him leave you."

"No!" Bridget gasped. "I'll wait for Ewen!"

The lady smiled sweetly, sadly. "My dear, haven't you realized it yet? He'll only return because of me. He never intended to come back here otherwise."

Bridget's eyes were so full of unshed tears that she saw the lady in a nimbus of floating light, until she looked to her like some kind of weird angel descended to spew spiteful, hurtful lies.

"He sends you messages, does he not?" the lady went on relentlessly. "He inundates you with them, I expect. No need to answer; the servants here complain they're run ragged with them. If he's running true to form, which I don't doubt he is, the next one—or at most, the one after that—would have contained some explanation of mysterious business he had to do, a long, perilous trip he must make."

Bridget's face paled.

"Ah, I see he's told you some mare's nests already, has he? I suppose the usual nonsense about his past, about why he was on the Continent so long? Forget it. He was there only because he couldn't bear to leave me, or leave without me."

"Then why *did* he leave you?" Bridget said, pouncing on that thought. "Because he did, didn't he?"

The lady shrugged slender shoulders. "Of course. I imagine it was his last roll of the dice. And see? It worked. I decided to follow him, after all. Did he ever speak to you of me?"

"Not often, not much," Bridget said, "but . . ."

"But never that I lived and thrived? My dear, how can you then believe anything he said? And as to those messages he's been sending you, they fit a pattern, if you only open your eyes to see it! First they're impassioned—aren't they? Then he begins telling you all sorts of reasons he can't return. Ah, I see, it's come to that stage, has it?"

Bridget held a hand to her mouth, although she couldn't have said a word. The lady nodded with satisfaction and went on implacably. "Then depend on it, the next message would be sure to have another such tangled tale in it. But this one would also enclose a cheque—to see you through until he could come personally. Which, I promise you, would be never. He is gone from you, my dear, and once Ewen leaves a mistress, he is gone from her forever. The best thing you can do now is turn the tables on him and deny him that pleasure by leaving him before he can shed you. It will increase your value, I assure you."

Bridget blinked.

"Ewen's friends are wealthy men," the other woman explained. "Many are happy to . . . attach the women he grows tired of. After all, he never keeps them very long. And as you have that disfigurement—trust him to seek diversity!—I imagine it won't be easy for you to find another protector immediately. But if the word gets out that you left Ewen, why, what a coup! I don't doubt you'll be able to find another admirer—of your audacity, if nothing else—before the sun goes down."

She smiled encouragingly at Bridget, who'd been sitting in a silent, aching morass of despair. Until her last words. Then Bridget's head shot up. Her eyes blazed. The mention of her scar changed everything for her.

She'd been taking insult and accusation, unable to counter them. How could she prove what she knew to be the truth and yet now feared to be a lie? She'd never had a lover, much less an unfaithful one. She didn't know how to deal with unthinkable betrayal. She refused to accept that Ewen would deceive her, and was dazed with the effort of trying to refute it.

But she'd lived with the scar and the misery it caused her all her life. *That* she knew how to fight. The lady's insult woke her from the numbing terror of the accumulating evidence against Ewen. It was a deliberate cruelty. *That* she could deal with.

She rose from her seat, shaking with rage. "He's told everyone you're dead," Bridget cried, "*everyone*! If what you say is true, why would he say that?"

The lady's expression didn't change, but her blue eyes went flat and cold. After a stunned second she sat back, smiling a chill smile. "My dear," she said calmly, "to whom has he said it? Not to his intimates, not to relatives or friends of his heart, of that you can be sure."

Bridget didn't know those people. That was her first fear and a constant source of dismay. She still hadn't met his family or dearest friends. Her heart sank—but then she remembered. "His friend! His redheaded friend was at our wedding," she said triumphantly, "*and* Baron Burnham and his lady, and—and two other gentlemen who work with him were there, too!"

The lady's laughter was bright, clear, and cold as cascading ice. "Oh, my dear! Not that rapscallion Rafe! He's up to every rig. And Burnham? A riper rascal does not exist. And two gentlemen who work with Ewen? What work is that? Were they croupiers? Or tavern keepers or racehorse owners? Our Ewen works at play and nothing else. Or did he tell you differently?"

"He said he sometimes works for . . . for the government," Bridget said carefully, as fearful of betraying Ewen's confidence as she was of his betraying her.

"England's ruler may be many things, but even he is not that mad, my dear!"

Bridget cast around for some weapon, some proof. "And his cousin Drummond was here last week!" she cried.

"I know, I was told. He stayed to visit, as family would, of course."

"He would have, but he didn't know we were just wed."

"Oh, that makes more and more sense. Ewen's own cousin didn't know of his marriage."

"It was because we had to marry so quickly, because of Ewen's father being so ill."

The lady nodded. "That at least is truth enough. But you still haven't explained why Drum didn't visit."

"He—he came with inappropriate company," Bridget said wildly.

"I heard about that. Is it the new fashion? I can't have been out of England *that* long. A gentleman, a nobleman, is now expected to come calling on his newlywed cousin in a coach filled with rakes and their doxies? Come, my dear, he didn't stay because he knew what you were, even if you say you did not."

Bridget thought hard. She sensed a flaw; she wasn't sure what it was and so tried to sound it out as she spoke it. "But if Drummond knew what I was, as you say . . . and he had other such women with him, then . . . then why *wouldn't* he stay?" She smiled in victory.

The lady smiled, too, and it was a real smile at last. She looked at Bridget almost tenderly. "My point exactly. He didn't stay because he was afraid Ewen would think he was poaching. You told him you'd only just met Ewen. You were fresh meat, so to speak. And as such you were untouchable—to everyone but him. Can't you see? Everyone knows about his patterns in such matters. *Everyone.* Except you, of course. But now you do, and now surely you can't want to stay here!"

Bridget kept staring at her visitor, unable to speak. The room grew quiet. She couldn't answer. She couldn't say a word yet. But she knew what she wanted to do. She only hoped she could decide what it was that she *should* do.

18

"And here are some of the invitations," the woman who claimed she was Ewen's wife said, lifting a packet of yellowed cards tied with ribbon from the little chest resting on the table in front of her. "Over a hundred were sent out, but I'm lucky to have even these few in my possession," she said smugly. "Most of the guests kept theirs as souvenirs, since it was the affair of the season. But since some of them weren't well known, at least in the countryside—though they were famous in London, of course—their cards were given to the butler as they arrived so their names could be announced. I kept them. I am *such* a sentimental creature."

Bridget touched them with a trembling finger. The flowing script on the top one bore the names of an earl and his lady. She licked dry lips and raised her eyes to the serene blue gaze of the woman.

"But these could be name cards responding to anything—invitations to a dinner party, a concert, a dance," Bridget said. "I have only your word it was for a wedding."

Silently the lady handed her another packet from the box. Bridget read the top card, or at least she did until her eyes blurred with sudden tears.

The honor of your presence is requested
at the nuptials of
The Honorable Elise Honoria Elizabeth Evans
daughter of
Lord Henry Thomas Evans and Lady E. Evans
to
Ewen Kenton Philip Sinclair,
Viscount Sinclair, Baron Paige, son of

Bridget read no further, but kept her head bent, trying to think. There was so much to take in. She'd asked for proof. No sooner had she asked than the lady summoned her servant and asked her to bring the little gilt chest from her room. The drab woman scurried to her bidding. Then she'd stood back in the shadows behind her mistress, awaiting further orders.

Lady Elise carefully opened the little chest and one by one showed Bridget her yellowed souvenirs, each with a story linking her to Ewen. Pressed flowers from her first ball; dance cards from a dozen assemblies with his name scrawled on every one of them; place cards from her bridal breakfast; and now invitations to her wedding with Ewen.

So much evidence of the past, Bridget thought miserably.

But she had evidence, too, evidence she couldn't deny or disprove. She saw Ewen's face before her. She remembered his kiss, his touch, the gentle way he'd loved her, the fiery way he'd taught her to love him, the things he'd told her, the steady look in his eye when he'd left her, the essential power and force and truth of the man, and his caring for her. She raised her head. Her voice was steady now and her eyes were clear. It was as though she could still hear Ewen's low, loving voice in her ear.

"I've seen all your mementos," she said defiantly, "all except for one. The most important one. I haven't seen your wedding lines. If you have them, I should like to see them."

"Should you?" the lady asked with a cold smile. "The audacity of the chit!" she commented over her shoulder to her silent servant. "So you should, I suppose, so you should," she mused, tapping her slender white fingers on the little gilt chest.

Then her blue eyes blazed. "But you shall not! Do you think I'm daft? Why, you might snatch them and throw them into the fire! Not that it would matter. The world knows who I am. But they are precious to me, if only because I am a sentimental fool. Once I loved him, you see. If I didn't have his faithfulness, at least I have his name. And so I will keep my wedding lines safe—from him, and from his . . . familiars.

"Look you, my girl," she said, snatching the cards from Bridget's hand, tossing them into the box, and slamming it closed, "I've dallied with you long enough. I've been beyond fair about this. And see how I'm served for my pity, eh?" she asked her servant, rising and handing her the chest.

"I will not put up with this any longer," she told Bridget, wheeling to face her again, "There's no reason for me to put up with this. You must leave. And at once."

"Ewen asked me to wait for him," Bridget said stubbornly, rising to her feet to face her.

"Have you no pride?" the lady demanded.

"Oh, pride in plenty," Bridget said, lifting her chin, "but faithfulness, too. I'm also a woman of my word. I told him I'd wait for him, and wait I shall."

"I can have you thrown out, you know," the lady said furiously, "and I will. But I'd rather not. I don't need more gossip, or a scene, good God, not a scene! I've my Louis to consider. He knows his father is a rake, poor child, but a scene on the doorstep of what I've told him is to be his new home? And after all I said about his father's promise to reform? It will not do!" She paced the room once and then came to a stop in front of Bridget.

"Listen, and listen well," she said, shaking a finger in front of Bridget's face. "I'll give you until morning. That's only fair. This must have been a shock to you; you haven't had time to think clearly. I understand that. I give you until tomorrow morning, then. You may think I'm cruel, but I am trying to be fair, too. I could simply cast you out; there isn't a servant here who wouldn't obey me in that. *You* are the interloper, my dear. I am their mistress—not Ewen's. I am his wife.

"But I choose to be charitable. After all, I believe you are more sinned against than sinning. Although to run off with a man of Ewen's reputation . . . the thing speaks for itself. Still, there are no coaches leaving at this hour, anyway. I'll see you're taken to the coaching station first thing in the morning. Shall we say at first light? That way you'll have ample choice when you get to the station. And hear this. I'll give you funds for your fare, and more, though not immediately, to go toward establishing yourself in London—or wherever you care to establish yourself. Simply give me your direction and I'll be sure it gets there after you go. But go you shall. And remember: You can have the money only if you leave tomorrow morning, and not a second after.

"If you think you'll get more from Ewen by waiting for him, do not deceive yourself. I'll raise such a fuss he'll be afraid to give you tuppence! He's been waiting for me to come home for a decade; I hardly think you can have a stronger claim that that! And I do think you'd want to spare yourself the indignity of being bodily removed— you and those grimy creatures from the slums.

"Oh. I see you've forgotten them," she said, watching Bridget's expression change to fear at the thought of any harm coming to Betsy, and then change again, to terror, as she realized what would happen if Gilly flashed out with her knife against a noblewoman.

"Well, I have not," Lady Elise said, her blue eyes narrowing. "It's a shame and a scandal that they're here at all. Ewen's perversions must have become quite rococo— I don't want to know about them!" she said, raising a hand to stop Bridget's protests. "Well, but I am here to put a stop to that, too. Once he has me, he said, he'll want no others. I'll test him. That's what this visit was intended to do, and well he knows it. But before I do, I'll have them tossed out with you. Oh. I see you don't care for that.

"But I ask you," she said, stopping and staring into Bridget's eyes, "what would you do if you were me?"

"And the thing of it is," Bridget said as she paced her own room in front of Gilly and Betsy moments later, "I'd do the same if I were her. Wouldn't you?"

"Me?" Gilly asked, amazed. "What would I do if someone tried to take *my* place? I'd trounce her, I'd pound her, I would! She'd be lucky she still had a scrap of hair on her head when I was done with her! But see, there it is," she added craftily, "proof she ain't got a real claim on this place. See? She's giving you a chance to go by yourself, *and* she's giving you money, *and* she's letting you stay the night under her roof. Why? 'Cause it ain't her roof! Was it hers, she'd turf you out right out. It ain't. That's why she's so nice. She's *too* nice."

"No, there *you* are. There's her best proof. It's because she's a lady," Bridget sighed, "every inch a lady."

"Hah!" Gilly said. "Lady or no, if she was sure of her ground, you'd be out in the cold right now, you would. Bet on it. Why ain't she furious and raging and shrieking at you, eh?"

"Because she's a lady," Bridget said, but Gilly laughed.

"The more reason to carry on," Gilly replied. "You're a lady, and were it you, why, you'd turn and leave and not come back until he threw her out himself and begged you to forgive him for having her here in the first place. Wouldn't you? Or else have the servants toss her the minute you seen her here. You wouldn't waste words on her, would you? Ah, but not her. What does she do, huh? She chats with you. She listens to you and then she goes and listens to the servants. She did, din't she? Then she tries to bargain and bribe you out. Now she's trying to scare you out. She ain't all she appears to be, that I can tell you."

"The servants said so?" Bridget asked eagerly.

Gilly looked at the floor. "Nah, well, but they couldn't, y'see. Only Hines says he remembers her clear, and he's the only one can say it, 'cause he's the only one got a clear look at her. The others? The rest wasn't here then. Since them days, the footmen and maids is all different—some went to the city, like so many's doing these days, some got married, some just up and quit. Them kinda servants don't hang around too long, leastways not at a house what don't see much activity—guests coming and going, to tip them for service, y'see."

"But the housekeeper," Bridget said, "surely she was here then."

"Aye. And she looked at his lady, too. But she din't see her. Couldn't. Her eyes are a scandal."

"But she does such neat mending!"

"That's all she *can* see. Put her nose on a hem, she'll sew like an angel. But unless she put her nose right on him, she couldn't see the Angel Gabriel in front of her if he came to call."

"Cook?" Bridget asked. "What about her? What does she say? She's been here forever, too, hasn't she?"

"Aye, but what's a cook got to do with a fine lady come for one night before she takes off on her honeymoon?" Gilly asked scornfully. "She just got a glimpse of her. All's she remembers is a elegant lady, all blond and smiles."

"But the boy," Bridget asked, "her son, Louis. Did you speak with him?"

Gilly exchanged a worried glance with Betsy. Bridget's spirits plummeted.

"Aye, for all the good it was worth," Gilly said, head down and scowling. "He don't speak to servants, says he. I asked him if he'd care to put up his fives with a *servant*, and he said he'd have me tossed out on my arse if I din't leave 'immedjit.' He don't speak like no foreigner, there's that. But he don't speak like no honest Englishman, neither. Anyways, he shut the door on my nose. They must have told him not to talk to no one. Whatever they done, he din't need no icing on his nasty, and there's truth."

"I didn't see his eyes from close enough," Bridget said nervously. "Tell me—are they blue or . . . hazel?"

"They ain't neither. Muddy is what I'd call them," Gilly snarled.

"Ah," Bridget said, another hope fading. They weren't so different from Ewen's to make the lady's claim laughable.

"So what are you going to do, Miss Bridget?" Betsy asked tremulously.

Gilly looked up, waiting for her answer, too.

Bridget paced one way and then the other.

"I could go to London to look for him," she muttered as she walked back and forth. "But he said I should not, so I can't go there. Not that I'm afraid I'll find him with another woman—not that at all. But he said I should wait for him. I can't go to his father—not because I fear him, but because it would be embarrassing, you see. And Ireland is *so* far away, and I so need to see him now. . . ."

She paced some more. Then she turned tormented eyes to Gilly and Betsy. "Whatever I do, I think I have to go," she said finally. "She insisted, she said she'd put me out if I didn't go quietly. And both of you, too. No, don't say it! I know you can fight, Gilly. Yes, Betsy, I know you can shout the house down. But it would only make it go harder for you. She has the right, you see."

"Does she? What about your right, Miss Bridget?" Gilly said passionately. "What about all them things you said about trusting the man you love, eh? All them things about a good man's gallantry and nobility, and code of honor and all, and about you knowing what you was doing when you trusted him? Huh? What about that?"

She argues like a child who doesn't want to hear there's no Father Christmas, Bridget thought in astonishment.

"Gilly, I know those things," she said, "and they're true. But—but the thing of it is that he's not here now, and she is, and Hines supports her, and I don't want an embarrassing scene . . . or worse. Why, she could call in the local magistrate, and I have no friends here except for you. And no relatives either, anywhere in England. No one but the Viscount, really, and he's in London somewhere and he's told me not to join him, and I don't know when he'll return. The truth of it is that no matter the right of it, she *looks* like a viscountess, Gilly. And I look like a . . ."

The words "poor, scarred, foolish, deceived woman" hung in her mind, and from Gilly's expression, it was as though she'd said them aloud.

Gilly's eyes went blank and she shrugged. "Aye, well, we'll stand by you, Miss Bridget, no matter what you decide to do."

"But you said you loved him and he loved you," Betsy said, her chin trembling.

"So I did," Bridget said, kneeling to hand Betsy her handkerchief. "That won't change. And when he returns, why, then I'll speak to him, and you'll see, things will be right again."

Betsy looked doubtful. Gilly's mouth turned down, and she looked as if she thought Bridget had just told the biggest lie of all. And perhaps, Bridget thought as her heart grew cold, she had.

"So," she said too brightly, rising to her feet again, "are you ready to leave at dawn, with me?"

"We ain't got much to pack," Gilly said simply. Taking Betsy's hand, she left the room with her sister.

Bridget wished they hadn't gone. There was a whole afternoon and evening and night left to get through, to think and pace and wonder through. She looked around the bedchamber. The sunlight shone through bright windows, but Ewen's shadow was everywhere in the room. *That* was what she didn't want to leave. But that, too, was what she had to pass the long hours alone with, so she could copy it into her heart.

She walked through the room, trailing her fingers over the empty bed, the vacant chairs and settee. Here his head had rested. There he had sat sometimes and joked with her. Here was where he woke her with a kiss, and there where he settled her to sleep in his arms. Here, he had lain with her, there he had laughed with her. Would he be as real to her anywhere else?

Bridget's head went up. Why had she thought that? Did she believe she'd never see him again?

She no longer knew what to believe. She sat by the window finally, looking out over the drive, thinking about Ewen, wishing he would suddenly appear there and solve her problems as easily as he had caused them.

*　　　*　　　*

Ewen woke before first light, as he always did these
days. He didn't bother waking his valet. He dressed
himself, slipped from the townhouse, and went riding
out into the mists of morning. He galloped his horse
down long green paths, riding hard, as though he were
pursued by the Furies. He raised few eyebrows from the
other early riders in the park. They'd seen the tall, dark
gentleman riding like that every morning for weeks now.

He rode until he felt his horse's sides heaving, and
then they walked down the damp paths, smelling the
sweet summer scent of broken grass and damp earth.
When the sun broke through the haze of dawn, he rode
back home again. He gave his horse to the stable boy,
then went back to the house to wash and to atone to his
valet by letting him help change his clothing.

He sat only long enough to have biscuits and coffee
and then left, walking the several streets to Monsieur
Delacroix's academy. There he passed an hour fencing
with the master himself, applauding his opponent and
taking his praise in return. They shook hands at the end,
declaring another draw, before he put on his jacket and
left. Once in the street, he rolled his shoulders to ease
the tightness he still felt there. It was only a few more
streets to Gentleman Jackson's. A *good sparring match*, he
thought.

But glancing up, he saw the height of the sun. He
reluctantly turned and walked to the discreet townhouse, so near the palace, where he'd spent each afternoon for weeks now.

As he took the stairs to his office he wished he'd
taken the time to have gone a few rounds after all. He
still felt edgy, tense, and restless. But he knew there
was nothing that would ease him. Not riding, sparring,

fencing, drinking . . . he'd tried them all in recent days. Nothing could cure him but her. He needed to get back to her, to talk to her, to tell her, to explain. And then to take her in his arms and let her take him far from himself and all the mistakes he'd made and would try to make up for.

He sighed as he opened the door to his office.

"About time you arrived," the man sitting in his chair said with a crooked smile.

"Rafe!" Ewen shouted.

The two men embraced, laughing like boys. Then they spent some time slapping each other on the shoulders, pounding each other's backs.

"Well met!" Ewen finally said. "You're back. The mission was a success?"

His redheaded friend frowned. "Devil take it, no. Don't know much more now than then. The damned little emperor may be planning something, and he may not be. Colonel Campbell says he's there to stay. Campbell's a good man and the right one for the job; I trust him to keep that devil in his place. But I'm not so sure he's right, Ewen. Bonaparte's too clever by half. He could charm birds from the trees, because he's half snake. Imagine—I met him face-to-face."

Rafe laughed mirthlessly. "That was all I dreamed of doing—all those months in the peninsula, all that time I was in hospital there. I dreamed of facing him and blowing his damned head off. Still do, but I couldn't do more than shake his hand when we did meet. So I can't say the mission was a success in any way."

"But it was," Ewen said, smiling. "You're back, fit, and just as sour as you were before. I'd say you thrive. But best of all, my dear dour friend, I'm free now."

"Free?" Rafe frowned.

"To go home, of course."

"How does your father do?" Rafe asked at once.

"He's well, I assure you. I'm not going there right away. I've a stop to make at Brook House first."

"Ah." Rafe's craggy face grew grave and guarded. "Brook House, is it? How is the lovely Bridget?"

"I don't know for certain," Ewen said. "That's the point. She's there now, where I left her. I got word of your trouble and tore back to London by myself. I've been here since." He looked at his friend measuringly, his expression thoughtful. "What are your plans now, Rafe?"

"A bit of this, a taste of that. My usual ramblings, I suppose. Why do you ask?"

Ewen sat back on the edge of his desk, looking at his friend. "I thought perhaps you might like to come with me."

"What? But you said your father's doing well. What do you need me for? You've got lovely Bridget. I'd be like a fifth leg on a horse at your little hideaway."

"Not exactly," Ewen said. His eyes were troubled, though he kept his voice light. He glanced down at his sleeve and brushed at an invisible spot there. For that fleeting second, the cool, urbane, ever facile Viscount Sinclair seemed uncertain and awkward. It was so strange that Rafe blinked. *Like seeing a cat miss a step*, he thought, intrigued and a little worried now.

"I'm going to have to talk with her," Ewen said, avoiding Rafe's fascinated eyes, "and when I'm done I'm going to need a friend with me. Two, I think, now that I see you again. I've already asked Drum to come along. I told him the whole truth about Bridget—and Elise," he added simply.

Rafe stared. "You told him?" he echoed.

"Well, but it was time. You were right. None of this has been what I'd thought it would be—no. Rather, Bridget isn't what I thought a woman to be. It's no longer a matter of what's prudent; it's become a matter of the heart—my heart, paltry thing that it is. She helped me discover it again, you know. I'd hidden it away so long, I think I'd forgotten about it."

He twitched one broad shoulder, as though the sentimentality in his voice disturbed him. "In any event, I haven't told her either."

Rafe went still.

"Yes, I know, I'm a fool. I meant to, I would have, but events conspired . . . in short, I didn't. And so," Ewen said with a shrug, avoiding his friend's eyes, "I must, and then ask her pardon. And in this case I don't know if my words alone will do the trick."

Rafe's eyes widened. He had never thought he'd ever hear Ewen Sinclair say such a thing.

"I need you to support me after I speak with her," Ewen went on. "Specifically, I need you and Drum to tell her"—Ewen raised his changeable eyes to Rafe, and there was rueful amusement in them—"that I'm not such a bad fellow after all, no matter what I've done. Do you think you can do that for me?"

"Of course!" Rafe snapped. "I think it, so I'll say it."

"Hold!" Ewen said. "A fine sentiment, but it may not be so easy. There is the matter of my reputation to dance around."

"Reputation? You've done some mad things in your time. Who has not? But I've never known you to be cruel or unfair." Rafe frowned. "Oh. The rake thing, is it? Well, even that isn't such a bad thing. Shocks the blue-nosed. But it was for the good of us all."

Ewen gave a short bark of a laugh. "Cut line, you
know me better than that. They said I was a rake, and it
helped our cause. True. But my dear friend, I practiced
what I played. I *was* a rake."

"Well, there you are," Rafe said stoutly. "You pay for
your pleasures and always take responsibility for them.
A rake? Maybe. But you're an honest man for all that."

"No, not such an honest man, as it turns out," Ewen
said softly, sadly. "And apart from that, a rake is never
completely honest, not really. Not with himself or his
consorts. Not a successful one, at any rate. And I was."
He gave his friend a long, steady look. "It's been easy for
me to acquire women, Rafe. Too easy. And there were
too many of them. Such simplicity. And such a simple
act I always achieved with them. A meeting of two bodies and a moment of pleasure. Dogs, I think," he said
with a twisted smile, "make more of it than that.

"But me and my light ladies?" He laughed. "*Light* is an
apt description. All of it had no more weight than a
feather. Airy love. A simple offer to a simple act, easily
done, more easily forgotten. A pretty face or a stimulat-
ing shape, and it begins. A few hours later, the thing is
done, and what of it?"

"Easy for *you*," Rafe grumbled.

"For you, too. Here, I give you my formula," Ewen
said with a mocking smile and a short bow. "These are
the ingredients: A man. A woman. A look of apprecia-
tion, followed by a knowing smile. Let it sit in the
moonlight until the air thickens. When there's a flutter
of an eyelash or a fan, smile again. When there's an
answering smile, add a tribute to her eyes or nose, or
whatever appears to be her proudest possession.
Sprinkle with pretty phrases, blend with meaningful

gazes. Stir her with a whisper, fold in an embrace, drop a light kiss—as sample of pleasure to come. Don't add a pinch, whatever you do; it must all go smoothly. Only stroke and caress lightly, then make the assignation, quickly followed by an act of what we chose to call love, for want of a word that won't get us shown immediately to the door.

"There you are. Done. A tasty way to end an evening or start a day. Simplicity itself. But as for me, once my simple aim was achieved, I simply always forgot why I'd wanted it so badly. I suppose they did, too. But not this time."

His hand made a fist, and he stared at it. "I didn't understand what intimacy was. Everything was going as usual, and then . . . I found her, I wanted her, and because she was in difficulties, I—" His voice caught and he paused. He bent his dark head.

"Rafe," he said, urgently, his eyes glowing, "she turned me round. It's an astonishing thing. A responsibility and an honor. Something I never thought to find: a friend and a lover." He shook his head and straightened. Rising, he started gathering papers from his desk. "Anyhow," he said over his shoulder, "you're back, so my job here is done. I'll speak to the old gentleman and be gone from London by sunset."

Rafe's rusty eyebrows went up. "Leaving London in the evening? Riding through the night? Gad! You *will* need escorts. My bags are still packed, my pistols primed, too. I'll be ready to ride. But . . ." He hesitated before he spoke again. That was so rare Ewen looked up at him.

"Ewen," he said with difficulty, "how the devil do you think she'll take it?"

"She's clear water, Rafe. Pure and good, and completely honest. She'll be shocked. Dismayed that I didn't tell her, of course. But I think in the end, she'll understand and forgive."

"And if she doesn't?"

"Then I don't know her after all, do I? But I do. She trusts me, Rafe, I know that, or I know nothing in this life at all. With all I've done, she trusts me. As I do her. She's been anxious and fearful, and why not? I suddenly left her alone in a strange place, on what was supposed to be her honeymoon. I've been gone a long time, so long that she keeps writing, begging me to let her join me here. But I've told her to wait for me. She is waiting, because she trusts me. And so whatever I tell her, I don't think she'll disappoint me. She won't let me down."

The moon rose over the trees, and Bridget finally got into bed. There was no more sense in pacing and plotting and planning anymore. Everything she owned was packed and secured, and ready to leave. So was she, at last.

19

They took the Great North Road and left London behind them, riding quickly and silently into the deepening night. Many men would have been afraid of leaving London in such a fashion at that late hour. There were only three of them, after all, and all of them on horseback, instead of riding in a carriage, with coachmen and outriders to see to the dangers on the moonlit roads.

But these three men didn't worry about highwaymen; they themselves were lethal. Two had been trained in ways of swiftly and silently taking the enemy down, and the third had played with instruments of death all his life, as many men of his age and class were trained to do. They were all experts, all fearless, all able-bodied. One of them was dead set on getting to his destination as fast as he could, and damned to the hour or the season. The other two valued him so much they would have followed him into hell itself, much less the English countryside.

Not that it was that easy. Especially in the black velvet folds of a late summer's night.

They didn't speak at first, and then as the hours wore on, they fell under the spell of their friend's urgency and the dreaming night itself. They rode without complaint, only stopping when they had to—they had more consideration for their horses than themselves.

The spoke together at the first stop they made, at an inn near a tollbooth two hours' ride from London.

"Good thing you've got fair weather," Rafe said as he took another swallow of ale.

"He'd race through a hurricane, the way he is now," Drum said. "Don't you see that look in his eye?"

"We're crazed as he is," Rafe said darkly, "and will pay for it, I reckon. At least we'll make someone happy—aside from Ewen. There are probably hordes of robbers in the hedgerows, just waiting for fools like us."

"Sorry to disappoint you," Ewen said dryly, "but this is England, not Italy, my friend. There are no highwaymen here."

"Ha!" Rafe grunted. "Famous last words."

"Famous indeed," Ewen said, "or rather, infamous—and historical, too. They're a century past, a world away, my friend. Spiders nest on their headstones now. Bow Street put an end to that sport. There's the odd road robbery these days, that's true. But even then, most self-respecting highwaymen insist on inconveniencing at least a coachful of victims for their trouble. Who'd bother to lurk on a dark road in the middle of the night in hopes of some stray madman happening along?"

"Too true," Drum commented. "And if they did see us, three men pounding down the road riding like they were pursued by devils through the night? They'd probably beg *us* for mercy. As I do now beg you, Ewen. If there are no highwaymen, perhaps we could take it easy. I don't want to break my horse's legs, or my own. It's like riding through ink out there."

"We'll keep to the main road," Ewen said, "and the ink is the disappearing sort. The moon's up, half full. Ride straight and no harm will come."

"But where's the sense in it? Everyone will be sleeping when we get there, anyway."

"You can stay here, then, and meet me later," Ewen said, putting down his empty tankard. "But I must be going."

"Damn," Drum sighed, rising, too.

"There's sudden storms at this time of the year," Rafe offered. "I saw some stars put out by clouds a while back. You sure you want to go on further tonight, Ewen? This isn't a bad place. If it's not far enough along for you, there's a neat little inn near Wallingford."

"It isn't far enough by half," Ewen said. "I want to keep riding until I get there."

"We're not birds. We don't have to be there before first light," Rafe complained. "We can get a good night's sleep and be there in the morning."

"Everything looks better in the morning," Drum said with a jaw-cracking yawn.

"I want to be there sooner," Ewen said, drawing on his gloves.

They left.

But, in the end, they did have to stop for the night. Ewen's horse pulled up lame. There was no question of leaving the beast alone on the road. Ewen rode double with Rafe, until that gentleman's I-told-you-so's drove him to share Drum's horse with him. Drum's incessant grumbling about the madness of his own actions persuaded Ewen to take rooms at the inn they finally reached.

"Be there after breakfast, a civilized hour," Drum said contentedly as he signed the register for a sleepy landlord.

Wordlessly, his dark face like thunder, Ewen paced up the stairs beside his friends.

"What's so magical about dawn, anyway?" Rafe yawned.

Ewen said nothing as he left them. He didn't say how magical it could have been for him. He didn't tell them how he'd dreamed of arriving at Brook House to find her sleeping, warm and drowsy in their bed. Or about how he'd planned to tiptoe into their bedroom, strip off his clothing, and slide into bed, joining her there. First he'd have stayed quiet beside her, letting the chill of his night ride leave his hands and body, warming himself by watching her sleeping face, reveling in the very fact of her nearness again. Then he'd have wakened her, slowly, luxuriously, his hands soft and stealthy as they stroked her soft body and her small, silken breasts, his lips feathering over her smooth, warm neck, her sleep-flushed cheek, her slightly parted dreaming mouth. At last he'd take her soft surprised cry into his mouth, and bear her back into the bed with him.

But these were not thoughts to serve him well when he was trying to sleep.

So he didn't. He couldn't. He was in that state too well known to travelers, halfway to his destination, his heart still racing as fast as his body had been, his mind even busier with thoughts of what he had to do when he got there. He stripped off his clothing, lay on the bed, and groaned. It would have been difficult to sleep even if the bed were comfortable. It was not. He was a big man with a long body. The bed was designed for the average traveler and had been used by so many of them it had conformed to every shape it had known except for his, he thought wryly as he turned, trying and failing to get comfortable.

But that was impossible. It had little to do with the bed, really, only with what wasn't in it with him. So he lay wide-eyed, hands linked behind his head, staring into the dreaming night, waiting for morning and the task he'd set himself.

He couldn't wait to get back to her. He'd missed her, and not just her body. That astonished him still. So many women, so many welcoming bodies, so many pleasures, and not one of them to compare to what he'd found with her.

He liked women, always had. He'd even loved a few. His mother, in the brief time he'd known her. Those first few females who'd shown him kindness: his nurse, an aunt, a cousin or two. And when he'd become a man, he'd even thought he'd loved the way a man should. He'd had his first infatuations. They'd all ended in sighs, but not sighs of repletion, because they'd all been gently bred girls, and because he'd come to know them too well to stay infatuated—or they'd found other men to love. That hadn't surprised him. He'd been a bashful youth, though no one could know it now. Few realized it then. He'd covered it with the glaze of smiling boredom, as so many young men of his age and rank did.

He'd had some women friends in those days, and still did. They were friends of the mind, not the heart: wives of friends, or confirmed spinsters who offered carefully intellectual friendship to him because they'd seen that he was a man who respected any good mind of either sex.

But as for love? He hadn't precisely loved Elise. He'd been awed by her and eager to wed her. He'd meant to be a good husband, but where that had led him? He turned in his lumpy bed again, wincing at memories of his marriage bed. Then, of course, Ewen the rake had been born, and had loved so many women—and not truly loved a single one of them.

But then . . . He thought of Bridget again. Who would have thought such felicity could spring from a light-hearted, lust-driven offer? He'd seen her and wanted her. She'd shone out from the sad company she'd been sitting in; he'd glanced across the room and seen the wallflowers and dowagers and . . . her. That lovely face, blazing with life and intelligence, yet also filled with sadness. So vulnerable—and so desirable to him.

What had he been thinking? he wondered now. That he'd be doing her a favor because of that scar? That damned, blessed scar that had preserved her for him by keeping fools from seeking the loveliness behind it? No. Impossible. Because he hadn't seen it at first. Not until she'd seen him staring and had raised that small chin and turned to him full face, staring back with challenge, pride, and defiance. That and not the scar was what had made him determined to have her.

He was a good hunter. He'd watched from the corner of his eye, carrying on a dozen dull conversations and limping flirtations, all the while alert to his opportunity, awaiting his chance. It came when her blasted aunt had seen his interest. As soon as he could, he'd followed her into her exile and broached his offer to her. She'd refused him with spirit and intelligence—and just a trace of longing. That had been enough to make him try and try again. But by their first real meeting he knew he could have her.

He had, and yet it was not enough for him. He wondered if it would ever be. He wanted her entirely, but she still withheld a part of herself. She was open with him in so many ways, but wary, too. He'd wooed her. That was easy. He'd won her, but that was something else again. It was a thing he could do. But what had he won from her? She seemed to care for him, but with all they'd done, she'd never declared her feelings for him in anything but her actions. That had never bothered him in any of his prior relationship with females; it had never even *occurred* to him before.

He laughed bitterly to the empty night. What right had *he* to demand all of her secrets? Well, but he was going to correct that matter now. He was on his way to do it. Thinking of it kept his eyes wide even though all he could see was the blindness of the night and the doubts in his future. Thinking of her kept his heart racing.

He cared about what she thought of him, found with him. Not only in their bed, not just what she thought of his skill in the act of love. He'd known too many women to worry about that. Any man with experience and expertise could pleasure a woman. Or could appear to—with a woman who pretended it. He'd had enough of that, too. The women he'd brought to his bed in the past had been like the bed he lay in now—too accommodating to too many other passing strangers, and so never exactly right for him. He hadn't known it then. He knew it now. Since Bridget.

Any willing woman could bring a man pleasure. Many had brought it to him. None had ever brought him ease before, or such laughter, or peace. Her presence made him feel right and whole. There it was, he thought. He felt uncomfortable here—he'd feel so anywhere she was not. She made him feel at home, at last.

It was that simple. And that difficult. And that unexpected. Because even with all his wide experience, he'd never known that before, and so had never guessed what a risk it was. But with all he was, he wasn't a coward. He waited for morning, when he could go to her and tell her everything he'd thought tonight. At last. No matter what happened afterward.

Bats flew home across the face of the setting moon. No bird sang. The crickets hadn't ceased their slow pulsings yet; they still counted the minutes left to the ebbing night. But Bridget knew dawn was coming. She rose from her bed as the stars began to fade and the sky turned milky with a hint of the dawn to come. She saw the slight changes because she'd watched through the night. She hadn't slept. She'd stared into the darkness, thinking, wondering, and then finally deciding what had to be, definitely, no matter how hard it would be.

The decision had been made. Now she had to be strong enough to implement it. But she *was* strong, she told herself, and rose from bed at last.

She rubbed eyes gritty from a night of wakefulness and washed her face. She dressed hurriedly. Then she looked across the room once last time. It was gray in the half-light of approaching day. Now all the rich colors in the silken coverlets on her high bed, the fine furniture, even the paintings that hung on the wall were muted to the same pale shadows of dawn. It looked like the ghost of the room she'd known. And so it was.

Now it was time for reality. She nodded to herself and raised her chin. Everything that belonged to her was in the traveling bag by the door. Nothing of hers remained here now—only everything she'd ever wanted and loved. She turned her back on it.

She cracked open the door, stepped into the hall, and stumbled over a body on her doorsill.

"Wha . . . ? Oh, it's you," Gilly said with a huge yawn, sitting up and rubbing her ribs.

"You slept here?" Bridget asked in astonishment.

"I slept in worse places," Gilly said cheerfully as she rose to her feet. "Leastways this way I din't miss you, did I? Well, then, so you meant it, eh? Leaving with the light, like that bitch asked, are you? Well, I don't blame you. Can't say I'd do different. Needs must when the devil drives, like they says. But if it makes you feel any better, I'm that sorry for it. On that head . . . listen, Miss Bridget, one thing afore we go."

Gilly sounded embarrassed, uneasy. She occupied herself with scratching under the loose man's jacket she wore, looking down at the heap of clothing she'd slept on as she did. "Thing is," she said hesitantly, "I been thinking. How you going to earn your way now? That witch downstairs is sure to spread the story 'cross London, and so from now on you can bet no one of the quality is going to let you in their back door to scrub their floors, much less be a companion no more! And Ireland is a far piece, to be sure. But see—if you come to London with Betsy and me, I could find you a job of work.

"Wait, listen," Gilly said fervently. "I know you're not in the game. But a good girl can be fooled, or there wouldn't be so many poor bastards cluttering the streets of London, would there? No, it ain't work on your back, or *with* your back neither, nor is it work with your hands, 'cause you're not used to such. You're a lady. At least, to me you are. And so I know you'll be that to them what I know, too."

Bridget frowned. Gilly talked faster, trying to explain. "See, the world's changing," she said. "A man with coins to jingle in his purse can move up now. I ain't saying he's going to be invited to tea with the Queen, mind. But if he's got the gelt to do it, he can live on a street next to gentry, can't he? He can dress up fine and go to Vauxhall and rub elbows with them, too, if he wants. And he wants, believe me. His wife can go to the opera and sit right across from them. And if he sends his kids to the right schools—why, who knows what can happen someday?

"*If* he knows how to behave, that is. Look, Miss Bridget," Gilly said, looking up at Bridget at last, "Betsy purely loves you and you and I get along, don't we? What I'm saying is that there's plenty of them what would like to rise in the world, and they got the gold but not the language or the manners to do it. You could teach them! I could see to it. You could make good money at it, too. So, why don't you come live with us, Betsy and me? We could do fine together, us three. Well, how about it?"

Bridget started to speak, but her voice caught in her throat. All that came out was a choked gulp. She cleared her throat, blinked back tears, and tried again.

"Gilly, I'm so honored. I thank you so much. I've been

doing some thinking, too. I don't want us to part, either."

"There we are," Gilly said almost gaily, though her face was strained and white. "Well, let's collect Betsy. I promised her I'd come soon as I saw you." She stooped, scooped up her clothes, and rolled them into a bundle. "Got all I come with," she muttered. "That's all a body can expect to leave with, right?"

"No," Bridget said, drawing a deep, painful breath. "That's all a lucky person can leave with. I'm going downstairs. But I'm not leaving so soon. I'll wait for the lady instead. I have some things to say to her now. I don't know if Betsy ought to be there when I do."

"Ha! Nothing she'd like better than to hear you tell her a thing or two, I promise you! Be good for her. Though I think she knows better words than you'll use."

Bridget smiled. "No, not this time. This time I think even you'll be surprised, Gilly." She squared her shoulders. "Let's go get Betsy," she said.

Experienced travelers, both Rafe and Drum slept deeply in their separate beds. But they both rose before dawn, if only because even in their sleeping minds they knew Ewen would ride on without them if they didn't. They didn't want to miss a thing that happened at Brook House. Ewen was a driven man, Ewen was a changed man, but he was the same man they both valued as a friend. And they were wildly curious.

They dressed in the dark and ate a hurried bite of breakfast in the rising gray of the broken night. They saddled and rode quickly, making such good time that they reached the long drive in front of Brook House as the sun began to brighten the morning mists from gray to pearl. They swung off their horses, to the shocked surprise of the stable boys who were standing waiting in the drive. Ewen's country coach stood there, too, but he didn't spare a glance at it as he went up the steps to the front door. Rafe and Drummond were a foot behind him and so saw him beginning to smile, slowly, in sensuous expectation.

Ewen paused only a moment, realizing the extent of his disheveled state. He tugged down his jacket and ran a hand through his thick wind-tousled hair. He brushed dust from his breeches, straightened, and, finding the door already open, went inside, his friend and his cousin following on his heels. They stepped into the vast glass-enclosed courtyard, blinking. The brightness of the rising sun was amplified by the glass dome, and the brilliance of it temporarily blinded them.

But that wasn't what stopped them. They halted in their tracks at the sound of a strident female voice.

"So," the cold, clear voice said, "you're here. That's good. I came to be sure, you see."

Rafe and Drum looked around quickly and so didn't see Ewen stand arrested, the color draining from his face. But the voice wasn't referring to him or them.

"You're a clever girl," it went on, speaking to someone they couldn't see. "You've done the right thing. I've a purse for you here. You'll find I haven't been stingy. You'll get the rest when you reach your destination. Just send word back with the coachman. He's waiting. I bid you adieu."

There was a silence.

"Come, come," the voice said impatiently, "the price won't go up if you resist. The sun is well up. Time to leave. Now, take the purse and go!"

The men narrowed their eyes against the radiant brightness, straining to see who was speaking and who was being urged to leave. The voice seemed to be coming from above them. They looked up to see a tall, golden-haired female in a flowing robe of white standing straight-backed on the stair, looking like an angel outlined by dazzling light. As they squinted they saw three other figures entering the room, walking slowly into the glowing light, hesitant as new souls tentatively entering heaven. The woman on the stair looked like an avenging angel, ordering them out again.

She spoke again, her voice impatient. "Come along now! Nothing's changed. A delay will only cost you. I don't care if you miss your coach. But I vow your slippers will!"

"No," Bridget said, stopping opposite her, "I think not. I got up early, too, but only to be sure to speak to you personally. I'm not here to bargain, either. I'm not leaving, you see."

Gilly and Betsy paused at her side, looking up at her.

"And so," Bridget said firmly, her head held high, "if you want me to go, I suppose you must put me out. Because I won't leave of my own free will. Ewen brought me here, and here I stay until he himself puts me out."

"And you think he won't?" Lady Elise asked from her position on the stair. She laughed, the brittle sound echoing around the bright glass room. Ewen's hands closed to fists at his sides. But he neither moved nor spoke. He couldn't. Because he couldn't believe his eyes or ears.

"Very well, very well," Lady Elise said, her voice simmering with fury. "I you don't care about the shame of it—and why should you, being the creature you are?—

then I suppose I must. But I won't just put you out. Oh, no. I don't want you hanging about the place, sleeping in the barns, peering in windows, distressing me and the servants and my poor dear Louis. No. I'll send for the local magistrate and have you evicted—and incarcerated in whatever jail they have here.

"Think carefully. You think Ewen will come to free you? He won't. Not just because I won't allow it, and he wants above all else to please me now. But because I know him of old. I'll meet him in London or at his father's estate. There's been enough gossip here, thank you—and thanks to you, too. I'll tell him what happened. Knowing him, he'll leave you wherever the magistrate puts you for a month—at the least—for a lesson. Although he won't put it that way. Oh, no, not he. When he finally has you let out, he'll send a note filled with apologies. The man is good at apologies! Haven't I heard them often enough?"

Bridget swayed a little. Her hands were trembling and her mouth was dry. She knew Ewen, she'd swear she did. But this woman was so convincing.

"The note will be filled with insincere guilt and many excuses," the lady went on, "and a far smaller payment than I'd give you now. That, at least, I can promise you! You ought to be compensated for his pleasure, I don't deny that. But I'll see that you starve if you try to hold me up for more now. Well? Last chance. Leave now and take the coach far from us. Or take the consequences."

"I'm staying, and I'll face the consequences," Bridget said. "Whatever you say, whatever ancient bits of paper you show me, whatever proofs you do or do not offer me—I'll stay and wait for Ewen. He would *not* lie to me. He—"

She stopped because Betsy was tugging at her skirt and pointing.

"Very well," the lady said furiously. She reached for the bellpull at the side of the stair to summon servants . . . but her hand paused on the cord. She turned her head to see what Bridget and the two girls were staring at.

Three tall men stood in the last shadows by the door. One stepped forward, his hands closed to fists at his side.

"*Ewen?*" Bridget cried in a glad voice. He was here! He and his redheaded friend, and his cousin, too. But it was Ewen! She took a step—and stopped, because he was standing straight and still. He was staring at the lady. And she at him. And she was smiling.

"Ewen," the lady said in a silken, satisfied voice. "It is you! Lord! I scarcely recognized you—you have changed. For the better, I must say."

"Elise," he said in a deep, dark voice, and Bridget could feel her blood chill in her veins.

"Yes," the lady said, smiling, "it is I. I'm back, as you see. And not from the dead, as this . . . person said you told her."

Bridget couldn't read his expression. He had none at all. "Ewen?" she asked, her voice quavering. "You know her? She is Elise? *Your* Elise?"

He didn't answer. His eyes were on the woman in white.

"Ewen?" Bridget said again, her own face white, her heart pounding so loudly she could scarcely hear the words she said.

She shook her head, as though that might clear the confusion and pain she felt thrumming through it. She could not, would not ask if he had lied to her. She couldn't ask if he was married to another. That would be asking if everything they had together was a lie. Looking at him now, at that dear strong face, feeling the strength of his presence, she couldn't doubt him or herself. She could only address the thing a lie at a time. She knew they were lies. She refused to believe they were *his* lies. She forced herself to ask what she had to, in the only way she could.

"Ewen," she said, "*she* says you married her."

He turned his head from the lady finally. He looked at Bridget. His face was taut, his eyes glazed with pain, alive with a wild light. His voice was strained when he finally spoke. But it was deep and slow and clear.

"I did," he said.

The lady laughed. Bridget swayed on her feet and would have stumbled if Gilly hadn't been there to steady her . . . and if Ewen hadn't strode forward to put his hands hard on her shoulders, gripping them tightly.

He looked down at her. A world of betrayal and loss was clear in her eyes. She raised a hand and touched his face lightly, as though to convince herself that it was he. He was troubled; it made him look younger, more vulnerable than she'd ever seen him. But he also looked tired, and his eyes were stricken. She saw how he'd be when he was very old and weary with life.

"You did?" she whispered, hoping she'd misheard him.

He nodded.

"She is your *wife*?" she said, anguished.

"No," he said, shaking his head, his voice shaking, too. "No, my dear. *That* she is not."

20

"**Y**ou married her, but she isn't your wife? What are you talking about? I don't understand, it makes no sense," Bridget murmured wretchedly, searching Ewen's eyes for an explanation of the incomprehensible.

"It does," he muttered angrily. "God help us all, but it makes too much sense. What are you doing here?" he demanded.

He felt her slender shoulders stiffen with shock. His hands tightened and he rocked her gently to and fro, shaking her gently to banish her look of shock. "Her—I was talking to her. I heard what you were doing here," he told her in low urgent tones. "Thank you for your faith in me. I don't think you could have given me more.

"What are you doing here?" he repeated, raising his gaze to glower at Elise.

"What do you think?" Elise asked. But her voice was less assured.

"God alone knows," he growled. "I thought I'd never see you again. You knew I'd no wish to. I ignored your notes over the years. I directed them to my man at law. I certainly never thought to see you in England again. Have you run mad?"

Her head went up as though he'd slapped her. "I had to talk with you," she snapped. A second later her voice became gentle, soft, beguiling. "What sort of a monster do you think I am? When I heard of your father's death, of course I had to come, whatever the risks to myself."

Bridget saw the blood leave his tanned face, making it suddenly grim and sallow.

"We have our past, to be sure," Elise went on, "but I'm not an unfeeling monster. I know what you thought of your father. We do share that history, and so I knew you'd need someone to talk with. I thought you knew me better than that, Ewen," she chided him.

"Oh, be sure that I do. But how long have you been here? You were in France . . . I heard you went to Italy," he said slowly. "Or did you return here, in secret, before this?"

"Oh, no, I've been living abroad. The war made life difficult, but not unduly; we've too many friends on both sides. We do what we must. I managed to survive." She shrugged, as though her glowing looks and expensive gown were nothing to speak of.

"I only came here for you," she went on. "I'd a letter from Georgette Halliday. Remember her? An old friend. And one—the only one—who did not desert me. She wrote to tell me about how the Earl was at death's door.

Naturally, I packed instantly and came to offer you whatever comfort I could, whatever the danger to myself. I knew you didn't open my letters—at any rate, a letter is cold comfort, is it not? I arrived in London a few weeks ago, sought you there—rather, had my servants do that. They were told you'd gone to your father's deathbed. I'd have followed, but that's hardly the best place for me, you'll agree. But neither did I wish to be seen in London. I went to an inn on the north road and sent to find out when you'd return. When I finally heard you were here, I came straightaway, of course."

"Ah, I see," Ewen breathed, releasing his hard hold on Bridget. He nodded. "We must talk. And then you're leaving—as quickly as you'd have had Bridget leave." He frowned at her, his dark brows knitting. "That was badly done, even for you."

"I was merely doing another favor for you," Elise said. "She told me you'd wed her. I knew it couldn't be."

Ewen threw back his dark head and laughed. It was such a sudden, unexpected, and merry a sound in that tense moment that everyone in the room gaped at him. But he seemed genuinely amused. "Dear, dear Elise," he chuckled, "time hasn't changed you at all, has it?"

"Here," a low hoarse voice said. It was Gilly. "All very well for you to laugh, but I ain't. Is she"—she jerked a thumb at Elise—"your missus or ain't she? And is that sour-faced brat your son or ain't he? . . . your lordship," she added when she saw identical looks of shock on both of Ewen's companion's faces.

"To the point as ever, eh, Gilly?" Ewen said. "No, he isn't my son. And she isn't my wife—your friend Bridget is. Rather, your friend, Bridget, the Viscountess Sinclair. No, Elise," he said harshly when he saw her startle at his words, "she isn't the Countess Sinclair yet. And won't be for a long, long while, either, lord willing. He's recovered entirely. You didn't think of that, did you? Why should you? If you're running true to form, you probably didn't even ask about him once you got here."

The lady grew rigid. Her glittering blue eyes were the only things that moved in her face.

"Yes," Ewen said harshly, "that's the Elise I remember. Enough. Come, we must talk."

He swept out an arm, showing where he wanted her to go. Elise came down the stairway with measured tread, moving toward the salon with stately grace, her morning gown flowing behind her as though she were a queen or a bride walking down the aisle in a hushed cathedral. Ewen took Bridget's cold hand in his and began to follow. But she hung back, looking up at him with grave gray eyes. He closed his hand convulsively over hers and was about to speak . . . until he saw Gilly and Betsy standing by her other side, staring up at him. Rafe and Drum were behind him now, too, almost stepping on his boots when he stopped so abruptly.

Elise paused, turned, and saw them. "Really, Ewen," she protested, "I hardly think this involves anyone but us."

Ewen looked at the little parade he'd begun. "You're right," he told her, "in that it does indeed involve all of us. Drum and Rafe know all already, and Bridget must. Still, as for the children . . ."

He looked at Gilly. She stared back so defiantly, no one there could think of her as a child.

"Beg pardon," he said with the trace of a smile. "I mean 'as for those less involved.' Still, I don't doubt you'll find out anyway. But the little one?" he asked, looking at Betsy.

"She knows more'n me half the time," Gilly said with a shrug. "Folks forget kids has ears, but they're like dogs under the dinner table, always waiting and watching, 'cause they never know when they might be something in it for them."

Ewen smiled one warm and genuine smile. "I do not doubt it. So she may as well come, too. After all, why not? I suppose the more that know, the less chance of this ever happening again."

"I hardly think—" Elise began.

Ewen cut her off in a hard voice. "The secret *was* kept, Elise, as per our bargain. Rafe knew because he trusts me with his life, and has done, as I trust him with mine, and so he had to know all my secrets. Drum only just found out. But apart from those first chosen few no one else knew, I kept my word. That was my mistake. Secrets are damnable things, because they can become weapons in the wrong hands."

"Ewen," Elise cried, "I never meant to hurt you!"

"Perhaps not," he said with a twisted smile, "but you certainly meant to help yourself. And somehow that's always meant hurting someone else, hasn't it?"

They sat quietly, ranged round the room, waiting for Ewen to begin. Elise sat in a small gilt chair by the hearth, her head high as Ewen paced before her.

He looks weary, Bridget thought. His dark hair was disarranged, his high brow was lined by a frown, his face was still pale beneath his tan. The dust of the road coated his high boots; his shirt and neckcloth were gritty with a film of it. He looked nothing like the suave gentlemen she'd met in London. He looked both more dangerous and more desperate. Still, the power of the man was astonishing. He was here at last, he filled her eyes, he filled the room for her—even if he was now as a stranger to her. Because he paced in front of Elise and hadn't a word to spare for anyone else since he'd entered the room. Bridget clasped her hands together in her lap to keep from reaching out to him. He wasn't looking at her; she wondered if he even remembered her.

Her gaze flew to the Lady Elise, sitting proud and pale, her blazing blue eyes fixed on him, too. How could he remember her, or even consider her, Bridget thought miserably, when he had this fairy-tale princess come from across the sea to comfort him? A lady who had married him? And yet was not his wife. She didn't understand, and suddenly was afraid to.

The silhouettes of the two gentlemen who had arrived with Ewen were as still as graven images against the long window where they stood waiting and watchful, too. Betsy and Gilly shared a deep chair, sitting back in it, scarcely breathing lest they be told to leave.

Bridget watched Ewen, yearning for him. She began to hate herself because of it, because she needed all her resolve now. She had to hide away her heart and use her head because it was her life and her future he would talk about now. One thing she knew: Despite how much she loved him, if he had betrayed her, then she must surely rise and go from here without a backward look. So she looked her fill now—and knew it would never be enough. And knew it would have to be if he had deceived her.

"The thing is so damnably simple," Ewen said suddenly in a hard voice, shaking his head as he stared at the intricate pattern of the Persian carpet he paced. "So

utterly stupid, too. Worst of all, it could have been pre-
vented if I'd thought about it. I promised to keep a
secret. That was my only mistake. No," he said sadly,
"no, not my only mistake. I was young and callow. I
might forgive the boy, but not the man. I never lied to
you," he said, looking up at Bridget. It was only then
that she realized he was speaking to her now.

"I was lying to myself, you see," he told her. "I gave
my word to keep a secret, and forgot it was a boy who
gave that word." He tilted one shoulder in a shrug. "It
may be that I had no choice, because the only way to
really keep a secret is to forget it, and I did that—too
well. If it's any comfort, I remembered at last. I was
going to tell you."

Elise laughed shrilly. "Oh, to be sure!" she said with
bright bitterness, "and I was going to tell her the truth,
too. Really, Ewen. You have changed. The boy I knew
was at least honest—to a fault."

He shifted his head to stare at her. "Honesty's never a
fault," he said. Then he turned his broad back on her.
"The thing of it is that I was young, and so was she," he
told Bridget, his eyes steady on her. "Neither of us was
too honest even then. If I had been, I suppose I'd have
wondered why such a lovely young girl would have been
so eager to marry me in the first place."

"Why should she not?" Drum cried, but Ewen waved a
hand to cut him off.

"No, Drum. I was old enough to be wed, but too
young for my years. I'd led a sheltered life. Taught at
home, unused to sophisticated company. When I finally
did go away to school, I was fine with other young men,
but totally at a loss with the ladies. Although how could
you know that?" he mused aloud, his gaze growing

vacant as he stared at something only he could see. "Although I actually blush to think it now, I was actually a v—" He paused, looking around the room at the fascinated company.

He laughed, a flicker of the devilish Ewen that Bridget knew so well in his voice and face now. "As I was saying," he continued, "I was a very inexperienced lad, to be sure. Indeed, I grew sweaty palms when I but danced with a pretty girl, and I stumbled over my words as well as my feet at every assembly or dancing party."

It was hard for Bridget to imagine that. Ewen tongue-tied? Ewen gauche and graceless? Ewen at a loss with a woman? Any woman? No matter how she tried, it was impossible for her to imagine that.

He sighed heavily. "And so you may imagine that when my father introduced me to Elise, I was dumb-struck. She was the Incomparable of that long-ago season, fair and fairylike, always in demand, full of easy laughter, glib and gay, so facile, her dance card always filled. And yet she deigned to dance with me! It even seemed she favored me. I paid court. What a fine suitor I must have been," he said wryly, "stammering and then yammering for hours when she actually sat moon-eyed listening to my drivel—my plans, my thoughts, my unformed philosophies."

"Nonsense!" Drum finally said, the pent-up word bursting from him like steam from a kettle as he leaned forward, both hands tight on the back of a chair. "I admired you then, Ewen, everyone did. You were a bit poetical, to be sure. But you were so well read, so steady and even-handed in your dealings with your friends. More than that, you were a model of gentlemanly behavior, in manners and in manner. Why, you were a bruising sportsman, an excellent pugilist, a neck-or-nothing rider, a fencer . . ."

"But not a swordsman," Ewen said ruefully, laughing a little. "At least not the kind I came to be later. Because women awed and terrified me then—with a certain glad terror, you understand. They fascinated and inspired me. Surely you remember, at school, I never went out of an evening with our friends to sport with the kind of females that were so easily available to wealthy young men like us?"

"We respected you for it!" Drum said. "You were a man of taste and discrimination."

"I was a boy with illusions," Ewen said harshly. "I avoided whores because they seemed to me mockeries of all I admired in ladies. And how I admired ladies! But I lost all my finesse when I was with them. I thought them such supreme creatures, and Lady Elise their personification."

Bridget bit her lip.

"Yes, that I do remember," Elise purred. "But Ewen, how could you think I could forget? You loved me," she said, casting a sidewise glance at Bridget.

"No, not at all," Ewen corrected her. "I adored you."

Bridget's eyes opened wide on a sea of pain she hadn't thought existed.

"There is a difference," Ewen said, gazing at Bridget. "I've only lately found that out, in fact. Enough wordplay," he said harshly, unable to keep looking into Bridget's stunned eyes.

He took a turn around the carpet again, fretful, restless even though he kept pacing. When he spoke, it was to the room. "The sum of it is that I discovered the lovely Elise not only willing to wed me, but eager to do so. My father exulted. Her father celebrated. It was a perfect match. Plans went forth with haste—in fact, with such haste that some thought it unseemly, wondering if it was a necessity. Idiot that I was, I was flattered both by her impatience *and* their assumptions for the reasons for it. I was full of myself and my pride and as eager as she for our wedding day."

Bridget closed her eyes at the thought of their wedding night, Ewen's long body entwined with Elise's slender, supple one. That dark head bent over that fair face, his strong hands cupping her head as his hazel eyes burned with tender love—not just lust—as they gazed into the vivid blue of Elise's. The two of them, enrapt, both elegant aristocrats, bred from the cradle for each other. She hadn't allowed herself to see that, not once in all the nights she'd laid in her lonely bed thinking about the two of them. Now she did. It was almost unendurable.

"Over a hundred at our wedding," Elise said dreamily. "You were there, Drummond, you recall. It was May, and there were roses, bowers of them—and lilies of the valley and sweet flag, and meadowsweet. Everyone said how cunning it was to mix the elegant with the common, the cultured blooms with wildflowers. But then, the whole affair was done beautifully. Some guests vowed to write it up for other brides to copy, they were that enchanted. And why not? No expense was spared. An outdoor breakfast for the guests, and such guests! The crème de la crème. Hundreds of them . . ."

"Yes," Ewen said, "and only the two of us on our wedding night. Remember that, too?"

Bridget stiffened. But Elise stopped talking. She glanced down at her fingers and inspected her nails with sudden interest.

"Well, but of course I believed my lovely young bride would be too weary after such a celebration," Ewen went on, his deep voice filled with sarcasm. "And of course, I understood that such a gently bred girl would not wish to tumble into . . ." He paused, looking over to where Gilly and Betsy sat, enthralled. "So we rode on to London," he said roughly, turning back to Elise. She still avoided his gaze.

"Then, of course," he said sardonically, "I understood she wasn't used to such hard travel and needed her rest. We took the packet to Calais, and the motion of the boat made her so sick she had to keep to our bed in our cabin, alone except for her maid, as I paced the deck worried sick for her. Such a gentle flower that she was," he said with irony, "of course it took days for her to recover from that, too.

"I was filled with understanding," he said, pacing again now as he had then. "Females are such delicate creatures. Hadn't my own mother been an invalid? I worried for my young wife. So young, so fragile, so gently bred that she trembled at my lightest touch, fluttered her lashes in agitation when I but kissed her cheek, and actually flinched when I dared touch her lips. At least your emotions were true, I give you that," he growled to Elise.

He took another agitated turn about the carpet, then stopped and confronted her, his dark head high, hands on his hips, his stare direct and cold.

"And I was not a monster, was I? And certainly not man enough, or bold enough, or bright enough, to broach the matter too often. In fact," he mused, "I wonder now if I was not relieved at the delay, for fear I'd bungle matters.

"But that was then. And after a while, even I began to wonder. We were in Paris, we were at a grand hotel. Weeks went by, and yet you were still ill, and so I called for a physician."

"How could I tell you?" Elise said simply, finally raising her bright blue eyes to look directly at him.

"How could you *not*?" he demanded.

Bridget looked from Ewen to Elise, her heart growing cold. They were still fighting about something that had happened over a decade past. It was as if the years had never intervened. Such heat could not come from a cold hearth.

"I thought that, in time, when events took their course—" Elise began.

"They did not," Ewen said grimly. "And now I thank you for it. Because you could have achieved it, you know. I was young and smitten and totally without guile—and certainly not expecting any from you. You could have been as calculating as you obviously had planned to be. I see that now. How would I have known it was anything but maidenly terror and not the disgust it was? How could I have known I was not your first lover?"

"I did like you!" Elise cried, bolting to her feet. "I was willing to try, but I was so damned ill—I wasn't lying about that!"

"Then that was the only thing you weren't lying about," Ewen said scornfully, as cold and contained as she was wildly angry now.

"I told you all!" she shouted back.

"Only when you had to," he countered.

"I didn't have to—but I liked you well enough by then to be honest with you," Elise said, trembling with rage.

"You turned from my embrace and vomited in my lap.

I think it was possible you owed me an explanation," Ewen said bitterly. "Your stomach was truthful, at least. Never was a man so sincerely rejected."

"I could have said I was ill," she protested.

"You'd have had to say you were dying," Ewen said with a grim chuckle. "That didn't mean I would have believed it. Why should I have? We weren't at sea, nor on the road; it was a bright morning and you were very fit—warm and rosy with health—and very willing in my arms until then. There was nothing for it but the truth then."

"But then I told you all," she said, sitting again, calming her voice, visibly gathering herself again.

"Only after I called you a slut," he said bitterly.

"I recall the word you used was *whore*," Elise reminded him.

"Yes!" he said with something like triumph, wheeling around to face her again. "Because kinder euphemisms rolled right off, didn't they? But then—and only then—did you at last tell me you weren't a whore, that you were a respectable female. How you defended your honor!" he said with a bitter chuckle. "Oh, yes, a very respectable female, and no whore at all, you said, it was only because you were already married. And so quite *respectably* with child."

Bridget blinked, but when she looked again she only saw the same bizarre truth. He'd loved his Elise. He'd wed her gladly. But it had turned out that she was pregnant with another man's child . . . and was still married to another man. So, then, she and Ewen had been married—and yet had not been married? It all began to make sense, terrible sense.

"*Respectably*—oh, to be sure. Even though your new

husband had abandoned you," Ewen went on relentlessly, "doubtless remembering that slight oddity about your nuptials—the fact that no one but you and he knew you were married at all."

Elise's lips grew tight. "Nevertheless, he accepted responsibility."

"After your father and mine had him tracked down and pinned down to it," Ewen said, prowling the room again, throwing the words at her as he passed her. "Cut line, Elise. He couldn't bed you without marrying you, but you couldn't bear his child without a husband. Hence me. I can't blame you for what happened to you before we met. He was a dashing officer when you met him. You couldn't have known he'd be faithless to you once he discovered that your father had plans for you and your dowry that didn't include a cashiered army officer. Nor could you have known he'd be discovered cheating at cards and drummed out of the uniform he wore so handsomely."

He gazed at her with something like sympathy. "You were young. You were frightened. I accept all that—now. But it was a damnable thing to do to me. What if we had consummated our false marriage? How could I have known I was raising the son of another man—a man who was not above blackmailing anyone who could pay his bills if the need arose? If I owe you anything, it's gratitude that at the last your will—or your body— thwarted your plans."

"Gratitude?" Elise spat. "Yet then you abandoned me!"

Ewen wheeled around to face her. "Did you really think I'd stay with you after I knew? Even if I'd felt something more for you, how could I? You were a bigamist! That's a crime punishable by death. Granted, they mightn't hang a female, and hardly one with your wealth and connections. I was a dupe, but you were a criminal. It would have been transportation for you, at the least. I doubt you'd have enjoyed living in the Antipodes with the other convicts. Then there was the matter of the scandal. We weren't even married. I'd been a fool and would have looked one, so I deserved it and the scandal that would have tainted my name. But your family didn't.

"I came back to England to seek advice. I found that, and more—proof of your duplicity. My father achieved that; he was the one who returned with me and made you produce your real marriage lines. But it was *your* father who sent you into exile," he told her. "Remember that. It was he who demanded that, after he agreed to support you and your lawful husband—whom *he* located and sent to you. You went with him gladly. Remember that? I do. God help me, but I can hardly forget, can I?"

His face was set in hard lines and his eyes glittered like topaz crystals. Elise sat still, white as a statue on a tombstone, gazing into his face without answering.

Bridget watched the pair of them. Surely she thought, Elise still cared for him. How could she not? She'd traveled so far to see him again to console him—and, finding him remarried, had tried to cast his new wife out. That was the act of a jealous woman, a woman who was still willing to fight for what she'd lost. Surely he still cared for her, too.

Bridget heard the bitter hurt beneath his every savage word as he fought with Elise again. He was usually so clever with words, so cool, so contained, so urbane. It was his hallmark. But he couldn't control the hatred in his voice, and he was anything but calm. And hate was, after all, only the bitter, rejected bastard twin of love.

Which meant that whether he was still wed to his fair Elise or not, his heart was still hers, and always would be, she realized. Because Ewen was a good man, a man of his word, a man a woman could trust for all time. Hadn't she been telling Gilly and even Elise herself that all these past days? Hadn't she been telling herself that, too? And she'd been right—in a way.

It came to her suddenly. So suddenly that she closed her eyes, trying to protect herself against the stab of unexpected revelation. He'd married Elise in good heart and good faith, pledging himself to her forever, whatever Elise had done. It was his way; she herself wouldn't have married him if he weren't that kind of man. She wouldn't have loved him if he were not.

And so the truth was worse than his having lied to her. Because he hadn't. He *had* given her his name and his protection in good faith. Whatever the facts of his married state, though, the truth was his heart could never be hers. But, she remembered as she sat in self-imposed darkness beneath her closed eyelids, despite all that he'd promised her, he'd never said anything about his heart, had he?

21

"Why?" Ewen demanded, shattering the silence that had fallen over the room. "Why return now? Is the gallant captain dead?"

Elise pulled herself up. "My husband is well, thank you. I came, as I said, when I heard your father was ill—dying. I do have a heart, you know."

Ewen sat back on the arm of a chair. For the first time since he'd come into the room, the tension left his face. He ran a hand over his eyes and smiled wearily. "Oh, lord, Elise. Give it up. It's over. I know you better than that. You heard my father was dying, and there was one thing he had that you wanted—and it wasn't his parting blessing."

"I don't know what you mean," Elise said. "I only wished to give consolation."

"Yes," Ewen said, "and get your wedding papers in return."

Elise's eyes grew wary. Ewen's shoulders relaxed. He sighed. "That's it, isn't it? Has to be. There's no other logical reason for this visit. Sorry you wasted your time. He doesn't have them anymore, my dear. He kept them as insurance against anything you and your dear husband might attempt in years to come. You thought that when he died you'd have a chance to get them? You remembered the youth you wed and how easily gulled he was? You thought if you came to me with tears and lamentations, some tale about your needing them—no, better still, some story about your son needing his parents' marriage lines for some pressing reason—a school to get into, an unexpected inheritance, perhaps?"

He watched her eyes widen and then narrow against all the thoughts she was busily concealing. "Yes. Good thinking." He nodded. "It might have worked—then. But an odd thing happened as the years went by. I grew up, my dear. Those papers are mine now, and safe with my man at law. Still, if your son really requires proof, I suppose you may have them back."

Someone in the room gasped. Not Bridget. She was too sick at heart to be shocked anymore.

"Because they weren't enough for me," Ewen said, rising to his feet again. "My father's a trusting soul. I, my dear, am not. Not anymore. I've worked in a strange arena, against people who make you look like innocence personified. I kept an ear to the ground to hear about you and your captain's adventures. If you'd wed me to protect yourself once, I felt you were capable of anything twice. I never opened your notes. But I knew what was going on: the gambling losses, the dealings with those on either side of the late conflict in order to pay them. Your morals, my dear, are even more flexible now than they were then."

"One has to survive in hard times," Elise said sharply. "Only gentlemen such as yourself can afford pure principles."

"Really?" Ewen asked quizzically. "Tell that to Drum and Rafe, and the good men we knew and lost. Those who risked the only thing they could not afford—their lives—for their principles."

He shook his head, the fatigue from his sleepless night evident in his face. "But that hardly matters to you, does it?" he said. "Remember, however, that I was aware of your unusual friendships and the reasons for them. It occurred to me then that you might someday return. That, failing to retrieve the papers, you might claim they were forged. That you might yet threaten to bring shame or scandal to my door. So now I've even more proof. I went to that little church in Scotland where you were first wed—"

Now it was Elise who couldn't control a gasp of surprise.

"A charming spot, just over the border," he commented. "Very romantic, I agree. I have written statements by all the witnesses as well as the vicar, and the actual ledger where the marriage was recorded. It's sworn to by all involved. And to cap it all, I have a statement signed by your father."

Elise's eyes widened.

"Yes, my dear, he, at least, is a man of principle. And he knows you, too," Ewen said. "But there, I think, is your answer. If funds are tight—and they must be if your husband is running true to form—I suggest you apply to your father. He's a difficult man, true, but a lonely one. If you went to him discreetly, promising to leave with the same stealth, and told him your problems, you might find you still have his affection. Or at least the route to his purse. The years blunt some hurts—and he did dote on you once upon a time.

"But," he said, covering a jaw-cracking yawn, stretching his long body as though he hadn't a care in the world but to get the kinks out of his back, "I must ask you to leave. Immediately. And why not? There's nothing here for you."

Elise stared at him. "You have changed, Ewen," she finally said with reproach—and grudging admiration.

"Thank you. I have, thank God," he agreed.

"But wait!" Bridget cried, shaking her head. "It's not settled. It can't be. If money's all she wanted, why lie to me? Why tell me to leave? Why try to turn me against you? I don't understand!"

"Oh, Bridget," Ewen said sadly. He came to her side, dropped to one knee, and took her two cold hands in his. "Can't you see? Because you were a formidable enemy. She hadn't heard I'd wed. Oh, as to that—" He reached into his inner pocket, withdrew a folded sheet of newsprint, and laid it on her lap. "Fresh from the printers, a notice of our marriage from the *Times*. You had me so transfixed I actually forgot," he told her ruefully, "never realizing what mischief it could cause."

"But how could I have known?" Elise protested.

"Oh, I believe you understood clearly enough," Ewen said, without turning his head to look at her. "You sounded out my wife's situation, doubtless making her volunteer some of it. The rest you got from servants. But

I can't prove that. For that reason, and that reason alone, I won't detain you . . . or worse. Can't you see?" he asked Bridget, his eyes searching hers. "She needed you gone. She probably thought to sell me the information about where you were. Remembering the man I used to be, she must have also hoped I might turn to her. But if you were here, she knew, I'd have no eyes or ears for her."

"As if I'd be jealous of her!" Elise said scornfully. "Really, Ewen, I thought with your new reputation as a rake—although I allow, I couldn't understand that before I saw you again—you'd choose someone with breeding, with background, with beauty! At least to match mine!"

Ewen didn't turn his head. His eyes were on Bridget. "She has more than you ever had, Elise," he said softly, "and more than you ever will."

"Have you no eyes?" Elise spat. "She is scarred! Disfigured!"

"Have you no ears?" he snarled, turning his head at last. "Get out, Elise. I owe you no explanations. But one thing I will tell you. My wife has no defect. Except," he said to Bridget, a small, sad smile on his lips as he gazed at her ashen face again, "she has no faith, I think, in herself, or her power over me."

Elise and her son were gone within the hour. Ewen's guests watched from a window to be sure. Ewen himself did not look; he was eating his breakfast without seeing it, because he could only look at Bridget.

She wanted to look at him, too. But to her surprise she discovered she was as shy with him now, here in the light, as she'd been with him that first night in his townhouse. It made no sense to her. She'd waited for him for so long, and doubted him even longer. Yet now that he was here, and now that she knew he'd never deceived her, she was wary of him. Or wary of her reaction to him, she realized in surprise.

All her doubts were gone. Now she saw they had muted the full force of her desire for him. With them gone, the enormity of her emotions frightened her. He was hers, and he was here, her husband, her lover. She'd always wondered about his sincerity, and then was made to question his honesty. Now that the clouds of distrust and fear had been dissipated, there was nothing to shade the stunning truth of her love. It was astonishing in its intensity. It overwhelmed her.

"Nice touch, that," Rafe said from the window as the carriage pulled out of the drive, "sending Hines with her. Old wretch!" he grumbled as he sat at the table again. "To think he'd side with her! How much did she pay him, you think?"

"Nothing," Ewen said, putting down his fork, his eyes still on Bridget as he drank in the pleasure he felt in her presence. "He was, in his way, doing his job, or so he thought. He remembered she was my wife, and that was the reason behind his every act. How could he know otherwise? No one else in England did. Elise and her family realized she was better off supposedly dead than wed to two men. I'd only have to cope with embarrassment; it would have been the prisoner's dock for her.

"Hines knows the truth now. He is, for all his sins, a faithful man. He's coming back when he's absolutely sure she's safely gone. He owes me that much, he said. He's very sorry, he said. He's very old, and very repentant. What choice have I but to believe him?"

"I'd'a scragged him," Gilly commented, with her mouth full.

Drum shuddered. "Doubtless," he said.

"When do we leave for your father's manor?" Rafe asked Ewen.

"In the morning," Ewen said, watching Bridget's expression, seeing how her skin glowed in the morning light, approving again that delicate small straight nose, noting with increased interest a pale freckle he hadn't seen before, to the side of her soft, full lips. "We've traveled far enough today."

"Amen!" Drum said fervently.

"If that's all right with you?" Ewen asked Bridget. "You must be sick to death of this place by now."

"I am," she admitted, looking at him, and then at her plate, "but you're here now. Tomorrow is fine for me, too."

"Well, then, I guess we'll be shoving off, too," Gilly said, getting to her feet and grabbing her hat. "Thanks for the grub, but it's time for us to get going."

"*We*?" Bridget asked, confused. "But things have changed. Why must Betsy leave now?"

Gilly's face grew pink. She fidgeted with her atrocious hat, holding it in front of her, looking down at its crumpled brim, "Well, y'see, I missed her something fierce," she said. "I don't know I can let her go again, and I do know she don't want me to."

"Then join us," Ewen said.

"Me? In the country? Nah. How'd I earn my bread?" Gilly asked, but she sat down at the table again.

"You won't have to, my dear," Ewen said gently. "There are good people who will take you in with Betsy, help you find a better life than you've known. I'll help you find them. And don't think it's because I've designs on you—I owe you much for supporting my bride in her time of need."

Drum snorted. "As if you'd have designs on a scrubby lad. How much ale did you have on an empty stomach, Ewen?"

"The lad," Rafe said, watching Gilly, "is a lass."

"Are you mad?" Drum demanded.

Rafe grinned. "Maybe a lord can't tell a female without her petticoats, but you can't fool an army man."

Drum plucked a quizzing glass from his waistcoat and stared at Gilly. He saw a skinny, unkempt tow-headed youth in baggy workman's clothing, and winced at the hat the lad was turning in his work-worn hands. He looked longer. He noted the hands were small-boned. He raised his eyes and saw the fine features set in a scowl, the badly cut shock of platinum hair brushed back impatiently, the golden eyes that glowered at him. "Extraordinary," he breathed. "It may be so. But if she is going to travel with us, she needs suitable attire. I've no wish to enact a scene from *Twelfth Night*, and she is no Viola." He sniffed. "Rather more like an onion, I'd say."

Gilly's small hands fisted, but Ewen disarmed her by saying gently, "There's no more need, Gilly. I promise you that."

She hesitated and looked at Bridget. Bridget saw the mixture of hope and fear—a mixture she knew too well—in the girl's eyes. That, and Gilly's hesitation, told her all she needed to know. She nodded in agreement. "That's the old life, Gilly. You'll be safe with us. Please stay. You know it would be best for you and Betsy. She won't take up a new life without you, and you know very well how much she needs to."

"And Drum is the perfect man to help you pick out

your new clothes," Ewen said. "There's a shop in the village, Drum. See to it that she has everything she'll need for the trip, and afterward."

"I'll come along," Rafe said, after looking at the way Ewen was watching Bridget. "There's things I need, too."

"I dunno," Gilly said nervously.

"Do you imagine I'll be driven mad with lust at the sight of you in a gown?" Drum asked scornfully, looking down his nose at her, making the idea sound about as palatable to him as eating mud, and about as probable. "Enough of this maidenly dithering. Are you coming?"

"*Maidenly!*" Gilly said, bridling, because it took her mind off her second thoughts and made her forget the dizzying combination of relief and terror she felt at the idea of what she was about to do. "C'mon, Betsy. Maidenly, huh?" she asked Drum, looking up at him fiercely. "I can work hard as any male, harder than any *gentleman* I ever seen! Can you lift a keg of nails, huh, can you?"

"Easily," Drum said loftily.

"Like to see it," Gilly said as she marched to the door with him, Betsy at her side. "How about a crate of turnips, huh?"

"With no difficulty at all," Drum said, stepping aside and bowing, indicating that she should go out the door before him.

Gilly frowned. Then, nose in the air, she swept out the door in front of him. "But a barrel of ale," she said as she went, though her voice was light, breathless with surprise at herself and him. "Like to see you roll a full one into a taproom, I would."

"Would you?" he asked as he followed her. "I shouldn't wonder. I can do it with grace and ease."

Their voices faded as they went out into the hall. Rafe looked back at Ewen and Bridget and grinned. Then he slapped on his hat and went out with the others.

The room seemed very empty without them. Ewen turned to Bridget and smiled. Then he frowned, because she was looking at the plate on the table, at her cup, at a spoon—everywhere but at him.

He cleared his throat. "Well," he said, rising, looking down at himself, brushing at his jacket, "I washed my face and hands, but I seem to have the whole North Road on my shirt and britches. Indeed, I'm sure I tasted it in my eggs. I think I ought to go up and make use of that Roman bath again. I missed that; it's the best thing about this place, you know. Apart from you, of course."

She stood up quickly. "I'll—I'll come upstairs, too."

He showed her through the doorway before him. Her skirt brushed his boots, her perfume teased his nose, but they did not touch or look into each other's eyes.

Speak up, fool! Bridget told herself as she walked up the stair with him, *Talk about anything, and the things you want to say will come tumbling out.* "It's strange," she said, "but though I wrote to you every day, and thought of you all the time, I—" She looked at him, her eyes troubled. "I find myself at a loss for words now."

"Only natural," he said calmly. "So much has happened, so much more needs to be said."

She nodded. They went to their room in silence. When they came to their door, Ewen opened it and waited for her to step in before him.

Like a damned footman. Oh, very suave indeed, Ewen, he told himself angrily as she swept past him. *Be cool and correct and set the seal on the loss of her confidence, that's very wise,* he castigated himself. But he couldn't just take her in his arms, as he yearned to do—as he'd wanted to do for more days than he could tally, more years than he'd known. She was like a stranger to him now.

His heart clenched when saw her go busy herself at her dressing table, turning the scarred side of her face from him, the way she did when she felt vulnerable.

Will she ever forgive me for not telling her? he wondered, drawing a breath against the surprising pain he felt for her—for himself. *Do I deserve to be forgiven? What must she have endured, what doubts, what fears—and yet against all odds she believed in me. I heard her with my own ears. Now she's avoiding my eyes. Have I lost her after all? No. I will not, cannot let her go*, he thought fiercely. *But how does a man go about seducing his own wife? Strangers were easy game, but this is no game.*

Think, man! he told himself angrily, shucking off his jacket. *Use your head, follow your heart, there's so much to say. You're supposed to be so damned good with words.* But those had been easy words, spoken for light reasons. This was only his whole life he had to recapture. He tried to think how to do that as he began pulling his shirt over his head.

He's here, he's back, he's been true to you, and all you can do is dither like poor Gilly when she was offered a chance at a new life, Bridget scolded herself. *What is the matter with you? There's so much to say, as he said; so much to tell him, to rejoice in.*

She turned to him, to tell him how much she missed him, how much she needed him, how glad she was that things had turned out so well . . . and saw him standing there, his shirt in his hand, his eyes on her. Here at last, in her room, in *their* room . . . in her heart.

Wordlessly she went to him. She stopped in front of him. He looked down at her, saying nothing, scarcely breathing. She placed her hand on his naked chest and felt his heart's sure, steady beat, the tensed muscles under that warm skin. She tilted up her head and looked into his eyes. So much to say . . .

And none of it was said.

He touched her cheek, her hair. Carefully, watching her eyes all the while, he lowered his head and touched her mouth with his. She stepped into his embrace and took his light kiss. She opened her lips and turned it into something hot and deep and delicious, drinking him in as if he were something she needed to nourish her. Indeed, she thought, he was. She put her other hand on his neck and pulled his head down, crowding close to him, pressing herself against him.

He laughed, he groaned, it was the same. He took her in his arms, he shivered with need. His lips on her mouth, her cheek, her neck, he breathed in her ear, "I'm filthy, dusty, reeking of horse and haste. Come, come with me. We'll bathe together, we'll—"

She went to their bed with him instead, because it was the nearest place they could lie together, and they needed that above all. Swift, intent, she helped him remove the last of his clothing. He couldn't wait for her to take off her gown, so he did it for her. They paused to look at each other. He was a man so often driven by lust and so long denied release. Yet he was nevertheless stopped short by the incredible pleasure of the thought that it was *his* Bridget in that delicious, necessary form.

She saw the embodiment of all her desires, and the evidence of his desire for her. She stared, thrilled and proud, because he obviously needed her as much as she wanted him.

Then their hands reached. They touched, they kissed,

there was a flurry of movement and sensation. It was like no seduction he'd ever known, like no daydream of their reunion she could have imagined. They were two halves intent on being whole again.

No word was uttered, no sound except for their breathing, and then the cry she made when he entered her, and the murmurs of pleasure and his harsh breathing, and his cry and hers. Because at last they were together as they'd both longed to be for longer than they could endure.

He held her even as he withdrew from her. Nothing could have made him let her go a moment before, nothing would make him leave her now. He stroked her back as she curled against him, stunned with pleasure and new realization.

"I'm sorry," he said in a deep voice, breathless from the pleasure he'd had. "It was too fast, I was too eager. Did I hurt you?"

"Oh, no, never, it was grand, Ewen," she said. "That was—that was—I never felt anything like that, I mean to say. At the end, it was . . . remarkable."

"Never felt anything like that?" he asked on a breathy chuckle. "Has my Bridget learned to lie while I was gone? I swear I showed you the way of it before."

"Oh, that," she said, and smiled. He felt her lips turn up against his neck. "Well, yes. You did. But that was what you brought me to in our play. I never felt this, at the end, I mean. It was cataclysmic."

He laughed, as delighted as he was proud. "Such lucky creatures you are. Yes, there can be two. We poor males have to make do with the one. And such a one as you gave me," he said, and kissed her again, because he too had never felt anything like it.

They stayed in bed a while longer, congratulating each other, caressing, reveling in the fact that they could. Then he rose to his knees and swung her up in his arms. "Now!" he said. "We're still alone, and with my worthy friends in charge, we will be all afternoon. So now, a proper seduction, in a proper setting, the kind I dreamed about all those lonely nights in London."

But there was none. Satiated, too pleased and at ease with each other for that now, the idea seemed to amuse rather than titillate them. He carried her to the Roman bath. They splashed, playing like children in the perfumed waters. They dried each other and walked arm in arm to their bedchamber again. There they made love again, just as rapidly, with no less pleasure. They'd dallied in the bath but couldn't now. It seemed they had no patience for it. Nor could they say all the things they had to say to each other. They spoke to each other with their bodies instead. They needed each other too much to risk words.

No one would have guessed it at dinner that night, or so they thought. They were content, calm, in control. But Rafe and Drum exchanged knowing looks when they saw their host and hostess holding hands, stealing glances, sharing secret smiles.

Betsy was too happy with her lot to notice, and her ever-observant sister was not so observant tonight. She was too involved with the fact that she wore a gown. It was white, with a high waist, the skirt falling to her new slippers, in the current fashion. She was bathed and clean, but that was about the only improvement anyone could see. In fact, all privately thought she'd made a better-looking lad, because she was awkward in women's clothes, and now it could be seen that she was thin to the point of emaciation.

Her hair, her one grace, had a single flower pinned to the back, as if in apology for the lack of curl or length. The flower only pointed up the fact that her hair looked as though it had been chibbled by rats. But she carried herself with dignity, and no one said a word in praise or censure of her looks. They were too kind for that. And perhaps, as Drum confided to Rafe, no one dared.

No sooner had dessert been served than Rafe yawned theatrically. He ran a hand through his flaming hair. "What a day! Up since dawn, then racketing about all afternoon. Time for bed for me," he said, yawning some more.

No one mentioned that a hardened soldier might have been used to more exertion than waking early and then taking a trip into a local village with two girls.

"Indeed," Drum agreed, rising from his chair. "And we have to be up at the crack of dawn tomorrow."

"Aye, I'm for my kip," Gilly declared, "and our Betsy's half asleep in her pudding."

They were gone from the room before the footmen could come in to clear the last plates. Ewen grinned at Bridget.

"We have excellent guests," he told her, offering his hand.

"And an excellent bed," she agreed, and smiled when she saw his eyebrows rise.

"That, my dear, was mine to say," he said indignantly, ruining the effect with a warm, loving look.

But she was sitting alone on the window seat in their room as the moon flew high. She'd wrapped her arms around herself and was staring out into the night, watching the shadows cast by the moon, thinking deeply as the night grew old. She heard a stirring from the bed and heard him rise. She felt him settle down in back of her. He pulled her close against himself, his long arms covering hers, his warm body absorbing the slight chill of the night from hers. He nuzzled her neck and then put his lips to her ear.

"What?" he said, his voice thick with sleep and loving. "I thought you well loved, and to my knowledge, a well-loved woman sleeps well, too."

"You made love to me very well, and you know it, but . . ." She couldn't go on. She felt his chest heave with a sigh.

"I see," he said, settling her closer to him, gently smoothing back her hair from her ear so he could put his lips there. "You have every reason to be angry with me, of course. Can you believe that I'd buried Elise's bigamous secret so deep it was as if it never happened? You made me remember. You made me forget. For what it's worth, I was about to tell you when I was called away.

"I never thought you'd have to deal with her villainy. I was angrier at her today than I was the day I learned how she'd deceived me," he marveled, "because I saw how she'd hurt you." He put his cheek against hers. "I wouldn't have had you hurt for all the world. Can you believe that?"

She nodded.

"Then what?" he asked.

"Ah, well," she said, thinking, *Here is my chance, here in the night. I'm too tired to care; I can't wait anymore. It must be said, and it's now or never.* "You said 'well-loved,'" she blurted, glad she couldn't see his face, because hers was growing hot. "I was well pleasured . . . but I don't know if I'm well *loved*, you see." And then waited, scarcely breathing, for his reply.

"Ah," he said, and paused. She heard nothing but the thrum of her pulse in her ears. "Then after all I've said and done," he finally sighed, "you still doubt it?"

"Yes," she said in a rush, "because you never said it."

"Said it?"

"You never said 'I love you,' and that's very important to a woman. But if you don't, I quite understand. It's just that you never did, not once, you know."

He went utterly still. When he spoke again, his voice was calm, but she could feel the acceleration of his heartbeat against her back. "Did I not?" he asked. "How odd. Especially with the way you are always declaring it to me."

"What?" she said in turn.

"No," he said bemusedly, his voice calm in spite of his inner turmoil. This was the question he'd wondered if he ever could bring himself to speak. "Now I recall," he said slowly, "you never said it to me, either."

She blinked. She swung around so fast her hair flew in all directions, some fine strands catching in the short stubble of his newly grown night beard, so it seemed they were linked by spider silk there in the moonlight. "I never said . . . I never said! Oh, Ewen . . ."

He cupped her face in two big hands. "No," he said seriously, trying to read her expression in the faint light, "you never did. Oh, I heard many a 'Yes, Ewen' and 'Ah, Ewen, yes,' and I'm glad of that. I suspected gratitude, and know pleasure when I hear it. But I never heard more. It may be important to a woman, but a man needs to hear it, too. Even a man who seems impervious to such things. Because he isn't. No man is. This man, most especially not."

He waited, very grave, very quiet.

"Oh, Ewen," she cried, aghast, "but I love you! How could you doubt it? I wouldn't have wed you else. I wouldn't have lain with you. I love you entirely, even when I thought you might have—well, not that I ever believed it. But even when I was made to think you had deceived me, I loved you, though I hated myself for it. I love you, oh, I do! How could you think otherwise?"

"Perhaps because you never said it."

"Well, but neither did you, and I didn't dare because I thought you'd married me for pity or—"

He put his hand over her mouth. "Never, never," he said softly. "Your situation gave me opportunity. It didn't compel me. Only you did that." His thumb moved, gently tracing the scar. "You bear this scar, my love. It's where the world can see it, but they can't see how it has made you so strong and clever, and so very brave. I bear a scar that can't be seen. I dared to woo a lady, and my touch made her sick to her stomach. It made me vow to show the world that no woman could resist me. Of course, I also made sure no woman could know me—until you. I risked that for you. I'm a very lucky fellow. We both survived our injuries. I wish I could heal yours as you healed mine, if only for your sake. But as for me, I can't regret it, because it brought you to me."

"And yours to me," she said, raising a hand to his face, "but I'll never believe you were an artless boy. Never. I'm sorry she hurt you so much."

He took her hand and put it over his racing heart. "She hurt my pride. Not this. She couldn't. I hadn't given it to her or any other woman—until you. And no other woman shall ever have it, or any part of me. I suppose I deserved what happened. A man ought not marry for any reason but for the one I wed you. I lusted after you, true, but then, to my wonder and delight, I found I loved you."

His voice grew softer, his fingers brushed against her cheek, his eyes held hers. "I burned for you, yes, of course, you knew that, how well you know that. But the reason I rushed you into my bed so soon after we wed . . ." He sighed. What he wanted to say would leave him open to her entirely. But what of it? Now he was entirely sure it was right and necessary. He spoke quickly, before he could remember how hard it was to say. "The truth was I didn't want to lose you, not for any reason. You see, I decided if there was to be a babe, it would be mine, with no questions asked."

He hushed her gasp with a quick, light kiss, and when he spoke again his voice held a smile. "You gave me none to be answered. Yes, I was very lucky. But I already loved you by then. Bridget, I do so love you." He paused. He cocked his head and smiled widely; she saw his teeth gleaming in the moonlight. "I've never said that before. How good a sound. I love you, Bridget, and there you are."

"No, there *we* are," she said, and held him close. "Now," she said after a moment, battling back tears, forcing control, "now then . . ." She snuffled and cleared her throat. "Now we live happily ever after, don't we?"

"We can but try," he said tenderly.

"Oh, Ewen," she said, "you can do better than that."

Laughing, joyous, more the lost boy she'd never met than the cool man she'd come to know, he carried her back to their bed and did his best. And then she helped him do better.